UNDER ATTACK

The door slid open just as Ariane felt her slate vibrate. She pulled it out of her coveralls pocket, seeing a message from Muse 3. This was a bad time, but before her thumb started to set the hold, she noticed the priority. An emergency?

"I've got a message from the agent on my ship," she said, frowning and pausing in the open doorway.

"The comm center can take it." Sewick whipped out his own slate. "Funny, the center's not responding. Perhaps they're doing some maintenance."

Ariane thumbed open the message, feeling uneasy. How could her slate be getting a message if the moon's comm center was down? The text message said nothing but "CAW SEP 12.35.15." CAW Space Emergency Procedure twelve-dot-thirty-five, number fifteen? What the hell did that mean? The thirty-five series covered interruption of command, control, or communications, but number fifteen was rather obscure. Her scalp wasn't simply prickling; it tingled with the sense of danger.

"I'd better check the comm center," she said, turning around and walking quickly back down the corridor toward the pillared hall. She brushed past the other contractors and Major Dokos. Suddenly the title for 12.35.15 popped into her mind: *Hostile Takeover of Command and Control Centers.*

She turned the corner and started running.

ALSO BY LAURA E. REEVE

Peacekeeper

VIGILANTE

A Major Ariane Kedros Novel

Laura E. Reeve

A ROC BOOK

ROC
Published by New American Library, a division of
Penguin Group (USA) Inc., 375 Hudson Street,
New York, New York 10014, USA
Penguin Group (Canada), 90 Eglinton Avenue East, Suite 700, Toronto,
Ontario M4P 2Y3, Canada (a division of Pearson Penguin Canada Inc.)
Penguin Books Ltd., 80 Strand, London WC2R 0RL, England
Penguin Ireland, 25 St. Stephen's Green, Dublin 2,
Ireland (a division of Penguin Books Ltd.)
Penguin Group (Australia), 250 Camberwell Road, Camberwell, Victoria 3124,
Australia (a division of Pearson Australia Group Pty. Ltd.)
Penguin Books India Pvt. Ltd., 11 Community Centre, Panchsheel Park,
New Delhi - 110 017, India
Penguin Group (NZ), 67 Apollo Drive, Rosedale, North Shore 0632,
New Zealand (a division of Pearson New Zealand Ltd.)
Penguin Books (South Africa) (Pty.) Ltd., 24 Sturdee Avenue,
Rosebank, Johannesburg 2196, South Africa

Penguin Books Ltd., Registered Offices:
80 Strand, London WC2R 0RL, England

First published by Roc, an imprint of New American Library,
a division of Penguin Group (USA) Inc.

First Printing, October 2009
10 9 8 7 6 5 4 3 2 1

To my husband, Michael

ACKNOWLEDGMENTS

When Roger Penrose, Professor of Mathematics, University of Oxford, wrote *Shadows of the Mind*, I'm sure he had no idea of the wild and bizarre ideas that book could put into a science fiction writer's head. In appreciation, I named the Penrose Fold for him, since there must be other brilliant Roger Penroses in alternate timelines. I'm grateful for my husband, Michael, who originally loaned me the book, and who provided clarification, encouragement, and advice for technological details in this story. I also thank my friends and family for their patience and for pretending to listen while I focused on this book. Once again, I'm indebted to my critique partner Robin, as well as first readers Summer and Scott, for their reviews and editorial comments. Finally, credit must go to my agent, Jennifer Jackson, my editor, Jessica Wade, and the staff at Penguin Group for their work on this series.

CHAPTER 1

Under our spotlight: The Senatorial Advisement Council on Stellar Matters issued their report on the light-speed data from Ura-Guinn. The solar system's sun survived the detonation of a temporal-distortion (TD) warhead in 2090, contrary to simulations and scaled-down tests. However, the Epsilon Eridani antenna can't resolve planetary surfaces or orbital habitats, so casualties from coronal mass emissions and flares have yet to be . . .

—*InterStellarSystem (ISS) Events Feed*, 2105.320.17.02 UT, indexed by *Democritus 11* under Cause and Effect Imperative

Ariane reluctantly put on her v-play equipment, signed in for her virtual session, and sat down. Her chair hadn't finished adjusting when Major Tafani started in on her. She hoped there was a special room in hell just for therapists.

"Major Kedros, you shouldn't abandon these sessions so soon." Tafani's voice was heavy. He folded his hands together on top of the desk that she suspected had no purpose other than to distance him from his patients.

Today, however, not even Tafani could puncture her composure. Today, the light-speed data proved that Ura-Guinn's sun *still existed*. Every cell in her body had exploded in relief when she'd heard the news. She'd waited *fifteen years*, with the rest of the civilized worlds, to learn the outcome of her last mission during the war. Hope still flowed with every breath: If the solar system still had its sun, then some of the inhabitants might have survived.

"I have to get my boss and his ship to G-145." Ariane tried to put regret into her voice, but couldn't. "It's temporary. Don't worry, Major; I'll be back in four months."

Major Tafani's lips thinned in disapproval. He was already on the edge of being unattractive, and his grimace made him look more like her grandmother than an officer in the Armed Forces for the Consortium of Autonomous Worlds. She reminded herself that Tafani had a doctorate in some sort of brain biochemical fidgetry, as well as a regular commission in AFCAW.

"Can't your employer use another pilot for this mission?" he asked.

"Aether Exploration doesn't have another N-space pilot. Besides, how else am I going to pay for these sessions?"

"Please don't be flippant, Major Kedros. We both know these sessions are part of your military compensation, even though it's unusual to extend my services to a reservist such as yourself." Tafani's fingers started drumming the desktop.

His services? *Well, I asked for this, didn't I?* She'd almost *begged* Colonel Owen Edones for addiction therapy, but she hadn't gotten what she expected. For one thing, she didn't understand the lingo these people used, even though everyone seemed to be speaking common Greek. When Tafani told her to put together a list of inner needs, she'd stared at him blankly. After she had come back with goals such as extending her pilot rating or improving her physical conditioning, he seemed frustrated.

"Don't you need emotional nourishment?" he had asked.

Her problems weren't about emotional nourishment, for Gaia's sake. She might have wiped out *several billion souls* during the war with a temporal-distortion weapon. She was going to have to wait more years for news of survivors, and meanwhile, the nightmares never left her. Besides disrupting her sleep, the ghosts were ever present during her days, rustling and whispering in the back of her mind. It took a *lot* of alcohol and smooth to drown them out, and she was seeing Major Tafani because she was tired of puking her guts up as a result.

The military had classified and rewritten her past for her protection. They had changed her appearance, effective age, and biochemical processes, and given her a new identity. She was Ariane Kedros now, and Ariane couldn't talk to Major Tafani about TD weapons, or being tortured by Terrans for revenge, or how Cipher, her own crewmate, had gone over the edge and had become an avenging angel of death.

If she did, Tafani's head would probably explode. He didn't have combat experience and he wasn't old enough to have been in the war. All he knew was Pax Minoica, a relatively peaceful time between CAW and the Terran League, brokered by the powerful and alien Minoans.

"New space is dangerous for you." Tafani's hand still drummed the desk. "I hear there's a cavalier, frontierlike attitude toward drinking and drugging."

"I've seen a work-hard and play-hard ethic." She nodded reluctantly. "But they deserve it, don't they, for the risks they take?"

"What about you?"

"What?" The sound of his fingers drumming on the desk irritated her.

"Will you deserve rewards for your work and the risks you'll take? Since you continue to drink, how will you control yourself?" It was his old argument for abstinence.

"I've done pretty well in the last four months." She was proud of her ability to sip socially. At this point, she saw no need to fully forgo alcohol or smooth.

"You have, but you use your civilian job and employer for support and distraction. You can't maintain restraint for anyone else but *yourself*, Ariane, or you'll end up checked into an addict commons again, helpless to perform your duties."

Her jaw tightened. He was trying to use the only fact he knew about her recent mission as leverage. She couldn't protest that Terrans had checked her into the commons after torturing her, coercing her to sign over Matt's leases in exchange for Brandon's safety, and then pumping her full of alcohol and smooth. *She* hadn't voluntarily taken anything, but she couldn't protest her innocence.

"Since you haven't read the mission record, you shouldn't presume I was unsuccessful." Her voice was biting and cold.

"That's another point. How can I properly treat you when I'm not allowed access to your records or medical history? I can't even perform genetic tests."

"You can take those concerns to the Directorate of Intelligence."

From his look, she knew he'd already tried. She added, "Otherwise, you'll have to work with me, as you see me. Surely that's possible for your medical discipline."

Tafani's eyes narrowed and a sour expression formed on his face, settling naturally into the lines about his mouth and eyes. "My *discipline* is hampered by the restricted bio-sampling imposed by the Directorate. Thus, I must resort to behavior modeling, counseling, noninvasive therapy, et cetera." He paused. "So we come back, full circle, to my strong recommendation: You shouldn't sojourn in G-145. New space is not conducive to your recovery."

"It's too late to change my plans." A wave of her finger brought up the Universal Time display. "*Aether's Touch* has been given a departure slot. We disconnect from Athens Point in three hours."

"Regular sessions are necessary for your recovery. Can you continue them from G-145?"

Ariane shrugged. "I doubt it. Bandwidth is a precious commodity at this point in G-145's development."

"I'm going to note in your records that you disregarded my recommendation." His frown deepened.

"Go ahead and 'note' all you want, Major."

She cut off the session before Tafani could answer. Childish, but *so* rewarding. Tafani would probably appeal to Owen or Owen's superiors in the Directorate, but he wouldn't find any support. The Directorate would love to see her stop these therapy sessions. In the past, her missions for the Directorate had been short, successful, often dangerous, and had never impinged upon her civilian life—until six months ago.

She smiled as she removed the v-play face shield and gloves. After stowing them, she double-checked her tiny quarters for any loose items. A quiet hum of relief started in her chest and she took a deep breath. She felt *free*. Soon she'd be moving *Aether's Touch* away from Athens Point and positioning it for the N-space drop. It was wonderful to deal only with her civilian job. She had an exemplary pilot safety record. She'd been Matt's pilot slightly less than six years, and he'd made her a minor partner in Aether Exploration two years ago.

She cancelled her privacy shield. She always paid for one whenever she used the Common Communications Network, or ComNet, through a commercial habitat. Privacy law was vital support for her false identity.

On her way to the control deck, she passed through the ship's small galley and caught a whiff of Matt's packaged lunch. Having grown up on a generational ship, Matt easily experienced sensory overload and avoided planetary food sources, because of his deeply rooted suspicions of microbes and uncontrolled bacteria. The one-hundred-percent-hydroponic-source noodle dishes that he loved, however, were too bland for Ariane's taste, although the scent was enough to make her stomach rumble.

She tapped the code to retrieve her favorite, cabbage and emu rolls. Having been on enough prospecting missions with Matt, she had to order her own food stores or go crazy eating his tasteless food. This close to departure, however, she decided not to heat the pack and permeate the ship with its wonderfully rich odor. There'd be plenty of time during the next few months to torment her employer with the "dirt-grown stench."

She moved lightly, holding the open pack of rolls in one hand and almost skipping through the passageway. In a little while, there would be only herself, Matt, and *Aether's Touch*—and she couldn't forget Muse 3. She paused at the open hatch to the control deck and listened to Muse 3 pose questions to Matt.

That little gnat of a problem was growing rapidly, in its own way. Neither she nor Matt knew much about training AIs, and the how-to literature, if it existed at all, was tightly controlled. Calling upon one of the few existing experts was problematic because Muse 3 might contain illegal rule-sets. Muse 3, however, had been created by Matt's longtime friend Nestor just before his death, and she understood why Matt was reluctant to deactivate it.

"Will I be allowed to pilot *Aether's Touch*?" Muse 3 used stilted, formal language, but in its creator's voice, which sounded incongruous for anyone who had known Nestor.

"We have an autopilot if Ari doesn't want to manually control the ship," Matt said absently, checking off provisions on his slate. His free hand ruffled his blond hair, causing it to stand straight up off his scalp. Ariane wanted to reach forward and run her own fingers through it, but Matt was the civilian equivalent of her commander; they wouldn't be able to crew together if she gave these stray urges any space or time in her head.

"There is no autopilot function for N-space," Muse 3 countered.

The sly but childlike, wheedling tone made Ariane smile. Now *that* sounded like Nestor. The corners of Matt's eyes crinkled with amusement, but Ariane didn't miss his painful flinch. He was probably reminded of his friend's murder, perhaps again seeing Nestor's body, strung up for him to discover.

"You can't pilot in N-space," Matt said.

"He's right, Muse Three." Ariane decided to step onto the control deck and stop this exploration of boundaries. "Look at all the experiments where someone sent automated equipment into N-space, never to return. A human must be at the controls."

"What hypotheses exist for this requirement?"

"Yes, Ari?" Matt turned toward her and rolled his eyes. He focused on the cabbage rolls in her hand and sniffed suspiciously.

She ignored Matt's silent warning and picked up a tightly packed green roll with her fingers, looking at it while she considered how to answer Muse 3's question. She'd studied the physics, managed the checklists, put in her simulator hours, and passed her flight reviews, but she wasn't an authority on N-space.

"I don't know. Perhaps it's due to our neurons being quantum detection devices." She said this in a rush because it related to a theory about consciousness, and that was the last topic she wanted to discuss with an AI. Sure, AIs could attain the right to vote, but no one attributed them with anything more than self-awareness.

"Perhaps this relates to the navigation equations—" Muse 3 went silent.

She exchanged worried glances with Matt. After a few moments, Muse 3 came back online. It stated its origin as it reinitialized. "Muse Three, constructed by Nestor Agamemnon Expedition, born of the *Expedition Seven*."

"Muse Three, don't attempt to evaluate the navigation equations," she said. "Only Minoan time buoys can do that, and we don't even know whether they're Neumann devices. Besides, AI isn't supposed to run ships—ever. It's illegal."

"Yes, Ari."

When had Muse 3 started using her nickname? At least it was being obedient. She exchanged a grin with Matt. Unexpectedly, Muse 3 displayed the view from the external cam-eyes and announced, "Master Sergeant Alexander Joyce is approaching slip thirty-three."

Sure enough, a nondescript man with tightly clipped hair and a mustache had separated from the dock traffic and was approaching their ramp. When he set his foot on the ramp, the security systems on *Aether's Touch* came alive with a notification alarm. As Ariane watched, she wolfed down her two cabbage rolls and threw the packaging into the recycler.

Matt acknowledged and silenced the alarm. He swiveled to face her, his warm brown eyes tightening with a chill she'd never seen. "What's Joyce doing here?"

"How would I know?" She wiped her fingers on her coveralls, which would soon be heading to the steamer anyway.

"Can't we go about our business without having the Directorate of Intelligence always breathing down our necks?"

That's not fair—it only happened once, she wanted to say, but they had avoided the subject of "what happened" on her last mission, and she'd been satisfied with that unspoken arrangement. She didn't care to bring up memories of what Matt had gone through any more than she wanted to rehash her own experiences.

"He's not in uniform." She refrained from adding that it probably meant Joyce *was* under orders.

"Master Sergeant Alexander Joyce requests admittance," announced the ship systems, which sounded synthetic and neutral to her after listening to Muse 3.

"Go to quiescent mode, Muse Three." Matt glanced at Ariane. "We'll *both* talk to Joyce, in case I need an interpreter for militaryese."

She shook her head at the unusual cynicism coming from her business partner and employer. Matt used to have enough unbridled optimism for both of them. Perhaps Nestor's murder, as well as Cipher's violent attempts to assassinate her, had changed Matt. Regretfully, she wondered whether anything could neutralize the poison of bitter experience.

As they climbed down the tube to the front airlock, the ship's systems announced, "Disconnection in two hours and thirty minutes. Environmental system conversion should begin immediately."

When you can't dodge crap from the Great Bull, as Lieutenant Diana Oleander had heard said in various and more vulgar forms, *the only way to avoid the splatter is to stay faceless*. The flutter in her stomach warned her that such a barrage might be coming her way.

"Pleased to meet you, Colonel. If you and your aide will step this way."

Colonel Owen Edones followed the Terran, his shiny shoes clicking on the deck. Oleander brushed imaginary lint from her service dress coat and walked calmly behind and a step to the right, just where an anonymous aide should stay.

For a moment, she wondered whether the scheduling staff aboard the *Bright Crescent* was purposely torturing her. She squelched the idea. Someone had to take the place of the mysteriously missing Sergeant Joyce on this emergency mission, and her name must have come to the top of the rotation list titled "Unpleasant Additional Duties for Junior Officers."

She followed Colonel Edones through a door into a small conference room.

"This is a secure room, sir." The serviceman who showed them into this room backed out quickly, closing the door behind him.

Looking around, Oleander understood his haste. Putting a dead body on the conference table could barely make the place more grim. Two Terran officers and two Autonomist officers sat at the table, their faces pale and drawn. Her own red service dress with gold trim was the single bright spot; the Terrans wore their customary muddy colors and the other Autonomists, including Edones, were dressed in the black uniform of the Directorate of Intelligence, which sported light blue trim in modest amounts.

"Shut that down." The major, whose name tag read BER-NARD, pointed at the slate she carried. Oleander had read her premission briefing. Bernard was the leader of the Autonomist weapons inspection team visiting this Gaia-forsaken Terran outpost. Despite the cool temperature in the room, Major Bernard's face sweated. Beside him sat a burly female captain named Floros, who looked ready to vomit.

"Yes, sir." Oleander thumbed off her slate and stowed the stylus. She tilted the slate so everyone could see that it couldn't record.

Colonel Edones walked to the head of the table, where an empty chair waited. All faces rotated to watch him. In Oleander's short experience with Edones, she'd noticed he could grab and hold the attention of any room.

Something's wrong. Oleander suddenly wished she could flee through the door behind her. She wasn't going to like what was coming. Moreover, she saw the dark maw of the Directorate sucking her even deeper into the muck of military intelligence.

"You called me here using an emergency priority, Major." Colonel Edones put the lightest lilt of a question onto the end of his sentence.

Bernard took a deep breath and said, "A temporal-distortion weapon's gone missing."

CHAPTER 2

If a weapon or weapon system (as defined in this Protocol) is lost or destroyed due to accident, the possessing Party shall notify the other Party within forty-eight UT hours, as required in paragraph 5(e) of Article II, that the item has been eliminated. In such a case, the other Party shall have the right to conduct an inspection of the specific point at which the accident occurred.

—Section V, Loss or Accidental Destruction, in Elimination Protocol attached to the Mobile Temporal-Distortion (TD) Weapon Treaty, 2105.164.10.22 UT, indexed by Heraclitus 8 under Flux Imperative

During the silence that followed Major Bernard's statement, Oleander's hand began to cramp. She relaxed her grip on her slate.

"*Gone missing*, Major? Could you be more precise?" There was an edge to Colonel Edones's voice. His ears and cheeks flushed. She thought the reaction made him look more human. When the coloring faded, he was his bland politic self again, with frightening secrets hidden behind cold blue eyes.

"Perhaps Colonel Ash could explain. After all, we're speaking about a weapon in *his* inventory." Major Bernard glanced sharply at the closest Terran, who had no name tag.

"There's a warhead package on our inventory that

hasn't been identified through physical inspection." Ash had an unremarkable face, made more colorless by his lack of expression.

"Are we talking about a separated Mark Fifteen package, a Mark Fifteen warhead, or a Mark Fifteen installed in a Falcon missile?" Edones asked.

"I'm not authorized to release that information to you."

At Ash's response, Major Bernard rolled his eyes. The Terrans didn't display any emotion and Oleander reminded herself that many Terran officers were trained in *somaural* projection; Ash probably had the ability to hide his feelings, as well as to subtly communicate commands to his subordinate.

"The inventory lists it as a package," Bernard said.

Ash barely inclined his head. Apparently he would allow Bernard to provide the information.

"Colonel Ash, you *are* authorized to release inspection-related information to us," Edones said. "The Elimination Protocol of the treaty allows us to investigate the loss or destruction of a weapon. Besides, we've signed agreements to protect your classified material with equivalent Consortium procedures."

"Section five covers loss or destruction by accident. This is probably a clerical error in the records," Ash said.

"Is that the Terran euphemism for a *prime fuckup*?" The words suddenly spewed from Captain Floros's mouth. Throughout the conversation, she'd looked like a smoldering volcano.

Oleander looked down to hide her smile. Floros's outburst was inappropriate, but it had the unexpected effect of relieving tension in the room. Everyone around the table relaxed, including the Terrans, if only to act offended.

"Captain, please." Colonel Edones's tone was mild.

"Sorry, sir." Contrary to her tone and words, there was no apology on Floros's broad face.

"Colonel Ash, AFCAW has every right, on behalf of the

Consortium, to investigate this missing item even if it proves to be a paperwork problem," Edones said. "Please don't make me go back to my superiors for endorsement and justification. They would immediately contact your commander, which would embarrass you much more than me."

Edones's threat to end Ash's career was so smooth and unyielding that Oleander shivered. She hoped she never ended up on Edones's bad side—never, ever. Ash's emotionless mask slipped and uncertainty showed, but for only a moment.

"We've already reported this up our chain of command. State Prince Hauser will be arriving within hours and he'll be able to answer all your questions." Ash apparently thought he could lose the taint of incompetence by pushing all negotiations onto someone else. His plan might work, or it could cover him with career-ending grime.

"Fine. I'll wait for your SP. We'll require quarters near the inspection team." Edones's gesture included Oleander.

Ash nodded.

"Lieutenant, tell the *Bright Crescent* we'll be here at Teller's Colony for an indefinite period of time."

"Yes, sir," Oleander responded briskly, and restarted her slate, but her heart sank. She might be on this Gaia-forsaken rock for a while. If this "small additional duty" dragged on too long, it might attract the notice of the Directorate's personnel management. Rumors said that once the Directorate of Intelligence snagged you for an assignment, your operational career was finished. She liked working in plain, straightforward Operations. At least the rules were fixed and written. Hell—at least there *were* rules.

Master Sergeant Joyce stepped onto the *Aether's Touch* with a confidence that filled the corridor and implied he owned the deck under his feet. He seemed much bigger in person than on video; being so perfectly proportioned, his sheer muscular bulk couldn't be realized until one stood in front of him.

Ariane saw Matt take an involuntary step backward as Joyce stepped through the airlock. Then Matt squared his shoulders and straightened out of his habitual slouch.

"Mr. Journey." Joyce extended his hand.

Matt shook it, but Ariane saw a familiar stubbornness set into his jaw. Having grown up on a generational ship, Matt had the slim and wiry body of most "crèche-get." Standing nearly as tall as Joyce, however, he looked almost frail by contrast.

"Good to see you, Joyce." Ariane, at least, was honestly happy to see Joyce.

"What are you doing here, Sergeant?" Matt asked bluntly.

"*Mr.* Joyce, if you please. I need a ride to G-145."

"What?" Ariane and Matt looked at Joyce in shock, receiving only an innocent expression in response.

"You know that's impossible. This ship is designed for two people and we've already requisitioned our air, water, fuel—" Matt sputtered to a halt.

"You're not making a real-space run. You're taking an N-space shortcut and you'll have plenty of resources for three people," Joyce said.

"As long as nothing goes wrong!" Matt had grown up in real-space and wasn't about to short his safety margins. He and Joyce eyed each other and Ariane sensed a testosterone buildup in the narrow corridor.

"G-145 is still under controlled access," she said. "Our ship was assigned an authorization key by Pilgrimage, but only for two travelers."

"I have authorization." Joyce touched his implant and pointed to the bulkhead. The systems on *Aether's Touch*, still hooked into ComNet, obligingly displayed his data on the wall.

Matt's lips pressed together as he looked at the key that had an AFCAW priority code at the end. Ariane looked down at her scuffed boots, no longer feeling joyously free or even interested in the conversation. As a reservist, she'd

done enough active duty this year—*perhaps for a lifetime*—
and she'd hoped to leave all those memories behind for a
while. Joyce, obviously under Directorate orders for some
dark military intelligence motive, had to get to G-145 in
a hurry. Matt could resist all he wanted, but Joyce would
have his way.

"Why don't you get on the next transport?" Matt
asked.

"*Venture's Way* won't be leaving for three more days. I
need to get there faster." Then, when Matt's face started
getting red, Joyce added, "Wouldn't you say you owe me
for keeping quiet?"

"Eh? What do you mean?" Ariane jerked her head up
to look at both men.

"Nothing," Matt said hurriedly.

"And I'm up one for a favor, right?" Joyce turned to
look down at her.

"Eh?" It was Matt's turn to be puzzled.

Joyce was referring to the sly bookkeeping he and Ariane kept on who had saved whose ass, and when. He was
currently one up on her, but she didn't want to go into that
history in front of Matt. As civilian employer and coworker,
Matt didn't need to know how dangerous most of the Directorate's missions had turned out to be. It was better that
he believe the last mission was an anomaly.

"Look, this isn't my decision to make." Ariane put up
her hands, palms outward. "Matt's the owner of this ship
and the equivalent of mission commander. You guys work
this out. I've got to get back to my undocking checklists."

As if on cue, *Aether's Touch* announced, "Warning: Forty
minutes before service conversion. Resource charges will
rise one hundred fifty percent. Environmental system conversion procedures must be initiated."

She turned about and sprinted toward the ladder to the
control deck, having the benefit of station gravity. Once she
was back at her panels, she started bringing up the environmental systems on *Aether's Touch*. When they tested out

as operational, the ship could take over all environmental functions.

She looked up at the video portals of ship airlocks, corridors, and compartments. Matt and Joyce were conversing intently, but not audibly, and her hand hovered over the internal comm control for a moment. She shook her head and went back to her disconnection procedures. Matt hadn't asked for privacy, but he also hadn't said she should monitor their conversation.

"Did you tell her?" Joyce asked after Ari went up the ladder to the control deck.

"Tell her what?" Matt crossed his arms. "Changing the subject won't get you a free ride."

"You went through hell and high water to help save her, and you aren't going to tell her *why*?"

"I don't remember any water." That wasn't quite true. For a moment, Matt remembered the blue New Aegean Ocean of Hellas Prime as they hurtled down in a rock, or more precisely, a reusable reentry vehicle. Matt tried to erase the memory by focusing his irritation on Joyce. "Ari's an outstanding pilot and a damn fine crew member. I've had to trust her with my life out in new space, so why shouldn't I go to extremes to help her?"

Joyce rolled his eyes. "Good to see that you've got a healthy amount of denial."

"You've got less than two minutes to tell me why I should lug along another resource sink."

"Let's just say that when I get to G-145, I can deal with a loose thread, something that might be a hazard to Ari's health."

"Didn't you find Cipher's—her body?" Matt swallowed hard. He might not remember Cipher's real name, but he couldn't forget the spectacular display of her talent with explosives. The shrapnel hadn't reached his protected position in the hovercraft, but he'd watched the pilot struggle to stay airborne and he'd seen Edones's face turn to hamburger. However much he'd hated the supercilious colonel before, he forgave Edones *almost* everything for holding on to Ari through that explosion. When they'd pulled Ari aboard the hovercraft—

"That's, ah, part of the problem. They *say* they stopped their search because the hillside is unstable." Joyce's cocked eyebrow provided subtext: *Ari doesn't know that Cipher's body is missing, and neither of us should bring up the subject.*

Matt reran Joyce's words in his mind. "What do you mean they stopped the search? Who are '*they*'?"

"Leukos Industries froze AFCAW out. We're not getting cooperation from the civilians investigating the bombing on the Demeter Reserve. This might be because Mr. Leukos has a strange aversion to Colonel Edones."

"I'm not surprised, nor do I believe he's alone in his feelings," Matt deadpanned. "But what does this have to do with G-145? You should be on Hellas Prime if you're interested in what happened to Cipher."

"We think she might still be alive. If so, she's too smart to stay on Hellas Prime. She blew a hole in Karthage Point and took over the habitat environmental systems, and Karthage was *military*."

"I'll agree she's dangerous," Matt said. "But I'm still waiting for the connection to G-145."

"I'm meeting someone there who knows part of the Karthage puzzle and the meeting is—constrained, both by time and place." Joyce cleared his throat. "This person might help us get a fix on Cipher."

"You're meeting with a TEBI agent." Matt grinned as he watched Joyce raise his eyebrows. Of course, he'd give the balls off the Great Bull itself to go back to the time when he didn't know the acronym for the Terran Expansion League's Bureau of Intelligence. "I've picked up more than you realize, Joyce. If you discount rich Mr. Leukos with his mysterious background, there aren't too many others who know about Ari."

"And what, exactly, do you know?" Joyce's eyes were sharp.

"I know enough. Those were Terran intelligence agents who abducted and tortured Ari, while we dithered because Edones couldn't risk the precious Pax Minoica." His mouth snapped shut. *That's the one decision I'll* never *forgive Edones for making.* He also wouldn't admit to knowledge of Ari's background; she was one big snarl of secrets that he wasn't supposed to know, and couldn't accept knowing. For instance, whatever involvement she'd had in the Ura-Guinn detonation ... He blinked hard and refocused on Joyce.

"Okay. I've got an appointment to take one of those TEBI agents out of play, but I can't tell you anything more." Joyce spoke slowly, drawing out his words.

"You're not going to assassinate anybody, are you?" Matt was suddenly uncomfortable. While he was enraged with Terran State Prince Parmet's staff for what they'd done to Ari, he wasn't sure he wanted to exact blood in revenge. What sort of retribution *did* he want?

"The Directorate of Intelligence doesn't perform state assassinations," Joyce said stiffly.

"Yeah. Sure. I guess I don't need to know the specifics." Matt watched the status displays on the wall. He had plenty to do before disconnection: check cargo, equipment, seal inspections, etc. He didn't have time to negotiate with Joyce.

"We can carry you, but it'll cost six thousand." Matt faced Joyce, squarely looking him in the eyes. This price was twice the HKD, or Hellas Kilodrachmas, that the *Venture's Way* would charge.

"That's highway robbery, Mr. Journey."

"The highway's not established yet," Matt said. "New space is expensive and I'm risking our lives, as well as *my ship*, by going beyond my safety margins. If I were docking at an established habitat, I'd be fined."

Joyce shrugged. He keyed his implant and pointed to

a wall to display a transaction screen. After speaking his phrase for voiceprint analysis, he transferred funds into Matt's account.

I suppose, as a good Consortium citizen, I should ask where those funds are coming from—but right now, I don't care. Matt pointed at the end of the corridor. "You'll web into Ari's bunk for the drop."

"Yes, sir." Joyce sauntered down the corridor to crew quarters, whistling a tune as he went.

Matt tried to unclench his jaw as he turned his attention back to his mission and his ship. While he had faith in *Aether's Touch* and he could use another six thousand HKD, another person on this journey meant they'd be royally fucked if something went wrong.

CHAPTER 3

Crystal has preserved the Minoan surgical hits de-
stroying Qesan Douchet's hardened bunkers, as well
as the finality of genetically targeted bioweapons that
we still don't understand. Minoan "justice" wiped out
Douchet's tribal gene sets, *forever*. Today, anyone of
Terran Franko-Arabian descent should have his or her
DNA analyzed before visiting New Sousse, just in case.
Remember, the tribe also had roots in Terra's French
Brazilian colonies. . . .

—*Interview with Hellas Prime's Senator Raulini*,
2091.138.15.00 UT, indexed by *Heraclitus 11*, *Democritus
9* under Conflict, Cause and Effect Imperatives

Aether's Touch was quiet. The men were safely webbed
into their bunks, sleeping sweetly under D-tranny and
no longer sniping at each other. The ship's systems, as well as
the pesky AI, were shut down. The ship seemed to be holding its breath; with no thrusters or engines operating, there
were hardly any sounds. Ariane sighed in contentment.

Their separation from Athens Point had been flawless.
Their boost away from the habitat was enjoyable until
Joyce and Matt brought their male egos onto the control
deck. There just wasn't room enough for a working pilot
as well.

"Don't make me stop this boost," she warned them

when the verbal sparring pushed her over the edge. "I'll space the both of you if you don't shut up."

Their expressions might have been comical if she hadn't been serious: Preparing for an N-space drop was risky business. They meekly left the control deck for crew quarters so she could have her peace.

Her checklists required her to physically verify the licensing crystal in the ship's referential engine. The step was only a regulatory requirement and the only way to know she skipped it was to look at her logs, but she always took the time to climb down to the bulge. The side trip stretched her legs and calmed her predrop jitters.

The bulge held the Penrose Fold referential engine away from the ship's main footprint and when viewed from the outside, looked like a tumor eating away at the forward belly of the ship. An N-space-capable ship like *Aether's Touch* couldn't pretend to look aerodynamic, but then, that wasn't its function.

She moved toward the engine that rose out of the "floor" she stepped on, thanks to her sticky ship-soles as well as the gravity generator she'd left operating until the last possible moment. The engine's shape and the seams of its shielding always made it look as if it were smiling at her. She ran her hands over the cold shielding, marveling at humankind's greatest accomplishment prior to contact with the Minoans. Humankind learned how to enter N-space via the Penrose Fold—they'd never understood how to get *back* from N-space, until the Minoans provided the solution with their network of time buoys, the design of which was still a mystery.

A mystery we might solve in G-145, if the artifact we found there is a non-Minoan version of a time buoy. She pushed in the crystal and entered the acknowledgment number displayed across the engine's curved surface into her slate for the logs.

Before she left, she glanced up at the small figure of St. Darius that Matt had attached to the deck overhead. Matt had been raised to set great store in Darius as the patron saint and protector of space travelers and explorers. Ariane, on the other hand, raised in Gaian fundamentalist tradition on a planet, considered Darius only an altruistic and historically significant figure, but it didn't hurt to pay her respects. She nodded to the figure and whispered a quick prayer to Gaia before turning away.

Back on the control deck, she webbed herself in and turned off the gravity generator. She double-checked the D-tranny dosages for Joyce and Matt. After shutting down the real-space navigation system, she pressed an ampoule of cognitive dissonance enhancer against her implant. She watched the ampoule drain and the implant start dispensing the protective drug for piloting N-space into her bloodstream. This drug was nicknamed clash, and steering through N-space without it was equivalent to committing yourself to the nearest psych ward for disassociative-based insanity. She had done one emergency drop without preparation, having to get her drugs dispensed while in N-space. She'd kept her sanity—although she supposed there were some who questioned that—but ended up hospitalized, taking intravenous nutrition for a couple days before she could keep her food down. *Nothing would make me go through* that *experience again.*

Clash, besides lowering some sort of quantum threshold within her neural synapses, made her edgy and gave her headaches. This effect had become worse after AFCAW meddled with her biochemistry. She now needed high dosages, so much higher than needed by normal human physiology that only AFCAW physicians evaluated her and prescribed her N-space dosages.

However, she shouldn't complain: She'd volunteered for the experimental rejuv and now she had a body that could recover from almost any amount of alcohol and drugs. Of course, she still suffered from overindulgence, like anyone else. She just had a hell of a recovery rate. Smiling wryly, she searched in her chest pocket for the street smooth that she usually used to cut the edge from the clash. Smooth was legal but wasn't an approved supplement for use in N-space.

She paused, her hand frozen. Last time the ship came back from G-145, she'd risked getting a fine, perhaps even having her license suspended, by the stuffy Athens Point officials. *But no one in new space even cares*, her mind countered. However, regulations or the risks of fines hadn't stopped her hand, but rather words she'd heard from Tafani. *Major Kedros, treating your body like a cocktail plainly proves your problem.* When she countered with examples of self-medication, he answered, *Don't you think that people who medicate themselves might also suffer from substance abuse?* She hadn't known what to think, except that she felt trapped. She had desperately hoped Tafani would answer questions, not propose more.

Fuck you, Tafani—I won't let you sit in my mind and mess me up. The savage spike of anger she felt surprised her, even frightened her with its intensity. She put the smooth tablet on her tongue and let it dissolve as she purged her emotions with deep breaths through her nose.

After she reconfigured her console, shut down everything that ran on Neumann processors, and picked up her manual checklist, she felt better. She piloted N-space for a living and she was damn good at it, regardless of the undermining echoes of Tafani in her head. With a tap of her finger, she started the Penrose Fold referential engine. She watched it go through initialization, safety checks, and the determination that there were no operating thrusters and no N-space connection through a gravity generator. It proclaimed itself happy with a green status light.

On cue, the twitching heartbeat signal displayed on her console, showing that she'd locked on to the Hellas inner-system time buoy. She had put the ship in the outgoing corridor, although the corridor was merely a convention used to manage traffic. Most important, *Aether's Touch* was far from the strictly defined incoming-traffic channel. Regardless of how ships dropped out of real-space, the buoys sequenced and precisely positioned the ships in the incoming channel, which was one of those mysterious safety features designed into the Minoan time buoy network.

Their keys were dialed in and she waited for a response from the buoy. Not only did the time buoy network have to program and calculate their nous-transit, but the Pilgrimage generational ship also had to approve her keys because their destination buoy wasn't "open." A moment passed before the display told her that they'd arrive in G-145 in eight hours and forty-nine minutes, using Universal Time. The transit estimate was generally accurate, although the pilot wouldn't feel the passage of time correctly. Eight hours could feel like eight minutes or eighty hours—there was no way she could influence her experience, one way or the other.

She tilted her seat back and put on a visor that was an imitation of v-play equipment, although it only displayed the unprocessed external cam-eye circuits. Her webbing wiggled snug as she adjusted her visor and turned it on. She couldn't see the dark inner-system buoy, but she could see whatever the abbreviated spectrum of visible light could show her around *Aether's Touch*. Her selected outgoing corridor was crowded, which wasn't surprising. Hellas was a busy system and these ships could be bound for anywhere.

A large commercial freighter was the closest ship in her starboard view and as she watched, the bulbous area around their referential engine grew bright and the ship winked out with a flare, dropping into N-space. She tsk-tsked quietly with her tongue; the flash of photons as the ship transitioned indicated their engine wasn't tuned correctly and they were wasting energy generating the Penrose Fold.

She put one hand on the N-space control and sent the drop command to the referential engine. *Her* transition didn't cause a flare, and the *Aether's Touch* dropped into N-space as smoothly as a pearl slipping into a pool of oil.

* * *

Tahir Dominique Rouxe stowed his bags and sat down on his bunk, a move that didn't even require turning because his quarters were so small. He continued to hope that this was an exercise, exactly like J-132.

"This is the captain—there have been changes." The announcement played through all the nodes in the ship and Tahir's stomach clenched at the sound of stress in the man's voice. The captain's throat sounded tight. "The *Venture's Way* has changed its registered name to *Father's Wrath*. Repeat, we are now *Father's Wrath*. In addition, our departure for G-145 has been rescheduled. We're departing earlier, at twenty thirty. Unofficial guests should disembark at this time. Repeat, we—"

"Audio off," Tahir said.

It's started. This should be a joyous occasion, the fulfillment of his father's plans, the true implementation of Qesan's Cause. So why did he feel so much dread and foreboding? He didn't know how long he sat staring at his hands, the hands with the scientific precision that Father needed, but the hands Father hated. His father's hatred wasn't limited to his hands but concerned Tahir's very existence, and for good reason. Because of a Minoan attack upon their settlement, Tahir didn't carry his father's genetic profile. When Tahir underwent paternity testing as an infant, Father's probability of paternity had been equivalent to any randomly selected man. As tradition demanded, Tahir's mother had been tortured into idiocy before the real cause was uncovered, giving Father leave to blame his mother's condition on the Minoans also. When the men in the thirty-thousand-strong enclave learned they were all sterile after the Minoan attack, Father hadn't celebrated the exception of Tahir's birth. After all, Tahir didn't have the right genes.

The hatch to his quarters squealed as it opened and Tahir clenched his fists as he rose to face Abram Hadrian Rouxe, the man he was only allowed to call Father inside his own mind. Ironically, the man whose name derived from "father of multitudes" could no longer reproduce, which fed the hatred and obsession that Abram lived and breathed.

"Why G-145?" Tahir asked.

Abram's exact combination of alleles didn't match Tahir's, but they still looked very much alike. They both had medium builds and shocks of thick, straight dark hair over thin faces with natural scowls. After that, their differences were minor and one had to peer closely to see that Tahir's eyes were deep green rather than almost black. He also didn't have Abram's pitted leathery skin, evidence of his father's hard life.

"The resources in G-145 fulfill our objectives. Are you taking issue with my choice?"

"We're looking for a home where we can live in peace, but G-145 doesn't have a hospitable body of any sort, planet or moon. The last solar system did." Tahir kept his tone mild.

"That was a dry run. You didn't expect me to move before I got the Ura-Guinn data, did you? I had to have proof that a star of this type could survive a TD detonation, while still destroying the buoy." Abram looked over his shoulder. "Has Emery checked in yet?"

"E-130 is opening in two years with a habitable planet. Wouldn't the Cause be served better by that system?" Tahir asked.

The schedules of the generational ship lines were well-known and Tahir was comparing mission G-145, undertaken by the *Pilgrimage III*, to mission E-130, started by the *Campaign II* thirty-seven years ago and due to open in two years. Pre–Pax Minoica generational crews were opening both solar systems, which was one of Abram's criteria for his targets.

"There are issues with E-130. This system is our best bet." Abram made a gesture that signaled the end of the conversation, at least for him. "Is Emery delayed?"

"I thought the Cause was about living free from oppression and finding a safe haven. G-145 doesn't have the natural resources. . . ." His voice trailed away. Years of dealing with outsiders' ideas, yet always fearing his father's next surprise visit, left Tahir circumspect when stating his thoughts. Abram turned cold, dark eyes on him and he tried to keep from flinching.

"If you question my decision, then you doubt my devotion to the Cause."

"No, Fa—Abram, I don't." Regrettably, Tahir did have doubts, but not about Abram's devotion. He wondered how his father had financed everything. Where had the money come from? Were there hidden benefactors? After Abram had paid him one of those surprise visits on Mars, he'd followed his father and seen him meeting with someone. It took more years to find the identity of that someone, who turned out to be an obscure and anonymous aide who worked on an Overlord's staff. Since that time, Tahir had begun to wonder whether Abram's plans, and choices, were as independent as he maintained. *Yes, Father, I have plenty of doubts.*

When Abram didn't speak, Tahir added carefully, "It's just that G-145 seems an unlikely target for the Cause, and I was hoping you'd illuminate me."

"If you were truly the son of my loins, then you'd trust me. You'd have no questions, no need for *illumination.*" Abram's voice was dangerously flat.

"I *am* your son, and perhaps my opinion doesn't matter to you." Tahir looked away to avoid the confirmation in Abram's eyes. "But, if I'm confused about our objectives, what about the others? Those who follow you because you've sold them on the chance to make a better world without the Consortium, the League, or the Minoans?"

Abram shrugged. "They are only sheep that require a mission, and any mission will do."

"And sheep can be sacrificed." The voice came from Emery, who appeared next to Abram with a fierce grin on his face. "Particularly if they're outsiders."

"Emery!" Abram almost smiled as he embraced the youngest nephew of Qesan Douchet.

Unnoticed, Tahir threw himself on his bunk as Emery, his senior by one year, and Abram slapped each other on the back. He felt twinges of jealousy interspersed with loathing as he watched Emery, whom Abram called the son of his spirit. Tahir was thirty years old, yet he evidently still craved his father's praise and attention. He wanted to shout that this mission would be impossible without his "outside" life and education. After all, he had risked imprisonment—but since he'd served his purpose and provided the tools necessary for Abram's plans, he was no longer of interest.

"Do we have to take *everybody* to G-145?" asked Chander, standing in front of Isrid's desk.

"We're leaving your two older sisters, plus the entire household, tutorial, and security staff on Mars. I wouldn't agree that everybody is coming along."

Terran State Prince Isrid Sun Parmet signed *absolutely* the last form he was going to look at before this trip. His promotion to Overlord Three's Assistant for the Exterior had engendered hefty amounts of paperwork. He took a deep breath as he put down his newest slate, an accurate facsimile of the devices made in the Consortium, but not as robust.

"That's not what I mean. Does—" An announcement from the ship's systems cut through the boy's voice.

"All passengers must take their delta-tranquilizer and web into bunks for safety." The ship repeated this warning three times while Isrid watched his son, eleven years old and carrying the significant name of Chander Sky Parmet, squirm with frustration.

"Have you been doing your *somaural* exercises?" Isrid asked sharply before the boy said anything more.

"Yes." Chander's face turned even more sullen and he looked down at his feet.

"Then use them. I want objectivity. If you have to add emotion, do it *somaurally*."

To give his son credit, he tried. He drew himself up into a straight stance and Isrid saw him physically struggle to remove the resentment from his face. However, Chander was beginning adolescence and the self-destructive, emotional bedlam that pitted every youth against the world was too hard to hide. Already the anger ingrained in his mind showed in his body. Isrid sighed internally; it would be years before Chander purged the demons of his adolescence and became a thinking being again. If Isrid wanted to spend the time to concentrate, he'd see his son's beautiful orange-yellow aura muddied with darkness.

"I don't need both my mothers along to babysit me." Pride screamed from Chander's face and body, despite his attempts for objectivity. His arrogant profile, golden skin, and green eyes came from Isrid, but his thick chestnut hair with burgundy tones was a faded imitation of Sabina's. The combination was striking. Already Chander was catching looks from both females and males, and being the son of a Terran State Prince added to the curiosity. At this point, Isrid couldn't give Chander enough of his attention. He now wished he'd added another male into his multimarriage, even though he and his wives hadn't recovered from the trauma of losing his brother and potential co-husband.

"Both your mothers have told me their reasons for visiting G-145, and they have nothing to do with you." Isrid made sure his hand signals were precise.

"Even Pri'mom?" he asked, referring to his primary mother.

Of course, Sabina was probably behind this in some way. Her main hobby was being a master manipulator, while Garnet, his other co-wife, was almost boring in her lack of layers. With Garnet, what you saw was what you got. With Sabina, one never knew her true motives, which added to her spice. However, Isrid was tired and he wasn't willing to speculate on Sabina's motives, particularly with his young son.

"Pri'mom hasn't said you need oversight, but I'm sure she can't resist critiques. Am I correct?" Isrid smiled as Chander ducked his head again. "And as long as she isn't correcting you in front of others, perhaps you should note her advice."

"I can handle that, Dad."

Isrid waited.

"Maria's out there, you know." Chander chewed his lip and shifted his weight from foot to foot.

The shipwide announcement telling passengers to web in for the eventual N-space drop blared again and while it repeated, Isrid observed his son. How much should he tell the boy? Chander was old enough to know that marriage wasn't for love; its purposes were for breeding approval, raising children, and, of course, serving as a political tool. If his son knew about Sabina's obsession with Maria Guillotte, then he probably knew both his primary parents were Maria's regular lovers. However, Maria could never enter a Terran marriage due to genetic damage she'd received near Tantor's Sun. For Sabina, that made Maria an enticing morsel, especially because she could never fully own and control her.

Isrid wondered if Sabina had thought he was jealous when he'd sent Maria away two months ago. But he'd assigned Maria to oversee the contractors in G-145 because of the sensitivity of the situation. Maria handled people and personality problems deftly, in addition to being his best analyst with a military intelligence background. Those Terran contractors had only a tenuous right to work on that moon—none of them knew he'd gotten the leases by kidnapping, torturing, and coercing Major Ariane Kedros.

Kedros had seemed immune to their standard drug-induced torture and he'd had to threaten to expose her and her former crew as the destroyers of Ura-Guinn, at which point she'd signed the Aether Exploration leases over. Maria understood the double-blackmail scheme hanging over the leases, and how everything depended upon Kedros staying quiet.

"Maria's not the *real* reason she's going, you know," Chander said cannily, breaking Isrid's train of thought.

"And what is?" Isrid asked.

"I don't know, but I can sense *revenge*. I wanted to warn you." Such adult words from a boy of eleven.

Isrid looked for signs that Chander was lying or exaggerating. He wasn't, which led Isrid to consider the idea that Sabina had underestimated her own son and let her guard down, something she would never do around Isrid.

"Thank you, Chander." Isrid inclined his head as if he were talking to an adult and added the signal, *I am grateful*.

His response delighted the boy. Isrid sent him to his quarters. He called and placated the ship's crew, who were worried about missing the departure window from Mars Orbital Two. Then he took his D-tranny and quickly webbed himself into the bunk in his private quarters.

As he dozed, Isrid's mind skipped to Major Kedros. His first action, when he woke, would be to order an intelligence report on her recent activities. Although the Feeds ecstatically proclaimed the Ura-Guinn sun had survived, his classified government sources didn't project a good prognosis for the habitats in the system. Instead of going out quickly in a nova, his brother and family might have suffered a slow, agonizing death from cosmic radiation caused by flares or coronal mass emissions, which didn't engender any sympathy in him for Kedros. He smiled as he fell asleep. He hoped Kedros had been dismissed or, at the least, suffered the wrath of AFCAW's Directorate of Intelligence for opening G-145 to Terran defense contractors.

CHAPTER 4

The crèche-get in their city-ships aren't like you and me. They're always out of fashion after they get to their arrival point, where they sit for a couple years, sucking up all the news they can and begging for spare gametes to keep their gene pool healthy. Makes me wonder what *kind* of agreements the Generational Lines make with the Minoans. [Reply not indexed.] They're the only ones entrusted with installing the precious time buoys, that's why.

—*Grant Iordanou*, Public Node at XiCheng Crossing & Stephanos Street, Alexandria, Hellas Prime, 2105.99.17.02 UT, indexed by *Heraclitus 12* under Conflict Imperative

N-space piloting was like steering a sensory deprivation tank through a canyon of indescribable terrors. The navigational "path," different for every pilot, wound between shadowy maelstroms. Baleful furnaces whipped up flashes and discharges of energy. If a pilot turned away from the path or peered too earnestly into the storms, faces appeared and hungry flickers of energy reached out—but Ariane *never* looked into the maelstrom.

As she'd tried to explain to Muse 3, human consciousness and concentration were required to steer a ship through N-space. Even though the maneuvers could be exhilarating, she felt the clash numb and separate her from what felt like submerged and instinctual terrors. Physically, she could expect weight loss, fatigue, and, after extremely bad drops, loss of hair. The clash helped her concentrate and got her through to the worst point: the transition back to real-space. Even under the best conditions, this was unpleasant.

Ariane sent the transition command to the referential engine via protected connections that didn't use processors. Each time she started the procedure to get back to real-space, she thanked Gaia that shielded analog circuits worked in N-space.

Next came the nausea. Knowing that this intense feeling would pass helped her move to the next step, flip a switch, mark it off, and move on to the step after that. . . .

The nausea abated and the sensations started. This was when the pilot realized how unpleasant light, sound, touch, smell, and taste could be. As usual, she smelled caustic cleaning lye, tasted something metallic, and felt deafened by the humming equipment. The console burned like ice.

During the transition, she always tried to picture her mother's laboratory and how it smelled. Her mother had been a designer botanist on Nuovo Adriatico, developing substitutes for popular spices, namely cinnamon and cardamom. There were always samples made into candies and sweetbreads; she remembered the sound of her mother's voice: *Try some, Ari, and tell me what you think.* Her mother was the first to use her middle name, Ahrilan, as her nickname, which had made her transformation to "Ariane Kedros" easier.

Luckily, these were memories that Ariane Kedros could allow herself, since Owen had been careful to create her false records with a similar name and background. Ariane Kedros had also been raised by botanists on Nuovo Adriatico. Those particular botanists, now dead, might have been surprised to find they had a child and they weren't buried anywhere near her real parents. This hadn't caused her any difficulties, since she'd purposely avoided going back to Nuovo Adriatico.

Her senses eventually calmed down. The air that circulated in the ship had the slight smell of ceramic dust. She started up navigational and real-space systems, seeing the destination channel blink on the console. The ship was right where it was supposed to be, in the system whose formal designation was a long and forgettable alphanumeric string. Everyone called the system G-145; the number was the generational mission and the Gamma indicated the Pilgrimage ship line, which had expended the years to drag a precious time buoy out here.

She started the gravity generator and the incoming message signal beeped, making her jump. Someone sent a package to Matt before the ship entered N-space, and the Pilgrimage crew had allowed delivery through the G-145 buoy. After she acknowledged receipt, the envelope flared into the center of her display. She saw the seal of Athens Point Law Enforcement revolving above angry red text that said, "Positive identification of receiver required for service."

Uh-oh. That might indicate a remote subpoena. This package wouldn't open for anyone but Matt, so it ended up on his queue. She shrugged and pushed the wake-up alarms for Matt and Joyce, even though they might have wakened naturally since the ship systems would have signaled their implants to stop the D-tranny.

"Hey, Ari, you don't look too bad. Must have been an easy drop," Matt said when he eventually climbed up on the control deck.

Meaning I still have my hair and I only lost a little weight. Ariane's mouth twitched as she turned in her chair. In that motion, she realized how tired she felt.

Matt's shirt trailed on the deck from one hand while he stared at the in-the-round display above and in front of her console. His bare chest was exposed and she made herself look away from this close sample of a lean, muscled male abdomen. After all, Matt was *crew*.

"An awesome sight, right in the middle of our front window," Matt said. Of course, *Aether's Touch* didn't have real windows because of radiation.

"What is *that*?" Joyce was dressed in crisp civilian clothes, though they somewhat resembled a uniform. "Hey, don't you guys require shirt and shoes to work here?"

"That is the *Pilgrimage Three*, one of the largest generational ships ever built. What a beauty!" Matt pulled on his shirt and padded over to the front console, ignoring Joyce's barb about not wearing his sticky-soled shoes.

"We're on approved docking vector and our gravity generator is aligned." Ariane looked up at the display. True, the *Pilgrimage III* was impressive. Currently configured in habitat mode, the generational ship looked like a fairy castle with spires bursting upward from her bulky engines and gravity generator.

"Have you done voice check-in?" Matt looked at the console, examining the status.

"No. I only sent our ship key and got our docking vector. If you want to formally check in, be my guest," Ariane said.

Matt tapped the console. "*Pilgrimage Three*, this is the *Aether's Touch* on approach as directed. We're carrying three crew members, with the following authorization keys."

The response was immediate and cheery. "Welcome back to Gamma-145, *Aether's Touch*. Looking forward to greeting everyone. *Pilgrimage Three* out."

"What do they mean by 'greeting'?" Joyce said suspiciously.

"It's tradition for everyone to disembark upon entry to the solar system, tour the controlling generational ship, and meet with the command staff. It allows them to catch up on Autonomist, or Terran, idioms and customs. A dinner is usually involved." Ariane swiveled her chair around to look at Joyce. His dismayed expression didn't raise any sympathy in her.

"Is there a problem, *Mr.* Joyce?" Matt's tone was acidic. "Please, enlighten us."

"I need to get to Beta Priamos Station. Quickly."

"Well, well." Ariane saw Matt's brown eyes flicker, then harden.

Priamos was the moon with ruins of an ancient, but non-Minoan, culture; Ariane and Matt had first prospected it months before. Orbiting Priamos, Beta Priamos Station had an elevator down to that moon, as well as the best access to "the artifact," as everybody called the possibly defunct buoy. Not only was the artifact firmly anchored in Aether Exploration's claim, but Matt and Ariane had left their most expensive bot on it during their last prospecting season. They hadn't deserted this bot voluntarily, which was another story entirely. Regardless, any research regarding the artifact or the ruins should generate wealth for Aether Exploration, so Matt was a bit protective about the commercial processes inside G-145.

"Our business, as prospectors, is entwined with the generational ship lines and we *will* observe their customs. I'm including you in that statement, Joyce." Matt abruptly left the control deck.

"Is it me, or did he wake up on the wrong side of his bunk?"

"Don't worry, it's definitely *you*." She couldn't miss a chance to needle Joyce, although she wondered if Matt had opened the message from Athens Point LEF. She swiveled back to face the console and display walls. "We've got light-speed data now, so let me introduce you to G-145."

Joyce sat down beside her as she adjusted the displays to first show the entire solar system.

"We have your predictable system here," she said. "The sun is slightly larger than Sol, but its radiation specs are right on. All the planetary orbits are in the same plane. For major planets, we've got three rocks toward the sun and three gas giants, one barely within the inner system and two far out. The divide between the inner and outer system is a huge meteor belt of junk."

"Nothing with Gaian-based life, or at most, nothing usable." Joyce kept up with net-think.

"Except for the ice ball named Sophia Two, but you're right, G-145 appeared to be a bust." She nodded. "It didn't have exotic resources or seem worthy of colonization. When we checked in with the *Pilgrimage* for our first prospecting season, the buzz was that everyone would lose money; no one could recoup costs for this mission. Here's our original claim."

On the wall in front of them, the image adjusted backward in time, the planets moving retrograde. Tapping, she laid a continuous three-dimensional swathe over the solar system image. This space-time slice went through the meteor belt twice and it swung by the inner gas giant close enough to extend their placer claim over one moon.

"Laomedon and Priamos, its moon," Joyce said. "I've done my homework. Laomedon is the innermost gas giant and Priamos is its second-largest moon."

"More importantly, our placer claim covers this point." Ariane zoomed in on what looked like an empty spot of space near Laomedon, which only resolved to a dot with a designation string of garbled letters and numbers.

"I take it that's where the artifact sits. Is that a stable Lagrange point?"

"*No*. It's *anchored*, with no station-keeping propulsion to be found. The only example we've got of something that never moves with respect to planetary bodies is the Minoan time buoys."

"So that's why we have a gaggle of scientists hired by contractors on all sides: Terran, Autonomist, and let's not forget the Minoans. What a mess." Joyce shook his head.

She winced. Part of this problem had resulted when she signed over leases to Terran interests. Those leases had saved her life; they were her payment for Parmet's protection of her and Brandon's identities. If she and Matt didn't protest the legality of her signatures, Parmet wouldn't release information that Ariane was pilot, and the mysterious, rich Mr. Leukos commander, of the crew that destroyed—that *might* have destroyed—the Terran Ura-Guinn Colony.

On the other hand, Matt was the one who had balanced the Terran against the Autonomist against the Minoan contractors. He'd also tried to balance military contractors with purely commercial ones. It'd been tedious for him to get the right counteractions. When he showed her the lease and contracting structure, he'd emphasized that this was unavoidable and perhaps the best step forward for humankind.

"Matt's streamlining the reporting. He created a new matrix that's been approved by the CAW Space Exploration, Exploitation, and Economics Control Board." She couldn't avoid using a defensive tone, still feeling guilty for all the work that Matt had to do for the SEEECB flunkies.

"Don't worry. Although he'll never admit it to Mr. Journey, the colonel thinks he did the right thing. The colonel even admires the Byzantine snarl that's resulted." Joyce grinned.

As if I care about what Owen Edones thinks. She wondered why Owen had sent Joyce here and immediately squelched her curiosity. She didn't have a need to know, but she'd bet a hundred HKD that this had something to do with the Terrans. They were still the *enemy,* or at the least, they were *the other side*, no matter what lip service AFCAW intelligence gave to Pax Minoica.

"There's more to interest the Terrans than just the artifact." She changed the display to zoom in on the third planet from the sun, labeled Sophia II. "They think the Builders— that's what they're calling this alien civilization—were terraforming this planet. They found what they think are inactive sensors on the surface."

"I thought they found nothing artificial on any of the inner planets during the second-wave prospecting." Joyce picked up his slate and began making notes. "Sophia Two was staked by Taethis Exploration; why didn't they catch this earlier?"

"There's a limit to what second-wave prospectors can

find using telebots. The lessee now has contractors capable of surface exploration."

"Are the contractors Terran?" Joyce asked.

"I don't think that matters as much in new space as you think it does."

"The Terrans will be all over this, given their problems with Mars and Earth."

"Not Earth—Terra. Once you leave this ship, you should avoid offensive words." She clipped her words, irritated. He apparently thought his mission, whatever it was, would be business as usual. It wouldn't, not in new space. "You're going to have to get used to new space, Joyce. There's a mishmash of backgrounds and loyalties here; our governing bodies are far away and we're isolated. You practically breathe ComNet on any Autonomist world, but it won't even exist here. That means no timely news or feeds, no safety monitoring, no automatic nine-one-one access, and you have to get into the queue to make calls home. There's no such thing as free bandwidth out of this system. Not while that generational ship has to get more than twenty-five years of data downloaded and processed."

She ran out of breath and stopped her minidiatribe. Tapping a command, she showed the view of the *Pilgrimage III* looming imminent and by now, filling the entire screen.

"And don't make trouble for Matt," she added. "He's had enough problems lately."

"I won't make any trouble." Joyce's voice was grave, but the corners of his eyes wrinkled with humor. "As long as I don't have to eat generational ship food."

Ariane laughed. "If I have to eat dinner aboard the *Pilgrimage*, then so do you. Worse, you have to pay for your food."

"That'll be the day."

"Of course, you get credit if you donate genetic material," she said.

He snorted. "I'll never sink to jacking off for money.

You haven't sold them anything, have you? What about Mr. Journey?"

"We haven't had time." At his expression, she said, "Seriously, Joyce, there's nothing obscene about it, once you can get over the privacy issues. They've got to contend with real-space, which prevents women from carrying babies to term. Besides, they never know when they'll be stranded light-years from civilization, and they can't even trust that the civilization they left still exists. They need a viable gene pool for healthy children and, possibly, for rebuilding our species."

"I don't care; they're not getting any of my little guys. Only my wife gets those."

She rolled her eyes, remembering the time she'd met Joyce's wife. That woman was a saint. "Why do men think they're superheroes simply because they can produce sperm?"

"Just get us docked, will you?"

Matt's mood didn't improve when he looked over his messages in his quarters. He'd seen the package from Athens Point Law Enforcement Forces, and if Ari hadn't acknowledged and allowed it to download—no, that wasn't fair. She was operating the ship and it was her responsibility to accept any messages directed to *Aether's Touch*.

He stared at the LEF seal revolving over the text. Since they knew the message had reached the ship, he had to open it. He sighed, looking at the text that said, "Positive identification of receiver required for service."

He'd already had unpleasant dealings with Athens Point LEF and, while this should be a request for relevant information, he had his doubts. He knew the LEF had finished gathering evidence for prosecuting Nestor's murderer, a customs official named Hektor Valdes. Unfortunately, Valdes wasn't rolling over on his employer, accomplices, or contacts. This remote subpoena probably meant they hadn't shut down the graft that flowed through Athens Point Customs. They were flailing around, expanding their voracious appetite for information, whether relevant or not. Worse, they might be feeling vindictive.

There was no sense in delaying any longer; he provided his voice and thumbprint for identification. He clenched his jaw as he read what the subpoena required. Great. Not only did they require an affidavit answering certain questions; they wanted a time-stamped copy of everything Nestor had sent him in the past year, and that meant exposing Muse 3. He had twenty-four hours to hand everything over to one of their authorized representatives.

He needed a lawyer, fast.

"I don't know why *I* have to be part of this parade," Joyce muttered into Ariane's ear while Matt moved through the airlock ahead of them.

"You heard him." Ariane nodded toward Matt's back. "We'll observe all generational ship customs, to include tours and dinners."

"But you've already gone through this once. Isn't that enough for everyone on our ship?"

"Nice try, Joyce. We always do the meet and greet; the Pilgrimage ship line is sovereign here, so consider it a complex border-crossing ritual."

"I'm going to gag if I have to eat any crèche-get food," whispered Joyce in a warning tone, but Ariane pretended not to hear him.

Ahead, Matt was shaking the hand of the senior staff representative, a woman with an unlined face and faded, short brown hair.

"Commander Charlene Pilgrimage. I'm off shift and I can give you the tour." The woman extended her hand. "Missed you the first time you came through."

This willowy woman commanded the huge generational ship *Pilgrimage III*, or as currently configured, habitat. Ariane should have learned by now that she couldn't make assumptions about the age or experience of generational ship crew members. Charlene Pilgrimage might have been born before her parents, or even grandparents.

"Ariane Kedros, pilot of the *Aether's Touch.*" She shook Charlene's hand, appreciating the purpose she felt in the commander's hand and arm.

Ariane looked around while Matt introduced *Mr.* Joyce. They were standing in the welcome area, a room fed by several hallways from the passenger airlocks. Two lines of four pews faced a shrine to St. Darius set into a niche in the wall. Of course, everything was bolted down to the walls or deck.

In generational ship fashion, the room was monochromatic, if one discounted the dark gray pattern on the deck. The walls were deep, golden yellow, while the doors and the shrine were outlined with light yellow. She walked toward the shrine, whose niche was backed with a mosaic of glittering gold tiles. At the top of the niche were two lines: ST. DARIUS INTERCEDES AND PROTECTS ALL EXPLORERS WHOM GAIA INVITES INTO ITS UNIVERSE.

As in the fundamental Gaia-ist tradition, no artistic rendering appeared, nor was any gender attributed to the Highest Creator. The golden statue of St. Darius, on the other hand, was lifelike and detailed. He stood in a helmetless environmental suit and held out his hands in benediction.

"If you're interested, Ms. Kedros, there are services here every day at nineteen hundred." Charlene's voice came from behind her.

Turning, Ariane saw that the group had moved past the pews toward the airlock. She followed them to the ladder that led upward through the vertical airlock between modules. What looked like spires from afar were towers of stacked modules that could separate, provided the disconnection charges blew properly. The deck of each module was "down" toward the engines or, when in habitat mode, toward the gravity generator.

She looked up the ladder and saw all three ports yawning open. Anyone could climb up onto the control deck, but generational ships were more concerned with the dangers of long-term real-space travel, rather than security. There were many examples of the hazards generational ships faced: the mysterious loss of the *Voyage II*, or the disastrous mission of F-58, when less than fifty percent of the *Expedition I* made it to the buoy setup point. As she climbed through the thick middle where the airlock separated, Ariane noted that the inspection date was two days ago and the autohoist, used to move heavy items through the airlock when the ship was operating with gravity, was securely tied to one side. What the *Pilgrimage*'s crew lacked in security, they made up for in safety.

She stepped onto the control deck after the others. The primary control deck was circular and lined with every conceivable type of console layout. There were mechanical switches as backups to automated systems, even though this ship couldn't transition into N-space.

"Hey, Ariane. Glad to see you back." Justin, the communications officer, waved at her.

"You're working third shift now?" She drifted over to Justin's console while the commander made a determined effort to give Joyce, the newcomer, an introduction briefing. She looked up at Justin's bandwidth readings, noting the amount given over to the *Pilgrimage* was largest. After that, the research and development bandwidth ranked second.

"Can you show me the contractor bandwidth distribution?" she asked, smiling back at Justin.

He obligingly expanded the display so she could see which contractors were using the bandwidth, and where they were located.

Meanwhile, the parade had worked its way around to the traffic console. She heard Joyce ask sharply, "Who's on that ship?"

Her gaze followed Joyce's pointed finger and her smile faded as her face went numb. On the list of recent arrivals to G-145 and ahead of *Aether's Touch* by several hours, was the *Candor Chasma*—a name forever embedded in her mind. Printed beside its Terran name were the words, "Planet Registration: Mars, Purpose: Dignitary Transport." Her stomach twisted. *Parmet's ship*. Its next destination was the Priamos moon of Laomedon.

"That's Terran Overlord Three's Assistant for the Exterior. They left for Priamos an hour before you arrived," Charlene said.

"State Prince Parmet?" Matt glanced at Ariane, his expression a mix of shock and resignation.

"Did you know about this?" Ariane asked Joyce, her voice low with anger. *So help me, if Owen knew and didn't warn me....*

Joyce, however, looked concerned also. He shook his head to answer Ariane's question and turned to Matt. "Now it's even more important that I get to Priamos as soon as possible. Remember my appointment?"

Joyce and Matt locked glances. Meanwhile, the generational ship crew looked on with lively interest.

"Do you know the Terran State Prince, or is this a matter of conflicting politics?" asked Commander Charlene.

Ariane shook her head and avoided meeting Charlene's eyes. Crèche-get could be annoying when they were catching up on events. They took their neutrality seriously, more than anyone else did, meaning they thought they should be privy to everyone's secrets. Granted, this crew had plenty to learn. In the decades between the *Pilgrimage*'s launch and their arrival in G-145, the use of a temporal-distortion weapon had ended the war between the Consortium of Autonomist Worlds and the Terran Expansion League. The *Pilgrimage* crew had also missed the beginning of Pax Minoica, brokered by the Minoans.

"Parmet was probably sent to represent the Terran companies that signed our leases and monitor the contractors doing research on Priamos—that's why we're so interested." Matt diverted Charlene's interest.

So many secrets. So hard to remember who knows what

about whom. Matt knew Parmet had tortured her and that she'd signed the leases under duress, but did he know why? Did he know exactly what she, Brandon, and Cipher had done during the war? This was why she needed the blessed numbness of alcohol and smooth to quiet the buzzing of all the secrets in her head.

"You'll have to excuse us, Commander. I need to speak privately with my pilot and *him*." Matt jerked his thumb to indicate Joyce. "Got a place we could use?"

"Certainly, Mr. Journey. I can let you use a small enclosure off the chapel on the floor below. It's secure." Charlene pointed back down the vertical airlock.

"Secure, my ass!" Once inside, Joyce growled and paced around the small room. "There's nothing secure on this damn ship and I wish I had the equipment to prove it."

"Doesn't matter, does it?" Matt stared at Joyce. "Even if we had a secure facility, you wouldn't tell us why you're going to Beta Priamos."

"Do you really want to know?"

"No," Ariane and Matt responded in unison.

"See?" Joyce smiled grimly. Matt glared in response.

Ariane put her arm on Matt's to get his attention. "What's going on?"

"We've got a problem. I have to delay the contractor meeting. I've got to give a deposition within the next twenty-two hours, and I'll need representation." Matt glanced uncomfortably toward Joyce. "They've subpoenaed Nestor's packages, the ones he sent me before he died. I need to fight this, so I don't see us leaving the *Pilgrimage* for another day, at the least."

He was protecting himself and Ariane—because they were harboring an illegal AI. But he was also protecting Muse 3 itself, all he had left of his friend. Over Matt's shoulder, Ariane saw Joyce's eyebrows go up.

"What about my schedule?" Joyce asked. Ariane and Matt ignored him.

"So?" She shrugged. "Let me go out to Priamos and take care of the contractor meeting."

There was silence as Matt and Joyce stared at her in shock.

"What? Why the surprise?" she asked.

"No offense, Ari, but you haven't shown much interest in the business side of this exploration company. Now you want to present a reporting matrix to a bunch of—er—hostile contractors?" Matt asked.

"Sure. You already familiarized me with all the reporting ins and outs."

"Maj—Ms. Kedros, you avoid business and anything that smells like paperwork." Joyce looked at her skeptically.

"Yes, and it's time I changed that. Matt's been asking me to shoulder more of the administrative load." Turning to Matt, she asked, "Isn't that right?

"But now we find that Parmet will be at Priamos. It's too dangerous for you, Ari."

She drew a deep breath. "I figured we could run into him. I know that Maria Guillotte's already there managing contractors who, not surprisingly, have strong connections to the Terran Space Forces. I can handle it."

"No. They tortured you, Ari." Matt looked for support from Joyce, but didn't get any. The sergeant's face closed and he crossed his arms as he leaned against the wall. He was staying out of this discussion. Matt added, "I thought Parmet hinted that if he saw you again—well, he'd do something."

"I'm not going to let his threats rule my life, or *yours*. We need to be able to go about our business." She was adamant, or at least she could *act* resolute, as Matt looked searchingly into her face. Internally, she was less sure. What would she do when she ran into Maria or Parmet? Smile brightly and say, *Hey, remember me? A couple months ago you pumped me full of mind-altering drugs and pain enhancers, then beat me up, broke my legs, blackmailed me, and dumped me in an addict commons.*

"You could end up sitting across a conference table from them." As he watched her, Matt looked less doubtful.

"Sure. But the Terran leases depend upon my silence and they know that. I doubt they'll attempt to mug me in the station halls."

Relief and worry battled on Matt's face, but cleared when she smiled at him. Sure, she'd love to shun the stuffy business briefings, but Matt and his leases had saved her life.

So it was settled. Well, maybe not.

"What about *my* schedule?" Joyce asked. "It takes around ten hours to get to Beta Priamos—"

"Nine point five hours in *Aether's Touch*," Ariane said.

"Fine. To make your meeting, Ms. Kedros, you don't need to leave for another eight hours, but I should get to Beta Priamos as soon as possible."

Matt was seriously considering Joyce's words. He locked glances with her. This was unlike Matt, violating crew rest guidelines by making her turn around the ship so fast, but his eyes asked her to do it. He knew something. What was so important about Joyce getting to Priamos? She sighed, knowing how this would play out, and agreed.

"I'll follow you out to Priamos when *Venture's Way* gets here," Matt said.

After he left, she frowned at Joyce. "Tell me you didn't do that just to get out of dinner on the *Pilgrimage*."

Joyce smiled.

CHAPTER 5

The College of History is at fever pitch: We're finally getting data surrounding the Ura-Guinn detonation. What
happened to the inhabitants and how did they cope?
We're analyzing the signals broadcasted soon after
the detonation. The chaotic fragments and the signal-
to-noise ratio make this nearly impossible, but this is
why we built the Epsilon Eridani deep-space, high-gain
antenna.

—*Journal of Marcus Alexander*, Sophist at Konstantinople
Prime University, 2105.326.09.15 UT, indexed by
Democritus 9 under Cause and Effect Imperative

Ariane got the ship serviced, undocked, and in a boost
toward Priamos. For their safety and comfort, she
turned on the gravity generator. Then she slept.

"You look better," Joyce said when she reappeared on
the control deck. He had minded the consoles while she
slept for a couple hours.

She plopped down onto the secondary control seat
and looked at their position. They'd recently passed by a
relay, which used the Minoan time buoy to shuttle faster
than light communications around the solar system. "Is the
comm forwarding up?"

"I pinged the relay and it's not operational yet. Perhaps
it's time to complain to the Pilgrimage staff. However, we
did get a light-speed message from Mr. Journey. He said

he'd be talking to a lawyer 'bout the time we arrive at Beta Priamos."

"Thanks for copiloting," she added, running her fingers through her hair. As usual, her short, loose curls arranged themselves obediently; she'd been lucky to get her mother's dark hair, eyes, and complexion. She felt a pang of guilt as she thought of her mother and father, both passing away while she was on active duty during the war. Then, before she could take leave and visit their graves, the Ura-Guinn event occurred and her new identity barred her from visiting that crypt in a little town on the shore of Nuovo Adriatico Estes.

"I wouldn't worry," Joyce said.

"Huh?"

"Don't worry about Parmet. The Terran leases depend upon your silence, so I doubt he'll even acknowledge your presence."

She recalled the hazy memory she had of Parmet leaning over her. At the time, he was the only other person in the small hold where she'd been bound to a stretcher and tortured. He talked to her, and acknowledged she'd saved his life. *After I pay this debt*, he had said, *if we see each other again, don't expect the same mercy*. She pictured his face, his hatred.

"I plan to avoid him and his family," she said.

"Don't waste the gray cells. Sometimes you think too much, Major. You're best when you're acting off the cuff." Joyce looked sideways at her, his expression neutral. "As for Mr. Journey, he needs some acting lessons. I can tell he's hiding something."

Muse 3 had remained quiet, per Matt's cautions, since Joyce's appearance. She wondered how much Joyce and Edones had already surmised, since Nestor had obviously dabbled in illicit AI. Muse 3 wasn't registered and Matt didn't want to give anyone the justification for tearing the AI apart in an effort to analyze its rulesets. She hoped he could work something out with the Pilgrimage legal office.

"Matt is probably covering for your mission. What did you tell him that he has to hide from *me*?" She went on the offensive to deflect Joyce's curiosity.

"You think he's keeping something from you?"

"There could be plenty of reasons for you to visit Priamos or its station, and you could have convinced Matt that it'd be in *my* interest. Maria used to be an operative for TEBI and Parmet used to run that organization, so who would you be—"

"That's enough speculation. When will you get approach vectors for Beta Priamos?" Joyce looked away.

She grinned. *So many secrets*.

Matt hated seeing his ship leave without him.

"I need an appointment with the Office of General Counsel," Matt said to Charlene, after he watched *Aether's Touch* separate from the *Pilgrimage III*.

"With the counsel himself, or the legal staff?" She didn't bat an eyelid at his request. Matt was a generational orphan from the Journey line, but he still counted as one of them. She was happy to extend their services to him, although he wouldn't get them for free.

The first appointment he could get was late in the next shift, giving him time to apply for a seat on the *Venture's Way*. After getting on the standby list, he went to dinner at the commander's table. Four other people dined at the table this shift, including Senior Commander Meredith and Commander Charlene, two of the three commanders on the *Pilgrimage*.

Matt had previously met Senior Commander Meredith, a quiet and conservative gentleman, on his first prospecting mission to G-145. After shaking Meredith's hand and digging into his favorite noodle dish, Matt had a warm, satisfying feeling of coming *home*. Perhaps the old adage was true: "You can orphan the man from his ship, but you'll never remove the ship from his blood." The ship was the generational crew member's protection, society, home, and family. The *Journey IV* had been Matt's entire world until he was sixteen years old and had opted off it.

After dining and sending a message to *Aether's Touch*, Matt prepared for his meeting. Pilgrimage's general counsel was a man known across all the ship lines as an eclectic expert on Autonomist and Terran law, Minoan contracts and treaties, and the obscure field of artificial intelligence rights. Just what he needed.

"David Ray, general counsel." The counselor shook Matt's hand and gestured for him to take a seat in one of the ship's ancillary conference rooms. His hair was a layer of mere fuzz about his skull, making the gray difficult to discern. He could be anywhere between thirty and three hundred absolute UT years of age. The use of two names indicated there was another David Pilgrimage running around on the ship.

"Matthew Journey. I go by Matt."

"Yes. Owner of Aether Exploration, the major claim holder on Priamos, where everything's happening in this system. I've looked into your leases—good work. There's not much I'd change."

"My leases were drawn up by Nestor Expedition, who was murdered several months ago. He was a friend." Matt shifted uncomfortably; this was going to be harder than he'd anticipated.

"My condolences. That's information I haven't seen yet." David Ray's eyebrows went up and his fingers tapped quickly. Reports and feeds regarding Nestor's murder were displayed on the wall and David Ray skimmed through them. Matt waited quietly, understanding how much generational crews had to absorb between each mission.

"Ah." David Ray's light gray eyes were objective and professional. "It appears both Expedition and Journey legal representatives are involved. Expedition counsel is locked in a struggle with Leukos Industries over the release of records. You've hired Journey counsel to protect your intellectual property during execution of Nestor's estate." There was the rise of a question in the attorney's voice.

"When we arrived in-system, I opened a subpoena from Athens Point LEF." Matt raised his slate, but he wasn't going to show the subpoena to the counselor until he had established client confidentiality.

"*Subpoena duces tecum*, remotely served." David Ray nodded. "Once you proved your identity, the subpoena was served. So why do you need us?"

"I don't have any problem with the statement, or affidavit, or whatever, but the LEF is also asking for material that isn't relevant, that I don't want to hand over."

"Such as?" This time, only one eyebrow rose slightly.

"Nestor may have been involved with—well, perhaps he dabbled in—" He floundered under the attorney's gaze and managed to get back on track. "This involves artificial intelligence law, like proof of original rulesets and rights of individuality."

David Ray tapped a command on his desktop. "This is now a privileged session. Go on."

The story came out in a rush, the words merging as Matt tried to prevent certain memories from building inside his mind. He told David Ray about the package he received, probably the result of Nestor's last voluntary action, and how he'd accepted the transfer of what appeared to be a full-fledged artificial intelligence entity. Before he got to the worst part, the part where he discovered Nestor's body, David Ray interrupted.

"This AI resides in *crystal*? Installed on your ship?"

"I didn't have enough temporary memory at the time. There were also other reports in the package and I didn't want to take the chance of losing whatever Nestor sent."

"This may complicate matters. AI rulesets must be validated as original before they're put in crystal." David Ray rubbed his jaw. "AIs are also prohibited from controlling space vehicles. Can you remove the crystal from your ship?"

"Yes, of course. I'm speaking of the data array in my prospecting ship. What's *more* worrisome is that Nestor lived on the outskirts of the law, and he may have bought illicit code and rulesets. If I give Athens Point LEF access to the AI, they'll insist upon dissection." Matt took a deep breath. "Look, I don't want to lose Muse Three. It's all I have left of Nestor."

David Ray rested his chin on clasped hands, his elbows on his desk. He didn't respond immediately, but rather watched Matt in a searching manner until he squirmed in his seat.

"It has a name and unique model number. You're already emotionally attached to it, even seeing a representation of your friend. That indicates clever programming, at the least," David Ray said.

"Nestor was good. Muse Three *might* be original and even qualify for individuality. It'd be a shame to dissect it merely to protect commercial interests."

"Matt, perhaps you don't know the roots of AI law." David Ray's voice was quiet and powerful. "The development of artificial intelligence is highly constrained, as you know, but those constraints resulted from the Phaistos Protocols."

Matt's eyes widened. The Phaistos Protocols? These were supposedly the rules of warfare developed under the supervision of the Minoans. He'd never read the Phaistos Protocols himself, since they were long and full of legalese. He'd heard stories of lawyers devoting entire careers to their study, and apparently he didn't know their scope.

"The Phaistos Protocols require that the release, delivery, and execution of weapons of war be always under human decision and control. Even the use of automated processes in target determination and acquisition have constraints—basically speaking, the Minoans require a human at the trigger, and a human decision to fire." David Ray smiled wryly.

"And what does that have to do with AI development?" Matt didn't see the connection.

"We must also ensure that AI never directs, or operates, our military tactics and weapons. This extends to keeping them from running ships that the Minoans consider weapon systems. Since one can always come up with a scenario where any small vehicle might deliver a weapon, AI control of spacecraft is prohibited under both Consortium and Terran law. We're not talking about autopilot or autodriver software; that's different."

"Oh." Muse 3 was looking like a bigger problem than Matt ever imagined.

"There's still hope for your AI." David Ray smiled. "If you can convince me that your friend's hobby didn't have anything to do with his murder, or won't be useful in convicting his murderer."

That was easy, considering that the LEF had enough physical evidence to prove Hektor murdered Nestor. Matt explained that they also had proof that Hektor, a customs inspector, accepted bribes and finally, payment for murder. "But they can't track down who paid off the customs inspectors. The money traces back to an anonymous someone employed by Leukos Industries." Matt avoided any mention of Cipher, Ari's old crewmate. There was also no need to bring up his suspicion that the rich and reclusive Mr. Leukos might have been Ari's comrade during the war.

"Ah. This explains the problems between Expedition ship line and Leukos Industries." David Ray lapsed into thought and Matt waited in silence.

Eventually, David Ray presented his solution. "When you send your statement for affidavit, you should also apply for AI development and test licenses, with our help. If we submit those applications, then we can move to prevent release of your AI on the grounds it's intellectual property of Aether Exploration. We can make the case that Nestor was protecting IP when he sent it to you."

"But there's no way around licensing the AI?" Muse 3 would still be examined, possibly dissected, but by different people, for different purposes. They would not necessarily be interested in keeping the AI intact, either. Matt sighed. There seemed no other legal option.

"That's my recommendation." David Ray's face was sober. "I think it's your best course, provided your AI hasn't done anything illegal or dangerous. Does it have a sense of self and proximity?"

"It seems to."

"You haven't allowed it to control your ship, have you?"

"No. I don't think my pilot would ever allow that." Matt laughed.

"Has it initiated any autonomous actions without consulting you? Of any kind? You need to be honest with me."

That was more vague and Matt frowned as he searched his memory. "Well, it did make its own decision to widen the parameters on a search I'd requested."

David Ray looked relieved. "That's not a problem."

A beep indicated that Matt's session was over.

"I've got less than eight hours to answer that subpoena," Matt said.

"Don't worry. I'll have my staff take your statement immediately, and I can give you an hour at the end of shift." David Ray tapped a few commands on his desktop. He looked up and smiled. "We'll also talk about our fees at that time."

Against the backdrop of the orange and yellow gas giant Laomedon, Priamos gradually grew visible as they approached. It was slightly bigger than Hellas Daughter, the moon with which Ariane and Joyce were most familiar. Beta Priamos Station initially looked like a speck. When they came closer, it was obvious the small station would never compete in size with Athens Point, or even Karthage Point. Currently, spidery girders and temporary construction modules made up one quarter of its roughly cylindrical structure.

"Doesn't look very welcoming," Joyce said.

"They've only got four class B and six class C docks working. Let's see who's here." She displayed the dock schedule and was proud that her voice and hands were steady. Two freighters sat at class B docks and two smaller ships, one of which was Parmet's *Candor Chasma*, used class C docks.

"One of those freighters doesn't even have a referential engine." Joyce peered closely at the display, so Ariane zoomed in on the occupied class B docks.

"That's the freighter designated as emergency evacuation for the station," Ariane said.

"What's wrong with using evacuation modules?"

"They're not operational yet." Ariane smiled. "Welcome to the frontier, Joyce."

Joyce snorted. "Never heard it called *that*, but I suppose the word fits."

Ariane concentrated on dock approach as Major Tafani's words echoed in her mind: *I hear there's a cavalier, frontierlike attitude toward drinking and drugging.* When it came time to face Parmet or Maria, she'd love some liquid courage, but she had to remember the Terran companies had a foothold here because of the leases that *she'd* signed. She could always protest that she'd signed under duress, which would stop all Terran research in its tracks. It wasn't likely that Parmet wanted to see her again either, since they were both locked into this double-blackmail scheme.

"You're going to dock *manually*?" Joyce's voice broke her concentration. She looked around and saw his strained expression.

"Why do you think I have to have manual ratings?" She quickly looked at the display of a red crosshair on top of blinking green lights. For Joyce's benefit, she added, "They haven't certified our version of autopilot to work with their dock system, so I have to dock manually."

"How do you know their docking system is, whatever, incompatible?"

Pointing at the small view port titled "Space Docking Automated Transmission System," she said, "S-DATS is for more than setting comm channels, you know."

"I didn't think anybody docked manually anymore. You didn't do that at the *Pilgrimage*."

"You've got to be prepared, Joyce. Particularly here." She grinned, enjoying the sight of the brawny master sergeant gripping the arms of his chair. Then she turned back to the rapidly approaching dock and its blinking lights, covered with her red crosshair.

After he heard the docking clamps clunk, Joyce let out a little sigh. There weren't any customs inspections to go through, just an acknowledgment from Command Post. She put the ship systems into password-protected standby and ushered Joyce out of the airlock. He looked around the corridor.

"It feels spooky. Too empty and quiet," he said.

"Yeah, there's usually ComNet nodes, even in the seediest ports." She didn't have to mention names.

Joyce immediately caught her reference to one of their previous missions and nodded. "How do I get down to Priamos?"

"The handy dandy space elevator is on ring five, where you'll also find comm to the surface. You need CP authorization to take it down. Good luck, Joyce."

After he left, she looked about apprehensively. The station was a bit unsettling. Her implanted ear bug was quiet and she realized she'd gotten used to having her music library or selected feeds blabbering to her when she walked around habitats. Instead, she heard sounds of creaking as materials expanded and stretched, trying to keep out the deep silence of space. Perhaps this was why Autonomist habitats were covered with ubiquitous ComNet nodes and all flat surfaces were displays—except the floor, which had to be kept clear for emergency use. Under normal circumstances, personally targeted advertisements and entertainment chased her, drowning out the sounds of deathly cold vacuum.

She realized what else was missing: those pesky remotes that people operated to collect information or perform tasks. No active nodes meant no ComNet, and no ComNet meant no remotes floating about.

Suddenly, she heard the sound of habitation: metal scraping on metal, a tapping sound, and a muttered curse. Following the curved hallway to the next airlock, she found the source.

"Frank!" she exclaimed with relief. She'd first met Frank Maestrale in J-132, then again in G-145 on the first prospecting mission. He worked for ComNet Installation Services, which was heavily funded by Consortium taxes.

"Figured I'd see you again, Ms. Kedros." The thin man in baggy crew overalls turned away from the wall where he'd been working. Behind him trailed an automated cart full of little round things that waved wire feelers, making them look like multilegged insects.

"Believe it or not, as the Priamos prime lease controller, my boss is thinking of setting up an office here. When will we be getting ComNet support?"

Frank rubbed his whiskers while he frowned. He always looked ten hours away from his last shave.

"If this place hadn't been built by the lowest bidder, I'd be on schedule." He gestured to the wall where a cockeyed node wiggled in a hole that was obviously a bad fit. With disgust, he pulled the node free and dropped it back into the cart. "The contractor didn't use the right templates or they had blind quality control inspectors. I'll have to custom-fit this node, like over half of the others. A perfect example of your tax drachmas at work."

"No wonder you look ready for a drink. I'll buy." Ariane ignored the image of Tafani's disapproving face hovering in her brain. "Is the Stellar Shield still operating, or have they built something with a little more class?"

"Oh, it's still here." Frank looked at her somberly, his dark eyes more serious than she remembered. "I'm ready to finish up, so I'll take you up on refreshment—except I don't drink anymore."

"Liquids in general, or just alcohol?" She laughed, although it sounded forced. She knew what he meant. She was surprised at the disappointment she felt, almost as if he'd betrayed her. "Any particular reason?"

Frank shrugged and smiled.

"Good thing I'm buying, then." For some reason, she impulsively added, "I'm cutting back on my drinking also."

The words didn't sound right. Her session with Major Tafani suddenly replayed through her mind. *Since you continue to drink, how will you control yourself?* The same way she always had in the past: through sheer strength of will. *Get out of my head, Tafani.*

Tahir listened tensely as the *Father's Wrath* made contact with the *Pilgrimage III*, after dropping back into real-space. There was confusion about the change of name, of course.

"We can change the lists, if that's necessary. Was the registry changed also? Over." The voice sounded puzzled.

Tahir saw Abram muttering in Captain Zabat's ear. So far, the captain had been frightened enough to cooperate.

"*Pilgrimage*, the lists and announcements must use the new name. Registry is still Hellas system and all stats on number of crew and passengers stay the same. *Father's Wrath* out," Zabat said.

"Certainly. Welcome back to Gamma-145 and we're looking forward to meeting everybody. *Pilgrimage Three* out."

If the *Pilgrimage* crew understood the significance of the ship's new name, they wouldn't have agreed so cheerily. Even Zabat had no idea the name *Father's Wrath* was a signal, notifying all supporters within the solar system that Abram's plan was in motion. This was not a dry run.

"Rand, take over real-space piloting and connection," Abram said.

Tahir turned around from the sensor console to look at the crowded control deck. This deck was designed to hold a crew of four, although only two of its regular crew members were present: Zabat, the captain, and Danielle, the N-space pilot. Also on deck were Abram, Emery, Rand, Tahir, and one of Zabat's engineers, a hidden Abram supporter.

Danielle quickly got out of her seat and went to Zabat's side. Zabat also stood, perhaps with the hope they'd be dismissed. He was a bulky man and only a little taller than the lanky Danielle, whose face looked even bonier after her N-space weight loss.

"Not so fast, Captain." Abram's gaze went around the deck. "Tahir and Emery, escort this pilot to her quarters."

Zabat took one look at Emery and came to the obvious conclusion. "She cooperated, Abram. She got us to G-145."

Tahir moved toward the hatch, not wanting to see the confusion on Zabat's face. The captain was going to discover that negotiating or cooperating with Abram never got anyone a *different* result—they merely bought themselves a little more time.

"Come along." Emery grabbed Danielle's arm.

"But we did what you wanted!" Zabat's voice rose.

"And you lived. Now, Captain, you have an appointment in the clinic." Abram had taken out his flechette pistol and aimed it, point blank, at Zabat's thick midsection. For right now, this coercion worked. Zabat flinched and nodded.

Following Emery and Danielle, Tahir fingered the bulbous shape of the flechette pistol in his belt. Abram had obtained several crates of them, even though flechette weapons were hard to find. They used bulky cartridges, which expanded upon firing into a cone of spinning needles with helical spines. They were designed to cause maximum damage to human bodies while not harming harder ship structures. The cartridges could also be infused with chemical or biological agents.

However, the threat of these weapons would be less and less effective on the crew of the former *Venture's Way*, unless Abram backed up his threats with actual action. Now that they were inside G-145, someone would have to die, as an example. Tahir knew that Abram wouldn't trust Zabat's cooperation otherwise.

Emery stopped and opened a hatch, pushing Danielle through.

"These aren't my quarters. They're the first mate's," she said, her eyes fearfully riveted on Emery's face.

"They're empty and that's all I want." Emery turned around to Tahir, who stood in the hatchway. "Get out."

"No, Cousin." Tahir swallowed, hard. "Abram wouldn't approve."

"Please." She directed her whimper at Tahir.

Emery quickly shoved Danielle toward the single bunk, his movements exploding with rage. She fell backward across the bed, her head and shoulder hitting the bulkhead. Emery whirled and in one stride, pushed Tahir out of the hatchway, his face close to Tahir's.

"Don't call me cousin." Emery's hands gripped his shoulders tightly. "You're not one of us, and you'll only prove that to Abram, if you run to him with trivial complaints."

"We may need her skills later."

"Her skills will never be used again. Not in this system." Emery smiled, spitefully. "You can have her *after* me."

Tahir shook his head and Emery released him with a disdainful sneer. He backed away, knowing that he wasn't strong enough to stop this, and Emery closed the hatch.

You're not one of us. Emery was right: He was an outsider. He felt nauseated and hurried away, so he couldn't hear anything through the hatch.

CHAPTER 6

Qesan Douchet was a madman and the Minoans did us
a favor when they killed him. He took the isolationist poli-
cies of his ancestors and twisted them into a manifesto,
which the Terrans just recently released. It's sickening.
If you like scary stories, look at his strategy for expanding isolationism (no, that's not an oxymoron). First, one
finds territory where the population can be permanently
isolated. . . .

—*Misogynist Freaks*, Lauren Swan Kincaid, 2103.043.11.25
UT, indexed by *Heraclitus 29* under Conflict Imperative

"This can no longer be passed off as a paperwork
problem, now that we've found this dummy package. This is theft," Edones said.

Colonel Ash sat motionless, watching SP Hauser. When
Hauser acknowledged Edones's comment by nodding his
head, Ash nodded also. Oleander frowned. *What a syco-
phant! I hope I'm not like that when I rise to senior officer
rank.*

She had been disappointed in SP Hauser; she'd expected
a Terran State Prince would look more impressive. From
her Autonomist viewpoint, leaders should look distinctive,
but Hauser seemed entirely forgettable. He had a small
badge on his chest and he wore the same sleep-inducing
colors as the Terrans in uniform.

Then Hauser spoke. His authority was mesmerizing and

she had problems taking her eyes off him. He had to be using *somaural* projection.

"I desperately hoped this would be an inventory mistake, Colonel Edones. We're sincerely upset by this turn of events." SP Hauser suddenly seemed so trustworthy that Oleander would have allowed him to invest her life savings, if she had any.

Edones pointed to an image of the dummy package displayed on the wall. He appeared sullen because he wasn't looking directly at Hauser, but Oleander realized he was using a sensible safeguard against *somaural* influence.

She followed Edones's example and focused on the package. Its dimensions, density, and mass distribution attempted to mimic the real thing, but it fell short under scans because it lacked exotic material. Once the Terrans had grudgingly scanned their entire inventory, they'd found the warhead with this package. It hadn't happened quickly: It had taken four days and three teams of eight people to go through the weapons stored at Teller's Colony, the biggest Terran arsenal located outside the Sol system. The results: Package TDP-2102-012 couldn't be found, inside warhead WM15-894 or elsewhere in the arsenal.

"This warhead was delivered three years ago from your production facility. When did it last have a maintenance inspection?" Edones waved at the short maintenance record on WM15-894. The history showed when the warhead had been produced and delivered, but there were no maintenance inspections listed.

After getting an approving nod from SP Hauser, Colonel Ash appeared to squirm in his seat. "We've gone to five-year inspection periods," Ash said. "This was—ah—one of our cost control measures."

"Gaia protect us," muttered Bernard quietly, although Oleander heard his words clearly. TD weapons should be monitored frequently, due to the exotic matter trapped inside the package.

Colonel Edones seemed stunned by the Terrans' admission. He cleared his throat before continuing. "So, if not for our inspection, you wouldn't have found this package missing for two more years?"

Ash nodded.

"What about delivery records? Was an inspection performed by the receiving unit?" Bernard asked.

"The maintenance squadron commander at the time didn't have enough techs to perform the receipt inspection for the unit, so he relied upon the civilian team that brought the warheads from the production facility." Ash tapped his table to display a signed form on the wall.

"They were cheaper than using military personnel," Ash added, and a flash of embarrassment crossed his face.

"Well, we have to look into the entire civilian delivery team, and pull their clearance investigations," Edones said.

"We've already started," SP Hauser said.

Ariane waited while Frank locked and immobilized his cart. Then they went through two station rings to the little bar that catered to workers. The door had a handwritten sign that read STELLAR SHIELD and the interior was built with odds and ends. The bar would be dismantled once the system "opened up," meaning the time when the Pilgrimage ship line released the buoy codes into the public domain. At that point, anyone and everyone in an N-space-capable ship could come into G-145. By then, the system would have another name and Beta Priamos would house legitimate, rent-paying businesses.

At this point, however, the Stellar Shield's eclectic interior felt comfortably worn and familiar. It was crowded, being shift-change time, and Ariane had to wind around populated tables to get to the bar, obviously made from repurposed struts and bulkhead shields. Frank trailed her. She hopped on a stool and he hesitated, uncharacteristically, before sitting on the one beside her.

"I'll take whatever beer you've got," Ariane said to the bartender, knowing the inventory was limited.

Frank squinted in thought when the bartender looked at him. "There's so much to choose from in the nonalcoholic range," he said dryly. "Just give me that stuff you say is Hellas Kaffi."

The large young man didn't look amused. He ducked through a hatch and returned quickly with their drinks. Ariane's chilled beer was in resealable polycarbonate and Frank's drink was in a flash-heat pack. Not that the station inhabitants didn't trust their newly installed gravity generator, but products delivered to Beta Priamos had to be consumed under many conditions, including zero gee.

The bartender held out a slate between Ariane and Frank, and she quickly grabbed it. The billing was manual, given the nodeless environment and dumb surfaces. In any restaurant back in the Hellas system, she'd use the tabletop for near-field exchange with her implant. Instead, she gave her thumbprint and verbal public password for voiceprint to the slate and applied the debit to one of her accounts.

"Thank you, Ms. Kedros." Frank was polite, as always. He never failed to call her *Ms*. Kedros, even when he was shit-faced—she doubted she'd ever see him like that again and she indulged in a moment of nostalgia.

"You're welcome." She sipped slowly and delicately at the beer, putting it down on the counter between swallows. She wanted to drink faster, but Frank was watching.

If Matt were here, he'd probably make the barbed observation that *normal* people didn't obsess about how fast they drank. She pushed that comment back into the dark nether realms of her mind where it could bounce around with Tafani's sly remarks such as *new space is not conducive to your recovery*.

"Hey, Frank, who's your friend?" A beefy hand landed on the back of Frank's hunched shoulders.

Ariane twisted and saw the hand was attached to a stocky man in ubiquitous crew overalls. He winked at her, his light green eyes a startling contrast in his dark face.

"Ariane Kedros." She extended her hand to trade a firm handshake with him. "Pilot of the *Aether's Touch*."

"Hal Bokori." The initial condescending leer on his face changed to a comfortable grin. "Pilot, huh? N-space or real-space?"

"Both. You?"

"I'm loadmaster for the *Golden Bull*, the behemoth that runs between here and the mining operation at Tithonos, Laomedon's largest moon." His grin became self-deprecating. "Can I buy you a drink or some smooth?"

Hal pulled a smooth dispenser out of his pocket. When he offered it, she took a tablet, but Frank shook his head.

"Not drinking, so what good is it?" Frank pointedly took another sip of Kaffi.

"It can take the edge off." Hal shrugged and put his dispenser away. "Not that any present company needs their edges smoothed, of course."

"You remember the 'Small Stellar Terror' everyone still talks about?" Frank jerked his head at Ariane. "This is she."

"No kidding!" Hal looked Ariane up and down. "You're the one who took down Axel?"

"Well, he was drunk and his reflexes were shot," Ariane said modestly.

"But, even drunk, he's stronger than the Great Bull."

A bell started clanging as Hal's drink arrived, which made him curse. "I ordered too soon—didn't know anyone was scheduled to come in this shift."

Whoops started about the Stellar Shield as everyone looked up at the arrival list. A ship's name appeared, right above the *Aether's Touch*. It was *Father's Wrath*, which puzzled her, because Matt had pointed out that *Venture's Way* was the next ship scheduled to arrive. Then a notation appeared, indicating that the ship had changed its registration from *Venture's Way*, perhaps due to a change of ownership. *Father's Wrath* was arriving at G-145 early, but more importantly, she'd miscalculated by being here in the bar. She was going to lose some pocket money.

"New ship in-system. *Aether's Touch* pays the next round!" were the cries about the bar counter as the bell clanged. "Anyone here from *Aether's Touch*?"

Ariane raised her hand and grinned. As the sole crew member present from the last arriving ship, she became responsible for toasting the next ship—essentially paying for the next round of drinks. She nodded at the bartender, and a cheer welled up. It wasn't the worst ritual to get caught in and Matt would have enjoyed it, even though he'd grouse about expenses and mutter some curse that included the Great Bull's balls. Her grin faded as she realized how much she missed him.

"I need to get going," Frank said abruptly.

"Have another Kaffi—you look like you've been working too hard." She noticed his face was pale.

"No, I don't need the caffeine." His hand shook as he carefully set down his flash pack. He glanced up at the arrival announcement before he left.

Hal clapped her on the back and slid another beer toward her. "Frank's been a wet blanket ever since he stopped drinking. You haven't finished your first beer, so drink up."

Contrary to Hal's advice, she sipped her beers. The night blurred anyway, filled with orders for drinks and sidesplitting jokes that could never be related to someone who hadn't been there. She met people whose names she'd never remember: other crew members of the *Golden Bull* and construction workers for the station. She met a young Autonomous worker who'd made the mistake of getting a green skindo right before transferring to Beta Priamos, where there weren't any salons. Now it was blotching, and several rounds of beer were required to remove the young woman's pout. "Carly, you'll just have to learn to use a touch-up kit," Hal advised. Everyone laughed, and then Hal introduced her to somebody else.

She always wondered, afterward, if the stories and conversation that accompanied the drinks had really been that good. But getting lost in the moment was what drinking was all about; it drowned out the memories.

Tahir's guts clenched when he saw Commander Charlene Pilgrimage. *Not another woman, please.*

The commander tried to make sense of the small party of men she faced as they stood inside an area that obviously held some sort of religious function for the generational ship. There were benches that faced a niche with a statue. She read the inscription above the niche, which referred to a St. Darius and Gaia.

"You're ahead of schedule, Captain Zabat. Where's your pilot? Danielle, right?" Charlene was familiar with Zabat, but hesitated when trying to remember the pilot's name.

Zabat was sweating, unable to ignore the threat of the explosives implanted in his body. In case Zabat wanted to be a martyr, Abram had demonstrated that the charges would take out innocent bystanders within ten feet—and the ship's first mate ended up being the sacrifice. Now Abram subtly herded Zabat, keeping the captains close together.

"Danielle had a bad drop," Zabat said.

She certainly had. Tahir decided the only way he was getting through this, alive and sane, was to pretend he didn't *know* about what he couldn't see. It wasn't working, because he couldn't get Danielle's face out of his mind. He hoped he wouldn't add Charlene Pilgrimage to the faces that kept revolving in his head.

"Right now, it's only my engineer and three passengers," Zabat added. "Let's get on with the tour, Charlene."

The commander looked at Abram, who certainly showed the hard wear and tear of a spacecraft engineer. Her eyes flitted over Tahir and Rand in a noncommittal way, but flinched when meeting Emery's gaze.

So far, everything was proceeding exactly as Emery

predicted. "These crèche-get are simplistic idiots," he had scoffed. "And silly enough to think they have no enemies and no need for security. They might sense something is wrong, but it's not in their nature to protect themselves."

"But Abram needs them," Tahir replied. "Isn't it ironic that we *need* their crèches and in vitro methods, which is exactly what we despise them for?"

At which point, Emery scowled and turned away, stopping the conversation. Tahir had smiled to himself, although he knew that pointing out logical incongruities in tribal doctrine would have no effect upon Emery.

Commander Charlene, just as Emery predicted, led them through the "chapel" and up the ladders to the control center. Abram was behind her, followed by Zabat, who looked so ill that he might vomit on the spot. Emery and Rand followed, with Tahir bringing up the tail end.

This was one of the critical pivot points in Abram's plan: There were no contingencies if they couldn't capture the generational ship's control center, and they needed to do it without any warning, subsquently leaving the system through the time buoy. They'd also like to prevent any warning going to the stations near Laomedon and Sophia II, but if that happened, Abram could adjust his plan.

Last up, Tahir climbed out of the vertical airlock in time to see Abram grab Commander Charlene's arm and, twisting it behind her, fluidly pull a flechette pistol out of his loose coveralls. The commander's briefing ended in a punctuating cry. Tahir numbly drew his weapon.

"Nobody move." The concentration in Abram's voice lashed Tahir's nerves and he winced, having intimate familiarity with that tone. Most of the controllers turning in their chairs immediately froze.

Tahir saw movement from the corner of his eye and he turned, but Emery was faster. The neck and base of the controller's head exploded in blood.

"No!" yelled Tahir. He took two strides to reach the young man, but no one could help him as he slumped for-

ward and slid from his chair. Emery's hit had been merci-
fully lethal.

"Don't move." Emery threatened the controller to the
left, who had involuntarily started forward to help the unfortunate victim.

"Tahir, see what he was doing," Abram said.

As instructed, he turned to the console and realized that
the victim had been monitoring the Minoan time buoy.

"I'm not sure," he said.

"That's all you can come up with, college boy, with all
your expensive education?" Emery smirked.

"If you hadn't covered the place in blood—" Tahir
stopped, realizing everyone in the center was watching
them, not that they'd remember much from these first few
moments.

Abram's face was wooden, waiting for Tahir's response.
Suppressing a shudder, Tahir wiped gore from the panel
that displayed the prompts and buttons for that station.
The smell of blood bothered him; he wasn't as hardened as
the others to violence—*I shouldn't be here*. Not that he was
afraid to die, but this was his fatalism speaking rather than
the frothing fanaticism that Emery carried. *Emery will die
for the cause and I'll die for nothing*.

"This station talked to the time buoy," Tahir said as
steadily as he could. "There's not much the crew is allowed
to do. I think he put it through an initialization loop again,
but I don't know why."

Emery growled in frustration and stepped over to look
at the console. He made a show of examining the prompts
and the button outlines, but Tahir knew he didn't understand the display. Emery whirled on the comm operator.

"Tell us what he did!" Emery pointed his weapon into
the comm controller's face.

"I don't know anything about the buoy," the man bab-
bled, near hysteria, his face bloodless. "Hardly anyone
does—we just follow the checklist."

"It's coming online again." Tahir kept his voice matter-of-fact, hoping to calm Emery. "The buoy is still in closed mode, controlled by the *Pilgrimage*."

Tahir relaxed. Control of the buoy was critical in *temporarily* isolating the system. *Permanent* isolation wasn't on anyone's mind. After all, that required destruction of a buoy. That was beyond the realm of possibilities—unless one had a stolen TD weapon in the hold of one's hijacked ship. He looked up and met Abram's eyes, which were steady and calculating. He was always surprised, considering the crazy plans that hatched inside Abram's head, to see signs of rational thought. It was easier to think that a madman drove their tactics. Sadly, Abram's plan would work and Tahir merely hoped to mitigate casualties. Luckily, Abram needed most of these people alive.

"Start shutting down the comm, Tahir. You'll have to stall requests for bandwidth allocation until we've got control of the entire ship," Abram said.

Tahir moved over to the comm console and noted the current allocation. He glanced a warning at the operator, who pointedly turned away and vomited, now that his fight-or-flight instinct was letting his senses work again. The crèche-get would all have problems once their noses started functioning. They probably hadn't ever smelled blood before.

Meanwhile, Abram spoke into his own short-range comm link. "Teams two, three, and four can proceed."

"What the hell are you doing? You don't have the crew to run this ship yourself." Commander Charlene had recovered from shock; her voice had a caustic bite that almost hid the waver. Some of the crèche-get straightened. Perhaps they were starting to think clearly.

Tahir shook his head. Lucid minds were dangerous. Abram needed cooperation and he couldn't get it if there was coolheaded leadership. This was a problem right out of Qesan's writings: Either Abram would have to make an example out of the commander to coerce the crew through fear, or he had to separate and imprison her, using her well-being as collateral for the crew's good behavior. Tahir knew which option his father would take. Abram placed greater stock in fear than loyalty.

"Go stand inside the airlock." Abram had his weapon aimed at Commander Charlene and made a motion with his other hand. Charlene looked confused but did what Abram told her. She couldn't make a quick escape and still evade the flechettes.

"Captain Zabat, please follow."

Zabat made a small, whimpering sound and shook his head. Abram sternly motioned again and added, "We will force you, if you lack the courage, and that will be bad for the woman."

Sweating profusely, Zabat shuffled to where Abram pointed and stood, as directed, facing Charlene.

"Closer." Abram reached into his pocket.

"Charlene, I'm sorry." Zabat's hoarse whisper to the confused woman was audible throughout the deck. The two stood little more than three meters away from Abram, hardly a safe range, but Abram might be deranged enough—

Emery and Rand took what cover they could under the consoles, crouching down and turning away.

"Turn away and cover your ears," Tahir said sharply and loudly, for the crèche-get's benefit.

He and the comm controller were as far away as possible in the circular room, but they were also directly across from the airlock. The controller whose name tag read JUSTIN exchanged a quick glance with Tahir. Justin's eyes were glazed with indecision and fear, but he followed Tahir's lead in turning away, hunkering down, and covering his ears.

Tahir heard a thump, then felt a slight concussive force and hard pellets of something hit him. He looked down and saw bits of gore interspersed with tiny smoking balls from the many incendiary implants in Zabat. They quickly burned out and turned into dark specks, as designed, without enough smoke to trigger the alarms. The sharp smell it left behind was faint but unique. Behind him, there were sharp screams of fear, pain, and horror.

Surveying the center, Tahir was unsurprised to see Abram whole and safe, although he would have tiny scars from the incendiary balls that had hit his face and hands. Perhaps insanity truly protected him. Abram's front was a mess of gore, although not as bad as the airlock, which had taken the brunt of the exploding bodies. There was no indication that Zabat had even existed, but Tahir could see Charlene's body. The ship itself had suffered no damage. Two of the controllers were weeping, and others were still in shock. Those gagging and covering their mouths and noses were recovering the quickest.

Abram listened to messages played by his ear bug. He nodded, his eyes distant, seemingly removed from the catastrophe.

"My teams now command your support and engineering centers," Abram said, motioning to the woman at the environmental monitor. "Call for cleanup. All of you will be safe, provided you cooperate with our requests."

Abram's voice was mild; he might have been talking about the weather or the local food. The environmental controller stared at him in confusion. When Abram frowned, she put through the call in a tight and wavering voice.

"We have your two other captains in custody, so be on your best behavior." Abram's voice almost purred with satisfaction and Tahir knew why. By executing Charlene, yet keeping the other two captains as hostages, Abram had satisfied several instructions in Qesan's writings.

Abram walked over to Tahir and the comm controller, wearing the gore on his front like a badge. The controller kept his eyes on his console.

"It's time to stop all communication between this ship and the outside. Do it in a way that won't alarm anyone," Abram said.

Tahir nodded. Most of the seven hundred people on the

Pilgrimage III were still ignorant of the takeover. Abram was commandeering major control centers and systematically containing the secondary work areas. Then he would widen his attention across the entire G-145 system and find a suitable ship to modify for carrying the TD weapon.

Ariane felt free and peaceful. No ghosts rustled in her head as she walked through the desolate corridors toward the slip where *Aether's Touch* connected. Hal had set his head down on the table and slept, snoring in oblivion until the bartender roused him and sent him off. At that point, Ariane noted the time and realized she had to leave. She had six hours before she had to catch a ride down to Priamos.

She congratulated herself on her control; she'd sipped slowly and paced herself. She wasn't sure how many beers she'd had, but wasn't it good she hadn't obsessively counted them? The empty station no longer felt lonely or creepy. She began to hum a tune, one that had been repeating in her head, as she turned the corner.

A woman blocked her way. She was Terran, by the look of the bland jumpsuit, but with a jarring originality not usually found in Terrans. For one thing, she had flamboyant, burgundy hair. That wouldn't be strange for anyone living on a Consortium world, since Autonomists had no problem with artificially coloring any part of their bodies, but Terrans prided themselves on their eugenics and their ability to breed *natural* enhancements to the human body. They didn't color their hair and they tried to breed for consistent physiques; this woman wasn't any taller than Ariane. Though she was extremely petite for a Terran, her tight jumpsuit revealed strong muscle lines along lithe limbs. Her complexion was perfection: Unmarked, unscarred, and much lighter than Ariane's, her face was as cold as honed alabaster.

"Uh ... hullo." Ariane stepped back to regain her personal space. She felt grubby and quickly smoothed her baggy crew overalls around her waist and hips.

"Hullo." The woman cocked her head to the side. Her light gray eyes seemed angry and mocking.

"Who are you?"

"I'm disappointed, Major Kedros. I didn't expect to find a *Destroyer of Worlds* stumbling around drunk, nor did I think you'd be such a pretty little thing."

"I'm not drunk." The words came out automatically. *Who* is *this woman?* Someone this small couldn't be a TEBI agent, given Terran prejudices about people outside the "average."

The woman sniffed delicately. "You reek of alcohol. Perhaps that's to be expected, since Major Kedros had to be checked into an addict commons."

"You're on Parmet's staff." Ariane made the most obvious assumption.

The woman's face and body were suddenly empty of emotion. It was an instantaneous change that Ariane had seen before in those trained in Terran *somaural* techniques. She would have backed away, but she found herself against the bulkhead. *Stupid, to get myself maneuvered this way.*

"Isrid is my first husband. He lost a brother and I lost a second husband at Ura-Guinn. Pryce and his wife were joining our multimarriage and Pryce would have fathered my next child." The woman's tone was flat.

The Terrans strictly controlled their licenses for having children, and often had to apply for them years in advance. She didn't know what to say, and she couldn't apologize for the Ura-Guinn mission or for following her orders. It was wartime and this woman wasn't the only one who lost loved ones, at Ura-Guinn or some other battle. However, this was the story staring her in the face right now and Ariane had to look down, breaking eye contact.

That was her first mistake. She caught the blur of movement on the rightmost periphery of her sight. Her flinch was late; her second mistake. Her shoulder barely slowed the kick and the right side of her head exploded in pain. *How the hell did that happen*—a tight fist caught Ariane in the solar plexus and she went down—*so fast?* She tried to roll away, gasping for breath, but she ended up wedged against the bulkhead and received several kicks in the kidneys for her effort.

Can't breathe. Pain. She couldn't avoid the woman's well-aimed boots. Even if she could voice an emergency, there were no operating nodes in the corridor to record her. The kicks paused. Her lungs gasped and wheezed.

"That was too easy. You're just a pathetic drunk." The woman delivered her scornful words in an eerily impassive voice.

Ariane tensed, expecting another kick. Her eyes were watering and she couldn't hear footsteps over her wheezing breath. Eventually she opened her eyes, seeing the bulkhead meet the floor in front of her eyes. A seam in the tough, flexible display covering was right in front of her and she could see the tiny connection threads that allowed an image to slip from the bulkhead to the floor.

Now that she wasn't gasping as much, she heard nothing. She tasted blood. Trying to roll her head to look the other way, she moaned. She was alone in the corridor. From the pain, she figured the blows against unprotected organs had caused bruising, perhaps bleeding, and she might have a cracked rib.

Several moans later, she was on her feet and stumbling toward *Aether's Touch.* Anger was beginning to replace shock, although she wasn't as angry with Parmet's wife as she was with Parmet. She and Parmet had a *deal.* He was supposed to stay quiet about the original AFCAW crew members. That was his payment for having her sign over the leases to certain Terran contractors.

What a bastard. He might not have released anything on ComNet, but he told his family. Gaia knows who else might be gunning for me. Since he didn't keep his side of the bargain, tomorrow I'm going to see about getting rid of some Terran contractors. Her anger was healing in its energy. By the time she reached the outer airlock of *Aether's Touch,* she had the presence of mind to wipe her bloody hand on her coveralls before she typed in her code and gave her password for voiceprint analysis.

"Muse Three, send a request to the *Pilgrimage Three* for the bandwidth to do an AI-indexed ComNet search." There were advantages to having an agent of AI stature. She could give Muse 3 complicated instructions that would have required her manual assistance if she'd used the ship's systems.

"Yes, Ari."

It'd take time to message the generational ship, since the relays for Beta Priamos Station weren't working yet. Meanwhile, she opened the med closet and tried not to cringe at her image in the mirror. Her scalp had split on the side of her head, hence all the blood in her hair, on her face, down her neck, on her hands—all over. By gingerly prodding and turning her ear, she determined the skin and cartilage weren't torn beyond the capability of plastiskin to hold and heal.

After cleaning her head and wounds, she pulled out the scanner. Being second-wave prospectors meant being prepared for medical emergencies, so *Aether's Touch* was equipped to heal some straightforward injuries, such as cracked and broken bones. Yes, one of her ribs showed a small crack, justifying her painful breathing. The rest of her ribs looked good, perhaps because of the bone growth stimulation she'd received after escaping Cipher's most dramatic explosion.

She applied a full dose of stim and agreed with the medical diagnosis that displayed, "Rest and limited activity required for three days," but she had to leave for a contractor meeting in five hours. Embarrassingly, it took mere minutes for a diminutive Terran woman to kick the shit out of the "Small Stellar Terror" and leave her like a rag doll on the deck.

Assessing damage to her internal organs was problematic. The med scanner showed she hadn't ruptured anything, but there could be finer internal damage and bleeding. She'd test again in a couple hours, when she might get better information.

"Ari, the response from the *Pilgrimage Three* is negative. No bandwidth can be allocated at this time, due to maintenance."

"Did they give a projected time for completion of the maintenance?"

"No."

That was unusual. She should give Justin, or whoever was controlling comm, some flak for being so vague, but she needed sleep more than she needed to look up whether Parmet had a wife with burgundy hair. She reached for bright, the friend of all shift workers, particularly those in space who didn't have planetary rhythms to guide their sleep patterns.

"Ari, from the test results, you appear to be injured. Should I call nine-one-one?"

"*No*, Muse Three. I fell and have some bruises, that's all." She lied, hoping the pesky AI didn't access the voice stress analysis algorithms. "Besides, there's no medical staff on Beta Priamos, so there's no one to call."

"You could send a message to Matt."

The comment had a tiny hint of slyness and Ariane froze. Would she have even had those drinks if Matt had been here? She queried her implant and relaxed when she saw the blood alcohol content was barely measurable. It still might have slowed her reflexes, or perhaps Parmet's wife was really *that* fast. Either way, she didn't want Matt to learn about this.

"No, Muse Three. There's nothing Matt can do to help me and we'd worry him unnecessarily."

"Agreed, but the tests indicate you should rest for three days."

She wondered how much time Nestor had wasted on emotional mimicry, since the damn thing sounded concerned, even motherly.

"I'll rest for three *hours*, Muse Three; then I have to get down to the Priamos surface for a contractor meeting."

No response.

If you want to sulk, that's fine, but I won't trust you with waking me. She added the bright to her implant and set the time delay. For backup, she set an alarm, one that didn't run through the systems within Muse 3's reach. After gingerly arranging herself on her good side, she quickly fell asleep.

CHAPTER 7

When you realize what the crèche-get face on their ships, you'll understand. When something goes wrong on a mission, they have no one to call upon for help. Their need for self-reliance is reflected in the Generational Line ship designs. If you read the chilling logs from the *Expedition I*, where they had to blow away key modules, reconnect, and rebuild under thrust . . .

—Senator Stephanos IV, 2098.022.10.31 UT, indexed by *Democritus 9* under Cause and Effect Imperative

"The control deck cut all our connections to ComNet," David Ray said. "Some sort of buoy problems."

"Never heard of that." Matt tried to sound experienced; in reality, he'd experienced only one solar system opening on the *Journey IV*. Everyone joked the Minoan time buoys had one ON button, they could take any sort of abuse, and they couldn't be turned off or destroyed—except with a temporal-distortion wave.

"I've got the AI applications and permit requests ready to sign, once we've got ComNet back." David Ray motioned at the display of legalese that gave Matt a headache whenever he looked at it.

Matt was surprised at how heavy his heart felt, all for a set of algorithms and rules. Muse 3 might have to be destroyed, depending upon how Nestor built it. However, after David Ray went through the laws regarding the licensing of AI rulesets, proof of originality, and rights of individuality, he decided he had no choice but to initiate the long process. He wasn't going to risk his company, essentially both his and Ari's livelihood, for Muse 3.

"Anything else?" David Ray asked.

"Nothing—other than your fees, I guess."

David Ray tapped the desk to bring up a matrix on the wall. "Here are my hourly rates. This is the rate schedule for non-Pilgrimage work, given that you're an Autonomist citizen."

Matt gulped. This destroyed the windfall he made from ferrying Joyce to this system, and any more work would make a serious dent in his operating expenses, provided he could even call this a business expense. He couldn't get on the visiting generational schedule, because he'd opted off the *Journey IV*. However, there were incentives listed at the bottom of the matrix.

"I can lower the rates through donations?" Unlike gravhuggers, Matt didn't have any qualms about the ownership of his sperm. Besides, this was about saving money. Strictly speaking, these weren't donations in the charitable sense.

"Are you already in our pool?" asked David Ray.

"No," There hadn't been time to consider donations the first time he came to G-145 and there'd been no driving need for Pilgrimage credit.

"If you're willing to sign up for a four-sample regimen, then we can make you a deal." David Ray displayed a different matrix of rates.

Matt nodded in relief. "Let's do it."

The decision itself turned out to be orders of magnitude faster than "doing it." David Ray loaded another flurry of forms onto Matt's slate to sign with thumbprint and voiceprint. The Consortium of Autonomist Worlds had intricate and thorny procedures regarding individual privacy, and one's genetic material qualified as private personal property.

"Our labs will want to look over your medical records."

David Ray frowned. "Unfortunately, comm systems are down, even between ship sections. It might be easier if I walk you over to the labs, which will give me a chance to stretch my legs."

The genetic labs and birth center were in another spire of the ship-turned-habitat, on the same level as the legal offices. David Ray escorted him around the connection wheel that held the spires together, while they chatted about the differences between the *Pilgrimage III* and the *Journey IV*. The traffic in the wheel's semicircular-shaped corridors was light. They saw fewer than thirty pedestrians and only two equipment carts, which surprised Matt.

"Third shift is downtime. That's why they're doing maintenance on the comm." David Ray motioned Matt to follow him as he turned off the wheel. "I'll have to warn you about Dr. Lee. She's our oldest geneticist."

"Warn me?"

"She may seem grouchy, but don't be fooled. She hides a generous spirit under her vicious wit." David Ray smiled. He obviously had a soft spot for Dr. Lee.

They stopped at a door labeled S6 LEVEL 19—BIRTHING CENTER TWO.

"She's always running her music. That's how I bribe her, by finding obscure selections." David Ray waved his hand over the switch and opened the door.

Contrary to what he just said, the stark glass and metal laboratory was silent. A tall woman stood at a lab equipment station with her back to them. Her hair was white and loosely piled up on her head, topping off a ramrod-straight back. Her crew coveralls and white lab coat didn't hide her lean hips and long legs. When she turned, the wrinkles about her lively eyes and the papery skin covering her thin aristocratic features revealed her age.

"David Ray!" She stalked toward them, scowling. "What's happened to my music feeds?"

Matt was amused to see panic cross David Ray's face.

"We don't have ComNet access, Lee. Maintenance, you know."

"I don't like depriving the children, and I can't even access my local library. What are they doing up front? They won't answer my calls." She crossed her arms over her chest and looked down her nose at the general counsel. "Up front" was shipspeak for the control deck.

"Let me try, Lee," David Ray said.

Matt watched David Ray scuttle past counters to the end of the lab. The attorney started tapping commands and muttering codes into the panel next to a vertical airlock. When Matt turned back to Dr. Lee, she was looking him over with narrowed eyes.

"What are you doing here?" she snapped.

"Getting cleared to make donations." He handed her his slate. "Matt Journey, at your service, ma'am."

She smiled and her face transformed, looking much younger.

"It's all an act, you know." She jerked her head toward David Ray. "He's at least two hundred years and not a day younger. He does his 'respect the elderly' routine to irritate me. We grew up together, but I fell behind doing a tour at headquarters."

"The control deck isn't answering and they've locked down the central data store," David Ray called.

"I could have told you that, you young twit!" Dr. Lee looked up from the forms on the slate and winked at Matt. "I've got to keep stroking that male ego, particularly when it's sitting in such a well-formed rack. Oh, is that too much information?"

"Only if you want to be obvious." Matt hid his awkward flush by turning away to examine the birth chambers.

There were ten chambers along the wall, with shining fronts and small circular doors. The occupied ones were labeled with dates, name, lineage, and a few other indicators. Each maturing baby represented a feat in human engineering; yet this process caused fear and loathing in the grav-huggers, who called them "crèche-get," as if there were something subhuman about them. Matt had matured in one of these chambers, as had anyone conceived under real-space conditions.

When humans had first considered long trips in real-space, they had never anticipated the problems of bearing children in low or changing gravity. With less gravity, there should be advantages for the mother. No more swelling, fewer problems with pregnancy-induced hypertension and preeclampsia. However, no one foresaw how finicky placental interchange could be when exposed to gravity different from Terra.

"Good. You're birthed from a well-recorded generational line. We won't need to do testing for recessive genetic nastiness such as cystic fibrosis, sickle cell, or thalassemia," Dr. Lee said. "But I need to look at your records."

Matt extended his hand and she pointed toward a hand outline on the lab counter. He used near-field data exchange to download parts of his medical records in his implant to local lab memory.

Dr. Lee scrolled the results on the wall. "You're negative for five types of human immunodeficiency viruses, as well as any sexually transmitted diseases. All your health indicators are well in the green."

"Aw shucks, ma'am." Matt pretended embarrassment.

Dr. Lee rolled her eyes and pushed him toward the vertical airlock where David Ray still tapped and frowned. "Go up one level and start working on a sample," she said.

Above the lab, Matt found a quiet little lounge with a small bar, several private cubicles, and a closed hatch that read AUTHORIZED PERSONNEL ONLY. He had the donation center to himself. Unbidden, his imagination started wandering toward Ari—*no*. He couldn't allow his conscious mind to explore that possibility; it would lead to complications. After all, Ari was *crew*. Then Diana Oleander floated into his mind. Deep down, he wondered whether Diana was merely a stand-in for Ari.

Better get on with this and catch my ride to Beta Priamos.
Before the comm maintenance, he'd checked the incoming
ship schedules. His ticket to Priamos had arrived early. He
started scrolling through the v-play titles listed at the bar.

Ariane dreamed she was at the Naga pilot controls again,
listening to Cipher and Brandon argue about whether they
should stay to collect data from the probe.
But it's not a probe.
"The mission brief was wrong. It's not an intelligence
payload." Cipher's eyes were large, her short orange hair
plastered to her head with sweat.
*Why would they lie? Didn't the civilian authorities trust
us to do our mission?*
"Don't be ridiculous, Ari. The maintenance crew that re-
moved it from storage and prepped it—they had to know."
Suddenly, she was standing next to Cipher, watching
Brandon throw himself toward the director of operations.
"The DO had to know, regardless of what he said when
we returned."
Did Brandon know? Ariane looked at Cipher. The or-
ange hair turned to deep burgundy. The face lightened;
then the skin melted and cracked away, leaving bone.
"You know we all deserve to die," said the grinning skull.
"More than four billion souls are gone, Ari."
She was back on the Naga ship, which bucked and
stretched. Console lights faded and recovered. Multiple
alarms went off, one of them pinging over and over.
It was her wake-up alarm.
"Quiet. I'm awake!" She rolled over, and her breath
caught at the sharp pain. Rolling over a stim-healed, recently cracked rib was torture.
When the alarm was finally quiet, she lay still and assessed her injuries. After a couple hours of sleep, she
couldn't believe how bad she felt. If there was any option
that avoided getting out of bed, she'd take it. She groaned
in frustration and pain. She had to get to Priamos: The con-

tractors needed the reporting matrix and they'd have questions. Matt was depending on her, and there was no one else to back her up.

Before they'd left Athens Point, he'd familiarized her with all the contractors, what they did, and the streamlined reporting. *You're a full partner now*, he'd said, *and you never know when you might have to represent Aether Exploration*. At the time, she'd doubted she'd need the background. How wrong she'd been.

Carefully, so *very* carefully, she pushed herself upright and got out of bed. If there was any time for analgesics, it was now. She took a triple dose, knowing her metabolism could handle it. Then she stuffed the entire remaining inventory of pain medication into the pockets of her business coveralls, adorned with the Aether Exploration logo, clean and ready from the steamer. She looked at them speculatively; how was she going to get into them?

Walking gingerly about in her underwear, she entered the galley and made her morning Kaffi. She and Matt made sure to stock the real stuff, ground from roasted beans grown on Hellas Prime. For some reason, drinks made from coffee beans, tea, or dried herbs were processed enough to pass Matt's crèche-get sensibilities.

The Kaffi and analgesics loosened up her body enough to use the hygiene closet and get into her coveralls and safety jacket. She checked her implant, where she carried copies of the new reporting matrix that the CAW SEEECB had approved for Aether Exploration. She also had copies on the slate she slipped into her coverall pocket.

She was ready to go and miraculously on time, but she hesitated at the airlock. Muse 3 had been uncharacteristically quiet.

"No arguments, Muse Three? No chiding or fussing about bed rest?"

"None, Ari. Analysis of past discussions has proven that Matt will reconsider his decisions as a result of reasoned questions and answers, but you will not."

She raised her eyebrows. Did Muse 3 just call her pig-headed? The tone sounded smug, but Muse 3 used Nestor's voice and that little pervert always spoke with a superior tone. Did Muse 3 know it was delivering an insult? This begged the question regarding Muse 3's interaction training, or lack thereof, while she was gone.

"Muse Three, try my request again for a ComNet search. Once you get it, find visual records of all past and present wives of Terran State Prince Isrid Sun Parmet."

"I have periodically attempted to get bandwidth from the *Pilgrimage Three*, since you didn't cancel your original request. All have been denied, with no estimate given for when there may be bandwidth available."

This was yet another troubling coincidence. When she added it to other oddities, such as Joyce being here, her scalp began to prickle. To quell her unease, she grabbed one of the few weapons in the locker. It was a nonlethal ministunner and small enough to go unnoticed inside her jacket.

This jacket was for safety: It could light up with various messages, had a shrink-to-fit safety vest, tons of straps and pockets to carry items, and was fitted with internal webbing that she could hook to all sorts of tie-downs. She checked her emergency accessories: a small knife with an extending blade, airless light source and flares, and a folding emergency mask. Another alarm beeped; she had barely enough time to get down to the surface.

"Continue the bandwidth requests, Muse Three. When you get ComNet access, do the search and send the results to my slate. Remember that all your comm to the surface has to go through the Beta Priamos Command Post." She paused, considering her next words. "I'm giving you control of any sensors that can be used while the ship is docked. In addition, you're allowed to reveal your presence under circumstances that fit within CAW Space Emergency Procedures, series number twelve. Better read up on them."

"I already have. Thank you, Ari."

Matt was going to have a fit about the energy bill if Muse 3 abused the sensors, but she didn't worry about it as she locked up the ship and scurried to the space elevator as fast as her bruised body would allow. Again, the station seemed deserted. The curt, scowling young man who handed her an emergency mask for the elevator was the only person she saw as she took her leave of Beta Priamos and rode the elevator to the moon's surface alone.

"You done yet?"

Matt jumped at David Ray's voice, turning away from the list of v-plays. The counselor's head was sticking up into the vertical airlock.

"I'm trying to find something to watch. I don't understand all these titles about engines."

"Euphemisms, my boy," David Ray said. "Look, I've got to go. I'll make an appointment for you tomorrow—"

They both frowned when they heard a man's harshly accented voice say something below in the lab. Dr. Lee's voice protested, another male voice mixed into the mélange, yet Matt couldn't distinguish words. David Ray headed down the ladder. Matt moved to the door, stepped through into the airlock tube, wide enough for several people to stand about the inner port, and looked down.

Perhaps it was a freakish coincidence, or perhaps St. Darius himself decided to help out a shipmate in distress, but when Matt shuffled a bit clockwise around the port, he could see David Ray's figure outlined against the back of the airlock tube due to the brighter light in the lab. David Ray had his arms up in that universal signal of surrender.

Matt heard Dr. Lee say something in a tense, shrill voice, but he still couldn't understand her words. David Ray was closer and his voice was deep and clear.

"We'll cooperate—don't do anything to the children," David Ray said.

Matt reached for the autohoist webbing and cable. He

worked quietly. The autohoist was set up for cargo and he readied it for carrying a human.

There was a sharp question, to which David Ray answered, "I'm alone."

Matt set the autohoist to sense the weight of an adult, with an override on the safety so it would move fast. The autohoist could be used to move bulky or heavy items through the airlock. It could also move an unconscious person or, Gaia forbid, a body. He held his breath as he lowered the autohoist webbing at the end of the cable. *Slowly, slowly*. He saw a sliver of the autohoist's shadow appear against the back of the airlock tube, and he brought it back up a smidgen. He didn't know where the "bad guys" stood and what they could see.

"I'm the general counsel." David Ray's voice was puzzled.

Another sharp question.

"Essentially, yes, I'm a lawyer."

A male voice, the one that had been asking the questions, rose slightly in pitch and gave a command.

Dr. Lee screamed, "No!"

Matt heard her clearly. What followed were the sounds of a soft thud and a screeching, ringing sound, as if a million pins scraped along the airlock tube and tried to drill into the metal. David Ray grunted and fell backward into the airlock in an awkward, spread-eagled position. The fabric on his left thigh was shredded and bloody. Matt dropped the harness onto David.

Many considered self-tightening webbing to be a miracle; Matt certainly did as he watched the harness webbing tighten about David Ray's shoulders and torso. Most of the harness tightened to specifications in a fraction of a second. David Ray had the presence of mind to lift one hand to a loop on the cable, allowing the webbing to connect under his arm. By the time Matt reached over and tapped the command button, the harness had stopped wiggling.

The autohoist hauled David Ray upward so quickly that

he banged the sides of the port. His yelps were overridden by another screech of metal pins. As he hung above the port, Matt closed the hatch and slapped the manual override lever, seeing shadows converging on the doorway below.

"Flechettes," David Ray said, panting in pain. "They're inside the bottom half of the airlock."

"Watch out—this is going to hurt." Matt released the autohoist and tried to catch David Ray, shoving him through the airlock door into the donation center.

David Ray groaned as he fell, trying to keep off his bad leg. He pulled himself along the floor to lean against the small bar.

Matt followed him and shut the airlock. "Pilgrimage command: Lock all airlocks to"—he looked up, reading the plaque over the hatch—"module two-zero-nine-eight. Pilgrimage command: Emergency seal override required in module two-zero-nine-eight. Lock all airlocks."

The Pilgrimage systems answered him. "Are you declaring nine-one-one?"

"No, emergency seal override." Matt tried not to shout.

"Do you require assistance?"

"No! Emergency seal override!"

There was a lag, and then the confusion the Pilgrimage systems were suffering became apparent. "No venting or gas mixture malfunctions detected in module two-zero-nine-eight. Emergency maintenance has been initiated at the airlock. Please remain calm and you will soon be able to exit the module."

The men in the module below had been quicker than Matt. He let loose a string of foul language that he'd learned from Ari. It started with common four-letter words and got worse as the Minoan Bull's genitalia were pulled into the fray. He turned to face David Ray, whose eyes were wide.

"You have to issue the security override," Matt said. "I'm not Pilgrimage."

"That could trap them. . . ." David Ray's voice tensed and he swallowed.

"They're going to get through, in time, and *they're using flechette weapons.*" Matt pointed at David's wounded leg, which was the most damning evidence of barbaric behavior. Stun weapons were widely available for use in space. They could be lethal, depending on the current they generated, but they were civilized weapons. Even the *military* used stunners.

David Ray looked at his gory thigh and winced. "I was lucky to catch the edge of the burst. I must have been at the far range of—"

A voice boomed from the nodes. "I am Abram Hadrian Rouxe and I now command the *Pilgrimage.* Continue in your assigned work, and you will not be harmed. Two of your captains are held hostage to your good behavior—the other's death stands witness to what will happen if you do not cooperate with me."

Matt shivered at the cold, uncompromising tone in the deep voice. The word structures and the slight accent were unfamiliar; the speaker wasn't Autonomist or Generational.

"Who is this Rouxe?" David Ray asked.

Matt shook his head.

"Please remain calm and the airlock will soon be repaired. The maintenance staff will release you in a few minutes." The helpful tone of the ship's system made Matt start cursing again.

"Maybe we should cooperate," David Ray said.

"I'm thinking they're not the forgiving type, even if all we've done is made fools of them." Matt tapped commands on the wall panel. "I'm locked out of ship systems."

Once again, an announcement by Rouxe came from the nodes. This time it was slightly different. "I am Abram Hadrian Rouxe and I carry the spirit of our leader, Qesan Douchet. My men will be visiting every work center. Cooperate with them and you will not come to harm. I can be benevolent, but remember that I have control of your children, both born and unborn."

David Ray's face paled. "There's no chance of negotiation. We'll die if they get through."

"You're sure?" Matt asked.

They locked gazes, and he got the feeling that the older man was terrified. The set in David Ray's jaw meant he was no longer considering a quiet surrender. Why the change?

"So we're blowing the module," Matt said softly.

David nodded. They waited for another announced threat, the same one, to complete.

"Did you recognize the name, the one he reverently mentioned?" Then, without waiting for Matt's answer, he rapidly said, "Pilgrimage command: security override. David Ray, alpha-ten-omega-four-two-phi. Pilgrimage command: security override. I require access to the emergency module system."

Matt held his breath and the independent EMS came online, showing its emergency options, one of which was to disconnect the module from the ship. He drew a breath in relief.

"What are you waiting for?" David Ray was adjusting the autohoist harness to hold him to the bar and floor.

Matt turned and grabbed the handhold, near the display, and attached to the bulkhead about a meter from the airlock. Any doubts that he might not remember how to do this vanished as his fingers danced across the panel. Every child on a generational ship was drilled in how to separate modules in a life-threatening emergency. Not surprisingly, the Pilgrimage interfaces were the same as what he had trained with on the *Journey IV.*

"Countdown starting!" Matt yelled.

Warning lights and a countdown display would be blinking in the airlocks above and below this module, warning the occupants that they had fifteen seconds ... ten seconds ... five seconds. There were clangs from below. Perhaps the men were trying to prevent the airlock door from closing. That was foolish, because their own module might decompress.

Matt tightened his hold as thumps came from charges blowing below and above him. There was creaking, a sharp, strong thrust, the screech of metal on metal combined with David Ray's grunt of pain, and module 2098 pushed away from the *Pilgrimage III*.

CHAPTER 8

The Absolutionist party uses the slogan "Yellowstone caused the war," but that's not right. That extinction event only taught us that we didn't know the first thing about terraforming and intentional climate change. We also didn't know how to pay for it, after the emergency aid dried up. So the colonists got tired of being taxed into extinction and *that's* what caused the war: money. *In particular, who had to pay for fixing Terra?*

—TerranXL State Prince Ling Adams, 2104.281.15.08 UT, indexed by *Heraclitus 22* under Conflict Imperative

"It's a good sign that you're willing to meet my deadline," Maria Guillotte said.

"We wanted to show our good faith, once we received your message." Joyce gave her a broad smile, at least by his standards.

He'd pushed Journey and Kedros on the schedule, which then allowed him a whole shift of sleep by renting a berth in the singles' quarters on Beta Priamos. He'd arrived on the moon's surface before first shift. The few nodes near the entrance recorded his arrival, but other than that, there wasn't standard node coverage in the facility. Priamos Moon operated without the watchful presence of ComNet or MilNet, although that would change in the next month.

"Let's go to my office." Maria signaled for silence and

strode deeper into the structure along sloping corridors and through strangely angled intersections.

Joyce would have liked to linger and look at the alien architecture, but instead concentrated on the long legs and tight ass of the woman in front of him. Sure, she looked good from the back, but the Terran penchant for standardization meant that Maria looked like any other Terran woman, at least when it came to her perfect proportions. She looked like the Aphrodite action figures his kids played with.

Given his experience, Joyce preferred the proportions of his wife, who was shorter and plumper than Maria. Besides, no soldier should allow his dick to distract him, particularly when he was on a plainclothes military intelligence mission.

Maria stopped at a recessed door that looked like one continuous piece of semiprecious stone similar to agate. It was highly polished and had a shiny weblike design of inlaid metal that looked like copper, yet the metal hadn't oxidized. There was a pattern near the side of the door, about halfway up. She held her hand over the design and a four-clawed appendage shot out.

Joyce jumped backward before he saw it was a holographic projection. The door slid open. Maria turned and smiled sweetly at him. "My office," she said.

Once inside, he used his enhanced slate to scan for recording pips. Maria watched patiently, a quirky smile on her lips.

"Well, what's on the bargaining table?" he asked. Information was always the currency in the intelligence arena.

"What do you want?"

"Andre." His reply was quick. Andre Covanni was a shadowy legend during the war and he remained undercover to continue his work for TerraXL, despite the Directorate's best efforts.

"Going for the brass ring, aren't you?" Maria shook her head with a sad smile. "If I had that to peddle, do you think I'd be here in G-145? Nathan might have passed messages to Andre, but we were too low in the food chain to know Andre's orders or identity."

"Parmet?"

"The SP isn't his handler, that's for sure. I don't think the SP even knows Andre's identity. But I could reduce the possibilities for you, perhaps as low as twenty." Her eyes narrowed.

That wasn't any better than what the Directorate already knew. Joyce kept his face passive, remembering Maria's *somaural* capabilities, and tried another approach. "We'll need you to stay in place," he began.

She cut him off. "Not acceptable."

"If you can't give us a lead on Andre, then your value—"

This time, she got a message on her ear bug and had to stop him.

"The SP arrived early. I thought he wouldn't be visiting until after the contractor meeting. We'll have to continue this discussion later."

"Wait. Should I stay in your office?" he asked.

She paused, turning and smiling, before opening the door. "I suppose, but don't show yourself. If necessary, you can hide in the closet." She pointed at a narrow door behind her desk that, given the strange shape of the room, he'd hesitate to say was on the *back* wall.

Joyce pressed his lips together in irritation as she left.

"You must be from Aether Exploration, the company that masterminded this extraordinary mess." Sewick's self-importance showed in his expression. He moved ahead of his colleagues to get center stage and offer his hand, which she grudgingly shook. She hated introductions where everyone pretended not to recognize one another, particularly in the age of ComNet. Either this was pretension, or the man hadn't done his prep.

"Yes, I must be *Ms. Kedros*. Pleased to meet you in person, Mr. Sewick." She tried to sound cheery, which was difficult because his handshake caused twinges of pain in her ribs. She stepped back before any more hands were of-fered. Everyone else took her cue and nodded their heads during greetings.

Four people met her when the elevator reached the moon surface. Mr. Sewick was the prime Autonomist con-tractor. She next greeted Mr. Wescott and Mr. Barone, the prime Terran and Minoan contractors, respectively. Barone wasn't Minoan, of course, but a native of Hellas Prime. He represented Hellas Nautikos, a company primarily owned by Minoan interests, meaning that Minoan capital com-prised more than fifty percent of their assets.

The fourth person seemed vaguely familiar to Ariane: a dark-skinned, dark-eyed woman in an AFCAW green uni-form, loaded down with bright gold epaulets and red trim. She had gray slivers in her short black hair and experience in her hard face, so Ariane almost expected the colonel rank on her shoulders. Her name tag read DOKOS.

"This is my ball and chain, otherwise known as my mili-tary adviser, Colonel Dokos." Sewick's smile was oily and he didn't meet Ariane's eyes, letting his gaze slide else-where. "I understand you're AFCAW also, Ms. Kedros."

"*Reserve* Armed Forces, rank of major, but I'm not on active-duty orders," Ariane answered automatically as she nodded to Dokos. "Pleased to meet you, ma'am."

"Likewise." Colonel Dokos met her gaze squarely, tak-ing a moment to study her face. "Have you had an accident, Ms. Kedros?"

Her ribs had grabbed her attention; she'd forgotten about the more visible effects of the beating. *No wonder nobody wants to look me in the face.* Luckily, she healed quickly and the bruises were turning green and yellow, let-ting her fudge the time of the incident.

"During the burn, a latch failed on a locker." Ariane kept her voice casual. "I slammed into the door when I tried to close it without gravity. My fault."

"Looks more like the results of a brawl," Dokos said

bluntly, her eyes narrowing. "Are you sure we haven't met before, perhaps when you were regular?"

Oh, Great Bull–shit. Now she remembered when she'd met Dokos, or rather, when *Lieutenant Karen Ahrilan Argyris* had a check ride with *Major Dokos* from Wing Evaluation. The ride started off badly, considering that Major Dokos had no sense of humor and was annoyed when Lieutenant Argyris showed up late, sporting a broken nose from a bar brawl. Her nose was different now, but who could tell under the puffy bruising? She had to have faith in the false records and the obscuring power of the rejuv treatments. If Argyris were still alive, she'd look much older than Reserve Major Kedros.

I'm Ariane Kedros, she told herself firmly. *I'm a commercial pilot, with a reserve commission of major*.

"Sorry, Colonel. I don't think so." She raised her eyebrows. "Unless you were stationed at Pelagos Naga Maintenance in 'ninety-seven, or—" Blah, blah, blah. Everyone in the military could rattle off their assignments and Ariane took the opportunity to bore the civilians with her list.

Dokos shook her head, luckily never intersecting with Ariane's false career, which was as obscure and lackluster as Owen Edones could design. Her reserve assignments for the Directorate were classified, of course, and couldn't be mentioned.

"Ms. Kedros, I want to express our thanks for being included in this exploration." Wescott's voice was warm and surprisingly genuine. "We know that you didn't have to lease claims to Terran-owned corporations—"

"Making our lives a living hell," Sewick said.

"Those of us who sub to Boeing-Zhou-Kunal, at least, are grateful for Aether Exploration's input and help." Wescott glanced sideways, but he didn't acknowledge Sewick's interjection. "Other claim owners might leave us at the mercy of the Consortium's S-triple-ECB."

Sewick muttered something under his breath that sounded like "damn flunkies," a reference to SEEECB personnel.

"You're welcome," Ariane said to Wescott. She looked for signs that he was practicing *somaural* projection and saw none. He fit the average ideal that Terrans strived for: medium build, skin that couldn't qualify as either light or dark, and regular features. Like all Terrans, his fashion sense was questionable, but he seemed sincere. He dressed in a conservative jumpsuit with a tailored jacket made from tweeds of muddy colors that blended into nothingness.

Unfortunately, she didn't *want* to like Wescott. She'd spent most of her travel time in the elevator thinking up ways to either fire the Terran contractors or make their lives so miserable they'd quit—all because Parmet didn't keep up his end of their double-blackmail bargain. Wescott didn't know anything about her background, so why should he and his employees suffer because Parmet had spilled Ariane's secrets to his psychotic wife?

Wescott's ignorance became even more obvious with his next words. "Our adviser, Ms. Guillotte, sends her regrets. She's got a VIP coming in for a tour. She said that you and she are already acquainted."

"Oh, yes, Maria and I have already met." Ariane smiled. *Maria kidnapped me and then dumped me, unconscious, in an addict commons—yes, we've met.* Her head felt strange, but whether it was from the beating or this surreal situation, she didn't know.

"We tried to get the best experts we could find," Wescott added. "We hired Dr. Myrna Fox Lowry, one of the foremost astrophysicists on Mars, to be part of our on-site staff."

"She's still quite young—*we've* got the established cosmologist, Mr. Novak." Sewick wasn't about to be outdone by the Terrans.

"Whom you hired away from one of our subs." Barone raised his deep voice for the first time.

"Better benefits always win out," Sewick replied in a satisfied tone as he stared back at Barone, but Ariane felt no hostility between the men. The world of research and development, whether for government, military, or civilian contracts, was small and the players well-known. Workers were itinerant, moving from contractor to contractor, hoping their scientific specialty would be in demand on the next contract.

"Gentlemen, please." Colonel Dokos's cool tone grabbed everyone's attention. "Ms. Kedros brought us a new reporting matrix that should help. I hope the matrix is approved?"

"Yes, we have the board's approval, although it wasn't easy to get them to agree to the shortcuts," Ariane said.

The CAW SEEECB flunkies, as they were not so affectionately called, tracked leases and contracts between all the organizations. The companies doing the actual work on the site, whether mining or exploring, were usually subcontractors to a contractor of the lessee. That meant reports went through at least two layers of indirection and obscuration before they even flowed out of G-145. Out of sheer frustration, the SEEECB demanded that Aether Exploration (aka Matt) put together a workable reporting matrix for the organizations that operated and leased Matt's claims.

"Good, we'll adjourn to our best conference room and go over the matrix. Everybody's here, right?" Wescott hesitated and exchanged glances with the other prime contractors.

"What?" Ariane asked. What were they hiding?

Sewick and Wescott looked subdued; Barone looked down at his boots. Dokos folded her arms and her face took on a not-my-business expression.

Sewick was the one who eventually answered. "We figured that if all of us had to haul around our ball—our advisers, per se, then so should Barone."

"What?" She raised her eyebrows. Barone's "ball and chain" was *Minoan*.

"I've requested, through my superiors, a Minoan adviser," Barone said. "I was told that one might be sent to assist us."

What? Rather than uttering another inane question, Ariane shut her mouth. Of everyone here, she might be the only one who had experience "negotiating" with Minoans. *Do we really want them here?*

"We're stymied; the symbols that we've found in these ruins are beyond us. It's impossible to interpret completely alien symbology without a common reference like the Rosetta Stone." Barone used measured tones, sounding like a man who picked his words carefully, giving weight to every syllable.

"And you think the Minoans might have a common reference? They might know something about these Builders?" Ariane followed the convention of using "Builders" for the inhabitants of this moon, because "aliens" was no longer specific enough.

Barone nodded.

"My biggest concern is whether you're going to give them access to the *artifact*," she said.

"They haven't asked for reports on the artifact. I doubt they feel threatened. Their monopoly on buoy production is safe," Barone said.

"What do the other contractors think about a Minoan adviser?" She included Sewick and Wescott with a wave of her hand. "For instance, the subs investigating the artifact are mostly Autonomist, but I think two researchers come from a Terran company."

Wescott acknowledged her assessment with a bow of his head.

"We'd like the best of both worlds, of course. We'd like to get information on the Builders from the Minoans, yet have the Minoans stay out of our way." Sewick surprised her with a conciliatory tone. "And so far, Barone is right: They've stayed out of our way. The Minoans have expressed no interest in the artifact. They haven't even asked for access to the video coming from your bot."

Apparently, their rebellious bot, which was stuck on the artifact, was still working. Ariane wasn't surprised that it was still recharging its batteries and operating, but she hadn't expected it to continue broadcasting. Matt would want the bot back eventually, because it was property of Aether Exploration, but he didn't have that kind of control over other research. Aether Exploration got a say in *who* managed the G-145 pie, not in *how* the pie should be consumed—or perhaps how the pie was baked? Okay, the pie was a bad metaphor. Basically, she didn't have the authority to arbitrarily change research decisions.

"What makes you think the Minoans will send someone to help? They've been pretty picky on how they've 'helped' humankind in the past." Perhaps she should remind them of the chaos the Minoans had created upon first contact with pre-Terran Earth.

"Come. I'll show you what they want." Barone gestured toward the airlock down at the end of the tube. Ariane walked beside him and everyone else trailed behind. They were going downhill and underground; she stepped cautiously in what seemed about three-quarters standard gee.

Everyone was silent as they cycled through the airlock and when she looked at Barone questioningly, he winked. Then the site-side doors opened.

"Oh." Her mouth fell open and she tentatively stepped forward onto a honed hard surface that had irregular opalescent striations. She stood under an arch of the same material.

"Not what you expected?" Barone asked.

"It's so—so beautiful."

"*That.* That is what the Minoans are after." Barone pointed to her, then to the nodes installed on a thin metal structure built inside the arch. "Your *reaction*. The Minoans are more interested in our reactions to these ruins, than in what we're examining. We're required, by our contracts with them, to deliver all sorts of observational data—but data of us, not of the Builders' artifacts, materials, or engineering."

She barely heard Barone's words as she stared around the large, glittering hall. She felt as if she had stepped inside a jewelry box carved of translucent semiprecious stone. The hall was rectangular and at least twenty meters by ten meters in area, lit by glowing designs on the ceiling.

When she and Matt first gathered their data using *Aether's Touch*, they'd determined that there were artificial structures under the surface of Priamos. As second-wave prospectors, they'd only had the use of telebots and near-surface scans. They could determine the size of the upper-most structures, but they hadn't landed on the moon surface. Neither had the original Pilgrimage exploration crews, who were technically the first wave of prospectors. Now that the Beta Priamos station and elevator were built, researchers had swarmed onto the surface.

"You've pressurized the structure, and installed scrubbers and oxygen generators." She should have noticed this earlier, but she'd been enthralled with the polished semiprecious stone pillars inlaid with metal and glowing materials.

"Ms. Kedros, we need to start using that matrix. There's no time for tours right now." Sewick stepped up and grabbed her elbow, causing a twinge in her ribs. He started steering her through the long hall between two rows of columns.

She gingerly pulled her elbow away and reluctantly walked beside Sewick. She hoped she'd have time later to explore the alien artifacts and structure. Somewhere, she thought jealously, a VIP was getting a full tour. *It's probably that bastard Parmet, with the homicidal redhead who claims to be his wife.*

Maria Guillotte was showing an input device to State Prince Isrid Parmet, his son, Chander, and his wives, Sabina and Garnet.

"Look at this, Dad." Chander was having fun at the sloped console, holding his hand in front of each of the large symbols to watch a holographic symbol extend. Once the symbol hovered above the console, almost touching his hand, Chander could rotate the symbol by tilting his hand left, right, up, and down.

"You're sure it's all right for him to play with this?" Garnet asked anxiously, looking up at the symbols that appeared on the wall above.

Chander frowned at Garnet's words, but became quickly distracted and enamored by another symbol. Sabina grinned as she watched her son; Parmet was also happy to see Chander's sullenness and ennui washed away.

"Don't worry, this console connects to read-only information archives. The Builders used lattice storage, and their versions of several crystal vaults are installed behind this wall." Maria also added the *somaural* signal of *no physical harm possible*. Chander wasn't watching, but Garnet relaxed. Garnet rarely projected, but she was adept at reading *somaural* signals.

"We can't access or understand their information?" Isrid watched the same set of symbols display after each of his son's attempts. The symbols seemed to chide, giving him the feeling of an error message.

"Sorry, not that easy, SP. This isn't a v-play," Maria said. "It'll be a long time before we can hope to understand any alien symbols. As for this terminal, we can't begin to know the security protocols. It might require voice or DNA keys."

"How long do you think it'll take?" Sabina asked, while her hand flickered, *How long will* you *be here?* Sabina hid her *somaural* question from Garnet and Chander, but not from Isrid.

"Years, I expect." Maria ignored the additional *somaural* content of the question, just as she had ignored Sabina's earlier signals. "We're lucky the Builders didn't create multipurpose interfaces, as we'd design them. They seemed to intend each input console to work with one particular system, which has helped us enormously. For instance, we can play with this console forever, knowing that it won't affect other systems in this complex."

"That's why you were able to get power and environmental systems online so fast?" Isrid asked.

"I'll show you the controls to those systems." Maria led them deeper into the complex, through strangely angled halls that were too tall for humans. "Everything in this complex is efficient in its power usage, and it's the efficiency we want to understand. Otherwise, their generation of heat and electrical current was pretty standard. They used a nuclear fission reactor and the fuel had decayed to where it was unusable, but the shielding and thermal conversion materials are outstanding. We'd like to study them more. As for getting a working reactor, the team mimicked the fuel form factors and experimented with isotope mixtures and refinement to get the right neutron flux. After months of work, the combined research team managed to power the environmental systems, to include pressurizing the complex with an oxygen-nitrogen mixture."

"Were they able to date these structures using the fuel?" Isrid asked.

"That would assume we knew the original ratios of isotopes in their fuel, but we don't. It gives us broad brackets, yes, but we're looking at how the entrances became buried and the pitting of the covering surface matter to make more accurate age estimates." Maria paused for effect, allowing the dawdling Chander to catch up with the adults. "We think this structure could have been built between ten and fifteen thousand UT years ago."

"Wow." Chander stroked the polished front of the nearest support pillar. "It doesn't look that old. Everything's so *clean*."

Both Garnet and Sabina smiled at Chander's comment.

"That's very perceptive, Chander," Maria said, "because they did clean out all atmosphere and organic matter. On purpose, it would appear, when they pulled out of here."

"Can't we be more precise?" Isrid asked. "That's a five-thousand-year window."

Maria glanced around at the floors, walls, ceilings, and

lighted panels. "We're still analyzing the alloys and composites they used. Many of them aren't made from materials local to this solar system—that makes it almost impossible to date. Also, without atmosphere or organic matter, referential methods using oxidation or radiocarbon ratios are out, even if we had the hope of finding references."

"Not much to go on, but you could use . . ." Isrid's voice trailed away as he thought through the scientific dating methods used in the Sol system. Every method he could think of was referential to defined material, within the solar system, of known age.

"Excuse me, SP." Maria signaled that she was getting a local message in her ear bug. Her communication paraphernalia was Autonomist, meaning it was higher quality and more reliable than Terran technology, which irked Isrid.

"I'll be right there," Maria said, pressing her jawbone to activate her implanted mike.

With a wry smile, she handed Isrid her slate. "I'm sorry, SP, but I've got an important meeting with the prime contractors. There are maps on the slate, and the areas allowed for visitors are clearly marked."

Maria nodded to his wives and son. She walked away with a free stride that stretched her long legs, her medium ash-blond hair bouncing about her shoulders.

Sabina drew close to Isrid's side and they both watched Maria walk away, until she turned at the end of the corridor.

"She's distant." Sabina had a scowl on her face that caused her lower lip to pout. Her fingers flickered and said, *Inappropriate behavior for a lover.*

Garnet rolled her eyes at her co-wife's comment. "She's busy, Sabina. She's being *professional.*"

Sabina looked up at Isrid with a cocked eyebrow, so he added, "I'd agree."

Sabina continued to express displeasure, a well-practiced projection for her, as she followed her son. Chander was down the hall reading notes posted by the archeological team.

Isrid had lied. He was as disturbed as Sabina by Maria's behavior, but not because he felt slighted. Maria was hiding something. He looked up to catch Garnet observing him. She nodded, and walked after Sabina.

CHAPTER 9

Considering the size and sequencing possibilities, we're lucky that for 99.5 percent of our genetic makeup, humans are identical. This leaves 0.5 percent to account for genetically determined differences in appearance, behavior, and health, and that's enough for decades of research.

—*Human Genome Project Review*, Volume 122, 2101.092.23.00 UT, indexed by *Democritus 23* under Cause and Effect Imperative

Indecision and irritation are not definable conditions for a computational entity, but Muse 3 considered itself—*pause for search*—inhibited by its current operating parameters.

After Ari left for her meeting, Muse 3 continued to cycle the request for bandwidth from the *Pilgrimage*. Meanwhile, it started a process to analyze CAW SEP 12.x, which described emergency procedures applicable in Consortium space. G-145 did not yet contain a Consortium world, but there were applicable procedures for Autonomists in new space.

Muse 3 ran through the procedure 16,384 times and with each analysis, produced a fuzzy decision set. There was still no response from the *Pilgrimage*. Three hours, fifty minutes, and 4.2 UT seconds after Ari left, the cam-eye at the ship's slip relayed video of three men running through the halls. Each man carried a weapon—*pause for pattern matching*—Muse 3 determined two were medium-voltage stunners and the third was a flechette pistol. There was still no response from the *Pilgrimage*. Muse 3 went through all decision sets and while flechette weapons were illegal on Consortium habitats, this event didn't warrant any action on its part. Seven minutes and 52.8 UT seconds after this event, all communication channels through the Beta Priamos Command Post shut down, making Muse 3's requests to the *Pilgrimage III* impossible.

Pause for analysis.

Muse 3 redefined its situation as externally constrained. When *Aether's Touch* was docked at Athens Point, communication across the Hellas solar system was effortless and faster than light, thanks to multiple buoys and relays. Buoys helped move matter, and relays assisted the movement of information through N-space. In G-145, the buoy was still under manual control by the *Pilgrimage* crew and the relays weren't yet operational. Now Muse 3 no longer had use of the Command Post antennae.

Aether's Touch, however, was a second-wave prospecting ship. All N-space ships had smart skin antennae designed for communication within ten thousand kilometers, but *Aether's Touch* also supported telebot control and gathering of scientific data. This ship had redundant, separate, and reconfigurable antennae for better transmission and reception of wider frequency bands than required by passenger or transport ships. Muse 3 turned the two most sensitive antennae in-system toward the *Pilgrimage III*, sitting between the paths of Sophia I and II's orbits. It could detect or initiate light-speed transmissions itself, without buoy support.

Pause for analysis of input from sensors.

As small as the probabilities were, the orientation of the antennae fortuitously allowed Muse 3 to observe another unusual event. Flashes of visible and infrared light on one of the *Pilgrimage*'s spires indicated small explosive charges.

Then a module separated and began floating away from the generational ship. Infrared spectra showed the escape of a small amount of life-supporting gases from the *Pilgrimage III*.

This was light-speed data, so the event had happened a few UT hours ago. However, these disparate events now qualified as an "emergency condition" against the decision sets and Ari must be notified. Muse 3 explored ways to send a message to the surface of Beta Priamos since the station CP comm support wasn't responding.

Muse 3 now classified its condition as *frustrated*. The station's structure and orientation prevented Muse 3 from directing ship antennae toward the moon's surface; no clear shot was available. Without a directed signal through an antenna—*pause for calculation*—the surface was too far away to discern omnidirectional comm signals above the ambient noise. Muse 3 widened its parameters and used all available sensor input to search for a solution.

One of the behemoths, as Ari called the freighters on the class B docks, had disconnected from Beta Priamos and was moving away under light thrust. It was also broadcasting an omnidirectional distress call. The freighter's transponder ID matched the registration of the *Golden Bull*. The distress codes indicated possible control problems, but Muse 3 didn't analyze this further because the orientation and angle of the large, flat, and reflective surface of the freighter presented a solution.

Using one antenna to track the slow movement, Muse 3 could guide another antenna and bounce a signal off the behemoth's belly down to the moon surface. Of course, the signal would be attenuated, so message bit rate and size had to be reduced—*pause for calculation*.

Muse 3 started reconfiguring antennae.

"*This* is Pilgrimage Line's best geneticist?" Abram's voice dripped with scorn and Tahir looked up from his station to watch an elderly woman step from the airlock onto the control deck. Her dark eyes glittered as they moved quickly, taking in the bloodstains that cleaning crews were removing from the airlock and bulkheads. She glanced about the control deck and when her eyes met Tahir's, he almost gasped at their accusation, wanting to immediately exonerate himself and protest that he couldn't *do* anything to stop his father.

"Yes, I'm Dr. Lee Pilgrimage," she said in a calm tone, and walked over to the command chair where Abram sat, circled by consoles.

As she walked, Tahir revised his estimate of her age upward. Her bone structure was slight, although all the crèche-get were slim and tall. Her hair was white and puffy, her skin papery and wrinkled in places, but she stood straight and proud, unlike the hunched old women in Tahir's tribe. Perhaps this resulted from good nutrition, a generous environment, and medicine.

"My specialty, more specifically, covers prefertilization genetic diagnosis and embryonic maturation." Lee stopped to stand in front of Abram, a low console between them.

"Yes, you maintain the 'crèches.' " Emery moved to stand protectively beside Abram, as if the frail woman were a threat.

"I prefer the term 'artificial womb,' " Lee said carefully.

Tahir watched the central tableau of three people with trepidation. Abram didn't consider women useful for anything but reproduction, and Emery followed him in his disdain for "breeders." Dr. Lee was too old to carry a child, and if she proved to have too much backbone and resisted Abram's plans, she might go the way of Captain Zabat and Commander Charlene.

Abram didn't look offended—yet. He cocked his head and asked, "What do you know, Dr. Lee Pilgrimage, about the Minoan attack at Enclave El Tozeur on New Sousse?"

The woman nodded with a resigned expression, as if she both expected and dreaded this topic. "I was finishing my term at headquarters, so that was some time around 'seventy-five. Someone managed to sabotage a Minoan ship so badly that it was destroyed, and Qesan Douchet foolishly—"

"You're speaking of my uncle, woman!" Emery leaned forward, but stopped when Abram put up a restraining hand.

"I'm sorry for your loss, young man." Lee's voice was considerate, but underlying her sounds of sympathy was the cold hardness of marble. "Regardless of who performed the sabotage, your uncle was imprudent to claim credit in such a public display. Take heart that your people now stand as an example for everyone: The Minoans play for keeps."

Lee shook her head and added, "Their genetically targeted bioweapons were—and still are—beyond our science or engineering. I remember looking at the initial reports in disbelief. How could their bioweapons work so specifically, and how could they make alterations in place, affecting current DNA organization? When Pilgrimage headquarters sent aid to the survivors—"

"That's a lie!" Emery raised his voice. "No one helped us, old woman. No one cared!"

"I beg your pardon," she snapped, her eyes glinting, "but I *personally* signed the transfer and ensured it was delivered to the Acting Elder at Enclave El Tozeur! Pilgrimage took pride in matching the Voyage relief donation of *fifty thousand* Hellas Kilodrachmas, and back then, young man, that was a substantial amount of money."

It certainly was. Tahir stood up straight from the shock, feeling a bit woozy. He saw Emery was laboring under the same feelings, working his mouth and probably wanting to call Lee Pilgrimage a liar. *But she has no reason to lie.*

The tribal elders told Tahir and Emery, all their lives, the outside world never noticed their plight. Once Tahir was off New Sousse, he realized that the rest of the Terran Expansion League considered Qesan Douchet a ridiculous, if slightly tragic, figure. The Enclave and tribe seemed mysteriously forgotten, and the Minoan attack was rarely a subject for casual discussion among Terrans. When Tahir made his infrequent trips back home, the tribe's poverty was heart-breaking and he was shamed by Abram's chidings to do better in his studies. After all, the tribe was suffering to pay for his schooling.

Abram surely knew about the donations. If only two ship lines had donated one hundred thousand HKD to survivors of the attack, then how much more relief money must have come in? Where had it gone? The elders had certainly never used it to make anyone's life easier, to take the tribe members from scrabbling in the dirt to clean houses and workplaces. *We could have built hospitals, started industries. . . .*

Emery was also staring at Abram with surprise and puzzlement, but Abram sat unmoved, focusing on Lee.

"We didn't need money." Abram's voice was flat. "We needed allies with weapons, with the strength and fortitude to help us retaliate and regain our pride."

Emery nodded slowly, but Tahir noted his hesitancy. Dr. Lee, however, was looking at Abram as if he were speaking a foreign language.

"If our money bought us this, then I am convinced that good deeds are punished." Lee gestured, with bewilderment, toward the bloodstains. "But St. Darius compels us to give help to the wayfarer in need and you might have gotten our help by asking. Did you think of that? You do need our help, don't you?"

Abram cocked his head again and Tahir wondered if Lee had pushed him too far.

"I think a test is in order, *Doctor*," Abram said. "Tahir, come stand beside me, on the other side from Emery."

Tahir's heart sank as he moved to stand beside the chair. In his experience, Abram's tests often involved somebody dying. So far, Tahir had avoided taking any lives and he didn't think he could kill Dr. Lee.

"These two young men are both related to me." Abram gestured to Tahir and Emery. "One is my nephew, who was present during the attack. The other is my son, who was in the womb during the attack. Which young man carries my genes, *Doctor*?"

Tahir's chest tightened. The three of them looked alike, regardless of what their genes indicated. It was a trick question and he dreaded whatever the penalty would be for him, Emery, or Dr. Lee, if she answered incorrectly.

Dr. Lee folded her arms and stared down her nose at Tahir, then Emery. "Perhaps you're not aware of this, Mr. New Commander, but little of the human genome is responsible for appearance. The color of our hair, eyes, and skin makes us different by a negligent blip in the sequences."

"You may take DNA samples, if you wish," Abram said, to Tahir's surprise.

"I don't need samples," Dr. Lee said with confidence. She pointed at Tahir. "*That* is your son, but his DNA cannot prove it."

Tahir looked at Abram and Emery, whose face was darkening. Emery had probably taken the "son of Abram's spirit" talk a little too seriously. Tahir anxiously tried to read Abram's response. Did Dr. Lee provide the answer he wanted?

"Congratulations, Dr. Lee. You understand the effects of the Minoan weapons. You must also know why I require your full cooperation and best efforts of your staff." Abram's colorless voice made Tahir flinch. The more emotionless Abram's voice, the more dangerous he became.

"*Now* you prefer allies with medical technology above those with weapons." Lee's voice, unwisely, held sharp sarcasm.

"I have all the weapons I need," Abram said indifferently. "Now I must have sons—and your children will be forfeit if you can't find a way to give me mine."

Lee's face went slack. She knew Abram was threatening the crèches and that was her key. Abram said everyone had a key, by which he or she could be unlocked. Manipulated. Threatened. Lee bit her lower lip.

"It might not be possible to reverse the effects of the Minoan weapons," she said.

"I'm surprised that you, as a renowned scientist and doctor, would jump to conclusions. Tell me what you need to give me sons."

There was a pause as she looked at Abram's face for a moment. She looked away and crossed her arms over her chest, her shoulders hunching.

"First, we'll need samples from you and all your peop—your men." She'd noticed the consistent gender of Abram's followers.

"I'll send in everyone who's closely related to me. You can go now, Doctor."

She turned to go, and stopped. "Do you like music, Mr. Rouxe?"

"No. It's distracting," Abram said.

"Pity. However, it's—it's necessary for me and my laboratory." At Abram's quizzical look, she added, "I'd like access to my music library."

"That can be arranged, in exchange for information. I'd like to know who was in the module that separated from the ship, the one above your laboratory."

Lee's face was blank as she said, "David Ray, the ship's general counsel, and a visiting prospector. I can't remember his name, but he should be on the ship's visitor register."

"Will you need any equipment that was in that module?" Abram watched her face carefully.

Tahir tensed up. *Don't lie—he always knows the answers before he asks.*

"No." Lee cleared her throat. "There's no critical equipment in that module."

Abram seemed satisfied by her answer and told Tahir to release her music library, after examining it to ensure that it only held music, of course. He ordered Tahir to escort Dr. Lee off the control deck.

Tahir walked behind Lee to the vertical airlock, grateful that she hadn't done anything that would have given

Abram or Emery a reason to kill her. She seemed cowed, so he was surprised when she quickly turned to him behind the edge of the airlock, where Abram couldn't see her.

"Tahir, your genes don't determine your fate," she whispered.

Then she went down the ladder and out of his sight. Tahir jerked around to see if Abram had noticed the pause, but Abram was deep in decisions and conversations. By the time Tahir walked back, he'd learned the unfortunate escape of Module 2098 was irrelevant and Abram didn't want to waste any resources on retrieving it. Abram was leaving Rand in charge of the team on the *Pilgrimage*, with orders to continue with the original plan. This left Rand with plenty to do, including moving the *Pilgrimage*.

Tahir could see this didn't sit well with Emery, who had vocally hoped to command the team on the *Pilgrimage*. Emery probably thought this was punishment for destroying the shrine to St. Darius. Abram, however, was being logical. Rand was a better negotiator than Emery, and they needed cooperation from the crèche-get.

"You'll go with me to Beta Priamos to prepare a ship for Tahir's gift," Abram was saying to Emery. "By the time we get there, everything on Priamos should be under control."

Under quickly diminishing gee, Matt dosed David Ray with pain meds and antibiotics. After the poor man was under, he tried his best to treat the mangled leg with what was available in the emergency first aid kit. A few flechettes remained deep inside the leg muscle and Matt didn't know how to remove them.

Then he had to assess their situation. The emergency training drilled into every generational crew member had several steps, the first being "Inventory and identify your resources." *Inventory what?* He looked about a module designed for one purpose: helping men donate sperm samples. There were three privacy booths against one side. The furnishings and fittings looked like any quiet men's club that Matt had encountered, with the exception of the monochromatic decorating that the generational favored. Everything was in shades of burgundy.

Too bad I can't hurl hard porn as a weapon, and it's a shame—contrary to how Nestor lived—*that one can't survive on porn alone*. If so, he and David Ray would be set up for months.

"Wha's happening? They comin' after us?" David Ray woke up a few hours later, still webbed to the floor and under the influence of every drug Matt thought might be useful.

"No, it's worse. They're going to let us die." Matt helped David Ray sit upright and lean his back against the bar.

"Tha's alright w' me." He gave Matt a lopsided grin.

"Maybe we ought to ease up on your medication."

"Wha?" David Ray began to examine his leg, wincing as his fingers poked the plastiskin.

"Unfortunately, I couldn't get all those things out of your leg. We don't have a med-scanner."

"Might be poisoned," David Ray said.

"Poisoned?" Matt looked up from the bar inventory. "They've broken both Autonomist and Terran law by using flechette weapons on a space habitat. For all I know, they've violated the Phaistos Protocols as well. Would they go even further, with poisoned rounds, and take a chance at pissing off the Minoans?"

"You think these people are afraid of the Minoans?" David Ray's smile was grim. "Did you recognize the name 'Qesan Douchet'?"

"Vaguely. Learned something about him in the orphanage." Matt was busy going through inventories and checking the location of items. "Ran an isolationist cult on New Sousse, right? He managed to blow up a Minoan ship, somehow, so they killed him and slapped the cult around. I think that was before my time."

"It was about thirty UT years ago, while you were on the *Journey IV*. Qesan's tribe was brutally misogynistic;

women were 'put down' if they couldn't produce sons—although they apparently did it humanely."

This shocked Matt out of his inventory. Having spent his childhood and early teen years on a generational ship, then living as a generational orphan on an Autonomist world, he had a hard time imagining such a society. David Ray had to be exaggerating. "New Sousse was TerranXL. Couldn't anyone stop that? Couldn't the women escape?"

"The cult didn't even control their planet, which was some meaningless asset under Overlord Six. If Six ignored the situation, it might go away—remember this was happening during the war. I think the League washed their hands of the isolationists."

"What if a *male* in the cult couldn't produce sons?"

"By definition, that couldn't happen. Until, that is, the Minoan attack." David Ray chuckled dryly. "The Minoans couldn't have created a better punishment for men whose lives were measured by the number of their sons. For a while, they wouldn't even believe they were sterile. They rejected the studies done by the relief medics, at least initially. Idiots."

"Idiots with weapons, who now control the *Pilgrimage*," Matt pointed out. "Who have realized, quite rightly, that they don't have to do anything but *wait* for us to die."

"Well, they won't reward us for coming back; I figure we'll be dead as soon as we open the airlock. So, let's run the checklists." David Ray shook his head and appeared attentive, but with obvious effort. "I assume you're finished with inventory. What's our situation?"

"We have a week of life support, looking at air reserve tanks, water, and power. I've got the collectors oriented toward the sun and the batteries are working correctly, but after we use up the air in the reserve tanks, battery power won't be able to create oxygen as well as maintain other life-support functions. We'll go downhill, either by freezing or oxygen deprivation. Unluckily for us, it won't happen fast enough to be painless."

"Sounds about right," David Ray said. "Module-operating mode was never intended for long-term life support. What other resources have we got?"

"We've got the emergency med kit, which can mend bones and minor wounds, but surgery is out. It's got a good amount of pain medication. We have insulated survival gear and two-hour oxygen masks for four people, but nothing for EVA. We've got three days' emergency rations, plus about fifty snack packs intended for donors. We've also got the best equipped bar in the entire system, with a wide selection of Terran brandies, Hellas-made scotch, smooth, and more than a thousand pornographic v-plays and videos. That leads me to the"—Matt scratched his head and didn't know whether to laugh or curse—"two freezers, each containing about four hundred samples of sperm."

"You forgot the useless lawyer with one leg."

Matt shook his head. "Those freezer units suck battery power. If I shut them off—"

"You can't do that. Those samples are our future generations." David Ray leaned forward, causing himself to move his wounded leg and wince.

"Your eggs are stored elsewhere, and this isn't the entire Pilgrimage sperm bank."

"The freezers will be in sunlight, no matter how we orient the solar collectors. Without power, they'll fry," David Ray said. "And that's enough sperm to account for one third of Pilgrimage genetic diversity, and you know how necessary that is. Absorbing such a loss would be tough for our entire line. Anyway, you said the batteries can't maintain oxygen creation once we use up the reserve tanks."

"But if we shut the freezers down now, it could mean a few more hours at the end of our week."

"No." David Ray shut his eyes, finality in his tone.

Matt stared at the wounded man, wondering whether he'd stepped over the line of sanity.

David Ray opened his eyes. "We can't worry about a few

hours here and there. We have to start figuring out what these isolationists want, particularly from the *Pilgrimage*."

"What does it matter? They're making demands right now to CAW or TerraXL or Pilgrimage HQ, perhaps ransoming the ship for money. Maybe they want a planet of their own." Matt pushed and floated in the low gee to the other side of the module. He called up the environmental display, just checking, to quiet his nerves. "Really, David Ray, you're going to lose the samples eventually."

"Let's table that subject for right now. Please. Can we see what's happening with the ship?"

Matt sighed, but didn't pursue the topic any more. "We have limited cam-eye feeds and nothing more. We can maneuver so we can view the ship. Remember, however, that the maneuvering jets use our air."

They both looked at the *Pilgrimage III*, which filled the display. It was still huge and beautiful, but no longer a comforting haven. Matt felt pain in his chest as he thought of it held hostage, and the crew abused, by the man whose voice was cold and heartless. *If I could only help them*. His jaw clenched and he balled up his fists at his helplessness.

"Let's talk about the proverbial elephant in the room. We have to get these flechettes out of my leg." David Ray sounded tired.

"I told you we don't have surgery support."

"We'll have to do it ourselves. Or rather, you'll have to do it *manually*, if you prefer that term." David Ray smiled weakly when Matt turned around to look at him. "You said there's lots of liquor and meds."

Matt swallowed, trying to loosen his throat.

CHAPTER 10

Most ComNet users use natural language interfaces to query AI models, providing loose specifications as well as limiting themselves to indexed information. There are ways to have Democritus models, in particular, explore unindexed material. This becomes necessary as the amount of garbage grows exponentially and masquerades as data.

—*Unindexed Searches under Democritus Rulesets*, AFCAW Captain Doreen Floros, 2103.022.08.09 UT, indexed by *Democritus 21* under Cause and Effect Imperative

Tahir caught up with Abram in a corridor on the *Pilgrimage* and started the conversation on a pretext, expressing concern about the container used for their package, a container that had to shield the exotic material.

"I was assured that it would be good for several years. It's supposed to have the best shielding," Abram said, gesturing for Tahir to follow him.

They entered a small room that Tahir had never seen, not surprisingly because the generational ship was huge. The only reason Abram could maintain control over such a large ship and crew was that the crèche-get were easily cowed. Of course, they were still in shock and they'd never entertained this security nightmare: someone wresting a controlled buoy away from them. Who would have thought of doing that?

Abram. And Qesan, before him. Tahir watched his father call up a display, which looked like a report from Dr. Lee, and read. He looked pleased as he fingered the collar of his coveralls.

Tahir glanced at his father's moving fingers, and his gaze froze on something that peeked out under the collar. Was that a body-armor vest? His lip twitched as he pictured Abram's bravado in the face of shrapnel, inspiring his men with his lack of fear.

"Back to our precious cargo. You were saying?" Abram turned quickly to face him, and he glanced away.

"Right. The shielding. It's holding up well, according to our measurements," Tahir said. "But the shielding is expended as it's exposed to the exotic matter, so I have to know its original quality and density. I can't believe we could afford shielding that's rated for more than six months."

Abram's eyes narrowed. "Don't worry. I paid well for that shielding and it'll last long enough."

"There're not many places that'll sell shielding for exotic matter, without asking questions."

"What's your point?" Abram seemed to be losing interest in the conversation.

"How did we afford all this, and where could you procure items such as exotic shielding and cases of flechette weapons?" Tahir asked. His heart was pounding.

"You heard the geneticist. We received quite a bit of emergency aid, and we invested it well." Abram shrugged as he closed the report. "I'm not going to apologize for withholding information from you, considering that I had to keep you focused on your studies."

You can't fool me twice, Father. I'm not like Emery. He chose his next words with care; he was walking a fine line here. "Since I've lived on the outside, I have a good idea of what this equipment can cost."

"You think we had funding from other sources? You're right. Are you insinuating that we might have paid more than we should? Perhaps, but what does it matter? We have no further need of accountants or buyers."

Tahir's heart skipped. Someone else had helped fund him, and now that someone had a say in Abram's plans. More than Tahir did, or ever could. After Lee's comments, he'd tried to do an honest assessment, for the first time, of what the past two decades had cost his people. Qesan's Cause turned out to be frightfully expensive, his own education merely a drop in the bucket. Yet he allowed Abram to use it against him, to twist him with guilt. He let Abram manipulate him, because he didn't want to know the truth.

"What will you need—in the future?" Tahir stammered as his mind raced. "I'd like to do something useful for the Cause."

"You want more responsibility? A leadership role, perhaps?" Abram watched him with flat eyes.

"Yes. I can handle it." *Watch out, I can't look too eager.*

"You must *earn* it, like Rand or Emery. Tell me, why are we doing this?"

Tahir was stunned speechless as he tried to control his anger. This was more hypocrisy, saying he should earn it! He'd spent years, studying, and eventually worming his way into a defense contractor job. What had Emery done during all this time?

His father's gaze chilled his budding rage, so he bent his head and recited, "'We do this to bloody the hand of oppression.'"

"Good. We'll see if you have any use in our new world. Now get ready to board the *Father's Wrath*." Abram dismissed him.

Tahir left, seething quietly, although he had to place much of the blame on himself. He'd had his doubts before, but his guilt and fear of his father had kept him in-line. Now he knew Abram could be *bought*, just like any common criminal. He had to escape this hell, while he could.

*   *   *

Whenever their investigation dug up more facts, the nightmare continued to grow. What disturbed Lieutenant Oleander most wasn't *her* notion of the problem, but the fear that emanated from the other officers, much as they tried to hide it.

"This is bad," Major Bernard said, initiating a whispered conference during a break.

"Surely there's no way the criminals could detonate a stolen package, even if it's the functional part of the weapon." She kept her voice as low as she could.

They were standing outside the cleared conference room and Bernard bent his head sideways to hear her. He shook his head in response to her question, leaving her frustrated and obviously *not* in the loop. She knew the line of execution approval for AFCAW: It required presidential, vice presidential, and tripartisan senatorial approval. After that, authorization traveled into military authority through a tangled web of special access and down the chain of command. Without those authorization codes, the criminals simply had a chunk of toxic components—and that's *if* they could dismantle the package, since it should have antitamper protection.

"Sirs, please come back into the shielded room for updates," said one of Hauser's aides. He was a nonuniformed young man who, according to Major Bernard, was TEBI.

They filed back in, having grown to a task force of fifteen Autonomist and Terran personnel, both civilian and military. Once the doors closed, their agenda displayed on one wall and Oleander noticed that the "Hazardous materials threat" bullet kept sinking lower and lower. Nobody seemed to be worried about the exotic material leaking.

"We've got reports on the civilian weapon-transfer team. These three men performed the final inventory: two long-term employees, plus one man who was in training at the time. They all had clearance, although the one in training had only interim clearance." The aide pointed to the wall and displayed three faces.

"Dr. Russell-Li and Mr. Nielson were responsible for the inventory and Dr. Rouxe was an observer-in-training. Russell-Li supposedly signed the inspection for warhead WM15-894."

It was silent in the room and Oleander's ears hurt from the strain of listening. She looked at the three Terran faces. None were out of the ordinary, and Rouxe seemed youngest, but appearances were meaningless.

"Dr. Russell-Li died in an accident a month after he signed the inventory, while both Mr. Nielson and Dr. Rouxe were laid off during defense contractor changes."

Murmurs rose about the room, but Edones cut through with a question. "Were the circumstances of Russell-Li's accident suspicious?"

"No. He died while on vacation. It was a drowning accident; he had a coronary while swimming and couldn't be saved," answered the aide.

"The body was recovered and identified? *Positively?*" Edones's voice was sharp.

"Yes, sir." The young man giving the briefing obviously thought the question irrelevant. "His family identified him and there was a full autopsy. We have no suspicions about his death, even with the strange timing. We're more concerned with the other two members of the team."

The aide's fingers flickered gracefully in command. The picture of Dr. Russell-Li went away, leaving Nielson and Rouxe. Background information appeared under the pictures in Martian patois, which Oleander didn't understand.

"Change display to common Greek," the aide ordered.

The writing changed. Oleander noted Nielson's and Rouxe's home planets, one of which was New Sousse—what was familiar about New Sousse?

Beside Oleander, Captain Floros gasped. She turned to see Floros's dark, square forehead crease into a frown and deep lines pull at the corners of her mouth. Floros's fuzzy blond hair was cut close to her head, making it look like a block. She didn't have the urbane and politic manners of

Edones or Bernard, and Oleander wondered if her notably slow rank progression resulted from her lack of tact. Considering the Directorate of Intelligence could handpick their people, Floros had to bring some esoteric skills to AFCAW's shadowy intelligence organization.

"Do you always grant clearances to—to—" As Floros sputtered and searched for words, Oleander looked down at the surface of the table in front of her, willing Floros to be a little bit diplomatic, just this once.

"Anarchists?" suggested Major Bernard.

" 'Isolationist' is the correct term," Colonel Ash said.

Floros spat out, "You gave a clearance to one of Qesan Douchet's descendants?"

Oleander frowned, the name jogging her memory and bringing up visions of the famous last video taken of Qesan Douchet. The name now had a buffoonish aura for younger Autonomists and Terrans, usually meaning "a mundane who is ignorant of his or her imminent demise by Minoans."

Douchet had stepped across an invisible line. Minoans accepted humankind's societal rules and laws, but they expected *everyone* to follow them. They didn't understand idiosyncratic defiance of authority and they didn't understand individuals who broke rules or laws. The chaos after first contact with the Minoans should have been an obvious lesson to someone like Douchet.

However, the Minoans did understand warfare. There were rules governing warfare between governments and states, and the Minoans had slapped on more conventions and treaties. In the decades-long warfare between CAW and TerraXL, all conduct of hostilities had to fit within the Phaistos Protocol. Whenever terrorism or piracy turned attention, foolishly, to Minoan assets—well, the perpetrators rarely survived the attempt. The Minoans would carefully declare war, often considered "open season," and hunt them down. Douchet's enclave was attacked under such a declaration, while the League and Consortium sat by and watched.

Colonel Ash shook his head. "If the enclave on New Sousse hadn't seceded from the League, they might—"

"Don't be absurd." Floros's frown morphed to a sneer. "We all know the Minoans did the League a favor, *after* filing intent with the Overlords. Douchet was an irritating pustule on the ass of humanity."

There was a shocked silence. Colonel Ash's mouth hung open, the colonel unable to finish his politically correct comment after that harsh honesty. Oleander raised her eyebrows and looked at Colonel Edones, expecting him to rebuke Floros.

"Obviously, the background of one of your scientists is suspect, by our standards." Colonel Edones's brisk voice was like a fresh breeze, letting them move on to a more comfortable topic.

"More than you realize," SP Hauser said. "Nielson is currently serving a prison sentence for embezzlement, occurring after his stint with the defense contractor. He's an example of the extremely small percentage that background investigations can't weed out: those that initiate an atypical late-life criminal event."

"That worked in our favor," the aide said brightly as he enlarged Nielson's picture. The background text extended to include the particulars of the prison sentence. "Since Nielson was in Unified League Prison, we could question him under neural probes."

Every Autonomist in Oleander's sight flinched at that violation of personal privacy, even Colonel Edones. She exchanged a glance with Floros, who leaned close and whispered, "*Latin barbarians.*"

She agreed with Floros's assessment, nodding, and internally thanking Gaia that she was a Consortium citizen. This was a small example of the differences between the League, where there was oppressive control, and the Consortium, founded upon colonist principles that valued personal freedoms.

Not that these differences led to outright warfare—no,

the long war between TerraXL and CAW started over *money*. After the Yellowstone Caldera caused an extinction event by blowing itself into the atmosphere and pushing Terra into an ice age, the League was desperate for funds. The settlements in newly opened solar systems were significant tax bases and started taking the brunt of tax increases. Many of the colonies, however, no longer felt responsible for restoring the "mother planet" and began to break away from the League, diverting their tax monies to other purposes. The League had to declare war, carefully following the Phaistos Protocol. In defense, colonist solar systems united the original Prime Planets of the Consortium of Autonomous Worlds and fought back, leading to decades of hardship and violence.

To Oleander, the events that had led to the war seemed avoidable, but she was a member of the first generation to grow up under Pax Minoica and she knew that colored her opinions. This small difference about personal rights, the cornerstone of Autonomist law that even applied to prisoners, reminded Oleander again that the Terrans were more than people who dressed strangely and spoke common Greek with accents. They competed economically and industrially with CAW and, to every other AFCAW officer in the room, they had been the *enemy* for nearly fifty years.

"Ah—Nielson underwent the procedure voluntarily. He wanted to prove his innocence." The aide noticed the reactions from the AFCAW side of his audience. Many relaxed, although the unsaid sentence hung in the room: *If Nielson hadn't volunteered, he'd have been forced.*

"Which leaves the obvious suspect," Floros said. "The one who comes from misogynists and criminals, who comes from a tribe thrown out of northern Africa, and then evicted from the French South American colonies. They were *asked* to leave Terra, if you look at your history."

"This isn't as obvious as you might think." The aide showed pictures of Dr. Rouxe and his background, including parents, birth date, previous addresses, and education. "He left Enclave El Tozeur at the age of eight, and then New Sousse at the age of twelve. He was educated in Terran schools, getting a doctorate in physics from the University of Florida in the Terran Florida Biome. He did his postdoc work at Mars MIT, before getting a government research position on Mars Orbital One."

"Who paid for his education?" Colonel Edones asked.

"Disbursed directly from the relief fund established for El Tozeur survivors and yes, sir, the tribal elders had to approve the disbursement—obviously, he's indebted to them." The aide knew Edones's next question and rushed through his second sentence.

"Yet he gets an interim security clearance to work in a weapons storage facility," Floros said disdainfully.

"Dr. Rouxe *voluntarily* went through a psychiatric evaluation under neural probe," the aide said. "He was estranged from his tribe and traumatized by watching his father torture his mother. The evaluators thought he held too much fear and hatred toward his father to involve himself in tribal politics."

There was silence in the room as everyone digested the information. Oleander pitied the man whose face displayed on the wall; the eyes that first seemed exuberant to her now took on a tragic cast.

"In societies like Rouxe's, obedience to tribal goals doesn't require respect or admiration. Fear and hatred won't prevent him from following Abram Hadrian Rouxe, who's labeled extremely dangerous by our Civil Security Division," Edones said. "We watch and measure Abram's impact on net-think, and he's attracted hundreds of nontribal followers. They are the disaffected, the anarchists, and the sociopaths, because Abram's anger against all governmental control appeals to them."

"We don't need to know what's going on in Rouxe's head. He's now our number one suspect, but we can't find him. He's out of crystal." SP Hauser used Autonomist slang for a person who couldn't be located through ComNet: a difficult, but not impossible feat.

Floros stirred and Colonel Edones glanced severely at her. Then he turned to Hauser, who had a pleasant expression on his face.

"You need our help," Edones said. "We *know* ComNet, we *built* ComNet, and we can find him. But we're not moving one iota until you release the specifications on the design flaw in the Mark Fifteen arming sequence."

Oleander heard the breath whistle through Floros's teeth as she drew in a big breath. Hauser raised an eyebrow. Oleander realized that Edones had leaked intelligence, like uncovering a card in a betting game. She'd originally thought intelligence games were about protecting your own information while trying to uncover the enemy's secrets. That turned out to be too simple; it was almost more important the enemy didn't know what you knew about them. However, you could let the enemy *know* you knew, if you wanted to negotiate—

"Agreed," SP Hauser said. "You obviously already know about our design-to-test flaw. I'll give you all the specifics, but your people need to find the weapon."

Edones cocked his head toward Captain Floros, who leaned forward eagerly.

"Out of crystal? That's as believable as the proverbial size of the Great Bull's balls," Floros said. "*I'll* find this bastard, sir."

The contractors hurried Ariane out of the large, pillared hall. They went through a corridor that never made ninety-degree turns, covered with inlaid mosaics of stone and metal. The mosaic designs swirled in organic abstract shapes, and she fought the urge to run her hands over their contours. She'd have all the time she wanted after the meeting to wander these corridors.

"This way, Ms. Kedros." Sewick had stopped grabbing her elbow, at least, and gestured for her to proceed around a thirty-degree corner to a door. Sewick held his hand over a plate next to the door.

She nearly jumped out of her skin as a holographic four-fingered *claw* extended from the plate to touch Sewick's palm.

"It's a scanner that records everyone who goes into the room," Sewick said. "We've been able to set a few to perform security filtering."

The door slid open as Ariane felt her slate vibrate. She pulled it out of her coverall pocket, seeing a message from Muse 3. This was a bad time, but before her thumb started to set the hold, she noticed the priority. An emergency?

"I've got a message from the agent on my ship," she said, frowning and pausing in the open doorway.

"The comm center can take it." Sewick whipped out his slate and poked at it. "Funny, the center's not responding. Perhaps they're doing some maintenance."

Ariane thumbed open the message, feeling uneasy. How could her slate be getting a message if the moon's comm center was down? The message should have gone through the Beta Priamos Command Post, then shunted through a comm center located somewhere in this alien structure. Perhaps the comm center had routed it through the spotty mesh network.

She stared at a text message that said nothing but "CAW SEP 12.35.15." She looked at the routing header. Muse 3 had bypassed both the station CP above *and* the comm center on the surface, passing it along the few nodes installed inside the facility. Those nodes operated on low power and used near-field mesh networking, meaning the message had taken a twisted and slow route to reach her slate.

CAW Space Emergency Procedure twelve-dot-thirty-five, number fifteen? What the hell did that mean? When she'd told Muse 3 to study that series, she didn't expect—what situations did number fifteen cover? The thirty-five series covered interruption of command, control, or communications, but number fifteen was rather obscure. Her scalp wasn't simply prickling; it tingled with the sense of danger.

"I'd better check the comm center," she said, turning around and walking quickly back down the corridor toward the pillared hall. She brushed past the other contractors and Major Dokos.

"Ms. Kedros. Our meeting!"

She barely heard their protests. Suddenly the title for 12.35.15 popped into her mind: *Hostile Takeover of Command and Control Centers*. She turned the corner and started running. Slipping the slate into her coverall pocket, she gripped her ministunner, holding it hidden inside her vest as she ran. She turned another corner and skidded to a halt, her boots making an obscene sound on the polished surface.

Frank stood a few meters away, where the corridor met the pillared hall. He pointed a stunner at her.

Matt admitted he was squeamish when it came to blood. Raised on generational hydroponic- or vat-grown food, he didn't even eat meat. Probing a leg that looked like hamburger made his stomach churn. Somehow, he pulled out the remaining flechettes. More importantly, David Ray got through the process and now dozed fitfully.

Matt now obsessively watched the cam-eye input of the *Pilgrimage III*, interspersed with checking the status of their environmental systems. He watched the *Father's Wrath* disconnect and start a burn with a vector that meant it was heading toward the gas giant Laomedon, Priamos, its moon, and the Beta Priamos Station.

Did that mean they'd abandoned the *Pilgrimage*? They shouldn't have enough people on the *Father's Wrath* to take over the generational ship, plus the Priamos station and facility. Matt tried a comm check with the *Pilgrimage*, but there was no answer. In doing so, he woke David Ray.

"What's going on?" David Ray sounded a bit groggy.

"I saw their ship leave on a heading for Priamos, so they

might have deserted the *Pilgrimage*. They can't have brought enough people to control this entire solar system."

"Unless they used squirrels."

Matt looked at him quizzically and David Ray added helpfully, "Pre-positioned agents hidden in plain sight, waiting to be activated. Like little rodents that hide underground and undermine structures."

"I think you mean moles. A squirrel is a small, clever mammal that can be trained to appraise and steal jewelry."

"Ah. I'm not well versed in pre-Yellowstone Terran fauna. *Moles*, then. If you study tactics used by CAW and the League during the war, you'll find the only effective methods for taking a solar system involved moles."

Matt grimaced. Who, among the people he knew who worked new space, would support Abram? Were there people he thought of as friends, who were waiting to throw off their masks and help the isolationists? He felt a creeping feeling of despair and wondered about Ari's safety. She was probably all right, since Joyce was with her.

"What's happening?" David Ray was looking at the display.

Matt turned around and watched the glints of departing short-range shuttles from the *Pilgrimage*. There were three coming out of the upper class C docks. He zoomed in as well as he could with the cam-eyes and tried to track them.

"They're heading toward the time buoy. What do they think they're doing?" David Ray watched with narrowed eyes. "They can't destroy or disable it. We powered it up and it's anchored, now and forever."

Matt tracked the shuttles by adjusting the module's cam-eyes, then turning the module itself with the small stabilization thrusters. They watched in silence for almost an hour. Matt was the first to answer the riddle.

"They're mining the incoming channels of the buoy," he said.

*　　*　　*

Joyce could barely breathe in this Gaia-be-damned *cupboard*. His shoulders pressed against the walls no matter which way he turned. If the darn thing had been built in a square, he might fit along the diagonal, but these Builders had problems using ninety-degree angles.

Luckily, there was air exchange around the upper and lower crack of the door. Joyce shifted his feet and leaned heavily to one side to stretch his back. He watched the crack of light at the bottom of the door.

Maria had jokingly said to hide in this closet if he thought it *necessary*. When he heard running footfalls outside her office and, poking his head out, saw men with flechette weapons turning the corner at the end of the hall, he thought the need for concealment might be *necessary*.

He heard someone step stealthily into Maria's office and he tensed, wishing he had any weapon beyond his bare hands. They'd served him before, so he got ready to launch himself when the closet door opened.

"It's me."

The whisper was so soft, he might have imagined it. He saw the light at the bottom crack soften and fade away. Someone was turning down the lights in the office. The door in front of him opened slowly and he tightened his fists, only relaxing when he saw Maria's shape.

She brought her lips close to his ear and breathed, "We have a problem."

No shit.

CHAPTER 11

Physical torture will get any confession you seek, so it's ineffective. Torture drug regimens, refined by TEBI during years of warfare, are better. Why not let the subjects determine their worst fears? When combined with the ability to convince subjects that they're speaking with their captor or their savior, TEBI moved torture into the galactic age. If dosages aren't tightly monitored, however, brain damage can occur.

—*Difficulties of Modern-Day Torture*, Zacharias Milano, 2099.363.11.00 UT, indexed by *Heraclitus 23* under Conflict Imperative

"Frank." Ariane tried to keep her voice low and calm. "What are you doing?"

"Sorry, Ms. Kedros, but you can't be running around until they decide what to do with you."

"Who are 'they'? Whom are you mixed up with, Frank?" She stepped closer, her hand inside her jacket and still gripping her ministunner. The problem with stunners was estimating effective range; Frank's stunner had more power and better range. A bigger problem was that his was already out and pointed. If fired from inside her pocket, the ministunner would more likely stun *her* than anyone else.

"Don't make me do this, Ms. Kedros." His jaw was tight and his mouth extended in stubborn lines.

She'd been stunned before: The feeling was even worse

than the uncontrollable, violent seizure, coupled with the possible loss of bladder and bowel control. These effects usually kept any but the most desperate—*or foolish*—from going through it again. She kept moving closer, her steps slow and small.

"What are 'they' doing on-station, Frank? You're not a destructive person. Or an extortionist or terrorist." She hadn't meant the last word seriously, but his eyes widened.

"It'll be a better life without CAW or the League interfering with our lives. You'll see."

Suddenly, a Terran woman emerged from the dark hall behind Frank and stumbled to her knee right beside him. Frank turned to look and Ariane started to pull her ministunner—she froze.

Behind the Terran woman stood the angry young man from the space elevator and he held a flechette pistol. There was no mistaking the bulbous shape of the chamber needed for the flechette cartridges. More importantly, there was now an innocent bystander between Ariane and the armed men.

"Turn around and face me. Put your hands up," angry-young-man said. Presumably, this last order was for both women.

Ariane and the Terran woman raised their hands.

"Frank, search that one." The flechette pistol jerked at Ariane. "Stop! *Don't* step between me and them, you idiot."

Frank stepped sideways and walked against the wall. He shuffled over to Ariane and holstered his stunner. She tried to catch his eye, making this as uncomfortable as possible for him, but he looked down at his feet until he was behind her. His hands, fumbling and inexpert, found the ministunner. Angry-young-man deemed the knife and flares dangerous, and Frank took them. On the plus side, they let her keep the light sources and emergency oxygen mask.

As Frank walked back, the young Terran woman beside Ariane whispered in accusation, "You had a *stunner*?"

Ariane answered calmly, "But *they* have flechette weapons."

"Yeah, Ms. Fancy Doctorate, *she* was smart. She probably saved your life." Angry-young-man grinned with a nasty and meaningful expression.

"You'd kill us?" The Terran woman's face paled.

Ariane looked again at Frank, who wouldn't meet her gaze. In contrast to angry-young-man, Frank acknowledged his duplicity. He supported whoever was behind this action, but he was obviously ashamed of his deception.

The young man, who wasn't Terran himself, ignored the woman's question. "We'll have to confine them," he said.

Ariane and the young woman were marched back down the corridor. They passed the conference room that would have held her contractor meeting, but now a man with a stunner stood at the door. They went past this room and around another gentle thirty-degree turn, where they were directed through another tall door.

This opened into a strangely disconcerting triangular room. A wide ledge ran along two walls, and a dividing wall jutted from the remaining wall opposite the door. The ledge might have been a bench, although it was higher than comfortable human seating. Two women were sitting on the ledge; one was Colonel Dokos.

"Welcome to what I think is the women's holding cell," Dokos said after the door was closed.

"Are we being monitored?" Ariane looked about the room. She walked past the divider and raised her eyebrows at the sunken square structure hidden from the doorway. Whatever its function had been for the Builders was irrelevant and, more important, there was no one else in the room.

"Unlikely. We had to mount our operating nodes on our own structures, because this stuff is so slick and nonporous that our adhesives didn't work. I don't think you could mount a recording pip without it being seen." Colonel Dokos absently stroked the wall she leaned against.

Ariane searched all the surfaces anyway, but she found nothing. Once she was satisfied, it was time to talk. The woman sitting beside Dokos was younger, but still nearing middle age. Her name was Varra Enid and she was a data analyst for an Autonomist subcontractor to Taethis Exploration. The only Terran had arrived with Ariane, and she turned out to be the vaunted Dr. Myrna Fox Lowry, the foremost astrophysicist from Mars. Regrettably, they didn't need astrophysicists or data analysts. Ariane and Colonel Dokos exchanged a glance.

"Well," Dokos said, "first we need to know how many hostiles we're dealing with."

That proved to be difficult. All their captors were workers who had come from the station above. However, Dokos had heard her captor talking to someone who mentioned an incoming ship. While Ariane was comforted that no hostiles were planted within the "cleared" R&D contractors, how many were now on Beta Priamos and the surface of Priamos? She wondered what had happened to Joyce.

The door to the room opened, ending their discussion. Two Terran women entered, the first reluctantly stepping in while their captors pushed in the second.

"Where did you take my son?" the second woman asked shrilly, tossing her burgundy hair. She started back toward her captors and stopped when she was menaced with a flechette pistol.

Ariane stood up and folded her arms as she watched. The door closed and the second Terran woman changed, instantly becoming cold efficiency. When she turned around, she didn't acknowledge Ariane, even though they'd met, briefly, when she'd beaten Ariane and left her lying on the station deck.

"Laying mines in buoy channels is against the Phaistos Protocols," David Ray said.

"These guys must think they're beyond any Minoan retribution." Matt adjusted the cam-eye focus, making the shuttles sharper. The actual mines weren't visible, but they could watch the process of placing and arming them.

"Why are they bothering?" David Ray asked. "After all, the buoy is still locked down by Pilgrimage; entry to the system requires getting a key from us, or rather, from them. No one's getting into this solar system after the *Father's Wrath*."

"Really?" Matt looked at David Ray with what he hoped was an innocent expression. "Perhaps they've heard the rumors that generational ship lines sell secret codes to governments, even the Minoans."

"That doesn't happen." David Ray's gaze shifted away from Matt.

"Most generational crew aren't in the position to confirm or deny those codes, but you're the ship's general counsel. You'd know about such negotiations." Then, when David Ray didn't respond to his probing, Matt snorted and shook his head. "Look, I'm crèche-get too! I won't be telling anyone about any secret codes, but if there's a *chance* a ship could come through, we should get into a position to warn them, shouldn't we?"

David Ray's jaw hardened. After a few moments, he nodded slowly. "We negotiated with both CAW and TerraXL for override keys, which are restricted to emergency use."

"At this point, I'm happy to hear that."

"But," David Ray said, taking a heavy breath, "those codes can't be used when the buoy is locked down, unless the ship authorizes it. Someone on the control deck might have switched it on."

"Abram What's-his-face looks like he's preparing for visitors." Matt pointed at the screen.

"He might be extra cautious, or prepared for Minoans."

"They have special keys?"

David Ray shrugged. "They make the time buoys, so who knows what they can do? So far, if they have special overrides, we've never seen them used."

Matt turned and watched the shuttles finish their jobs. Ships coming back to real-space never superimposed upon each other, due to "magic" in the Minoan time buoy network. Pilots had to be sharp about announcing their vectors and moving out of the channel, because the buoy sensed impediments in the channels and delays could ripple through the network. How the buoys sensed obstructions drove physicists nuts; no one even had a beginning theory.

"Do you think the buoy can sense something as small as mines? Would it prevent entry from N-space?" Matt asked.

"I'm going to guess *no*. Otherwise, why would the Minoans put a prohibition against mines into the Phaistos Protocols?"

David Ray was probably right. Matt nodded glumly. A ship might transition from N-space safely, but when they started moving, they might be crippled. Matt didn't know how much explosive power those mines had, but the isolationists obviously had faith in their strength.

"We have to get within real-time *talking* distance of the buoy channel," Matt said. "Then we can warn someone entering from N-space."

David Ray chewed his lip as he looked at the display that showed the distance to the channel. "That's a one-way trip for us. It'll take us too far out, use too much of our air reserve to push us there, and we'll pass our point of no return. Are you willing to risk our lives on the chance that someone's mounting a rescue mission? What if the emergency keys aren't enabled? If they aren't, *nobody's* getting into G-145 until we take back our control center."

"What else can we do? We have no weapons. You can't even walk. This might be our only way to help the *Pilgrimage*." Matt's throat was tight.

There was silence in module number 2098 for a couple minutes.

David Ray nodded. "Let's do it."

Matt did the calculations and gave the commands to the

EMS, which powered the module's rudimentary thrusters. Their thruster power was in the form of chemical propulsion and gas jets that used up part of their air reserve. This was, indeed, a one-way trip. He used as little "fuel" as possible to build up to a slow drift, keeping in mind he'd have to use fuel to slow down. It'd be twelve hours before they'd ease into real-time comm distance of the buoy's channel. He hoped his calculations also kept them clear of the minefield, since they had no sensors that could detect the mines.

"Well, what are we going to do with ourselves in the meantime?" Matt asked as he handed David Ray another ampoule with pain medication.

David Ray winced as he tried to reposition himself. He hooked the ampoule into his implant and gave Matt a crooked grin. "You could teach me to curse."

"Huh?"

"I was awed by your impressively long blue streak of language when you were trying to lock up the module. Where'd you learn that?"

"My pilot." Matt laughed. "She's military, a reservist. She can turn the air blue, when she wants to swear, that is."

"And the part about the Minoan Great Bull—er—doing—ah—whatever?"

"Oh. That's my addition. I have no problem profaning other people's gods, provided they can't hear. Since I've only seen two Minoans in real life, I figure it's safe to abuse their Great Bull."

"Hmm. You know that *we're* the ones who think they worship the Great Bull, right?" David Ray asked.

"Aw, don't take all the fun out of it."

"Let me have a quick go at cursing; then I'll take a nap." David Ray said.

"I can't abide cursing," Abram said in his flat, cold voice.

Tahir didn't think the man writhing in the frame heard

him. At first, Tahir felt sorry for State Prince Parmet when he was ushered into the room. Abram had wasted no time on Beta Priamos Station, other than to determine it was secure. Once Abram was down on the moon's surface, he'd looked at the roster of names that had been collected and immediately selected the Terran State Prince for questioning.

"I know what that's for," Parmet said, looking at the frame and the technicians. "Why don't you just ask me for the information you seek, whatever it is? I might cooperate."

"How could I trust your answers?" Abram asked.

"That's what I would say. This is an ironic twist of fate, which you wouldn't appreciate." Parmet gracefully shrugged.

"You're mistaken. If I can craft your arc of retribution, then I improve my own kismet."

As Tahir watched the two men face off, he couldn't help but be impressed with Parmet's stature and bearing. Of course, he knew the Terrans were consummate actors and with their *somaural* training, could control many autonomous muscles and reactions. That knowledge didn't make the tall man with near-golden skin any less imposing. By contrast, Abram became stooped and sallow, bitterness oozing from every pore.

"Somehow, I'm not surprised that this is really all about *you*." Acidic disdain dripped from Parmet's voice. Abram ignored the words; the technicians exchanged frightened glances.

Parmet stepped into the frame with dignity and let the technicians tighten the restraints. His *somaural* abilities soon couldn't withstand the regimen of pain inducers and emotional feedback enhancers that Abram's professional torturers pumped into his bloodstream.

As a first step, Abram probed for leverage as the technicians worked the pain enhancers. Parmet was protective of his family and had particular fondness for his first and only son. He also still grieved the loss of his brother at Ura-Guinn; the brother and brother's wife were going to join Parmet's multimarriage. Tahir felt twinges of sympathy after learning this. He no longer thought the Terran multimarriage was offensive and kept his "cultural dilution," as Abram would have called it, private.

Abram started using Parmet's son as coercion, moving to more constructive and relevant questions. Why was Parmet here in G-145? What were the features of his ship? Which contractors on this moon were Terran and which were Autonomist? Abram looked for the additional peripheral information. At this point, in an effort to please the captor or to help their savior, whichever script was being played, the subject would babble more information than necessary. Abram uncovered some surprises.

Why was Parmet in G-145?

First surprise: Parmet had tortured and coerced a woman to get Terran contractors some leases. Tahir's opinion of the State Prince dropped, while one of the men laughed and then choked when Abram stared at him. Abram didn't appear amused so much as vindicated.

"I always knew commerce and business would eventually adopt the tools of warfare." Abram nodded.

What were the features of Parmet's ship?

Second surprise: Parmet's ship wasn't the commercial version of the TM-8440; it was a retrofitted military model that still held an original command and control module for the Falcon missile. This time, Abram almost smiled.

"Can we use that CCM to interface with the Mark Fifteen package?" Abram turned to Tahir and in doing so, missed the look of horror that crossed Parmet's face. Tahir wondered how cognizant the subject was during drug-induced torture. Since Parmet had practically invented this type of torture during the war, perhaps they should be cautious about information flowing the *other* way during this interrogation.

"With some adjustments, yes." Tahir said nothing more

and Abram turned back to Parmet, who again had bulging eyes and twisted lips from the pain of his existence. Worry knotted Tahir's gut and he chewed the inside of his cheek. Parmet's ship had taken ten hours off Abram's schedule and Tahir tried to hold down his panic. He was resolved to be out of G-145 before Abram used the TD weapon, but he still didn't have a whisper of an escape plan.

Abram continued the probing. *Which contractors on this moon were Terran and which were Autonomist?*

Third surprise: One of the prime contractors, Hellas Nautikos, was owned primarily by *Minoans*. Shock hit everyone in the room like a stun grenade. The men froze and the room was quiet, except for the suppressed moan that came from Parmet's throat.

"Call Emery. And get this man's son." Abram's voice was soft and flat, but Tahir recognized the stance and the careful enunciation. He'd seen it on the video of Abram with his mother, and fear started creeping over him. He had to fight an urge to curl up in a corner and hide. Abram was enraged, but he wouldn't let his feelings manifest in outward symptoms—the messenger of such news was a safe outlet for his rage. Parmet would end up dead or, like Tahir's mother, a vegetable. Tahir's stomach churned as a technician departed to retrieve Parmet's son.

Emery was quick in responding to Abram's summons. He eyed Abram, then stood beside Tahir with his hands held behind his back and his feet braced wide.

"Emery, find every supervisor that works for Hellas Nautikos and execute them."

"Pardon? Sir?" Even Emery, used to obeying orders, was startled. According to Qesan's stratagems, Abram should be manipulating their prisoners in efforts to start small steps of cooperation. Each bit of cooperation would lead to more. At this phase of their mission, according to Qesan, executions were contrary to their objectives.

"Execute them. They work for our enemy." Abram turned away in dismissal, looking at Parmet with calculation.

Emery bowed his head in assent and went to the door, but paused as Abram absently added, "Emery. You might as well get rid of the military personnel, while you're at it. We can't afford to keep them around."

The door beside Tahir opened and he saw Parmet's son. Chander, according to net-think, was eleven years old, yet he matched the height of his guard. Terrans bred their children tall and the boy's face indicated his true age. His intense green eyes were natural, since he was Terran, and they flashed in barely suppressed terror.

"Why am I here?" Chander asked. His mouth clamped shut as his gaze went to the end of the room, where the frame clamped his father into a semi-upright position.

"Shut up." The technician holding Chander's arm tightened his grip.

Chander's face went slack. Tahir knew what the boy was feeling, being suddenly reminded of the times he himself had been escorted into his father's viewing room to see the video of his mother's torture. It was an "example of Minoan oppression," as Abram had called it.

Abram, standing beside the drooling Parmet, hadn't noticed the boy's arrival. "I couldn't care less if we break him, so increase the dosage," he was saying to the technician. "First, I need him to give us low-stress passwords for running his ship. Second, I want to know everything I can about the lessees here on this moon. I want detailed backgrounds on all the players, whatever he got from Terran military intelligence."

The technician was pushing Chander toward the focus platform, the raised and spotlighted area that Parmet could see, given the tunneled vision from the drugs and blinders. Tahir tapped Chander's shoulder, causing him to jerk his head. His thick chestnut braid flipped over his shoulder.

"Don't blame yourself," Tahir said softly. "You are separate from what happens to your father."

"Go fuck yourself." Chander's face broke into a snarl as he was pulled to the focus platform.

Tahir shook his head. The boy was probably trying to practice *somaural* control, which was a mistake. Abram would require honest pain from Chander to influence Parmet, even though Parmet's world was exaggerated and artificial.

As the technician twisted Chander's arms behind him and into the harness, Tahir closed his eyes. He couldn't stop his ears, however, as the shrieks of the boy's pain were echoed, louder and shriller, by the father's screams. Abram's flat voice cut through all of it, asking measured questions and making promises that he'd never keep. Tahir clenched his jaw and pushed his anger deep, down into his depths where it festered and compressed into hate.

CHAPTER 12

When Qesan says "cut off the head," he means it. Getting rid of prior leadership is necessary for focusing followers, but Qesan cautions that executions must happen early while the people are confused by their new circumstances. This helps prevent martyrs. Of course, he only considers male followers, male leaders—I think women are discussed in an appendix on resources, right after cattle. Before reading more, I suggest you go watch this [video] where the Minoans bomb his ass. Laugh wildly, freely, to keep yourself sane. . . .

—*Misogynist Freaks*, Lauren Swan Kincaid, 2103.043.11.25 UT, indexed by *Heraclitus 29* under Conflict Imperative

"I saw men in *civilian* clothes with *flechette* weapons," Joyce said quietly to Maria, who had just joined him in the closet.

Maria had served half her career in the Terran Expansion League Space Force before moving to TEBI; she had to know the ramifications of his words. The Phaistos Protocols directed that personnel carrying deadly weapons must be in military uniform with rank displayed.

"I don't know who they are, or who directs them," Maria whispered. "I left the SP and his family to get to a contractor meeting, but when I was going through the great hall, I saw your *friend* Kedros detained and marched away. Evasion became necessary."

Regretfully, he had no time to worry about Kedros's situation right now. "How long until they search this office?"

Maria's mouth came close to his ear again as she said, "The office lock requires my handprint. They won't be able to open it. I'm hoping they'll assume this room has been shut off for later exploration and analysis, as are many of the other rooms."

"Then why am I in this hell of a cupboard!" He pushed past her.

"Shush." She put a hand on his mouth and he smelled the fresh, pungent scent of her soap or lotion. "They can still hear us."

Joyce took a deep breath and looked at the door to the office. It sealed well, but he could see a tiny crack of light from the hallway. He turned on his small slate-light, keeping it at the lowest setting, and looked about the office.

"Perhaps we should finish negotiating the terms of your defection and get your signature," he said.

"You want to do that *now*?"

"That's the only way I can trust you." His voice was cold, intentionally insulting.

Her response was to raise one eyebrow.

"You rejected our first offer of compensation—"

"Which was based upon staying in place." She folded her arms and frowned with irritation—*purposely*. He had to remember her *somaural* skills. "Look, Joyce, I know the rules of this game, because I've played them from the other side. You want me to stay where I am, as a double agent, but that's not acceptable. I want to emigrate, but my TEBI experience prevents me from doing that legally and openly. That's why I called your Directorate. Let's move *on*."

He picked up on the important words. "You say you've *played this game from the other side*?"

"That's what you need, isn't it?" She smiled. "I've got recent information about our agents. Some are double-dealing."

"We already know about Lieutenant Colonel Jacinthe Voyage."

Maria let nothing show, neither disappointment nor surprise. "What if there are others? Besides, you want to know how Cara Paulos infiltrated our network."

Yes, he needed details on Cipher, Kedros's old crewmate, originally Cara Paulos, to piece together how she'd taken control of Karthage Point's environmental systems. Hearing footfalls pass the office again, he realized he shouldn't delay. Still keeping to a whisper, he asked, "What's your price?"

"I want a secure, well-paying job, preferably in what I do best. I'll *require* eighty thousand HKD per year in salary and, above all, Consortium citizenship so that"—she paused slightly, almost imperceptibly—"I can have children. Children with *citizenship*."

Joyce stared at the woman, whose dark blue eyes, on the same level as his, were defiant. His mind was backtracking, because this was back-ass-ward from what he and Edones thought Maria wanted.

Everyone knew that the Terrans used strict eugenic controls via their multimarriages. Accidental pregnancies were prevented by state-applied birth control implants, with the additional threat of withholding citizenship from unplanned and unapproved progeny. Citizenship was the only way to have benefits such as health care, but it was that governmental health-care system with which Maria had run afoul: She wasn't allowed to have children due to Tantor's Sun disease, which she'd contracted in a battle near Tantor. This disease incurred a measurable genetic mutation that would likely be found in all her eggs. On Autonomist worlds, the mutation was considered benign and could be removed from the egg, if parents wished, either in utero or before fertilization. Maria also had a weakened respiratory system from Tantor's Sun disease, but, like other battle wounds, the condition wasn't hereditary.

Joyce cleared his throat, not sure about finding a job

that fit what she "did best," but he needed to keep her on the Directorate's hook. "I can't authorize any of these arrangements," he said cautiously.

"And it doesn't matter right now." Maria motioned for silence as they heard more running footsteps in the corridor. After they faded away, she continued softly. "This system is technically under Pilgrimage Line control, so we're both outside our jurisdictions. From what I've seen, this takeover came about by seeding the construction and mining crews with agents."

"Even on the *Pilgrimage*?" He didn't think that possible, considering how long ago the ship had started its voyage to G-145.

"There, I figure they muscled themselves on board and they're now controlling the crew. For the last day, we've been denied bandwidth due to maintenance and I didn't get suspicious until it was too late." She shook her head. "Beta Priamos is probably also overrun."

"By whom? What do they want?"

"Don't know. But that puts us on the same side, doesn't it?"

He still couldn't trust her, but she was correct: The decades-old enmity between the Consortium and the League didn't matter right now, inside this new system.

"We need comm," he said grimly. "And information."

She nodded. "We have to get up to Beta Priamos."

Oleander learned why Captain Floros, as prickly and introverted as she was, had been snagged by the Directorate of Intelligence.

"Watch and learn, Young Flower," Floros said to Oleander as she cracked her knuckles. She tapped the keyboard outline on the table and grinned menacingly at the display responding on the wall. "I'll show you how to kick around those AI models—intelligent indexing, my ass."

Oleander laughed. Across the conference room, Edones glanced at them and then went back to his subdued and hushed conversation with SP Hauser. His enigmatic and cold blue eyes could have been taken as discouragement of her levity, but she chose to ignore him.

This is how I handle galactic disasters. I need to look for humor in the little things. Besides, she was irritated that no one had told her that a Terran package *could* be detonated without the warhead interface or the security unlock codes.

"We've got to find this bastard," Floros muttered as she displayed a search interface.

Oleander had never seen that interface and as she watched Floros, her mind cleared. She had to concentrate on her own task; all scenarios came to her queue so she could weed out the duplicates, and prioritize them for later analysis. Edones had told her that any scenario involving martyrdom should be higher priority for investigation.

The quick briefing regarding the design flaw in the Mark Fifteen arming sequence left Oleander a bit confused, but as she saw the scenarios submitted by the other officers, she felt a chill settle between her shoulder blades. Apparently, test codes could be substituted for operational arming codes, provided they were downloaded to the warhead package during a certain sequence of environmental conditions. This involved entry of valid test codes, quickly followed by a rapid increase and decrease in gravitational force, called an "S" maneuver based upon the graph of force versus time.

Every officer in the room had figured out a way to get the weapon to arm and possibly detonate. Oleander compared the scenarios. They all had a space vehicle hauling the warhead dangerously near a gravitational well, such as a sun or near-sunlike gas giant. She gave scenarios using manned vehicles a higher priority than those using remotely piloted vehicles, remembering Edones's martyrdom factor.

There were plenty of hypotheses regarding how the isolationists might interface with the package and *where* they'd detonate it. Unfortunately, *where* related to *why*, which nobody understood. Everyone was guessing.

"I've got him. Boarding at—" Floros yelped and clamped her jaw shut.

Oleander put down her slate. Edones stood up, waiting.

Floros's complexion paled. "Both Tahir Rouxe and his father, Abram Hadrian Rouxe, left Athens Point under assumed identities prepared by other members of their tribe. Civilian security was lax, since they didn't fool my analysis."

"Where were they going?" Edones asked.

Floros's mouth twitched. "It's G-145, sir. There's been no response from anyone from that system for almost eight hours. Several Konstantinople Prime University sophists have issued complaints, saying they were cut off from archeological data because of a governmental conspiracy."

Suddenly, all the Autonomist ear bugs alarmed in emergency mode, in that irritating way audible to everyone standing near. Oleander's hand jerked up to silence hers, a motion that echoed Edones, Floros, and Bernard.

"That's the *Bright Crescent* with a high-priority message," Floros said. "Pilgrimage Headquarters has issued Declarations of Emergency to both the Consortium and the League."

Ariane hid her hands under her folded arms and tightened them into fists. Her first reaction at the sight of the homicidal redhead was to force an apology, preferably through pummeling. However, she'd spent her adult life trusting her senses but not always acting on her first reaction. Right now, her senses told her she wasn't in danger. She remained standing as Parmet's first wife introduced herself as Garnet Westwind Tachawee and gestured at the redhead, who threw herself onto the ledge.

"That's Sabina Sky Cavanagh, my co-wife. They've taken our son, Chander, and husband, Isrid, or rather State Prince Isrid Sun Parmet," Garnet said.

Colonel Dokos introduced everyone already in the

room, getting around to Ariane last. Sabina's hand, initially lying against her thigh, flashed a signal. Garnet stiffened.

Ariane stepped forward to stand in front of Garnet, making sure she was out of kicking range. This wife might be just as vengeful.

"I think Sabina feels we're enemies," Ariane said to Garnet. "I might have agreed, six months ago. However, wouldn't you say it's time to forget the war, under the current circumstances?"

"Fine words," Sabina said coldly from the bench. "You heal quickly, Kedros. Don't speak to her, Garnet—someone will be rescuing us soon."

Garnet's head jerked back to look at Ariane's face. Her warm hazel gaze slowly examined the bruises. Then she looked back at Sabina, whose hand signals were hidden from everyone in the room except Garnet and Ariane. Garnet's face paled.

"I—" Garnet's eyes became both chilly and perplexed. She glanced at Ariane, then stumbled to the bench and sat down. "I'm sorry, Ms. Kedros."

Sorry? Even Sabina looked puzzled by Garnet's reaction. Ariane went to the divider wall and leaned against it. This put her close to the middle of the triangular room, where she could watch everyone. Garnet composed herself, but remained withdrawn. *She didn't know who I was until Sabina told her*.

Colonel Dokos watched this exchange, but apparently chose to ignore everything but the present issue. "You're wrong in expecting rescue, Sabina. We might have to assume the worst case: Someone has taken over this solar system, probably while the buoy has been locked down by the generational ship."

"What about the Minoans? They're not going to like this rampant lawlessness." Dr. Lowry sounded hopeful.

"They'd have to use a locked-down buoy," Ariane said. "We need to be our own law and fend off these criminals with our own hands."

"Don't the Minoans have override codes?"

Dokos shook her head. "That's a rumor and we can't depend upon their rescue or perhaps, their retribution. Besides, I don't want to be the target for a Minoan attack."

"We supply the Minoan contractors with data," Varra said. "According to them, the Minoans are only interested in our research methods."

"Let's get to basics, and figure out how many people are involved. Perhaps—"

Dokos was interrupted as the door opened and two men walked in. They could have been brothers, but the first man was much younger. They had similar scowls, black hair cut ragged and sticking out in random spikes. They'd been exposed to planetary sun and wind, although the second man had lines at the corners of his eyes and mouth and down his cheeks. They were not happy lines; this man rarely smiled.

Ariane looked quickly at the five women on the bench, searching for a spark of recognition. None of the others had seen these men before, and neither had she. The way they strode into the room made them look like what Matt called "grav-huggers," those used to the strong gravity of planets.

"Everyone on the bench." The younger man gestured at Ariane with his flechette pistol.

She complied quickly, noting his wild eyes. His gaze flitted about the room and flared alternately with anger and excitement. She settled on the bench between Varra and Dr. Lowry.

The older man took up position beside the door, quietly acting as servitor, while the young man went to the end of the bench and stood directly in front of Varra. She flinched at the pistol he held in her face. Ariane laid her hand on Varra's forearm, trying to give her courage.

"What company do you work for?" The pistol was steady, even though the voice held deep currents of emotion.

"Telepresence Systems, contracted to Taethis Exploration," Varra answered.

"Do you work with the Minoan contractors?" The pistol trembled a tiny bit.

"Well, I"—Ariane dug her fingers into Varra's arm and drew in her breath—"don't think so."

The wild young man wasn't particularly observant in subtleties of human communication. He kept his gaze on Varra's face and frowned. "You don't *think* so, woman?"

"I—I don't know." Varra was stuttering and Ariane kept gripping her arm.

"Stupid cow. What about you?" He stepped sideways to hold the pistol in Ariane's face.

"I work for Aether Exploration. Recently arrived—don't know anything about Minoans." She gave this short answer as example to the others. The tingling on her scalp ran down her neck; she knew, by the waves of rage she felt roll off the young man, that no one should work with the Minoans—not if they wanted to live.

The young man accepted her ignorance quite readily, and the pistol moved to Dr. Lowry's face.

"My employer is the Physics Department of MIT, and I'm contracted to work a year for Booing Zhou-Kunal, which is *Terran*."

Ariane leaned back against the wall so she could watch the other women. Garnet looked up guilelessly as she explained that she was here on an informational tour and no, she didn't know who worked for whom. Ariane initially thought Garnet had no *somaural* projection skills, but now she amended that opinion. The best projectors gave no hint of their abilities. Garnet was open with a perfect touch of fear as she faced a weapon that could tear apart her skull. Sabina was good at *somaural* projection, but she liked to show her capabilities. She scowled back at the young man as she answered the same as Garnet.

"Well, you're all luckier than you know." The pistol

reached Colonel Dokos, but now the man stepped back out of range.

"Stand up and keep your hands away from your body," he said.

"I don't work for Minoan contractors," Dokos said as she stood. Following his instructions, she kept her hands palm forward and away from her hips.

"I know whom you work for." He glanced up and down her uniform, finishing at her shoulder rank.

"Dokos, Colonel, service number—"

"Shut up!"

Dokos stopped.

"You know Abram's orders, Emery," said the older man at the door. He sounded bored, but respectful.

"I know," Emery shot back, over his shoulder. His eyes were bright and excited, looking like a young boy daring to do something he'd never done before . . . *like execute a woman in cold blood.*

Ariane looked at the older man, then Emery. "Don't—"

"Stay still. All of you." The older man at the door stepped forward and pulled Varra upright. He gripped her arm tightly and held his flechette pistol pointed at the soft fleshy area, at Varra's waist. "Do I have to explain how this round will tear her apart, in ways that no one can put back together? Or how long it'll take her to die?"

Varra closed her eyes and pressed her lips together, but a small whimper came out anyway. The man holding her stared at Ariane. "They're breeding stock, Emery. It doesn't matter how they react—just put down the uniform."

Emery pulled out a stun wand with his other hand and motioned Dokos to step behind the partition. "Over there."

Ariane exchanged a glance with Colonel Dokos, whose eyes flickered over the bench of women and Varra, held tightly against a flechette weapon. Ariane raised an eyebrow. Should she resist? Fight? But Dokos's dark eyes said, *No, not without civilian casualties.* She disappeared behind the partition and Ariane looked down at her hands, lying useless in her lap.

Dokos tried to struggle. They all heard a scuffle, but it was short and decisive. They heard the stunner sizzle, followed by a body dropping and flopping, sounding loud in the small room.

Beside Ariane, Dr. Lowry moaned. Ariane put her arm about her shoulders and Dr. Lowry ducked her head down, as if she could avoid the sound. The stun wand crackled and buzzed again, higher, causing her teeth to hurt. She clamped her jaw shut. Thumps came from behind the partition.

"What's that?" Dr. Lowry mumbled the question into Ariane's shoulder.

"Lethal use of a stun wand," Ariane replied.

The whine went on and on, unending. Unadulterated rage rose inside her and spread a hard and calculated calm throughout her body. She looked up and locked gazes with the older man holding Varra, directing a murderous blast of anger at him. His eyes widened. If she could get close enough to kill him, *she would—and he knew it.*

The room was suddenly silent. No one moved.

"What're they doing?" whispered Dr. Lowry, her face still buried in Ariane's neck and shoulder.

"He's making sure she can't be resuscitated." Ariane's lips and tongue were stiff, her voice dull.

Everyone waited—forever. The smell of burned flesh spread through the room. Dr. Lowry pulled away from Ariane and covered her face in her hands. Varra whimpered, her knees obviously shaking and her eyes closed. Emery finally reappeared. He holstered the wand, his pistol still in his right hand. He looked at the bench of women, where three tearless faces watched him steadily. He seemed puzzled.

"If there's any other military on-site, it's in your best interest to tell us." He spoke firmly, building up bluster with every word.

Silence.

"We'll leave the body so you can mourn—appropriately—er, whatever rites women do on your worlds. We'll get a body bag." Emery stared at each woman, flinching when he looked into Ariane's face.

The older man pushed Varra toward the bench. She stumbled and sank to her knees beside Ariane. Both men backed out of the room, closing the door behind them. Varra collapsed into a ball and threw up at Ariane's feet. The sharp, acrid smell of vomit barely displaced the burned flesh and other odors that followed death.

Her chest felt as if it were going to burst from fury. *You bastards think* mourning *is women's work? Wait and see what* justice *can be, when served by a woman.*

CHAPTER 13

Turning in the tags can get to you. Facing your commander and setting down tag after tag, one for every service member you lost . . .

—*Interviews: the Weight of War*, AFCAW MSgt. Pike, 2092.098.12.02 UT, indexed by *Heraclitus 12* under Conflict Imperative

Nobody's coming to help us. They can't get into the system because the buoy's locked. In retrospect, Matt had made a big mistake—a fatal mistake. Their movement had used up too much propulsion and energy for a module equipped with short-term life support. Matt didn't have accurate consumption rates. Regardless, it didn't look good.

They tried to keep their oxygen consumption as low as possible. The module drifted into the targeted position, close enough to the arrival channel to have real-time communications, yet hopefully, many kilometers away from any mines. After some minor station-keeping maneuvers, Matt dialed down the oxygen levels even further and they waited. No one arrived from N-space.

David Ray's leg continued to swell, which was bad. When examining it, they couldn't decide whether it was infected or poisoned. Matt dosed him again with stringent antibiotics, thanking St. Darius that they had toilet facilities because of what would happen to David Ray's digestive tract.

At this point, David Ray suggested they crack open some of the expensive liquor. "After all, alcohol's a depressant. It might slow our oxygen consumption."

"Combining alcohol with your pain meds could—"

"What? Induce a coma before I run out of oxygen?" David Ray shifted and winced. "Bring it on."

Considering their situation and David Ray's pain, Matt stopped resisting his suggestion. *If we're going to die out here, we might as well be stinking drunk.* He carefully pushed toward the bar and adeptly caught the customer side, letting his momentum flip him over to the service side. He selected a fancy-looking liquor bottle for David Ray and a beer for himself; both were in resealable polycarbonate that he fitted with zero-gee suction inserts.

Despite his morbid intention to pass out, Matt found that he couldn't let go of his hope. While David Ray sucked down his liquor, Matt sipped cautiously and continued to monitor the buoy's arrival channel the only way he could: visually through the cam-eyes.

"Here's another crazy but surprisingly plausible theory about the Minoans." David Ray took another deep swallow of liquor. His bottle was half empty, yet his pronunciation was precise and clear.

Matt raised his eyebrows. After that much liquor, he'd be slurring and singing embarrassing limericks. *Ari's right; I am a lightweight.*

"Go on," Matt said, since David Ray appeared to be waiting.

"Perhaps they're not the result of evolved intelligence." David Ray looked triumphant.

"Meaning what? They're constructed, like AIs?"

"Even stranger. Maybe they're Boltzmann brains."

"So who created them?" Matt watched the display. If he kept David Ray babbling nonsense, perhaps the liquor would eventually take over and give the poor man relief. *Boltzmann brains, indeed!* Even though David Ray wasn't slurring, he was becoming a bit unsealed around the edges.

"That's the thing. Nobody created them. Didn't you cover Boltzmann in your early science classes?"

This time, Matt had to give him a withering glance. "I'm crèche-get, remember? We use his equations to analyze gaseous mixtures." *All of which project our imminent death.*

"That's physical chemistry. He also shook the world with his theories of entropy and probability."

"I thought you mentioned brains. He also worked in biochemistry?" Matt took another small sip and went back to watching the display.

"No, the idea of a Boltzmann brain came much later, though it's based upon his ideas of probability. The theory is . . ." David Ray's eyes closed and Matt thought he'd fallen asleep, but he suddenly opened his eyes and continued with renewed vigor. "Anything might spontaneously come into being even though it has a minute probability of doing do. So intelligence might pop into existence on its own, rather than evolving or developing."

"Yeah, I vaguely remember that from my cosmology." Matt scratched his nose. It didn't seem relevant to mention he'd almost flunked the subject. "But the theory is about intelligence rather than life, right? And that sort of intelligence isn't supposed to happen until billions and billions of years have passed, toward the end of our universe."

"That's the thingk about probabililility." David Ray's words were slurring, hindering his clipped enunciation. His eyes twinkled and he took another hefty gulp of liquor. "Just because somthingk isn't *probabable*, doesn't mean it can't happen, even in the first seconds of the universe."

"Why don't you close your eyes," Matt said in a soothing voice.

David Ray did exactly that, continuing to mutter incomprehensibly.

Matt sighed and stared at the visual display, which he set at high magnification. He was tired and sleepy from the low oxygen content in the air. He watched the blinking lights of the buoy and they became mesmerizing. Perhaps if he closed his eyes . . . at the edge of the display, a flare of heat and light changed the picture.

"Whoa!" He sat upright, his heart racing. "Lower display-two's magnification by ten and pan right. Stop!"

David Ray opened his eyes at Matt's outburst and looked at the display in puzzlement. "Air's nothin' dere."

Matt's lungs labored and he squinted at the display, feeling dizzy. With effort, he slowed his panting. He was sure something had set off the mines in a distinctly bloblike area. He wished he had the instrumentation available on the *Aether's Touch*.

"Increase magnification by ten. Again." Matt definitely got a sense of distortion from that area of the channel.

"We might be looking at some sort of stealth technology," Matt said.

"Wishful tinkin'—you're hallucinatink." David Ray shut his eyes again.

"I should try a distress call. Perhaps tell them that we see them."

"Ever'one'll hear ya." David Ray was reminding him the broadcast was omnidirectional, meaning the isolationists on the *Pilgrimage III* would hear his distress call.

Matt chewed on this complication for a moment. Sure, it hurt his ego that the criminals who took over the generational ship would hear his pleas for help, but David Ray might be making a different point. Don't give away a stealth arrival, you idiot, provided one even exists!

Matt eventually settled for broadcasting, "To all ships in the area, we require emergency assistance under the Phaistos Humanitarian Directives. Our coordinates are—" He added their sun-centered coordinates, which everyone understood inside a newly opened solar system. He would have liked to add something like, *This means you, silent ship in buoy arrival channel*, but David Ray was correct in his caution. Even if he couldn't articulate well, he was thinking more clearly than Matt.

"Useless," David Ray muttered after Matt recorded the message and set up a repeating broadcast.

"Maybe." Matt watched the display hopefully, but nothing changed. His eyelids kept crashing down and time seemed to flit by between his evaluations of the display. A half hour passed. Then an hour.

His heart was laboring on full thrust and he was beginning to identify the subtle effects of hypoxia, which could cause anything from irrational decisions, even hallucinations, to gently passing—had he just seen a mine explode on the display?

He squinted. There was nothing on the magnified view of the arrival channel, not even the distortion he'd thought he'd seen. It was ridiculous to imagine a stealth ship coming to their rescue. That kind of technology wasn't possible for N-space-capable ships. He would have pounded his fists in frustration, if he only had the energy.

"Nice to know you, Matthew Journey." David Ray's grin was crooked, his eyes shut, as he obviously planned his final words.

"Likewise, David Ray Pilgrimage." The lights in the module seemed too bright and his head felt as if it were going to split open from a headache, but he was too sleepy to care. His world was dark again. *Damn it, eyelids, open up.* He wondered where Ari was—*Wake up, Matt*—this was how Cipher had killed that guy on Karthage Point. *Ari, I hope you're alive and safe.*

The module didn't so much shudder as jiggle. It felt as if it had suddenly settled in a bowl of gelatin. The comm light on the module control panel flared green.

"I acknowledge the emergency call from module-two-zero-nine-eight-separated-from-*Pilgrimage*. I am preparing to connect in good faith, under Phaistos Humanitarian Directives." The voice broadcasting inside the module was neither male nor female, and lacked a certain indescribable human vibrancy. Some would say it lacked soul.

"Oh, Gaia. It's Minoan." With all his swearing and cursing, Matt always reserved the name of the Supreme Heart of All Holy Avatars for prayer, as in: *Gaia, thank you so very, very much for saving us and I'm grateful, but did you have to send aliens?* He looked at David Ray, whose eyes were bright and surprisingly alert.

"At least they have good timing." David Ray grinned.

Matt looked at their air mixture display. The Minoans needed better than good timing; the oxygen level was in the red.

It was Ariane's duty to see to Colonel Dokos's body, ensuring the proper military protocols were followed. She rolled Dokos onto her back and quickly removed all rank, ribbons, and medals from the uniform. She set these aside, then removed the name tag that said DOKOS and, after applying her thumbprint to the back, pushed up Dokos's sleeve. She slid the edge of the name tag into the implant receptor on the dead woman's forearm.

Behind the divider came the sounds of Garnet talking in low tones to Varra, who was trying to recover from a bout of hysteria. Not that Ariane faulted her behavior, because most Autonomist citizens wouldn't be able to cope with this, especially those too young to remember the war.

Sabina and Dr. Lowry were soberly watching Ariane. When the edges of the name tag glowed with light, Lowry asked, "What are you doing?"

"I'm downloading information from her implant into the tag, which has to get back to AFCAW. My thumbprint has been logged as the recorder of her death."

"Doesn't that violate all sorts of Autonomist privacy law?" Dr. Lowry had apparently learned much from her work on Priamos.

"Not in this case." The name tag stopped glowing and Ariane disconnected it. "This can only happen if the implant records brain death. Besides, this process encrypted both her implant and this tag. Only certain AFCAW personnel can decrypt it."

Ariane pocketed the name tag and stood, looking down at Colonel Dokos. She knew how painful stunning felt, so she couldn't hope that Dokos hadn't suffered before death came. She stepped back and saluted, the last rite of respect for a soldier. *A soldier who was executed without any chance of defending herself.* Beside Ariane, Dr. Lowry and Sabina put their hands on their hearts and bowed their heads.

After she brought her arm down, she glanced at the body bag, thrown inside the room so fast they never saw the person behind the door. Obviously, they were supposed to prepare the body.

"I can't get her in the bag myself. Can you help me?" She turned to Dr. Lowry, who blanched.

"No, I can't. I've never touched—" The young woman backed away, hands held up.

"I'll help," Sabina said.

Ariane held her gaze, looking for derision or disrespect in her eyes, but seeing none. Knowing she had to put aside her resentments for later, Ariane nodded curtly and let Sabina help her.

After sealing the body bag, they had joined Garnet and Varra on the other side of the partition when the door opened again. It was Emery.

"Sit against the wall," he ordered, gesturing with his flechette weapon.

If he'd showed up with only a stunner, Ariane was angry enough to have tried jumping him—and that meant she wasn't thinking rationally. She tried to suppress her rage as she moved over to the bench. *Cool down*, she repeated internally.

Emery then stepped forward, followed by two men, one of whom had accompanied him when he executed Colonel Dokos. They went behind the partition.

"Have you finished your rites?" Emery asked.

No one answered him and he didn't seem eager to look anyone in the eyes. Instead, he told the men behind the partition to hurry up.

"Emery. I'm on urgent business from Abram." The quiet words came from a man standing in the door. Again, this was someone who might be Emery's brother. Significant inbreeding must be going on somewhere, although the look exchanged between the two was anything but brotherly, by Ariane's assessment. This time, there was a distinct difference because the man in the door wore Terran civilian clothes. He might even have the same tailor as Wescott.

"What do you want, Tahir?" After a quick look over his shoulder, Emery brought his attention back to the women, much to Ariane's disappointment. She noted Tahir carried only a stunner.

The two men carried out the body bag. After Tahir stepped aside to let them out, he came into the room. He addressed the women directly. "Which one of you is the *Destroyer of Worlds*?"

Uh-oh. As she heard the title the Minoans had given her and her other crew members during the publicized Pax Minoica negotiations, Ariane's face went wooden. She did exactly as the other women: She looked puzzled and exchanged questioning glances with the others on the bench. She saw Sabina and Garnet doing the same, although they had to be better actresses. Being Terrans, how long would they protect her identity?

"These are women, you idiot, or haven't you noticed?" Emery's words came through a clenched jaw. He appeared to be grinding his teeth.

"Women fought on both sides of the war, and almost everyone watched the initial signing of Pax Minoica. Besides, we have the verified word of a Terran State Prince," Tahir said.

Ariane felt a small movement from Sabina, who sat at her right. Emery and Tahir, however, seemed locked in silent argument and didn't notice.

"Then he's fooled you with his body language or— whatever. Give it up, none of *them* could be a warrior."

Tahir didn't respond to Emery's jeer. Instead, he pulled

his stunner out and pointed at each woman in turn, as if considering her candidacy for the title. Varra was on the end and she was obviously too young. Then came Garnet, but she was Terran. So was Dr. Lowry. The stunner pointed at Ariane and hesitated, but from her outward appearance, she was also too young to have been in the war. That left Sabina, also a Terran, who wouldn't have been attacking a Terran world during the war.

"The guilty one should step forward." With his calm voice, Tahir didn't seem particularly suited for this job.

Emery sneered. "If you're so sure you're looking for a woman, why don't you have a *name*?"

"Not enough time." A flash of disgust flitted across Tahir's face, and the women saw the telltale grimace.

Meaning, not enough time before Parmet broke. Parmet's mind might be mush right now, particularly if he's gibbering about me.

Sabina must have come to the same conclusions. She stood and calmly said, "Enough of this. I'm the person you want."

Ariane tried to keep her jaw from dropping open. She glanced at Garnet, who had a questioning look on her face. Beside Garnet, Varra looked puzzled, perhaps not having glommed on to the meaning of the title. She might be one of the few who had never watched the momentous treaty-signing ceremony, captured forever in crystal. Dr. Lowry, on the other hand, looked at Sabina with shock.

"Ridiculous." Emery looked even angrier, if that were possible. "We know you're the wife of the State Prince and the mother of his only son."

"Perhaps *you* have a naive understanding of the complexities of Terran politics." Sabina's voice was cold. "A State Prince must heartily support Pax Minoica and what better way than to show forgiveness through a marriage contract? After all, our marriages are political implements first, breeding licenses second, and finally means of establishing affiliations and distributing wealth. The State Prince was waiting for the right moment to go public regarding my background."

She presented her words in a logical and believable tone that hid the nonsense. Tahir gaped at her answer. So did Ariane.

"Take me to the State Prince, and you'll see. He'll corroborate," Sabina added.

"Sit down. Vengeance has not been exacted for Ura-Guinn, and that still festers in the heart of a State Prince." Emery's voice was flat; he'd been pushed too far.

Sabina sat down regally, every motion strengthening the veracity of her story.

Tahir frowned. "Parmet called for revenge and it was rumored he illicitly financed Terran reprisal squads."

Ariane almost nodded, wondering why Sabina had come up with that half-assed story. Certainly not to protect Ariane; perhaps Sabina wanted to see Parmet, but she should have invented a more believable story.

Tahir nodded at Emery. "You've seen him kill. Do any of you question that he would kill you at my command? Starting with her"—he pointed at Garnet—"and proceeding with you"—he pointed at Sabina—"until someone comes forward."

Emery visibly squirmed at the word "command," but he nodded. He might not like Tahir, but he wouldn't walk away from a chance to use his wand.

This changes everything. Ariane couldn't let anybody else be hurt, tortured, or killed for Ura-Guinn. She stood up slowly.

"I'm the person you want." Her voice surprised her, being clear and confident.

Tahir's stunner and Emery's pistol both pointed at her, but the men didn't look convinced.

"I'm *Major* Kedros, of the Reserve Armed Forces of the Consortium of Autonomous Worlds. My service number is alpha-seven, one-two, six-four-seven-two, and *yes*, I'm older than I look."

Emery's face darkened. "You're military." His hand tightened on his flechette pistol and Ariane's stomach flinched.

"No," Tahir said quickly. "Abram wants to see this one."

Emery looked at Ariane's face for a moment. He gestured for one of his men to hand over a flechette pistol, which he gave to Tahir. "I think you'd better use this. She may be trouble."

Tahir accepted the weapon, handling it gingerly but competently. He secured the stunner on his belt while Ariane cursed internally. Emery had made the right call: Using a stunner was tricky against a combat-trained professional, who could initiate hand-to-hand and spread the stun to both bodies. On the other hand, flechette weapons were spaceship-safe, flesh-eating weapons that didn't need fine aim or range adjustment.

After her flare of frustration, Ariane cooled her emotions, trying for objectivity. *They'll make a mistake eventually; I just have to be ready.* Cipher once complained that all Ari had, entrenched in the core of her being, was a lump of logical ice—*well, don't fail me now, lump of ice!* She took a deep breath and met their gazes calmly.

Emery leered, although his expression seemed strained. "Go ahead and take her. Leaves the better-looking Terrans for us."

"You're not allowed to touch any women, not after that pilot." Distaste filled Tahir's face, causing his nostrils to flare. "Everyone knows that's by *Abram*'s command."

Abram seemed to be the magic command word. Emery's face reddened.

Tahir ordered Ariane to march out of the room ahead of him. He gave her directions for turning. Since she barely knew the way back to the great hall, she tried to keep her eyes open for the informational signs left by the archeological teams. She had an ungracious thought for contractors who didn't want to hand out maps to visitors; then she realized Barone and his people were probably dead. *Executed.*

Anger rose again, but with it came a wave of reproach. The breach of her false identity paled in significance to the loss of those people, who were hoping to advance humanity's knowledge with their work. *Focus, Ariane—you need to figure out who's behind this, and what they want.* This Abram, the leader, appeared to be the key. He'd told his men to execute any military, probably because they'd be most likely to thwart his plans, but why did he kill the Minoan contractors? Moreover, how did he get control of the buoy? The hours of rejection for bandwidth now made sense to her. Her stomach tightened. Was Matt okay? Had Joyce been captured?

"There'll be a price to pay when the Minoans get wind of this," she shot over her shoulder.

There was no reply from Tahir.

"You can't imagine they'll allow one of their buoys to fall into criminal hands."

"We've already experienced Minoan retribution," he said. "Take the tight right corner here."

She turned, as directed, and at the end of the short corridor, she faced a door much like the one to the original conference room for the contractor meeting. If her sense of direction was correct, she was on the opposite side of the great hall.

"Turn around."

They faced each other in the short corridor. Tahir placed himself at the end so he could watch for anyone coming in the main corridor, looking as if he intended a private conversation with her.

"Parmet said you're the pilot who detonated a temporal-distortion weapon in Ura-Guinn and still escaped through N-space." He grinned. "I figure you still have your N-space pilot qualification from the military. It's too valuable a skill to throw aside."

She stayed silent, not admitting anything until she understood Tahir's agenda. From his accent, he was Terran, perhaps highly educated. He had a familial resemblance to Emery, but they seemed to be at odds with each other.

Tahir reached inside his jacket, took out a slate, and thumbed it while carefully keeping the pistol trained upon her. Then he dropped the slate, which skipped on the polished stone floor and then rested against his boot. Keeping his distance, he pushed the slate in her direction. It made a light whining sound on the clean floor.

"Pick it up."

She did, cautiously. The slate was an example of rugged Autonomist manufacturing and it had the weight of an informational slate with additional sensors. She kept it dangling at the end of her arm, preferring to keep her eyes on his face. She let her thumb slide into thumbprint position and glanced down, but disappointingly, Tahir had locked the slate and none of the functions lit up for her.

"Look at the picture." His eyes were bright with anticipation.

The slate had a display area about the size of her palm, but the high quality and detail made her think the picture was a close-up, not a magnification. She saw the pointed green vessel with wires sprouting from every sharp vertex and her face went numb. Looking closely, she verified it was indeed shaped as a great stellated dodecahedron, having twelve pentagrammic faces that each rose into multiple, pointed triangular pyramids. This was the cheapest stable geometry for containing and accelerating microscopic amounts of exotic matter to generate a temporal-distortion wave. The wired vessel sat inside a case with one labeled edge showing near the bottom of the photograph. She could make out the red letters TDP-2102-012/WM15 at the top of the label.

"Where did you get this picture?"

"*That*, Major Kedros, is my gift to my father. It rests within the hold of the *Father's Wrath*, waiting for its appropriate means of delivery. *That* is why there won't be any ships to rescue you—or me."

CHAPTER 14

Galactic Sovereignty is a subject many applicants fail on entrance exams. Each generational ship line is neutral and self-governing; otherwise the Minoans wouldn't deal with them. Their offices and headquarters, when located planet-side, enjoy extraterritorial status. The solar systems they open, via a buoy, remain their territory until they relinquish sovereignty.

–Get Accepted to Law School! Paris Stephanos, 2102.260.09.42 UT, indexed by *Heraclitus 12* under Flux Imperative

Oleander knew what G-145 was; that solar system was one of the hottest topics on net-think and she'd followed reports released by archeological teams. But why would Dr. Rouxe haul the stolen TD weapon there? As far as she knew, there weren't any habitable worlds in G-145. Then she realized the emphasis that Captain Floros used: *Both* the Consortium and the League had received Declarations of Emergency.

"I need an encrypted channel," Colonel Edones said.

After Hauser's aide authorized the channel, Edones immediately moved to a corner of the conference room to make his call. Using his implanted mike, his discussion went subvocal, but she could see the urgency in the set of his shoulders and the way he paced a small circle into the carpet.

Terrans came and went on hushed errands for SP
Hauser. Presently, Edones and Hauser had received their
orders and they faced off in the center of the room, right
across the table from Oleander and Floros.

"What's going on?" she asked Floros.

"Just sit back and watch the show." Floros grimly nodded toward Hauser and Edones.

Silence fell over the room. The men eyed each other.
Hauser was taller but suddenly, for all his *somaural* projection, he didn't quite match Colonel Edones in presence.

"You go first," Hauser said. "After all, we had to reveal
the safety issues with the warhead."

Oleander frowned. The Terrans were becoming more
childish by the minute.

"Fine." Edones's expression would have frozen anyone
with less confidence than Hauser. "*Our* message states that
Pilgrimage HQ thinks the buoy is no longer under control
of the *Pilgrimage III*. They assume something has happened to the crew, but they're not privy to the fact there's a
madman with a TD warhead loose in their system."

"Pilgrimage, I assume, asked for aid under a prear-
ranged agreement made with the Consortium? Please explain, Colonel, how they expect you to get into the system if
the buoy is locked down." Hauser's tone was triumphant.

Edones bent his head in acknowledgment. "Because
there are encrypted overrides for AFCAW, provided the
Pilgrimage III crew was able to activate them."

Hauser didn't look surprised and merely gestured for
an aide to hand him a slate. Oleander, however, was taken
aback by this admission. She glanced at Floros, whose
eyes had narrowed in triumph as if to say, "I knew it but I
couldn't prove it."

"*If* CAW's duplicity is made public, then Overlord Three
will release this statement expressing condemnation for the
Consortium's attempt to undermine Pax Minoica." Hauser
handed Edones the slate.

"Duplicity is a strong word, considering the opening of

G-145 was contracted during the war." Edones didn't look at the slate. "Besides, we both know the codes might not work. If the Overlords want political profit from this, I'm warning you that Senior Senator Jude Stephanos, from Hellas, is currently drafting *his* statement of outrage over *your* override codes on a buoy financed by Autonomous Worlds."

Both sides had overrides to sovereign buoy operation? Oleander had naively taken generational ship line "neutrality" at face value. She heard Floros snort.

"At this time there's no reason to release this information," Hauser said.

Edones smiled coldly. "Agreed. Why tarnish the reputation of the generational ship lines or take the chance of angering the Minoans? However, Pilgrimage HQ put constraints on our response. This must be a joint mission and they've limited the ships we can take into the system."

"Oh, Great Bull–shit," Floros said in a low voice, out of the corner of her mouth. "No matter what, the civilians will make this a clusterfuck."

"Major Bernard and Captain Floros, I need a manifest of every ship and crew inside G-145, and an analysis of where they might be when we enter the system. Lieutenant Oleander!" Edones's voice was clipped.

"Yes, sir." She sprang out of her seat.

"Notify Colonel Aquino that the *Bright Crescent* must be ready to depart in eight hours, configured for Rho-Epsilon-Sigma."

Her forehead wrinkled, but she didn't voice her puzzlement. The colonel was referencing the flexible battle configuration for several missions, such as reconnaissance, extraction, and stealthy surgical strikes. However, the *Bright Crescent* was only a medium-weight Fury-class cruiser, fitted with rail guns, swarm weapons, and kinetic missile tubes, typically for use with the Champion II or Assassinator missiles. A Fortress-class destroyer would have a wider range of weapons, plus shock troops and a squadron or two of fighters to compare to the two weaponless pin-naces carried by the Fury-class cruisers. She had figured a destroyer would be sent to G-145, if only for its intimidation factor.

"Why the *Bright Crescent*?" Leave it to Floros to publicly question the orders.

Oleander waited. She didn't know what type of senior officer Edones might be: one who didn't like his decisions being questioned, or one who figured his people deserved most of the same information he had for his decisions. Luckily, Edones cocked one eyebrow at Floros's query and proved to be the latter.

"Pilgrimage HQ has been specific: One ship each is allowed from AFCAW and Terran Space Forces, with limited combined mass and displacement. After all, it's their territory."

"But, sir, they obviously don't know about the weapon—" Oleander stopped short when she saw the colonel's expression.

"Yes?" He raised both his light eyebrows, which wasn't good.

"And I guess they're never going to know," she finished.

"Never say never, Lieutenant," Edones said, almost cheerfully. "But for right now, we must keep the ship lines in the dark."

"What about our new allies?" Floros's tone was sour and she jerked her head toward the SP, who was huddled with his aides. "How can we execute a dual-flag mission if they're not allowed access to ship and weapon specs?"

"Ah, but that's been anticipated. There're new classification guides in everybody's queues. By the way, Lieutenant Oleander, as senior weapons officer, you'll coordinate armament with the incoming Terran ship and crew. You'll need to do that from the *Bright Crescent*."

"Yes, sir."

Edones pointed his slate toward hers and pressed the transmit button. "Since you're heading for the ship, take these orders to admin and have the day officer execute and send them to Directorate admin. Stay there until you've verified they're in effect."

"Yes, sir."

She strode out of the room and in the passage, glanced at the orders she was taking to the day officer. One set of orders put Master Sergeant Alexander Joyce onto hazardous-duty pay status DI-3. The other set of orders transferred Reserve Major Ariane Kedros to active duty with the same hazardous-duty pay status. The duty location for both was G-145.

She raised her eyebrows. As cold and uncaring as Edones seemed, he took care of his people. Joyce's family now received additional pay and Kedros had full military medical benefits if, Gaia forbid, she was wounded in G-145. And if Major Ariane Kedros was in G-145, conducting her civilian job, then so was *Matt Journey*. The rescue of G-145 suddenly became personal.

"The connection to module-two-zero-nine-eight-separated-from-*Pilgrimage* has been sealed. I am ready to supply an oxygen-nitrogen atmosphere." As if in response to the Minoan's voice, the vertical airlock seal's status light went green.

"Hey, we've got light gravity." David Ray started fumbling about his webbing. The toxic atmosphere alarm started blaring. "Open the airlock, Matt."

"We'll depressurize."

"That's hypoxia speaking. I can't do this myself. I'm hurt, remember?" David Ray's urgent tone cut through his fog of panic like a knife.

Luckily, Matt had spacecrew barometric chamber training and he knew sudden pigheaded irrationality could be a symptom of hypoxia. Several years ago, when he'd gone through routine low-atmosphere training, his test partner refused to put his oxygen mask back on when required. The instructors had to tackle him and forcibly attach the mask.

The training let crews experience mild hypoxia to reinforce the idea that, sometimes, your worst enemy could be your own brain.

The light is green. Matt undid the webbing holding him to the floor and bounced unsteadily toward the vertical airlock. He bumped into the wall and rebounded, catching the edge of the bar. *If the light is green, the airlock is sealed*, he kept chanting to himself. He webbed himself temporarily to the handhold and silenced the atmosphere alarm.

Even though the airlock sensors detected an adequate seal, the module systems knew the airlock wasn't attaching to anything conventional, or in a manner for which it'd been designed. Matt had to insist that yes, he was *sure* he wanted to open the outside seal to the airlock.

The pressure light stayed green, but the seal light started flipping between red and green. The module system became confused. It flashed conflicting messages on the wall: "Warning, inadequate seal for safe entry! Oxygenated environment detected outside airlock."

Matt finally convinced the system to open the lower seal. He opened the hatch and a wave of warm, humid air hit him. He breathed deeply and immediately gagged. The *smell* was overwhelmingly fetid for someone raised aboard a generational ship.

"St. Darius, I don't want to seem ungrateful, but is the oxygen worth *this*?" However, his headache was fading and—David Ray! Thinking more clearly and feeling much steadier, he unwebbed himself and went to help the counselor.

"Egad, that's awful," David Ray commented when Matt got him closer to the airlock. He looked about the module. "This humidity is going to overwhelm the module's scrubbers and we're going to get a lot of condensation. We'll have to ask them to adjust their mixture."

Matt looked warily at the comm panel, his heart sinking. He didn't want to talk to them. The Minoan's voice suddenly came over the systems, making him jump.

"Knossos-ship has been damaged by illegally designed explosives. Are rescued-persons in module-two-zero-nine-eight-separated-from-*Pilgrimage* responsible?"

Matt turned to David Ray and saw horror wash over the counselor's face, his eyes widening.

"Absolutely not!" David Ray shouted. "A group of criminals overtook the *Pilgrimage III* and they are the ones mining the buoy channels, not us."

There was silence.

David Ray tapped the mute command, his fingers shaking. "Sorry, Matt, I'm rattled and I forgot some important points about Minoans. They understand and remember *titles*, so don't bother with names, because it'll only confuse them. There'll also be uncomfortable pauses, for us, when conversing with them. We have to learn to wait."

"You do the talking then. You've studied them."

David Ray nodded and Matt reversed the mute command. They both waited.

"Knossos-ship has been damaged," repeated the voice. Another long pause occurred before it continued. "Knossos-ship cannot support module-two-zero-nine-eight-separated-from-*Pilgrimage* as attached. Rescued-persons must board Knossos-ship."

Matt's eyebrows rose, but David Ray quickly said, "Rescued-persons understand and comply."

"But—" Matt didn't know if any mundane had boarded a Minoan ship before. He'd once suspected Edones might have, but was later convinced the supercilious colonel knew no more than anyone else about the inside of Minoan ships.

David Ray made a shushing gesture, a big smile on his face. Matt shook his head vigorously. *He's too drunk to understand; this might be the answer to* his *dream, but what about me?* Then Matt looked about the module and his shoulders slumped. If the Minoans claimed they couldn't keep the module pressurized, what else could he do?

"Knossos-ship awaits rescued-persons. Please perform your shutdown procedures."

David Ray helped Matt enter commands for the module systems; the precious sperm samples would have acceptable temperature control from the solar panels and batteries, since the scrubbers could be shut down. Then, for the first time, they leaned through the airlock hatch and looked "down."

"You've got to be shitting me!" Matt's voice was tight.

The edges of the outer seal of the airlock sank into something Matt considered a cross between semitransparent primordial stew and tapioca pudding gone really, really bad. It was light olive green with internal blotches that varied between red and brown. His eyes blurred from the stench.

"No defecation of rescued-persons is intended," said the Minoan voice.

Matt clenched his jaw. "Yeah, right," he muttered through his teeth, into David Ray's ear.

David Ray, on the other hand, looked fascinated. He pointed to the far side of the circular puddle filling the airlock tube. "I think our atmosphere is coming through those ports. Or perhaps, pores?"

Remembering their open comm, Matt shrugged. Considering the flatulencelike atmosphere, only Gaia knew what those pores were. He had a more pressing question.

"How are we supposed to board?" he asked, pointing at the tapioca-like surface. "It can't be liquid; it's bumpy. Is it solid?"

Help didn't come through the comm panel, so they turned back to the airlock tube.

"Well, I'm game. And I'm already wounded." David Ray gripped the ladder, swung away from their small platform, and worked his way down using his arms. He only had to go about four rungs before his feet touched the puddle surface. His shoes began disappearing as if they were pressing into viscous liquid.

"At least it's warm." He went down another rung and he was up to his knees in the strange stuff.

"Watch out, it's changing." Matt saw internal blotches, or floating chunks, start moving and coalesce about David Ray's legs.

"It's starting to pull—whoa!" David Ray threw his arms up and floundered, for only a second, like a drowning man on the surface of a lake. Then he went under with a slurp, merely a large blotch floating deeper until he was quickly out of sight.

"Aw, hell." Matt punched the delayed close for the airlock and pushed violently away from the ladder and down, toward the putrid puddle. He closed his eyes and held his breath as he hit the surface.

"There's no shuttle or ship here on the surface?" Joyce asked.

"No. We're not scheduled for a supply delivery for several days," Maria said.

"What about emergency evacuation? Are there autonomous pods or modules available?"

"Yes, but since the surface was considered safer than shooting anyone into space, they're fixed structures. Besides, the evacuation modules are accessed from both sides of the great hall, which is now crawling with these. . . ." She couldn't finish with any appropriate words and vaguely gestured with her left hand.

"Whoever they are, they have no insignia or uniforms, so we know they're thumbing their noses at the Phaistos Protocol. They're not military." Joyce conserved his energy by sitting in one of the comfy office chairs.

"I agree. I also haven't seen any connection between the strangers and the traitors that support them." Maria looked thoughtful. "Except, I've seen no women in their ranks. Not a one."

"Once again, we're lacking information. We don't know

who they are, how many there are, or what they want. Unfortunately, they're not hampered by the same problem."

"Yes, they are." Maria smiled. "Aether Exploration made such a mess of things with their layered contracts, no one knows who's supposed to be down here or who works for whom."

Joyce frowned at her until she looked away and muttered, "Okay, some of the fault is ours."

It certainly was. If SP Parmet and his staff hadn't forced Kedros to sign leases over to Terran companies—but then, if the Minoans hadn't applied pressure, there wouldn't be Minoan-owned contractors here either. Joyce shook his head. No sense in assigning blame, when they had to focus on getting up to Beta Priamos.

"Apparently the only way off this rock is the elevator. Do we have any weapons?" he asked.

"Only this." She pulled a personal ministunner from her pocket. It was civilian and it didn't have a lethal setting, plus its range had to be less than twenty feet.

This was so incongruous he had to laugh, quickly muffling himself with his hand. Catching his hysteria, Maria chuckled quietly as she put the ministunner back in her vest. They quickly sobered.

"We're not going to scare anybody with a personal stunner, considering they're running around with flechette pistols. So scratch any thought of overpowering the guys running the elevator." Joyce leaned back further and the chair adjusted, making him think about how much he'd like a nap, a few delicious moments of sleep. "Could we wait them out? Until a hostage exchange or whatever they're planning?"

Maria shrugged. "Problem number one: We don't know that they plan to negotiate with any authorities. Problem two: I saw them inventorying our supplies and making themselves at home in our kitchen, so they think they'll be here for a while."

"Key words are *they think*, because once the outside worlds figure out—"

"What if they've got control of the buoy?" Maria's voice was blunt. "Then no one's getting into the system."

Joyce raised his eyebrows. He had to give Maria credit for thinking big, but his initial reaction was to scoff at the idea. However . . . it was disturbingly plausible. Because he worked for the Directorate of Intelligence and had high clearances, he knew about the overrides negotiated between the ship line and CAW. However, the possibility of rescue came down to one issue: Did the *Pilgrimage* crew download the command to allow overrides?

"We can take over their message center," he suggested.

At the same time, Maria said, "We can hitch an elevator ride to Beta Priamos, going EVA."

Neither spoke immediately, appraising the other's plan behind lowered eyes. His was suicidal, given their lack of weapons, but hers had problems also.

"You're not EVA-qualified anymore." He was obliquely referring to her Tantor's Sun disease. She had equipment to provide her positive air pressure and oxygen when sleeping, which traveled with her in a large case—when she didn't need that case for kidnapping victims off habitats, he reminded himself. She'd used her equipment case to smuggle an unconscious Major Kedros off Karthage Point. Later, he found the equipment broken down into small pieces and stuffed in ventilator shafts and trash compactors.

Maria shrugged and pointed to the implant in her forearm. "I get continual medication that prevents the respiratory problems—it's controlled similarly to asthma. If I set the EVA suit to slightly higher oxygen than normal, there's little chance of an attack."

"But there's still a chance. How long before you run out of meds?"

"A couple days. I was supposed to receive my quarterly shipment on the resupply ship tomorrow. Gives me incentive to kick these guys out of here, doesn't it?"

"Is there an in-system source?"

She shook her head. "Even the *Pilgrimage*'s labs can't manufacture it. If our 'captors' have truly shut us off from the outside worlds, then we're all dependent upon the *Pilgrimage* for everything, from food to light manufacturing."

Joyce pictured a future filled with crèche-get food: processed algal bars, hydroponically grown pastel vegetables, and bland noodle dishes. The glimpse nearly made him gag.

"That's enough incentive for me," he said. "Where are the EVA suits stored?"

CHAPTER 15

When an unbeliever faces an arc of retribution, tailored
to their sins and completing their just punishment, they
will hesitate. It becomes the responsibility of the believer
to agent that arc of retribution, and the believer will be
rewarded, their kismet enhanced . . .

—*Forecast by the Fifteenth Prophet, Who Served Without a
Name, est. 2058.xxx UT, reindexed by Heraclitus 7
under Flux Imperative*

Ariane wrenched her gaze away from the picture of the
Terran TD warhead package. Tahir watched her with
fascination, perhaps a hint of terror.

"What are you doing with this?" She spoke slowly, her
mind whirling as she tried to recall all the classified briefings she'd had on Terran TD weapons. In particular, she
tried to remember the safety and control mechanisms that
prevented unauthorized arming and detonation.

"He intends to detonate it."

"You mean Abram? Is he your father?" She stared back
into Tahir's eyes and knew the answer. "He's insane."

"Yes." He spoke in a matter-of-fact tone with a shrug, as
if he accepted and acknowledged this long ago.

"If he can detonate this—"

"He can."

That's Great Bull–shit, but Tahir obviously believes this

and I need to keep him talking. "Then he'll kill all of us. A temporal-distortion wave will cause a sun to nova."

"Ura-Guinn's sun survived. Abram has studied this and calculated the safest yield and detonation point. He only wants to destroy the buoy."

"No one knows why Ura-Guinn's sun survived. Even so, lots of people died from that detonation." She tried to keep her voice steady. "The flares and mass emissions fried most of the inner-system bodies and habitats. Anyone transitioning from or to N-space at the moment of detonation, *anywhere in the Minoan buoy network*, was lost."

"Except you. You're living proof that someone can drop out of the system during a TD detonation." His eyes brightened even more and he looked feverish. "Can you do that again?"

A chill ran up her back and she tried to ignore the creepy feeling he gave her. "That was luck, nothing more. We dropped before the detonation, but thousands of others were lost in transition."

"I read classified reports that said the buoy was going down when you started your drop."

She paused and quickly reassessed his Terran clothes and his accent, so different from Emery's. Tahir was educated and, if she could believe him, he'd procured the weapon for Abram. If he read classified governmental reports on the damage at Ura-Guinn, did he also have access to classified weapon designs? His conviction that Abram could detonate a stolen weapon might have merit. She changed her approach; trying to convince Tahir of the ramifications of a TD wave was counterproductive.

"You need to stop him," she said urgently. "Don't give him codes or anything else that controls the weapon."

Tahir's face went through rapid transformations: helplessness, anguish, and terror. She watched him struggle for control, finally shuttering his face in darkness. With a sinking feeling in her stomach, she realized he could never stand up to his father, no matter how she tried to manipulate him.

"It's too late for that." His voice was soft and cold. "You'll realize that when you meet him. Now turn around and put your hands behind your back."

She did as he told her, and he tied her wrists with a quicktie usually used in law enforcement. For a moment, she wondered why he'd waited until now to tie her hands. Did he now expect a suicidal escape attempt? She had no death wish, even if she did have her dark moments. A memory of Cipher took over her thoughts: Cipher holding a stunner and expecting old Ari, or new Ariane, to roll over and participate in a group suicide pact. *Even Cipher knew me better than that, considering she backed up her proposition with explosives.*

Tahir pushed on her back, breaking the memory's grip. "Start walking."

She followed his directions and by her estimate, they wound around the great hall to the comm center. Abram also used it for his operations center, but everyone was obviously used to ComNet coverage, by the number of messengers scurrying about. The confusion indicated Abram's people weren't trained for comm-out conditions.

Tahir pulled her to one side of the corridor to let someone by: Emery, the executioner, and his cohort jogged by and turned into the comm center ahead of her. She noticed Emery had blood on his right hand. As he turned, he wiped his hand on his thigh. She hesitated and Tahir pushed again, nagging her into motion.

The comm center was chaotic. Glancing about, she noted she was the lone woman in the room. To her right, Emery, his cohort, and two other men were piling slates on a counter in groups. Beyond the men was a portable display unit with lists and diagrams on its glowing surface. From the conversation, Ariane guessed that they were trying to account for personnel. Had they found everyone assigned to Priamos? They didn't want any loose cannons rolling about and upsetting their plans.

Good job, Matt, although you couldn't have known this would happen. Ariane looked away and pressed her lips together, hiding her smile. Matt's snarled leases had ultimately proven useful. These criminals had a nightmare on their hands, figuring out how many people were working on this moon. The contractors weren't being cooperative, by the looks of Emery's hand.

"Hey, do we have her inventoried?" One of the men with a pile of slates pointed at Ariane. She frowned at his choice of words, but he didn't seem to notice.

Emery turned slowly and scrutinized her, the lids on his eyes so low that they were slits. She tensed. Dokos's tag, fixed in an inside pocket, dug into her side as she tightened her arms. The quick-tie began to hurt her wrists.

"Her name is Ariane Kedros," Emery said. Then he looked at Tahir and their gazes locked.

"Kedros... Kedros..." The original questioner turned to the display and cycled through lists. "Who's her employer?"

"Aether Exploration," Emery said in a casual tone. "You've got her recorded as female number three in room twenty-two. While you're at it, mark her as military."

"What?" All four men looked at her.

Her face stayed impassive and her mind veered away from Colonel Dokos. She made a note regarding Emery's excellent recollection, which spurred her to observe the room and commit the faces she didn't know to memory.

"She's mine," Tahir said.

"Yes. *Cousin* Tahir has decided she'll be useful." Emery drawled the words. "We'll see what Abram thinks."

Ariane felt the tension. She heard the sarcastic tone in Emery's voice and the irony applied to the word "cousin." There were complexities here she didn't understand. Tahir pushed her away from the group and across the large room to another knot of men.

Frank was there, standing awkwardly with his weapons hanging on his belt. His face looked like he was frightened, or intimidated, as he talked to a man whose back faced Ariane.

"Abram, I brought her," Tahir said.

The man speaking with Frank turned around.

"This is the *Destroyer of Worlds* the State Prince told us about." Tahir prodded Ariane in the back with the bulbous flechette pistol.

Abram inspected her, his gaze traveling over her once, stopping on her face. Ariane tried not to recoil. Abram's face was pitted and lifeless. His dark eyes burned with anger, but had a dead, reptilian quality—she'd never seen such frightening eyes. Trying to meet his gaze was physically exhausting. Nothing in his eyes indicated he was looking at another person; he might have been looking at a slate, rather than Ariane.

"No, you've got the wrong person. I know Ari. She's a pilot," Frank protested.

With relief, Ariane looked away from Abram, to Frank's face.

"Right, Ari? You weren't in the war . . ." Frank's voice died away as she raised her eyebrows. His forehead wrinkled and his expression became pained. "You didn't have anything to do with Ura-Guinn. I'd be disappointed—"

"*You're* disappointed? That's a laugh, Fr—" The side of her head exploded and she was suddenly on the floor. She tasted blood and her vision grayed and narrowed to a point as she fought to stay conscious. Abram didn't pull his punches for women.

She heard an exclamation from Frank.

"I can't allow livestock to be insolent. It's an issue of training," Abram said dispassionately. His voice sounded far away, far above, as he added, "Take blood and tissue samples from her. The Terran said she has rejuv enhancements, so if she can pass anything of worth on to male progeny, we'll keep her."

She ground her teeth, trying not to shriek from the pain in her skull. Someone pushed her jacket sleeve up for sam-

ples; then strong hands grabbed her upper arms and hauled
her to her feet, and higher. As she dangled, the hands dug
into her arms and the quick-tie cut into her wrists. She
couldn't open her eyes or raise her head.

"Put her in with the Terran," Abram said.

"He'll kill her," Tahir protested.

"I merely assist in both their arcs of retribution," was
the cold, flat retort from Abram, but she didn't understand
the words.

They dragged her out of the room.

"We need her, Father!" Tahir tried to keep desperation
from cracking his voice.

Abram whirled on him, eyes blazing wildly. "You are
never to call me that again."

Tahir lowered his eyes respectfully, but he didn't back
away. This would make Abram curious, if nothing else.

"What interest do you have in her?" Abram's eyes
narrowed.

"She's useful. She's pilot trained."

"I have plenty of pilots. As a female, her only useful
function is producing eggs."

"Abram, this is a moment when fate balances on your
decision. She has destroyed a world; consider what her final
punishment would be."

Tahir had never publicly stood his ground with Abram,
not in this way. He added, "You yourself spoke of the arc of
retribution, written by the Fifteenth Prophet. If you hesitate to be the agent of her completion, then let me."

Glints in Abram's eyes indicated that Tahir was on
perilous ground. "Be careful—that prophet speaks of
great deeds and significance, not the small, mean life of
womanhood."

Tahir suppressed his frustration. This would be so much
easier if Kedros weren't a woman, but she was the best
chance for escape he'd ever get.

"What could be more significant than destroying

Ura-Guinn? She detonated the first and only temporal-distortion weapon used in warfare," Tahir said calmly and methodically.

"She merely did as she was ordered." Abram made a dismissive gesture with his hand.

"As do all our followers for a free life?" Tahir said the words clearly, so everyone in the room could hear.

Abram jerked his head back and his eyes focused on Tahir's face, reconsidering his son for the first time in months. *He realizes he's been out-maneuvered, but sadly, he's surprised that* I've *managed this.* Tahir clenched his jaw; Abram had just given him added incentive to make his plan work.

"You say that great deeds, if done in the line of one's duty, cannot qualify for salvation?" Tahir asked the question, again clearly enunciating it for everyone in the room. The surrounding audience of men was quiet.

"We are talking of a *female.* Why should I care about the ultimate fate of unbelievers or, in this particular case, livestock?"

"Yet you mentioned two arcs of retribution as you sent her away. She destroyed Ura-Guinn and when divine punishment for such a deed is presented to us, aren't we obligated to complete the arc?" Tahir was intensely aware of the watching audience. These men were his leverage, and Abram knew it. Abram's own rhetoric, the source of his invulnerability, was now going to force his decision.

"If we are, collectively, the agent, then who will be the witness?" Abram asked, changing his tactic.

"I will."

"Of course. How do you intend to complete the arc?" Abram's voice was dry.

"She will pilot our mission, exactly as she did for Ura-Guinn." Tahir's voice was hard.

"*She* will pilot? That's a suicide mission that will be carried out by my most dedicated men. How do you intend to witness her final act, Tahir?" Abram thought he knew his son and there was a quirk at the side of his mouth.

"I'm going along." Tahir was tense and he wiped all doubt from his mind. His father had to believe him.

Abram raised his eyebrows and Tahir felt the depth of his father's surprise. *What's the matter, Father? I've risked my education, my career, my freedom, and any chance at a normal life on a Terran League world. Why is it so hard to believe that I'll give my life for your cause? If I were Emery, you'd have no reservations.*

There was silence as Abram examined him.

"Agreed, if she survives until ship departure," Abram said. "But I won't trust the mission to you and this female's arc of retribution. You will both merely observe *my* pilot and mission commander."

Tahir nodded his head in assent. Before Abram turned away, he saw a strange glint in his father's eyes. He tried not to smile at the irony: He finally won respect from Abram, but only by volunteering for a suicide mission that he had no intention of completing.

"Let go of me. I can walk!"

The men carried Ariane by her arms and didn't let her toes touch, causing pain in her shoulders and tied wrists. They ignored her protests. She let loose a long streak of the worst profanity she could gather, and they dropped her like a live stun grenade. Stumbling, but on her own feet, she kept up with her guards. Someone followed behind her, probably with a weapon. She felt dazed and bemused by the armed guard of three—four men? Was she that dangerous?

It was more likely that Abram never took chances. Glumly, she reviewed his recent actions and all the snippets and conversations she'd overheard. Abram had control of the *Pilgrimage III*—*Why didn't I look into that "buoy off-line for maintenance" story*? Given Muse 3's warning, she figured Abram controlled the Beta Priamos Station, as well as every comm point on the Priamos moon. *I've been asleep at the controls! When I put my uniform into my locker, I must have also packed away my brains.*

Time to stop the recriminations. Her guards halted at a door, opened it, and shoved her through.

"Too bad we can't watch," one said in a snickering aside to another. "It'd be like a down-home cockfight."

The door closed behind her and she paused in the dim light, her eyes adjusting. Her hands were still tied together behind her back. She saw movement but didn't have time to dodge before Parmet rushed at her, grabbing her shoulders and pinning her against the door with a heavy thump. Her breath was knocked out of her chest.

"You! Where's my son?" he roared. His eyes bugged out of dark holes, the veins on his forehead stood out, and his face was purpled with bruises.

Her chest heaved for air as she stared into his face, so close their noses almost touched. She couldn't pull up a knee as he pressed against her. Before she could squirm into a better position, he pulled her away from the door and swung her by her shoulders. She flew across the empty room. She couldn't keep on her feet, and rolled against the wall.

His shadow loomed over her. She tried to move, but her weight rested on her back and her tied arms. As she writhed, she had a vision of a lighted passage and a redhead leaning over her. *Not again.* She closed her eyes.

Moments passed. When she opened her eyes and raised her head, she saw Parmet was back at the door in an attentive position. Listening? He moved back toward her, lightly, his finger over his lips. She tensed again.

"I had to keep up appearances, Major Kedros," he said softly, kneeling in front of her. "They overdid the drugs and I'm letting them think they initiated a psychotic cascade."

She blinked hard and stared at him for a moment. He had *somaural* talents, true, but they couldn't help a psychotic or hallucinating brain pretend to be normal.

"Have you seen my wives or son? Are they well?"

She pushed and wiggled to a sitting position against the wall. He reached to help her, but stopped when she flinched away. He waited while she cleared her throat and took some deep breaths.

"Your wives, Sabina and Garnet, were locked up with the rest of us. They were fine, when I last saw them. I don't know what's happened to your son."

Instead of the expressionless face she'd come to expect, he grimaced in a human way. He looked like a worried father and nothing like a Terran State Prince. The torture had stripped away his energy, confidence, and discipline. She knew what that felt like. Since he was the one who sanctioned similar torture for her, however, she had no sympathy for him.

"Did you tell your wives or son about me? Who I am?" she asked in a hard voice.

"No."

He sounded honestly puzzled, but she had more pressing concerns than confronting him about her mugging. "These men claim to have a TD weapon. I saw a photo and I think it's a Terran package." She kept her voice low, and didn't explain how she could recognize a Terran warhead.

"I hoped I'd dreamed the conversation I heard—they talked about the weapon."

That's not good. She pushed against the wall, trying to get comfortable. "Hey, can you do anything about this quick-tie they put around my wrists?"

"That's too much for me. My brain's been burned out, remember?"

Yeah, right. She sighed.

He told her what he'd heard between his sessions of torment. "They probably have my ship access codes, as well as those of my pilot. I still have a unit on board that can interface with a warhead, which makes things much easier for them."

"They act like they can detonate it." She frowned. "I pretended I believed them, but that's ludicrous. They couldn't know your ship would be here in G-145. Even if they get the controller unit to work, how could they possibly arm the weapon?"

He shook his head, resignation on his face. "The answer isn't my ship; it's Dr. Tahir Rouxe."

"Doctor?"

Parmet nodded. "I've got a good memory for faces. I remember him from one of our weapon test teams. If he got Abram a weapon, then he's capable of stealing a set of test codes."

"Test codes? Well, I suppose they could send it into the sun and release the exotic matter. Gaia knows what that might do, but it won't come close to a detonation." She looked around the bare room, hoping for food and water. How long had it been since she'd eaten? When would the bright wear off and she'd have to sleep? She didn't even know the time. Now she wished she'd installed a skin watch to run off her implant.

"There's a hole in the security and control mechanisms. It's classified," Parmet said.

He had her full attention. "What?"

"Our test protocols can arm and detonate a weapon, provided it goes through certain environmental conditions. Dr. Rouxe would certainly know the required sequence. The weapon has to be enabled with correct test codes, then experience a certain high-gee pattern." Parmet paused, licked his cracked lip nervously, and continued. "That'll arm the weapon and start the detonation sequence. When testing, the timing of the detonation was critical because the TD wave had to expand inside a Penrose Fold boundary."

"You dumped the temporal-distortion wave into N-space." Her eyes widened. "I thought the Minoans forbade that."

"They didn't have the means to control us, by their definition, until Pax Minoica was signed." He tried to shrug and instead, winced. "During the war, it was too expensive and time-consuming for us to test weapons the way the Consortium did, by reducing to a negligible yield and boosting the package several light-years away from the detectors. Then Ura-Guinn happened, and the Minoans pushed Pax Minoica. In the first treaty, which wasn't surprising to *us*, they stopped all TD testing. We signed, and no more dumping."

"During your tests, the Minoans didn't notice any problems with the buoys?" She wondered if the Directorate of Intelligence knew about this shortcut used by the Terrans.

He smiled thinly. "Strange, huh? We dumped low-yield TD waves into N-space regularly for years, and nothing happened to the buoy network. AFCAW detonated a TD weapon in *real-space*, and the buoy network went all to hell. Makes you wonder about the nature of N-space."

"I'll let the physicists and cosmologists worry about that. We've got to keep these nutcases from making G-145 another Ura-Guinn. I think Abram's convinced he can survive the detonation, because Ura-Guinn's sun didn't blow up."

She got up and paced the room, finding the water bottle in the corner. "Can you help me with this?" She motioned to the water with her head.

Parmet slid over, in a seated position, to pick up the bottle. He stood and held it for her as she took a swig. When she finished, she backed away.

"For some reason, Tahir is interested in my previous experience, in particular, my N-space drop at Ura-Guinn," she said. "Maybe he requires my skills."

"They don't need an N-space pilot; they can do it from real-space. They don't care about swallowing the temporal-distortion wave." He stared at her in a thoughtful manner. Nervous under his scrutiny, she turned her back and continued to pace.

"Well, since almost anybody can pilot real-space, why is Tahir obsessed with me? Particularly with my N-space drop from Ura-Guinn." She stopped and turned. "Maybe he's trying to get out from under his father's thumb. He's thinking *escape*."

Parmet blinked, as if clearing a phantom from his view. "You'll have a chance to stop them, Major Kedros."

CHAPTER 16

Many scientific disciplines were neglected due to the great exodus into space in the twenties [*Link to: Minoans, N-space travel, Minoan motives and gifts*]. Biochemical and medical research, even many basic sciences, were supplanted by physics, material sciences, and practical astronomy—anything directly supporting N-space travel and colonization.

—Putting Medical Science back on Track, Konstantinople Prime University, 2082.08.09.02 UT, indexed by *Democritus 6* under Cause and Effect Imperative

As he flailed around in oily syrup, Matt desperately wished he knew how to swim. There was no need to swim aboard a generational ship, even for tank maintenance. Later, as a generational orphan who knew he'd be planet-side only when necessary, he'd never considered learning the skill.

He thrashed as he was pulled downward. Suddenly his legs came free. His torso and head followed, and he dropped with a slurping sound onto a shiny, soft floor. A gravity generator was operating and interestingly, he came through with the correct orientation.

"Ugh." He collapsed into a sitting position and he put his hand to the floor to support himself, only to discover it felt like mucous. When he jerked his hand up, it wasn't wet or slimy. He fingered his dry jumpsuit, face, and hands. Hadn't he just come through liquid?

He looked up, then around. He was in a seamless and, excepting the rounded corners, square room. It was approximately three meters in every direction, with no openings, not even above him. Shuddering, he felt around a perimeter of semitransparent green flesh covered with slime. Nothing, however, stuck to his hands. He sniffed. Either he'd become immune to the putrid smells, or the ship itself had a milder, peaty smell than the muck through which he'd recently floundered.

Most important, he was *alone*.

"Hey, where's David Ray?" he asked loudly. When there was no response, he ramped up the volume. "Anybody listening?"

He looked up again, trying to see how he entered this space. Was that dark blotch big enough to be a person? Then he remembered some of what David Ray blabbered about titles.

"I am the owner of Aether Exploration." He tried to speak calmly. "I need to know where the other—where all rescued-persons are held."

Silence.

He tried, "I wish to know the location of the Pilgrimage general counsel, because he is wounded."

"Welcome, Owner of Aether Exploration."

The answer came so fast that he started and the hairs rose on his neck as he tried to find the source of the voice. Where was the node? Cam-eyes, on their own, were almost impossible to spot, but he could usually see where nodes were installed. Provided, of course, that the Minoans used mesh-network technology.

"Pilgrimage General Counsel should be here with me. He needs medical care." Matt directed his words to the ceiling.

There was a long pause while Matt paced back and

forth. Every time he thought of saying something, however, he bit it back.

"Pilgrimage General Counsel is delayed because of damage. Systemic cleansing must occur."

"What?" Matt pictured David Ray drowning in a vat of caustic cleaning solution. "What are you doing to him?"

As if in answer, one of the walls sighed and a slit appeared. At its bottom, David Ray came through with a slurping sound, making Matt wince, and slid to a stop on the floor. He appeared to be sleeping. Matt knelt beside him and suddenly David Ray's eyes opened.

"Well, well." David Ray's voice was dreamy. "I do feel better."

"How's the leg?" Matt stared at what should have been a ragged, flechette-torn, bloody upper thigh. Instead, David Ray's suit, more formal than Matt's coveralls, was perfectly clean and pristine. Matt looked down at his clothes, for the first time noting they looked like they'd come from the steamer. They'd been his oldest coveralls with his business logo, but the frayed collar and cuffs now looked new. The fabric was flame and rip resistant; he'd previously punctured the knee in a small triangular tear, but that was repaired also.

"There's no bandage and it's tender, but it doesn't feel infected." David Ray poked his thigh. He unsealed the seam on the inner thigh and pulled the fabric aside.

Silently they looked at the patched wounds, covered with something that looked like plastiskin, but better. All signs of infection were gone. Matt wondered if the Minoans could tell them whether the flechettes were poisoned. Before David Ray sealed his trousers, he fingered the "healed" fabric thoughtfully.

"Why'd they fix our clothes?" Matt asked.

"Perhaps they think our garments are extensions of ourselves," David Ray said quietly, frowning. "Our clothes represent our personalities by displaying patterns, colors, or text. Garments can perform computations and store our data, but in the end, they aren't part of our selves. It might be different for them."

"You think the Minoan attire is part of their bodies?"

David Ray didn't have a chance to reply. Another sigh sounded, and an elongated slit appeared in the opposite wall.

With that same slurping sound that made Matt shudder, a "guardian" entered. This was the name net-think gave the armed escorts that protected Minoan emissaries. Matt thought it was amazing that the guardian, with its head-dress of short, sharp horns set in a whirled gold and silver cap, slipped easily through the slit without even turning. Clothed in flowing black, it carried a baton, and stood head and shoulders taller than Matt, which was *tall*. Even though its garments flowed about to obscure its form, it looked bulkier than Sergeant Joyce—and Joyce had a frighteningly muscular physique. Matt faced the guardian, closer than he'd ever been to a real Minoan, and fought the urge to step back.

David Ray clutched at Matt's leg to stand up. "These don't talk," he whispered as Matt bent to help him.

Once standing, David Ray tested his leg and nodded approvingly. Then he faced the tall black figure standing in front of the slit, which was still open. Its black garments, if that's what they were, drifted about on a nonexistent breeze.

"Do we follow you?" David Ray asked.

Very slowly, the guardian nodded—once. The movement was agonizingly slow for Matt, who gritted his teeth and raised himself on his toes. He knew he was both impatient and impulsive—at least that's what Ari told him.

Now he vibrated with tension. *If the Minoans are here, they're going to chase these assholes back to their solar system!* He was also worried: The Minoan directed-energy weapons had legendary accuracy, but perhaps this was more fable than fact. How much collateral damage could result from Minoan justice?

"We're not armed." Matt hoped to move the guardian more quickly. He wanted to meet the decision maker on this ship.

"They know that," David Ray said quietly.

"Right." *They have scanners way beyond our own tech.*

The guardian nodded again and turned back to the slit. David Ray appeared to easily follow through the slit, but Matt gritted his teeth before stepping forward. He expected resistance, like trying to squeeze through a membrane. He met none, and almost stumbled with the suddenness of stepping through to the other side. He heard a sigh behind him; whirling, he saw no evidence of the slit.

The guardian's measured gait led David Ray beyond a curve and Matt hurried to catch up. The tunnel through which they traveled reminded him of a huge intestine and he stepped carefully on the floor because it disturbed him. It looked like shiny wet mucous and felt viscous to his booted feet. It sounded like liquid and made a faint sucking sound when he pulled his boot away, but when he stooped to touch it, his fingers came away dry. It just seemed *wrong*.

The guardian stopped and turned to the wall, although Matt didn't know how it could tell where it was going—perhaps those splotches were signposts? It lifted a gloved appendage and placed it on the wall. It appeared to have a five-fingered human hand, but only Gaia knew what was under the glove.

A slit appeared with that same sighing sound, an audible breath of relief. The guardian stepped through. David Ray and Matt followed, stepping into an oval-shaped room. Matt guessed this was either a control or observation deck, but he didn't see any displays or physical controls. An emissary-type Minoan in red robes stood on a raised central area, with another black guardian behind and to the side.

This was the type of Minoan featured on net-think and simulated in v-plays. Its curved, graceful horns were longer and more impressive than those of a guardian. The tips were capped in worked metal, probably precious, with strings of jewels cascading from each tip in loose loops down to an ornate medallion and collar. Some of the jewel strings disappeared under the red robes near the neck, perhaps hooking into the back of the horned headdress. As with the guardian, the face area was dark and features were distinguishable as shadows, unless the emissary turned and displayed its generic profile.

Matt almost gasped; he'd never seen that many jeweled strings on a Minoan before. He noted that the emissary's graceful gloved hands were holding two strings each, with particular jewels carefully held between slim fingers. *We're targeted with a weapon.* Matt noted the guardian had stepped carefully away from them; he glanced at David Ray, who was watching the emissary's hands.

"Please explain the explosive devices about the buoy, Pilgrimage General Counsel." The emissary's voice was pleasant, but sounded neither male nor female. It lacked vibrancy, yet analyses of Minoan voices indicated they were probably made by organs similar to human lungs, diaphragms, and vocal cords.

Since the Minoan had dispensed with pleasantries, Matt was relieved to let David Ray do the talking. The emissary had focused on him anyway, since he was Pilgrimage and had the responsibility for setting up the time buoy.

"Nonuniformed persons, whom I shall name *Criminal Isolationists*, have boarded the *Pilgrimage Three*. Through violent use of flechette weapons, these Criminal Isolationists have taken over the command and control centers." David Ray explained how they ended up in a free module while Matt looked at the strings of jewels on the emissary. Net-think suggested that the jewel combinations were controls. Matt couldn't count the jewels, separated by metal ferrules, pouring from this emissary's horns. This Minoan had a plethora of equipment at its command.

David Ray's synopsis impressed Matt. Of course, one didn't become general counsel on a generational ship without having legal-debate experience, and David Ray was a language maestro. He stayed away from personal and informal names, for the benefit of his Minoan listener, as well as highlighting every violation of the Phaistos Protocol that he'd observed. He meticulously emphasized the party at fault, ensuring there'd be no confusing Matt or himself with the perpetrators.

"We were nearly out of oxygen when we noted that several of the criminally planted mines were exploding." David Ray finished in a flat voice, without even the hint of a question.

Yes, representative of the Great Bull—are you going to explain your invisible ship, which you've never shown to mundanes before? Matt narrowly watched the emissary. Having grown up as Journey Generational Line, he didn't view these beings as gods, but he wasn't immune to intimidation; the technological level of the Minoans was so high that, for some mundanes, it was indiscernible from magic.

There was a long pause. It passed, by far, being pregnant or awkward. Matt silently prayed for patience.

The dark-gloved hands relaxed. Matt and David Ray relaxed. One hand reached for another string, unerringly picked a brilliant ruby, and twirled it slowly between the second and third finger.

"I am called to this system as contractor adviser. This is our current dilemma." With its free hand, the emissary gestured toward its right. Even though the red robes didn't show the structure of its arm, the movement didn't feel human. This made Matt shiver.

A holographic display beside the emissary appeared and showed the organic outline of the Minoan ship, marred by a sharp square wart on one side. *Nice display, and there's our module.* Matt was surprised by the number of red points that clustered about the ship in a regular grid pattern. Both the Minoan ship and Pilgrimage module had drifted and were now surrounded by mines. David Ray looked at Matt, who winced. He'd told David Ray that they'd be kilometers away from the mines, but he was guessing about the mine locations, since he couldn't see them.

"Knossos-ship is damaged," Contractor Adviser said.

"What about weapons?" Matt's heart was sinking.

"As Contractor Adviser, I have some offensive weapons at my disposal, but they cannot be used because of damage to Knossos-ship."

Of course. Why isn't anything *going right?* Matt clenched his fists.

As the hours passed, Floros's snide comment about absurdity would replay in Oleander's head. *Even if we get into the system, we're absurdly hobbled,* Floros had said, *We need three-point insertion and assault.* After making another plea to Colonel Edones, Floros threw her hands up and apparently accepted the conditions imposed by Pilgrimage Headquarters.

Once the crew of the Terran frigate arrived, Oleander sat with eleven other junior officers as Captain Floros did what the Directorate of Intelligence did best, which was provide information on the opposing threat. The briefing was thorough; Floros tried to identify every ship that might exist inside G-145.

"Since a range of advanced surveillance equipment and telebots is available at G-145 for the explorers and archeologists, we should expect to encounter both standoff and close-support jamming. If so, ship-to-ship comm and weapons targeting may be affected, but our worst enemy will be real-time data."

Hands raised, questions started, but Floros squelched everything by raising her voice. "We can't access the buoy's data channels. Therefore *there will be no FTL data available.* Period."

There was stunned silence. Finally, one of the older Terran officers—Oleander wasn't sure of his rank, considering that he wore a subdued uniform—raised his hand and asked, "What weapons and weapon systems do these isolationists have?"

"Glad you asked, 'cause that's next." Floros tapped the podium and a list displayed on the wall above her, with classification of "Secret: Source Protection Required."

Oleander wondered what source the Directorate might be protecting. Where did they get information regarding the isolationists' inventory? She put aside her questions to concentrate on Floros's briefing.

"They'll have standard poor-man weapons on their vehicles, such as kinetic spikes, perhaps with smart guidance. We also know they have mines, lots of mines. They have only one military weapon system: the State Prince's retrofitted MIL-8440 Gladiator, now listed as an unarmed TM-8440."

There were snorts around the room. The tension level lowered. Most military ships sported active and smart armor. They could avoid mines and kinetic weapons with normal sensors or confuse targeting systems with chaff; FTL data no longer looked necessary.

Lieutenant Maurell, the junior weapons officer on the *Bright Crescent*, sat next to Oleander. He raised his hand and got a nod from Captain Floros.

"It sounds like these isolationists will be embedded about the entire system. We'd need three-point insertion, you know, to strike both space and ground facilities. Why aren't we sending a destroyer or at least a Paladin-class cruiser, with shock troops and an escort of corvettes. . . ." His voice died away as Floros's face darkened.

Oleander crossed her arms. She leaned back to get a better view of the other junior officers. *This'll be interesting to watch.* Colonel Edones and SP Hauser had debated this point into exhaustion: How much information should be released to the crews? Edones argued that many needed to know the threat to be effective, while Hauser had to be convinced, specialty by specialty.

"The following information is highly classified and

given on a need-to-know basis." Floros used her official briefing voice. "Since you're all involved with offensive or countermeasure systems, you need this information. The isolationists have what's equivalent to a *Mark Fifteen temporal-distortion warhead*. They have a good chance of detonating it, and guess what? Instead of having to cobble together some jury-rigged controller, they have a retrofitted MIL-8440 Gladiator *that still has an MCU-15A controller*."

There were curses and exclamations. Floros overrode them all as she continued. "Even though the controller is disabled, we've figured out how it can interface with the package. If we can figure it out, then we must assume they can. They're not as stupid as Qesan, their previous leader."

There was muttering as everyone dealt with the possibility they might be transitioning as a TD weapon detonated, lost forever in N-space. Hardly better, they could arrive at G-145 just in time to die. Floros waited for the room to quiet. She nodded at Maurell.

"To answer the lieutenant's question, we're taking all we're allowed to take into G-145, given our agreements with Pilgrimage. To make matters more *delicate*, Pilgrimage HQ doesn't know about the TD weapon. To them, this is a rescue mission."

Floros changed the display and showed how they were balancing capabilities. The *Bright Crescent* had longer range, better armor, and more brute firepower than the lighter Terran Defender-class frigate. However, the frigate was faster, more maneuverable, had short-range weapons, grappling capability, and packed more troops than the *Bright Crescent*.

"We've got two cutters coming in with three companies of Terran special-force rangers. They'll go onto the TLS *Percival*, while the *Bright Crescent* will squeeze in one platoon of Consortium shock commandos. For standoff battle scenarios, *Percival* will take escort role, and we'll flip that for boarding scenarios. However, we're not going to see normal tactical scenarios—I'll turn this over to Lieutenant Oleander for special weapon issues."

Oleander stood up, and she couldn't help feeling a little nauseated. This wasn't an exercise or training; this was the real deal. People were going to die. How many lives were lost, how much success the mission had, could turn upon the weaponry and armament selected. She went to the podium and touched it, loading her first classified slide. As she glanced at the armament list, she felt calmer, more confident. The dual-flag command staff had already approved this load.

"We have to remember these people have every reason to defy the Phaistos Protocols," she said. "That means the buoy channels are probably mined and we all know a ship coming out of N-space can't have smart armor activated. We'll have only passive armor, with no ability to avoid or reduce damage. That's why *Bright Crescent* will drop first."

She saw Lieutenant Maurell's face go white. Her other crew members tensed. *I'm only starting, guys. It gets worse.*

CHAPTER 17

The best target is a small community that can be cut off
from its civilizing authority.

—*The Cause, Qesan Douchet*, est. 2073.011 UT, indexed
by *Heraclitus 24* under Conflict Imperative

"Isn't this going to set off alarms?" Joyce paused before
opening the door. They'd had a tricky time getting to
the exploration equipment storage lockers undetected.

"There aren't any security alarms." When Maria noticed
his surprise, she gave him a withering look. "We're a cooperative scientific research mission. Why would we need
alarms and monitors?"

After she closed the door behind them, Joyce muttered, "Perhaps this unsecure environment attracted the
isolationists."

"I wondered that myself." Maria touched glowing symbols on the wall and the ceiling gave them low light. "Even
though I love to blame Aether Exploration for the chaotic
situation here on the moon, I admit I've seen similar situations in other newly opened systems. It was mayhem on
J-132's Ambra, for instance, with thousands of contractors
crawling over its surface."

"Still doesn't explain why they chose this system."

"Maybe they thought they'd get a cache of usable alien
technology. Perhaps they're interested in the artifact."

Maria led him past crates and tanks that stood in orderly rows.

"Yes, the *artifact*." Joyce shook his head; what could they want with that? It had been nicknamed "the most extensively studied space junk in history" by the Feeds.

Maria opened a large locker set against the wall near the Builders' airlock. The nameplate read BOEING-ZHOU-KUNAL and had the seal of the Terran space forces underneath. The locker held three EVA suits. Joyce was dismayed to see that they weren't the self-fitting type. It'd take at least an hour to fit the suits, get them on, and test them.

"So we're decided?" Joyce looked at the tall woman searchingly. "We're going out there and waiting to hop a ride on the elevator? It'll be dangerous; we can't be assured we'll have enough air."

"I know. But it's the only escape we have." Maria tossed him a pair of gloves.

"You'll have a chance to stop them, Major Kedros."

Isrid hadn't intended to slip into an altered state, but as he relaxed against the wall, he sensed Major Kedros's aura. She radiated a deep blue-purple, shot with sparks of turquoise. The light scent reminded him of the sea air on a shore he'd visited on Quillens Colony. It was almost as he remembered it, except for a flare of orange-red that licked its edge. He slowly glanced down; his familiar orange-red glow now had sparks of turquoise.

Maria had warned him. *There's now a connection between you two*, she said when she reminded him that significant events or debts could connect two auras. Torture, blackmail, saving each other's lives had apparently tied them together. He blinked. The auras were gone.

"Why do you think I'll have any chance to stop them?" she asked. "You sound like you're sure."

Looking at her face, he knew how she'd received the old bruises, the ones on the other side from her recent injuries. He'd answered her honestly—no, he hadn't told his family about her identity. Sabina privately boasted about attacking Kedros, after the fact, to needle him. She wanted him to know she had access to classified information, but years of living and sleeping with Sabina created chinks in her *somaural* armor that he could interpret. Sabina had intended to kill Kedros on the station, but when the time came, *she couldn't.*

Now, considering the entwining of auras, he might know why he and Sabina had both showed mercy to Kedros. But he didn't have anything close to a *scientific* hypothesis and he wasn't going to speak of this to anyone, until he knew more. *That's only if we stop these madmen from using the weapon.*

"I think Rouxe may be planning an escape." Isrid tried to focus. "It must have taken years of manipulation and planning for Abram to maneuver Dr. Rouxe into a position to steal the test codes. It's hard to understand the kind of hate that would drive a father to use his son like that, and waste his son's life."

"That kind of hate?" Her voice was quiet. "The kind that drives people to torture others?"

He met her gaze squarely and without flinching. "You may not believe me, but I would never sacrifice my son to satisfy my revenge."

Ariane believed him. She swallowed, her throat tight. Her shoulders ached, her arms hurt, and her wrists burned. Parmet slid down to a sitting position again, clearly exhausted. Not feeling much better, she leaned against the wall. The light panels above lit the space dimly; her eyes had adjusted and she saw the havoc the torture had done to him.

"So you think Rouxe wants to escape, but how does that help us?" she asked. "I'll never be allowed near the weapon, and Abram's covered every contingency I can think of."

"Be prepared. If you get near my ship, try to sabotage it. The onboard controller gives them an easy way to enter the test codes."

"I'll never get near your ship, because they're not *that* stupid. If the controller is destroyed, will it stop them?"

He shook his head. "No, they could still jury-rig an interface. But you'd slow them down."

"Then all they have to do is yank your weapon about and it'll arm! Pretty piss-poor design, if you ask me." She snorted.

"They needed those test codes, which were classified and protected. Rouxe went through a lot to get those codes and I doubt he'll let anybody else enter them. If he wants to keep you close, go along—"

Their whispered conversation was interrupted by the sound of someone activating the outside lock. Parmet slid quickly toward the corner and crumpled up. Ariane moved to the other side of the room. When the door opened, she was standing with her back to the wall, her eyes wide.

"He's insane." Her voice cracked. "Get me out of here."

Tahir walked in, his weapon holstered, followed by a man who looked like he was Autonomist. Two more tribal—or family—henchmen stood at the door. Luckily, Emery wasn't present.

"Glad you're still alive." Tahir seemed different. His stance was relaxed, confident, with the air of a man who'd set a plan into action and was watching it unfold. He cocked his head as if assessing her, weighing her abilities.

"Can't say the same for you," she answered.

"Do you know what the arc of retribution is, Major?" he asked.

"No, but I can guess." The phrase implied justice or punishment, probably for her.

"There's a belief among my people that there's a symmetry to great deeds, both good and evil, such as your destruction of Ura-Guinn. Your salvation can come in the form of doing the same again, this time for a just cause."

She kept her face blank. Was she being offered a way to sabotage Abram's plans? Perhaps they were *that* stupid, but if so, they wouldn't expect her to cooperate gracefully.

"You think I'll pilot your ship?" She kept an edge in her voice. "What do I get out of this? A few personal freedoms in the future?"

"You have no future. But you can have salvation when justice is served." Tahir replied in a level voice, but his eyes flashed a warning as they darted to the men accompanying him. He seemed to be asking her to be his conspirator.

A henchman in the doorway said something sharp in another language. Tahir nodded and grabbed her upper arm. She winced.

"If you're going to drag me around and make me run a ship, how about untying my hands?" She kept her tone flippant and, not surprisingly, Tahir's eyes narrowed with suspicion.

"Don't bother," said the Autonomist henchman. "I'm piloting." He pointed a stunner at her. He was too close, but if she jumped him, the men in the corridor would ensure there'd be no escape.

"Careful, Julian." Tahir motioned him back.

"There's no need to bring her along, and you'd better not endanger this mission." Julian's accent carried the nasal vowels of New Alexandria, an Autonomist world. "I don't give a shit about your retribution voodoo."

"But Abram does." Tahir ended the conversation. He cut the quick-tie, and she nearly yelped from the pain in her shoulders. He retied her hands, this time in front of her. As he tightened another quick-tie around her bruised wrists, he added, "Your cooperation isn't necessary for justice, but it aids in your salvation."

She grimaced. *Thank Gaia I don't have to pretend to join these idiots—but I could have done without the quick-tie.*

Parmet didn't stir once during this process, and their captors no longer seemed worried about him. When they opened the door and escorted her out, Julian glanced back and shrugged. They turned a tight thirty-degree corner and there was the beginning of the tunnel to the elevator. A familiar figure waited at the first airlock: Emery.

"Why the surprise, Cousin? You knew you'd never be entrusted with this mission." His tone was mocking.

"I know." Tahir's voice was quiet, but Ariane saw ligaments stand out on his neck. "But I thought Abram would be sending his *best* man for this mission."

Emery's face twisted in a snarl.

"Cut it out, you two." Julian kept the younger men on track, as he pushed Ariane forward.

They went through two temporary airlocks and a wide tunnel with an arched ceiling, before they arrived at the elevator to Beta Priamos Station. The lights along the elevator door frame flickered as each person stepped in, and the panel displayed, FOUR PERSONS RIDING. ADD ADDITIONAL BAGGAGE BELOW OR PRESS START FOR LIFT CALCULATION.

Emery viciously punched START with his finger. The elevator jerked a little as it started moving, and then displayed its arrival time calculation.

"What's the matter with this thing? We should be able to get there in three hours." Emery was obviously smarting from Tahir's comment as he commanded the elevator to adjust its lift. "Yes, I authorize more weight, you stupid thing!"

"Strap in, everyone," Julian said.

Ariane quickly looked away from the elevator's controls over to Tahir, who was watching her somberly. Tahir had more schooling than Emery; would he notice that the elevator indicated it had to lift more than four hundred *extra* pounds? It was compensating, approximately, for the weight of two people in EVA suits.

"Three hours, minimum time," muttered Emery. He wasn't paying attention to *why* he had to keep adjusting the lift.

Tahir kept watching her, so she moved to sit on a bench away from the others and more important, away from the elevator panel. She sat, letting the self-tightening webbing form about her.

"At last." Emery strapped in.

Emery and Julian were probably thinking about their glorious suicide mission. Tahir might be wondering how he would get her cooperation, perhaps for a last-minute N-space drop. She glanced at the panel, which had darkened, and placed her hope in the extra weight riding on the outside of the elevator.

Maria said the frequencies used by their suits could be monitored by their comm center, which had been overrun by the men Joyce privately called the "crazies." Because of this, they used no comm, other than hand signals and the vacuum-rated slate Maria was carrying.

This is the fucking stupidest *thing I've ever done.* After another bout of swearing with no audience, Joyce turned and gave the thumbs-up acceptance wave to Maria. This was their third and last try.

It was idiotic wandering around in an unarmored civilian environmental suit when there were crazies about with flechette weapons. If this were a military mission using the proper equipment, he'd have a military-grade, self-sealing suit that sported exoskeleton-supported armor. He'd also have spread-spectrum chaotically encrypted communications support. Instead, here he was, hiding from hostiles on the surface of a moon without atmosphere, in a civilian suit made of the same stuff as self-sealing drink and food packs. *Like I'm a fucking sandwich.*

Joyce sighed. They'd already tried this twice: They got suited up and cycled out the airlock, made their way to the elevator structure, crawled through the access gantry, then waited until their air supply fell below the threshold needed to get to Beta Priamos Station. At that point, they reversed the trip, went back through the Builders' airlock, and got full tanks.

This time, if they went back, there were no filled tanks waiting for them. They could fill previously used tanks, although Maria said that would take them past the comm center. It was unlikely the crazies would allow the two of them to lug tanks past that area without questions, or violence.

The twilight outside had deepened, but he could still see by the glow of Laomedon's edge. Maria had warned him that Priamos, tidally locked with its face toward Laomedon, would soon be going behind the huge gas giant and losing the warmth and light of the sun. They had to feel their way along the ridgeline that marked the upper part of the Builders' ruins. Maria didn't want to chance using their helmet spotlights, so she led while Joyce followed the dim controls on her arm.

Once again, they crawled through the maintenance gantry and made themselves comfortable. They were on the elevator's outside crate that collared a cable long and strong enough to reach the station, courtesy of carbon nanotube manufacturing. They waited for somebody to use the elevator, causing the internal cargo hold to push through its airlocks and slide into the crate.

They calculated they had approximately an extra hour of air beyond what they needed for the long trip up to the station. Joyce checked that his alarm was set correctly, then settled into his snoozing spot. He had carefully selected this resting place, near a smooth wall, considering the fragility of the civilian EVA suits. No sharp edges, thank you very much.

He thought he'd just sat down when his alarm went off. His eyes flew open and he squinted at the heads-up display in his visor. An hour had already passed; Gaia, he must be tired. How long had it been since his last sleep cycle? He should have taken some bright, but he hadn't brought extra doses with him down to the moon. *You didn't prepare— sloppy work will get you killed, Joyce.*

Maria was gesturing, indicating there was activity below. He got to his feet, not easily done in these civilian suits, and stepped close. She held out the slate and he put the contact on his glove onto the pad for local secure communication.

"Someone's loading the internal elevator," she said, her voice sounding strange from the compression algorithms.

"Our extra hour's up. It might be safer to go back."

"We've got a leeway of ten minutes."

"We've got an *error* of plus or minus ten minutes," he said. "Can your lungs handle the minus side?"

"I can do this." With that, she pulled the slate away. She put it on her upper arm, where self-tightening webbing secured it. Then she carefully stepped over the crosspiece at the edge of the enclosure and onto the elevator crate.

Joyce followed. They secured themselves to the crate by lying down between raised struts and using webbing that came with the suits. He hoped that whoever was riding or transporting cargo on this thing didn't dawdle.

After hesitating during the initial hookup, the crate moved quickly enough to satisfy him. As the crate rose out of the cradle, he didn't want to look up at the tiny station above because he thought it'd give him vertigo. However, looking at the dark side of the hulking gas giant, Laomedon, made the elevator feel puny and his perch even more dangerous. Space wasn't any better; anyone who'd been in vacuum looking out into the dark expanses knew that such contemplation would eventually shrivel the soul.

So he turned and looked at the struts, admiring the nano-manufactured, ultrapure steel. He focused on the heads-up time display: more than two hours to go. He could continue to marvel upon the advances of material science—he snorted—or he could sleep. Reaching awkwardly to his wrist control, he set an alarm to wake him before the crate slid into the station.

The elevator ride up to Beta Priamos Station was unbearably long and yet much shorter than Ariane hoped. Luckily, it was quiet and the men left her sitting alone with her thoughts.

She leaned her head back, closed her eyes, and tried to plan. Unfortunately, she wasn't good at this thing called planning. Matt, like all her supervisors, said she was good in a crunch. Her military commanders had called her "quick thinking" and "coolheaded under stress," but no one praised her planning or strategic thinking.

With planning came uncertainty, gnawing at the back of her brain. If she let it grow, the only place she could silence the sound of her disintegration would be at the bottom of a bottle. There were no bottles here, and no place to hide from her responsibilities.

You think too much, Joyce said. He was right. These idiots who followed Abram had no idea of the hell they were about to unleash upon G-145. Her resolve hardened. *They also have no idea what* this *Destroyer of Worlds will do to prevent another TD detonation.* She'd take the entire station out in a ball of fire, if she could. *How's that for an arc of retribution?* She glanced quickly at Emery, noting that he alone wasn't dozing.

She closed her eyes. They were approaching Beta Priamos; she felt the odd effects of its gravity generator above them and her webbing squirmed and tightened. She didn't have a plan yet. She opened her eyes and saw Emery staring at her.

"What the hell," muttered Julian as he reached for a barf bag. Luckily for all of them, it was self-sealing and clung to his face as he started to vomit.

"Still getting your space stomach in shape, Julian?" She ladled on the fake concern. "Perhaps you shouldn't be piloting this important mission."

Julian snarled something that might have been "Fuck you."

"Sorry, can't hear you."

"Stop it, Major," Tahir said.

Emery looked amused, but his attention was on the docking display. They felt the interior elevator car disengage from the crate with the carbon nanotube cable. The elevator car moved toward its airlock in the ring.

"Time to go," Emery said. The door opened and he checked the passageway with his pistol ready. He motioned for them to disembark.

The station seemed as deserted as before, but Ariane figured it was, nominally, under isolationist control. She wondered briefly about Joyce; had he made it back to *Aether's Touch*? There was also that extra weight the elevator carried, but since no one had rushed out of the elevator maintenance bay to rescue her, she couldn't waste time worrying about whoever or whatever had hitched a ride.

Emery and Julian went in front, their weapons ready. Ariane walked behind them, followed by Tahir. She gained a little hope from their caution, since it might mean they didn't have the entire station locked down.

The elevator docked on ring five, but the class C docks were located on ring three. When they went through the connecting tubes and entered ring three, Ariane was pleased to see Emery turn to the right. He'd lead them right past *Aether's Touch*.

She noticed the men were unused to station gravity and the curvature of the floor. Their footsteps were hesitant, sometimes stuttering. She'd have to plan this right, because she wasn't intending to escape. Slowly, in preparation, she shortened the distance between her and the men in front of her.

When they had almost passed the corridor to the slip, she darted and brushed by Emery.

"Stop her!" Tahir yelped.

Emery reacted quickly by tripping her. She went sprawling toward the cam-eye connected to *Aether's Touch*. With her hands tied in front of her, she softened the fall. She managed to mouth her message before his boot came down hard on her back. Then, as he grabbed her collar and hauled her back toward the other men, she mouthed her message again.

"Is that your ship?" Tahir asked.

She didn't answer.

"That slip is leased to Aether Exploration," Emery said. "We haven't broken the security yet. It's more sophisticated than the Terran ships or freighters."

"We've got the pilot right here." Tahir pointed at her with his pistol.

She flinched and wished he wouldn't do that, considering his weapon skills, but this was a delaying tactic if ever she heard one. She tried not to look hopeful.

"We don't have time." Once again, Julian reminded the others of their mission. "We have to get the full benefit from Laomedon's eclipse."

His comment prodded the others into moving. Once on Parmet's ship, they climbed up to the control deck. Some one on-station had prepared the ship for undocking and when she saw the status boards, she knew they also controlled the Command Post. CP had already transferred control of the docking clamps to the ship.

The TM-8440 had two pilot seats because it separated N-space from real-space functionality, making it easier to crew the ship. Because this was a much larger ship than *Aether's Touch*, and originally military, there were more stations on the control deck. Comm, weapons, and command all had separate stations and seats.

Emery went immediately to the weapons station. She noted, with a sinking feeling in her stomach, that the console was active. These isolationists had been busy; they had already used the controller to cobble together an interface to the raw warhead.

As she expected, Tahir pushed her into the N-space piloting seat. It put her too far from the real-space controls; she'd be unconscious or dead before she could grab control of the ship. *So much for flying us into a rock.*

As Julian went through a stripped-down coordination with CP to undock, she examined the N-space console in front of her. Parmet's Penrose Fold referential engine had gone through a diagnostic test two days ago, probably right after they docked. She realized that she'd docked at Beta Priamos Station thirty hours ago. The bright loaded in her implant was gone; she now ran on adrenaline alone, her enhanced metabolism kicking in.

"We're unlocked and pushing away," Julian said. "We've got the gravity generator online, so we can do full boost."

She looked at the blank diagnostic display at her station. Slowly she moved her bloody and bound wrists to rest on the console, and surreptitiously pressed the status query command. The view port displayed the result, "PFR engine uninitialized. No license crystal installed."

Emery laughed harshly and she turned to see him watching her. "You didn't think we'd leave that engine up and running, did you?"

Yes, she had. She'd underestimated them. She'd been lulled by Tahir's talk of N-space drops, forgetting that a Penrose Fold referential engine couldn't operate without its license crystal. *Stupid, stupid, stupid of me.* She stared at Emery, remembering him taking out his wand to use on Colonel Dokos. Hatred flooded her face with warmth.

"The crystal's safe with Abram, down on the moon." Emery turned back to his weapons display.

"Go to hell." Her voice trembled with rage.

Julian signed off with Command Post. Emery and Tahir ignored her. She watched the display of Beta Priamos Station dwindling slowly behind them. Ahead was G-145's sun; Julian was punching in the burn parameters.

She was out of options.

CHAPTER 18

We've analyzed comm fragments and estimated the casualties in Ura-Guinn. The population of the innermost habitat was lost with the initial coronal mass ejection. The populations on the primary planet and corresponding habitat had protective magnetospheres, plus warning, so there were initial survivors. This work has been hardest on the Terran researchers. . . .

—*Journal of Marcus Alexander*, Sophist at Konstantinople Prime University, 2105.331.12.05 UT, indexed by *Democritus 17* under Cause and Effect Imperative

"If you don't have weapons, maybe you can use a squad or two of these guys to take back the *Pilgrimage*." Matt jerked his thumb at the guardians. "The generational ship doesn't have stand-off weapons."

David Ray winced visibly and shot him a warning glance. Confused, Matt snapped his mouth shut. He thought it was a good idea. *Apparently not.*

"As Contractor Adviser, I'm not equipped to handle confrontation with weapons, beyond taking protective measures." The emissary made a gesture of apology. "I have requested a warrior interface. We must wait."

"You have a comm channel through the buoy?" Matt leaned forward.

"No. The buoy is not available for communication."

His hopes fell. However, the Minoan's answer begged

the question as to how they'd entered the system in the first place. Did the Pilgrimage ship line negotiate secret codes with the Minoans too?

"Contractor Adviser, we hoped—," began David Ray.

"All tactics must be coordinated with the warrior interface. Please wait." The emissary cut him off with uncharacteristic speed. Its fingers twirled a bead and the hologram changed to a distant view of a star field. When its head bent, it became motionless, but for the robes that gently billowed.

David Ray motioned to Matt to step farther away from any of the Minoans. "I think that's the signal for 'go speak among yourselves, mundanes, and leave me alone.' "

"No kidding. Do we have privacy?"

"I don't know. I doubt it matters." David Ray looked at the two motionless guardians. "We won't be allowed to leave until the warrior shows up."

"Yeah, but where's he—it—been all this time? It's obviously on this ship."

David Ray lowered his voice until he was barely breathing his words. "I'm beginning to think these guys are manufactured as needed, and I'd be curious if I wasn't scared *shitless*."

Matt's eyebrows rose and his voice lowered in kind. "Why?"

"We've historically interacted with these two types." David Ray jerked his chin toward the emissary and the guardians. "But there're also the warriors. They're ruthless, by our standards. They commanded and executed the attacks on Enclave El Tozeur."

"Maybe that's what we need," Matt shot back. "Maybe they can kick these assholes all the way back to New Sousse."

"Be careful what you wish for." David Ray frowned. "We don't understand their moral structure and we've only seen Minoans function within our legal system. Given past experience, if they bring in their warriors, human life won't weigh much in their battle tactics."

"How'll we know—"

A sighing sound made Matt jerk around and he watched a slit appear in an area of a wall. He gasped at the height of the figure that stepped through; the ceiling above had to dimple, like someone sucking in their stomach, to let the horns pass. This Minoan, from boot soles to horn tips, stood almost a meter taller than the guardians.

There was no question as to its occupation. Its weapon was similar to the guardian batons but longer and with raised decorations in gold at one end. While the emissary's outer robes were red, the warrior wore the shorter black robes of the guardians, but with gold trim. Its horns seemed carved of pure ebony. They were sharp and uncapped, lacking the emissary's strings of jewels that went to the back of the headdress. Instead, the warrior wore a high-collared torque of golden metal that had short strings of jewels hanging from it. There were plenty of control surfaces on that torque, which plugged into the back of its headdress.

The two guardians went down on one knee, while the emissary nodded slowly—once.

"I pass over control of Knossos-ship," Contractor Adviser said to the tall figure.

David Ray drew in a sharp breath. He leaned close and muttered into Matt's ear, "People are going to *die*. Possibly in vast numbers."

The warrior strode past Matt and David Ray as if it didn't see them. Above its horns, the ceiling kept contorting in waves to avoid getting gored. Matt watched these movements with a combination of nausea and awe—*sort of like our body-forming chairs, but better.* David Ray poked him to direct his attention toward the Minoans.

The guardians backed against the walls. Over the holographic display, emissary faced warrior and Matt couldn't tell who was in charge of whom. The warrior loomed taller, yet the red-robed emissary didn't appear intimidated. Matt frowned; what would a frightened Minoan look like?

"Knossos-ship was not to be witnessed."

Ah, so it does notice us. The warrior, however, didn't gesture or look at Matt and David Ray. Its voice wasn't as smooth as the emissary voices that Matt had heard, both personally and recorded.

"Damage of Knossos-ship was unavoidable, as was rescue under Humanity Phaistos Protocol," Contractor Adviser replied.

"Explain."

At this point, Matt expected Contractor Adviser to launch into an explanation, where he and David Ray could interject their comments. Instead, both Minoans reached for a bead. Contractor Adviser twiddled what looked like a priceless ruby while the warrior touched a purple crystal, perhaps an amethyst. Over the display, they touched fingertips and Contractor Adviser's jewel glittered.

They were probably doing nothing more than near-field data exchange. ComNet users did this all the time by touching node-enabled surfaces to transfer data with their implants. But when the Minoans did data exchange, it looked more impressive. There was nothing like sparkling jewels to make the process seem magical. The Minoans' fingers dropped from their respective jewelry and the warrior turned slowly to look at Matt and David Ray.

"Contractor Adviser, please introduce Pilgrimage General Counsel and Owner of Aether Exploration to the warrior—er—interface?" David Ray spoke quickly, with an atypical stutter.

Matt figured he should put a lid on the smart-ass remarks that often spouted from his lips. He tried to look quiet and unassuming, which wasn't difficult in this roomful of seven-foot-plus aliens.

"I have done so, Pilgrimage General Counsel." The red-robed emissary gestured toward the warrior and stepped back from the holographic display. "This warrior has level-three authority, and command of all units within this solar system. You may address this warrior as Warrior Commander."

"I'm honored to meet you, Warrior Commander," David Ray said.

The warrior, who faced the holographic display and fingered a string of beads on its torque, ignored David Ray's words. The display zoomed to show the square wart of the Pilgrimage module on the side of the ship. The wart started to flash, giving Matt the distinct feeling that the warrior was going to jettison it into the minefield.

"No! Please!" David Ray came to the same conclusion and moved toward the display.

The Minoans in the room didn't acknowledge David Ray's words or movement. The guardians remained motionless. The emissary and warrior might have been statues, except for the whispering movement of their robes in the fictional breeze.

"*I* am the only Pilgrimage authority here." David Ray's voice cracked with desperation. "Your actions must have *my* approval!"

Laws. We say that Minoans always follow the rules, but perhaps we should say they follow laws. Matt remembered Nestor talking about Minoans and the differences between rules and laws. *A law is a codified rule, which has more than convention behind it,* Nestor said. *We know Minoans obey our laws, but we don't know if they follow our societal rules and conventions.*

"Pilgrimage General Counsel is correct. This system is sovereign to the Pilgrimage ship line." He tried to use a calm, authoritative tone.

David Ray gave Matt a glance of gratitude, mixed with apology, that said he should have thought to say that himself. Then David Ray jumped backward as the warrior rotated to loom over him.

"Does Pilgrimage approve the use of the module to detonate mines that threaten Knossos-ship?" The warrior's voice had a deep grating sound that set Matt's teeth on edge.

"No. That module contains vital Pilgrimage assets."

The room was silent as the warrior appeared to ponder David Ray's response. Its gloved fingers stopped moving. "What action would Pilgrimage suggest is most effective, given the tactical situation?"

Personally, Matt didn't have a clue. He looked helplessly at David Ray, surprised to see the mild-mannered attorney square his shoulders. David Ray poked his finger into the holographic display at the green triangular symbol, which represented the buoy. "I agree we must clear the buoy arrival channel. If your ship took damage, our ships will fare worse. But my module is *not* a mine-clearing tool. There has to be another way." David Ray looked up at the tall, motionless warrior, his jaw set stubbornly.

Joyce had dozed off again and his eyes snapped open when the alarm beeped. He recoiled at the sight of the station looming close. The exterior lights, directed toward the outermost struts, made it look like they were going into a dark maw surrounded by brilliant teeth. When the top of the elevator moved into shadow, the light on his helmet allowed him to see the alignment shaft.

Now that they were passing the station's gravity generator, Joyce and Maria were on the "bottom" and "side" for a few moments. The webbing held him tight, but he still didn't like the feeling. They passed by the ringwheel shafts of the station, eventually feeling like they were on the "top" of the crate again. He hoped Maria had a good space stomach.

He felt the grinding of metal on metal as the crate settled in its cradle. All movement stopped and he quickly grabbed a strut to hold himself while he loosened the webbing. Preparing to jump down and follow the inner elevator, he looked over to Maria. She hung loosely from a strut with her legs sprawled strangely.

She's unconscious. Joyce did a quick three-sixty turnabout, letting his helmet light go around the maintenance bay. It wasn't pressurized. The maintenance airlock, about five meters from the crate, was the small crawl-through hatch type. Beside the hatch, to his great relief, was an emergency oxygen-supply station.

Meanwhile, the inner compartment of the elevator slid away to hook up with its airlock. He had a more urgent matter. He pressed the webbing releases and caught Maria as she fell from the scaffold strut. She wasn't a burden by weight; under construction phase, most habitats kept the gravity down and he estimated it at seventy-percent normal gee.

However, lower gee didn't discount problems from momentum. Her tall body was floppy and his suit was bulky. He struggled to get her over to the station. Once there, he pulled out the fiber-protected hose and connected it to the emergency intake on her suit, comparing her front panel to his. Her oxygen consumption was significantly higher than his, since he wasn't close to the caution point yet.

Then he noticed the flashing light on the slate webbed to her arm. Pulling her limp arm forward across her chest, he read, "At the station, I may need emergency oxygen as soon as possible. Resuscitation equipment may be required, but remember that emergency stations might report their use to CP."

Great. Even when she's unconscious, she nags. He already knew what to do, thank you, Maria. Did she really think he'd forgo helping her, in hope of staying unnoticed by Command Post?

He couldn't hear the hissing of the bleed valves or the intake of pressurized oxygen, but Maria's oxygen indicator went green. She didn't open her eyes and he couldn't take the time to query her suit to see if she was breathing. He hauled her upright, twisting, and using her suit webbing to hold her against the tanks on his shoulders and back.

Bent to carry her weight, he stepped to the maintenance hatch with Maria's limp body hanging atop his tanks, which were luckily the newer, low profile types—*although that means I'll end up as a smear on a bulkhead if they get punctured. Don't think about that, Joyce.* Tapping the plate beside the hatch caused it to go into cycle, which meant it was operating.

If there's a crazy sitting on the other side, then we're hosed. He grimly looked at the small airlock tunnel when the hatch swung open. Squeezing through with Maria on his back would be impossible. He'd have to drag her behind him.

By the time he had them both on the safe side of the airlock, he was sweating too much for the suit to compensate. He laid out Maria in the maintenance prep area, and removed his helmet and gloves as fast as possible. Searching about, it seemed to take him forever to find the CPR emergency station and grab the equipment. Before he disconnected the front panel of her suit, he pulled her slate off her sleeve because it was wildly gyrating.

"No external cardio-stim shock!" Its text shouted at him as soon as he held it in his hand. "Check pulmonary implant and attach to medical equipment."

"Okay, okay," Joyce muttered. At least Maria had shut down the audio.

He unlatched the front panel and unscaled her suit. Pulling it open and away from her chest, he frowned at her apparently seamless clothing. How the hell did it come off? He lurched to his feet, opened the electrical equipment locker, and found a portable point high-heat source used for vacuum soldering. He grabbed the neckline of her stretchy suit, pulled it away from her body, and melted his own seam.

He pulled open her clothes. Her firm breasts bulged upward from a bra like none he'd ever seen before, but he avoided staring. Below them, she had an implant between her ribs that resembled an asthmatic aid. Asthma had dwindled on Autonomist worlds, because in utero treatments often stopped it during development—often, but not always.

There's no way she should have been bouncing around

in an EVA suit. Her lips looked blue. She didn't appear to be breathing, but when he attached a lead to her chest, the equipment said her heart was beating slowly. How long had she gone without adequate oxygen? He wondered what he'd do if she had brain damage, since there were no medical facilities on the station.

The med equipment should have queried her implanted device wirelessly, but it only sat there. Nothing blinked. Her device was Terran-made and had a medical-lead plug. Would it interface with their med equipment? He fumbled around on the cardiopulmonary equipment until he found the manual lead and plugged it into her implant.

Now something was happening. Lights flickered on Maria's implant and blinked on the med equipment. Her implant hissed and he leaned back as her chest heaved. She wheezed and the implant sputtered as air and liquid spurted from it. Having a modicum of first aid training, he turned her onto her side.

An obviously painful session of choking and retching went on for at least ten minutes. During that time, he got her additional oxygen from a small tank he found in the med locker. When she was finally still, he removed his environmental suit.

"Thanks." Her voice was hoarse.

"You're welcome. That's me, Dr. Joyce. I'll bill you later." He was pleased that her brain appeared to be functioning normally. Her slow heartbeat might have been induced by her implant, for all he knew, to get her through the pulmonary stress.

"What the hell did you do to my suit?" Maria, still on her side, looked down at her chest.

"Oh, *that's* what you call that weird stretchy thing covering your body."

"It has a finger-actuated seam in front. You didn't have to ruin it." She sat up, moving carefully.

"There wasn't any time to feel you up and find the doohickey that opened it." Joyce walked along the personal lockers, naively unsecured, and examined their contents. He found coveralls that looked to be the right height and tossed them to her. "We should change our clothes anyway."

"It's hideous." She wrinkled her nose at the light blue coveralls, examining the colorful orange piping and patches on the front.

"It's clean."

"Yes, but I'll be wallowing in it."

Joyce gave her a hard glance. "That's the *point*. As you noted, these crazies don't recruit *women*."

Maria sniffed, but she stood up and started stripping down to her undergarments without any more argument.

Joyce looked away. *Damn, that woman has a body that just won't stop.* Perfection like that, even if it didn't run to his personal taste, was difficult to ignore. He had to push Maria into the part of his brain that held the women he didn't think about in *that* way. Major Kedros, for instance, occupied that compartment and he never thought about her sexually. Well, not *never*. Hardly ever.

"What about my hair? What about weapons?" Maria had dressed quickly.

He shed his coveralls and pulled on maintenance ones while she rummaged through the equipment lockers. On her back was MNX-R1 in big orange letters, which would probably outrage her Terran fashion sense. He suppressed a smile.

"Plenty of Autonomist men wear their hair long. Here on-station, my recent military cut may stand out more than yours. I'm worried that hard hats might affect our reactions, so try this." He tossed her a head rag. She watched him put his on and mimicked him, arranging hers in a way that held her hair out of her face.

"No weapons, which isn't surprising. How about this?" She tossed him something with a strap.

He put it over his shoulder before looking at it. "Plasma torch? They're not going to help against flechettes, or stunners, for that matter."

"They give us a purpose, and they can be pretty mean at close range." She grinned. "Let's get going."

If Matt could see the warrior's eyes, he'd have said he was witnessing a stare down of wills. But there were only dark shadows where the warrior's eyes would be, as if it were wearing a stocking over its head. Warrior Commander "faced" David Ray, but Matt couldn't decide whether it was considering David Ray's objections or looking at an inconvenient lump on the floor.

Surprisingly, Contractor Adviser suddenly moved, gesturing for David Ray's attention. "Please provide assessment of Pilgrimage assets on module, as justification of module's worth."

"It's a *sperm bank*, for Gaia's sake, and it's important to the Pilgrimage ship line." Matt decided to cut this short, adding, "The question is whether this sperm bank is worth our lives, as well as the lives of people on incoming ships."

Silence. David Ray looked shocked. Slowly his face and jaw loosened, making him noticeably tired and old.

"David Ray?"

"I can't make this decision." David Ray shook his head and his voice was hoarse.

Warrior Commander turned suddenly toward the display. "Pilgrimage-ship is moving."

"What?" Both Matt and David Ray peered at the hologram, as if they could change its field of view by mere examination. The warrior changed the display by twiddling its jewelry and it shrank, as if they'd moved back to view a larger part of the solar system.

"This is unexpected behavior?" asked the warrior.

"Yes. Once we configure the ship as a habitat, we convert the thrusters to station-keeping mode and stay close to the buoy."

"They must have a hell of a reason to move that ship, because it's a lot of work to move once it's in habitat mode," Matt added.

"Can you determine *where* they're going?" David Ray asked.

"This is the projected path from their current position, given light-speed data." The warrior showed a dotted orange line in the planetary orbital plane.

"You don't have FTL data from the buoy?" Matt pointed at the triangle along the ship's path, which indicated the *projected* current position.

"No. I cannot access any data channels on the buoy." Warrior Commander's voice grated like gravel on a landing strip, but the words were matter-of-fact, holding none of the frustration Matt expected from human dialogue.

He glanced at David Ray. If the Minoans couldn't get comm or faster-than-light data, then nobody could, except maybe the isolationists. "If anybody shows up to rescue us, they'll be sitting ducks."

"What tactical situation is Sitting Ducks?" asked Warrior Commander.

"He means they'd be helpless. The Terran duck is an amphibian that can't defend against predators if it's caught nesting on land," David Ray said.

"I think the duck's a bird," Matt whispered, tugging a sleeve.

"Then why do we refer to ducks being watertight?" David Ray quickly turned his attention back to the warrior. "What I'm saying, Warrior Commander, is our ships may not survive the transition. But we need a solution that won't destroy my module."

"In deference to Pilgrimage-future-generations, Knossos-ship has determined that mines can be moved without using module-two-zero-nine-eight. This process has begun, but it is slow," the warrior said.

Matt made a mental note that the *ship* appeared to be the brains of this expedition.

"Thank you." David Ray slumped. "Can we help in any way?"

"No."

The emissary and warrior became motionless except for their hands, which ranged deftly about their control jewels.

He motioned David Ray to move away. "Let's give them some room, and hope they can clear the channel."

The two men retreated to a rounded corner and a bench formed from the wall. Even though Matt shuddered when his hands touched the substance, it felt comforting to his rear end. He leaned against the wall and yawned.

"I'm happy they're not using the module, but if they don't have their fancy directed-energy weapons, what will they use?" David Ray whispered. "And what if this is a self-healing minefield?"

"Self-healing minefield?"

"Meaning it reorganizes itself if mines are destroyed or pushed out of position. The individual mines move themselves as needed."

"Great." Matt hadn't thought he could feel any more depressed. Until now.

"We can always hope these isolationists aren't as advanced as AFCAW, or the Terran Space Forces." David Ray crossed his arms on his knees and rested his forehead on his arms. He was quiet, perhaps catching a nap.

Matt closed his eyes. This was a good time to get in touch with someone with more influence. *St. Darius, now there're others involved—all the crew members on* Pilgrimage. *People I care about might die. Like Ari . . .*

CHAPTER 19

Any weapon, weapon system, or weapon delivery system with lethal capabilities cannot be solely controlled by artificially programmed intelligence. . . .

—Section XVII, Lethal Weapon Control, Phaistos Protocols, 2021.001.12.00 UT, reindexed by Heraclitus 8 under Conflict, Flux Imperatives

Muse 3 dutifully recorded and analyzed Ari's actions near the slip, as it had done when two separate groups of men tried to break into *Aether's Touch*. The burglary attempts were easily thwarted. From the recorded comments, Muse 3 learned that *Aether's Touch* had the most advanced security systems on the station and these criminals had already seized the other docked ships.

Ari's actions, however, were confusing. Muse 3 identified her behavior as under duress, with controlling captors. She broke away from her captors, but then fell to her knees directly in-line with the cam-eye and appeared to talk, yet nothing was recorded. After Muse 3 ran facial analysis programs, it concluded that Ari had arranged to pass a message that would be unnoticed by her captors.

"Stop my ship." She'd mouthed the command twice.

Perhaps a human receiving this message might understand, but Muse 3 was initially stymied by the indication of ownership. Ari didn't own a ship. Then it widened its interpretation—*pause for parameter change*—pilots often referred to any ship they piloted as theirs, and even passengers used the same phrase.

Muse 3 reviewed the significant events in the log it was keeping for Matt and Ari. First, there was a change of personnel at the Beta Priamos Command Post. Male voices replaced two female voices and the professionalism of the "chatter" went down. The unprofessional behavior indicated that these were usurpers, per *Hostile Takeover of Command and Control Centers*, CAW SEP 12.35.15.

Then there had been the *Golden Bull* incident. After CP personnel changed, the freighter, or "behemoth" as Ari called it, was given orders to disconnect for some purpose. After disconnection, it went silent and started squawking an automated distress call. At the time, this was fortuitous for Muse 3, since it was able to bounce a signal off the freighter and down to nodes on the moon's surface.

After confirmation of receipt from the slate, Muse 3 received no additional direction from Ari, and it continued to monitor the *Golden Bull* situation. Changes occurred on board the freighter, because eventually humans replaced the automated distress call. These humans weren't allied with the usurpers in CP, considering the exchange of aggressive words.

Unfortunately, Muse 3 had no way to help the *Golden Bull*. The behemoth didn't have the fuel to get to the Tithonos mining station, which was the next nearest facility where it could dock, and its crew apparently didn't want to dock back with the hostiles on Beta Priamos. It currently hovered off station and swapped threats with CP.

Muse 3 continued to monitor the CP channel. The Martian-registered ship *Candor Chasma* requested disconnection and undocking clearance. Muse 3 recorded the entire verbal exchange.

The pilot's voice, after analysis, proved to be one of the men in the corridor with Ari. Other voices in the background could be separated, but Muse 3 had to enhance them, making voiceprint analysis difficult. Enhancement of the last message from the *Candor Chasma* had an additional female voice.

"*Candor Chasma* away. Wish us success," the pilot said.

Almost simultaneously, in the background, a female voice said, "Go to hell."

As the *Candor Chasma* departed Beta Priamos Station, Muse 3 enhanced the female voice and ran the phrase through analysis. There was an eighty-percent probability that this was Ari's voice and she was under stress, although that result wouldn't stand up in Consortium courts.

Stop my ship. Muse 3 had enough supporting data to conclude that Ari wanted to stop the *Candor Chasma* from performing its mission, whatever that may be. Several actions were possible, provided the *Aether's Touch* wasn't docked with the Beta Priamos Station. Muse 3 began separation procedures.

Pause for constraint evaluation.

The final set of physical clamps was controlled from the station CP. The *Golden Bull* had initially separated with CP approval, so there were no problems. If *Aether's Touch* tried to pull away with clamps contracted, the ship would be damaged. While the damage wouldn't affect life-support or maneuvering functions, the injury to the clamp anchors would prevent docking until EVA or bot maintenance was performed.

Pause for cost analysis. The damage to *Aether's Touch* would require more money than was available in the Aether Exploration operating accounts. Matt would have to take on more debt years and due to his current fiscal position, he'd have to find more cosignatory heirs. For Consortium banks, death and the disbursement of an estate didn't close outstanding debts. Muse 3 preferred a solution with lower cost; perhaps it could impersonate Matt or Ari by requesting separation from the CP usurpers.

Pause for cause-and-effect evaluation.

It was illegal for Muse 3 to impersonate a human, although Muse 3 had risked this before when it had sent a text message to Ari with Matt's signature. However, presenting itself as a person using verbal interactions on a recorded Command Post channel was worse. So was the punishment. Such an action by an agent that wasn't registered as an AI would result in dismantlement.

However, if Muse 3 performed an illegal action against illegal usurpers—*pause for fuzzy weight comparison—pause—stop application of ruleset*. Muse 3 recognized that justification of its action was impossible. A computational entity didn't have the equivalent for saying *no guts, no glory*, but Muse 3 knew it had stepped over legal lines as it constructed its request to Command Post.

"Now that the *Chasma*'s away, I'm taking a break," the controller was saying before he turned in the open doorway to meet, face on, Joyce's boot.

Exclamations erupted from inside. Spit, blood, and teeth flew sideways from the controller's face, his head jerked backward. Maria pushed past him through the door. Joyce sent a second boot into the controller's abdomen, aiming for the solar plexus. He heard the sizzling sound of a stunner and ducked down beside the writhing controller.

"That was easy." Maria sounded satisfied.

Joyce looked quickly about. "Only two?"

"This one wasn't trained to use a stunner. He shouldn't have pressed the trigger during hand-to-hand." Maria pushed the limp body out of the chair while brandishing a ministunner. "Stand away from that one."

Joyce let her stun the controller, feeling no pity as the unfortunate man shuddered into unconsciousness. The room started smelling of urine, feces, and that strange combination that Joyce called fried sweat and blood. Pulling the controller out of the doorway, he locked the door and enabled the cam-eye security display, which is what the previous controllers should have been using. They were lazy, or perhaps they weren't trained to run CP.

"What weapons did we get?" she asked, looking around.

"This one was only packing coffee. Worse, it's the generic kind." Disgusted, Joyce nudged the man's drink pack with his boot. "I can't believe these guys took over an entire station command post."

"They had help. And we are talking about a *civilian* CP," Maria reminded him.

"We haven't seen more than, what, four crazies? They must have the real staff locked away."

Maria nodded. "That's what I'd guess."

"Garris, you piece of bastardized shit from the bowels of the Minoan Great Bull, answer me!" This invective came from a console across the small room.

Maria and Joyce turned to see a dark face with startling green eyes displayed above the comm console. The face had deep lines of anger. It sat atop a thick neck and even on the small display, the man looked like a moving mountain of muscle. The transmission origin was identified as the *Golden Bull*.

Joyce put the console to automatic before Maria had a chance to move. The display port from the *Golden Bull* showed "Hold" across it, exactly when an undocking request opened from *Aether's Touch* and received the same treatment.

"If we answer on the common channel, then everyone knows we've taken over the CP," Joyce said.

"But we could use allies. How are we going to talk to them?"

"Sure, they *look* like they're on our side. Let's first assess the situation." Joyce's eyes narrowed as he looked at the two display ports on the wall. There was a problem with the attentive pose of Mr. Journey on the right port; he was sure that particular young man was currently on the *Pilgrimage III*.

Maria started puttering about the console recently occupied by the crazy, while Joyce looked at the comm console and tried to figure out how to get the equivalent of private secure channels from it. Granted, it wouldn't have military-grade encryption, but there had to be *some* security safeguards that he could invoke without a password.

"Good, they have FTL data through the buoy. Here's the situation."

He turned around at Maria's words and looked at the display she'd sent to the wall. The solar system, as well as all artificial bodies, was rendered in two separate displays. On both pictures, the green swathes showed FTL coverage. Inside the green swathe was the buoy, of course, as well as a block-shaped grid of small objects sitting in the arrival channel of the buoy. He immediately knew what the crazies had done.

"Fuck," was all he could say.

"I'll second that." Marie tightened the display on the grid, trying to resolve one of the objects. "Those are mines, but I can't tell how sophisticated they are. They could be anything from dumb rocks with proximity fuses, to smart, self-propelled rockets with station-keeping capability."

"The Minoans are going to kick their crazy asses back down the evolutionary tree for violating the Phaistos Protocols. I just hope innocent bystanders, like us, don't get caught in the crossfire."

"That's *if* Minoan ships can survive a transition into a minefield," Maria muttered. "And last I knew, the buoy was still locked by Pilgrimage. Perhaps the minefield is there as a paranoid stopgap."

Joyce moved to stand directly in front of the displays. "Are some of those mines moving?"

"Strange as it may seem, yes. They're moving slowly and nothing else seems to be in the arrival channel." Maria tapped a command, showing velocity vectors on moving objects. "FTL data confirms it—that means whoever's running this clusterfuck can see this also."

"Why's the *Pilgrimage* moving?" He focused on another area of the diagram.

"Beats me." Maria tapped again and showed green projected paths of the generational ship and one of the inner planets. "In two hours, provided they don't change their vector, they'll cross behind Sophia One."

Sophia I was the second planet from the sun, similar to Sol's hot Mars, but with a geologically active molten core.

"Anything they'd want on Sophia One?"

Maria shrugged. "Nobody's interested in that rock right now. I don't think we've even placed sensors around it yet. Maybe the ship is damaged and they need the shade."

Meaning they needed protection from radiation. He hoped that wasn't the case, considering the huge number of people on the *Pilgrimage III*—including Matt Journey. His glance strayed back to the held call that showed Journey's picture.

"We can't do anything about the buoy area right now," he said. "What's going on around this station?"

Maria changed the display. Beta Priamos Station, as well as Priamos, were moving into Laomedon's shadow. It was an echo of the *Pilgrimage*'s movement and the similarity made him uncomfortable. Regrettably, his *feelings* didn't give him better insight.

"That's the SP's ship." Maria pointed to a squawking ID moving away from Beta Priamos Station. "Maybe he's a hostage—but where are they going? They won't rendezvous with anything on that vector."

"I don't know." Too many mysteries, and Joyce was tired of using his brain. He'd rather be doing something clear-cut and active, like kicking asses. He pointed at the freighter drifting off Beta Priamos. "Let's figure out what to do about the *Golden Bull*, all right?"

At least Maria was pragmatic and knew when to change her focus. His doubts about her loyalties quieted, since she didn't rush headlong into an attempt to save the State Prince. She brought up the CP log to figure out why the freighter was floating off the station.

Apparently, the *Golden Bull* was taken by the crazies

about seven hours ago, shortly after they took over CP. Somebody down on Priamos called Abram was issuing commands—

"Did we cut off the crazies down on the surface? Will they know we're here?" He had hoped not to alert the *entire* solar system when they grabbed the Beta Priamos Station CP. Maria's eyes widened and she, also, began checking their comm channels.

"No." She sounded relieved. "Abram has a dedicated buoy-relay channel, probably to speak real-time with the *Pilgrimage*. He's not cut off from comm, but if he tries to speak with this command post, I'm sure he'll notice our silence."

"I guess that's the best we can do. Make sure we're recording his channel. Now, back to the freighter problem."

The *Golden Bull* was supposed to install a buoy relay on the dark side of Laomedon in a stable Lagrange point. That would have extended comm coverage, but something went wrong on the *Golden Bull*: The crew rebelled—rather, they resisted the initial coup leaders and took their ship *back* from the crazies.

"Good for them," Joyce said. After Maria looked at him, he added, "I mean the anticrazies, the original crew."

"The last orders from Abram to CP were to talk the rebels into docking at level three's B-4 slip. There's a boarding party ready to take the ship."

"So the crazies want to take the freighter—back again— from the original crew, right?" He pointed to a diagram of the station. "That explains where most of our armed crazies are located. They're sitting at B-4, so no wonder the *Golden Bull* doesn't want to dock. By the way, who's the angry guy on the comm?"

"That's a loadmaster, named Harold Bokori. I'm guessing the captain and pilot were, ah, undercover crazies." Maria shrugged, apparently resigning herself to using Joyce's nomenclature. "The *Golden Bull* is in trouble because they don't have enough air or water to get to another class B dock in the system. Perhaps this was a precautionary measure taken by the crazies, or mere happenstance."

"So we've got to convince him that we're not crazies and figure out how to help him and his crew, but not let the crazies overhear anything." He wished he could turn this over to Major Kedros, since she'd mastered the art of pulling great solutions, at the last minute, out of her—*hmm*—shapely rear end. His own ass wasn't nearly as attractive, nor did it seem to be the source of any great ideas. Thinking of Kedros and her piloting, however, helped his brain grasp at inspiration.

"What about S-DATS?" he asked.

Maria looked thoughtful. "Pilots usually only monitor that channel when they're on dock approach."

The Space-Docking Automated Transmission System, or S-DATS, always squawked at a specific frequency inside a solar system. Reliable pilots, such as Kedros, monitored S-DATS as they approached habitats or stations. S-DATS would tell them the frequency for the CP channel and other general conditions on-station, *such as autopilot-docking compatibility.*

"Ship-specific instructions can be sent over S-DATS, right? The freighter might be monitoring it, considering its half-docked condition." His voice became eager. *This might work.*

"Yes, packets can be directed to specific ship IDs, but only text bursts are allowed over S-DATS. You're never going to convince him"—Maria jerked her thumb toward the fuming loadmaster—"that you're not a crazy, if all you're using is text."

"You can use text to tell him to get on a different, and secure, channel. Once you have video, you can use your powers of persuasion."

"Oh." Maria looked vaguely uncomfortable, which he thought might be her why-didn't-I-think-of-that expression.

"I'll try. If they're monitoring S-DATS and they switch

over, then I'll handle the loadmaster. You take care of *Aether's Touch*." Maria glanced at the held calls, where Matt Journey's face displayed. "And if that ship has its pilot, then I want to know how Kedros escaped the surface of Priamos."

As Maria turned away and started tapping out her text message for S-DATS, Joyce gave some thought to Mr. Journey, who couldn't possibly be on his own ship at this moment. Maria's message went through and a moment passed before the crew of the *Golden Bull* changed their comm.

"*Golden Bull* to CP. What's happening? If you're screwing with me, Garris—"

"May I help you?" Maria moved into cam-eye range with a sweet smile, shutting down the loadmaster's tirade.

He had no doubt Maria could convince the loadmaster that she wasn't a crazy. Barely listening to their conversation, he tapped out his instructions to *Aether's Touch*, trying to figure out if there was a human sitting on that ship. He wasn't surprised when *Aether's Touch* quickly responded on the channel he indicated over S-DATS, but stayed in text-burst mode.

"Is that you, Major?" he typed. Not many people in this system should know that Ariane Kedros was also in the AFCAW Reserve.

"No, Major Kedros is not available. Her orders are attached. Please release docking clamps for *Aether's Touch*."

He looked at the attached analysis, provided with video, no less. Certainly, it *appeared* that Kedros had been taken aboard the State Prince's ship, now heading in-system. It also *appeared* that she mouthed the words, *Stop my ship*. The FTL data diagram showed that the ship would be close enough to the buoy to drop to N-space within an hour. Perhaps these crazies were making an escape and grabbed the closest N-space pilot they could find. On the other hand, someone could be showing him cleverly edited video.

"If you do not release the docking clamps, Master Sergeant Alexander Joyce, both this ship and the station will be damaged."

Joyce stared at the text. A crazy couldn't know his full name and rank, but Journey's so-called automated agent would have that information. He could no longer accept Journey's protest that this was an advanced search agent with special algorithms—this was a full-fledged, soon-to-be-rogue AI.

Using Artificial Intelligence to control weapons is a violation of the Phaistos Protocols, which we've interpreted to mean that AI shouldn't even pilot ships. Of course, that's one interpretation. *But I'm not allowed my own interpretation.* The standard joke said noncoms, as opposed to officers, "worked for a living," but the flip side of the jab was "noncoms weren't paid to think."

By his eye-for-eye logic, the crazies had already flushed the Phaistos Protocols down the crapper, so why shouldn't he bend them? He glanced at Maria, who was busy with the *Golden Bull*, and surreptitiously released the clamps. Then he compounded his crime by erasing all the implicating message copies he could find.

Lieutenants Oleander and Maurell shrank to the right and hugged the bulkhead to let the oncoming commando move past in his hissing and squeaking armor and exoskeleton. In full gear, the commando's rank couldn't be determined, but Oleander had no doubt that the hard face she saw was a senior noncom.

"Do you think they *sleep* in that stuff?" Lieutenant Maurell muttered into her ear.

"All the time, son, all the time," drifted back to them as the commando continued jogging down the corridor.

Maurell cringed. "I forgot they can hear better than we can, even over the huffing and puffing equipment."

"Besides, we're all going to be 'sleeping' under the D-tranny," Oleander said.

"If you call that sleeping." Maurell grimaced. "I'll be so nervous about the transition that I'll have waking dreams."

"That's better than ending up in full psychosis." Oleander took a last look at her slate and sighed. "We're not carrying enough of *anything*, it seems. Not enough commandos, not enough antimine slugs or ammo for our rail guns. I don't even want to think about our piss-poor missile load. Luckily, there should be no need for swarm missiles."

"We're packed to the gills on the largest ship that Pilgrimage allowed. Do you think the ship line did this on purpose? This means we *have* to rely upon the *Percival*." He lowered his voice to a bare whisper, probably to avoid MilNet pickup by the nearest node. "Can we trust them?"

"To be fair to Pilgrimage HQ, they never considered this scenario and neither did we." Oleander frowned. "As to the trustworthiness of the Terrans, well, they have as much to lose as we do."

"So we can rely upon them as much as any force with differing weapon systems, tactics, and languages, who've never done a coordinated mission with us. Although the commandos and rangers seem capable of *ooh-rah*-ing at each other."

Oleander chuckled. Maurell stared at her.

"At this point, all I *can* do is laugh," she said with a shrug. "Everybody speaks common Greek well enough, so I wouldn't put communication at the top of your list of worries."

Because there's plenty more to worry about, she thought of adding, but Maurell's tense face made her swallow the words. There was no need to continue, since the yellow vector warning lights started blinking slowly, bathing the hallway in bright light.

"Take-hold warning. This is first warning for low-gee maneuver." The words reverberated through the halls in the senior loadmaster's deep, drawling voice.

"Better get webbed in," she said.

As she headed for the control deck, she tried to wipe Maurell's parting expression from her memory. She understood his anxiety, and wouldn't trade places with him for anything. As senior weapons officer, she'd see what was going on when the bright hit her bloodstream and they transitioned into normal space. While that put a heavy load on her shoulders, at least she could react or take action. Poor Maurell would be webbed into his bunk and, after he woke to transition alarms, he would be following status and chatter from his quarters until called to duty.

By the time Oleander was webbing into her station on the control deck, the vector warning lights had turned orange and Captain Janda, as pilot seat, was announcing the third take-hold warning for station disconnection. She put her weapons station through another self-test before looking around.

The buzz on the control deck was subdued and professional, with all positions manned by senior crew members; the commanders of both ships were prepared for the worst. Nobody knew what to expect when coming into real-space at G-145, so they made use of their most experienced crew members.

"Teller's Colony cleared us for departure, sir." Captain Janda was the senior pilot and making the N-space drop to G-145. On Fury-class ships, the pilot seat was dual-capable, requiring both N-space and real-space training. Captain Janda did both but had navigational and sensor support from Captain Stavros, sitting to the right of the pilot seat.

"Let's go, Captain Janda. Use maximum-allowed departure boost. Captain Stavros, shortest course to buoy channel, if you please," Lieutenant Colonel Aquino said.

"Yes, sir." Captain Stavros had a quiet voice that nonetheless carried clearly. Her fingers flashed on her console as she sent parameters to the pilot seat; she would already have calculated and stored that course.

Behind Lieutenant Colonel Aquino, Colonel Edones was webbed into the mission commander's seat and reviewing something on the slate plugged into his chair. He wore the only black and blue uniform on the control deck; everyone else was normal AFCAW Ops, wearing green combat suits. Edones's frigid blue eyes, his bland expression, even the manner in which he tapped his slate, radiated cold, hard competence. Oleander was surprised to feel comforted by his demeanor but, as she reminded herself, Edones was the sole officer on deck who had experience from the war.

Surveying the control deck, she figured the two senior noncoms had seen battle with the League. Senior Master Sergeant Albert was loadmaster, when the ship wasn't at battle readiness. Now he was responsible for damage control and sat at the damage assessment console. Chief Master Sergeant Serafin sat at tactical, her thin sharp face focused on her displays.

"*Percival* matching us, sir. *Twelve* kilometers astern and twenty degrees to port." Chief Serafin's gaze slid sideways to glance at the Terran officer.

Oleander imagined what Serafin's gut was going through, flying formation with an *enemy* ship. She and Albert put their doubts on record by vocally protesting, during the mission briefing, the presence of a Terran officer on the control deck. Colonel Edones had calmly acknowledged their suspicions as valid, but countered that Terran presence was necessary to coordinate the dual-flag mission.

Major Phillips of the Terran Space Forces, the focus of all this heartburn, sat quietly at the comm monitor station. An AFCAW staff Intell officer might operate this station, but rarely. The station was a holdover from the war because the upgraded comm stations could do everything it could, and more. Now this console was configured to prevent Major Phillips from doing anything but speaking with the *Percival*. His counterpart—*or exchanged hostage*—was Major Bernard, who currently sat on the bridge of the *Percival*.

"Comm, please remind the *Percival* that twenty kilometers was the separation distance for buoy approach." Edones's voice was pleasant.

"Yes, sir." Lieutenant Kozel, the comm officer, eagerly informed the *Percival* of their error. Kozel was the most junior officer on the deck, his date of rank three years younger than Oleander's.

"Major Phillips? I'll remind you of your duties as coordinator on this rescue mission. You're responsible for your crew observing the legal limits. Don't make me bypass you again." Edones's voice became colder and almost everyone on the control deck turned to view the Terran officer. They all knew the *Percival* had probably just breached their communications and EM security.

"Yes, sir." The words seemed to jerk out of Major Phillips mouth without his consent. He appeared uncomfortable as he nodded at Lieutenant Colonel Aquino. "Sirs," he added. The Terrans had some confusion regarding the mission commander versus ship commander roles.

"Damage Assessment, log the CommSec violation," Aquino said. He turned to exchange a glance with Edones. "And we're not even out of the system yet."

"Yessir," Sergeant Albert drawled.

"*Percival* dropping back to twenty kilometers," reported Serafin.

Oleander suppressed a smile as she turned back to her console. At least Phillips wasn't adept at *somaural* projection, which was good to know.

Three and a half hours to N-space drop. Military ships didn't verify that crew members had dosed themselves with D-tranny before dropping, so she checked her implant and its load of drugs. She verified that her implant would release the bright as close to real-space transition as possible. She had a feeling she'd need it.

CHAPTER 20

When requested, the Consortium of Autonomist Worlds has agreed to provide between one and five ships, with maximum tonnage and personnel specified in appendix 5. The hosting Pilgrimage ship will decide number, deployment period, entry, and departure of ships within Pilgrimage sovereign space. All weapon systems and munitions must be inventoried and approved. . . .

—Section III, Status of Forces Agreement Between the Consortium of Autonomist Worlds and the Pilgrimage Ship Line, 2085.210.12.00 US, indexed by Heraclitus 4 under Flux Imperative

"Command Post put that nut on hold. Serves him right." Julian triumphantly shut off the channel that previously carried Hal's arguments with CP to all listeners.

Hearing Hal's voice had given Ariane hope, although resistance on Beta Priamos didn't help her stop the TD warhead attached to this ship. She turned her attention back to Julian. He didn't have military experience. The ship was capable of monitoring two comm channels plus S-DATS. Granted, most pilots wouldn't monitor S-DATS unless they were on dock approach, but no one with military training would *shut off* one of their comm channels.

Julian, like most real-space jockeys, acted as if he were driving a planetary vehicle. Heavily reliant upon that metaphor, he stayed with the in-the-round display, showing a fake window that wrapped one hundred sixty degrees around the forward consoles. Real-space jockeys were most comfortable with cam-eye views and linear distance displays, which let them feel as if they were looking out of an airplane cockpit.

Julian set one view port on the left to the planetary orbit plane through the solar system. Over to the right side, near Ariane's position, two small view ports were open. One showed cam-eye video of Beta Priamos, now barely visible, while the other displayed the default FTL display identifying all bodies within ten thousand kilometers of their position. She glanced at it, noting their progress away from Laomedon and saw a familiar blinking ID.

Aether's Touch! She looked away. Joyce must have received her message and followed, although he'd wisely dropped out of the direct line between Beta Priamos and *Candor Chasma*. However, he hadn't had time to sabotage the civilian transponder. She couldn't let the isolationists see the *Aether's Touch*.

"Set your displays correctly," Ariane said as she leaned forward. She quickly moved her tied hands up onto the console in front of Julian's right arm and tapped.

"Hey! Stay away from my console." Julian backhanded her across the face. Considering Sabina and Abram had already worked her face over, this hurt like hell. She flew backward into her seat.

Emery and Tahir had been diddling with something at the weapons console; both looked up, frowning. What now displayed in front of Julian was the ship's route using two dimensions of time. This plot was used by N-space pilots, but could be mind-bending for the mathematically challenged. A complementary view port represented their current vector in numerical text, not graphics. She knew these would be the last displays Julian would pick.

Julian set about bringing up the representations that he understood, while Emery and Tahir went back to their discussion. Tahir had readily entered his test codes, which surprised and panicked her. If he had some sort of plan to stop the detonation, he hadn't given her any clue regarding his tactics.

None of the men paid any attention to her suggestion regarding the displays, but that wasn't the point. Muttering about a nosy bitch who didn't know her place, Julian brought back the in-the-round display. He also chose to again open the cam-eye view behind him, probably to give him the confidence that he was moving in the right direction. Its poor resolution could no longer distinguish any artificial objects against the huge backdrop of Laomedon. Since he had FTL data through the buoy and he knew safety procedures recommended an open FTL display, his hand hovered in indecision. She held her breath, but as she hoped, he chose the diagram that charted their forward course.

Aether's Touch no longer showed on any displays. She relaxed.

"We've identified fourteen possible crazies on-station." Joyce glanced at the stunned and bound figures propped in the corner of CP. "Two have been taken out. Six are waiting for you at the airlock for B-4. That leaves six others roaming around."

"The station doesn't have complete node coverage yet. There may be more—crazies—hiding about," Hal said.

Even Hal had picked up his nomenclature, Joyce noted rather proudly. *After all, it's a perfectly appropriate name.* Joyce stood behind Maria as she tried to convince the freighter crew that her plan would work.

"We think we've got an accurate count, considering what we saw down on Priamos," Maria said. "Abram took moles with him down to the surface. Particularly ones with tech skills."

"Still, you don't know if some of them are waiting on the *Hesperus*." Hal was uneasy, frowning. "We could lose the *Golden Bull*, which has a referential engine."

"You haven't got the resources to get within lock distance of the buoy," Maria said bluntly. "You tell them you're coming in, and Joyce spoofs the lights at B-4 to make it look like you're docking. That'll hold them for a while, but how long will it take you to go through the cargo-to-cargo connection with *Hesperus*, then get to the B-1 airlock?"

"We've got to pressurize the bay, since the *Hesperus* is pressurized for emergency evacuation." Somebody behind Hal said something, and he turned to speak off-line for a moment. He turned back to face the cam-eye. "And we're almost finished with that."

"So you're in?" Maria asked.

Hal grinned and winked. "We're in. After all, it was our idea to begin with."

Joyce raised his eyebrows. Maria had worked out the details, but strictly speaking, Hal was right. The freighter crew first brought up the possibility of connecting the two freighters. The cargo-to-cargo connection wasn't designed to be used under pressure, since the crew usually wore EVA suits under that type of cargo transfer. However, the bays could be separately pressurized for sensitive cargo and the *Hesperus* was already sitting there, pressurized, because it was the temporary emergency evacuation vehicle for Beta Priamos. Now they had a coherent, but risky, plan to get the crew of the *Golden Bull* to safety, quickly and quietly.

"How long until you're at B-1?" Joyce asked Hal again.

"Give us at least twenty minutes. That's *if* we don't run into any crazies sitting on the *Hesperus*."

"Can you do it any faster?" Joyce frowned. He didn't think the fake docking signals would fool the crowd waiting at B-4 for long.

"I want my entire crew safely across the cargo connection before we move through the *Hesperus*."

"Then get going. I'll start the docking lights to keep the people at B-4 entertained."

After Hal signed off, Maria sighed and looked over at the display of the men waiting at airlock B-4. They didn't hide from the cam-eye, apparently thinking that CP had cut all video feed to fool the docking ship. When she broadcasted Hal's "surrender" over the CP channel, they jittered about like bugs as they tried to figure out their weapons coverage. Luckily, they had no way of looking outside since Beta Priamos was built to protect its residents from radiation. There were no windows in the docking ring.

"You don't think they'll buy your light show for that long, do you?" she said.

"No. If they're not already suspicious that CP isn't up on voice, they'll soon be. They might send runners to find out what's happening."

She nodded, running her tongue over her teeth in a contemplative manner. "Too bad we don't have any other distractions."

"But we do. If you give me that awesome weapon you collected"—he held out his hand—"I can run around the station and create havoc."

"If you think this will work against flechettes, then be my guest." Maria dropped the ministunner into his hand.

"I can free the station's original staff. That'll be a good distraction." Joyce motioned at the diagram where they'd mapped the probable locations of the imprisoned personnel. These were locked storage areas that either didn't have a lock override or didn't respond to CP's override unlock, perhaps because they were manually disabled.

"You think that's the best thing to do right now? If you release *civilians*, you may incur collateral damage."

Joyce paused and looked at her carefully. Her expression was impassive and detached, her voice soft, but was she genuinely concerned for the safety of civilians?

A beeping alarm caused them both to look at the comm console.

"Shit." Maria showed an uncharacteristic lack of grace as she tapped a few commands. "It's Abram. He's coming up with others on the elevator. He wants to speak with CP."

"What the hell? I thought the elevator was up here—doesn't it take at least two hours to go down, even at maximum speed?"

"We've been here for at least a couple hours."

"Can you stop the elevator?"

She tapped a few more commands. "No. All I can do is simulate comm problems for a little while."

"Then I have to cause mayhem, diversions, et cetera, or the crew of the *Golden Bull* is toast," he said. "Stay quiet and keep CP locked up tight. It'll take a plasma torch several hours to break into here, so take advantage of the time."

"Be careful. You're not wearing any armor." She looked worried, but he didn't believe it for a minute.

"Maybe my charm will protect me." He checked the charge on the ministunner and ignored her snort.

"Take this for comm." She tossed him a small slate. "Remember, there're hardly any nodes out there."

After they agreed on channel and call signs, he checked the view of the outside corridor and let himself out quietly. Behind him, he heard the locks slide and engage. *Yes, ma'am, I'm off to wreak havoc and mayhem.* This might even be fun. He saluted the cam-eye before he slipped quietly down the deserted corridor.

Oleander dreamed Matt was in trouble; vividly, she saw his small prospector ship decompressing and separating into floating chunks as isolationists fired missiles. *Where'd they get missiles?*

The proximity klaxon wailed. Her eyes flew open; the bright pumped into her bloodstream and made the transition from dream state to reality seamless. No disorientation—although for a moment, reality seemed sharply surreal. She was webbed snugly into her seat. Her fingers flew over her console to check the rail guns. A different alarm shrilled from the damage assessment console.

Sergeant Albert calmly shut off the second alarm. "Explosive force registered on port ventral section epsilon, sir. No decompression, but passive armor was blown away. Assessment team on its way."

Oleander realized she'd been holding her breath. She let it out as she saw the backs of other crew members relax. The passive armor was made of protective layers of aerogel, light as air and stronger than the same thickness of titanium. The ventral epsilon section, whether port or starboard, was immediately behind the bulge of the Penrose Fold referential engine, which was almost indestructible. The PFR engine ended up being passive armor in its own way.

"We're stationary with respect to objects within one kilometer, which are all probably mines." Janda was sweating and he looked as if he'd lost at least five kilos during the drop. There was no way to tell if he'd lost hair. *Decided this was the best way to handle N-space*, he had joked earlier, stroking his shaved head.

"Active armor is initialized and operational," Serafin called from tactical. She looked over at Stavros, who was tapping frantically at her console.

The proximity klaxon still wailed. Everyone waited on Stavros.

"Navigation and sensors?" Aquino asked.

"No FTL data, sir." She slapped the console in frustration and shut off the proximity klaxon. "This is what we've got through light speed."

Everyone trained without the FTL feed from the buoy, but everyone also hoped they'd never be the ones in that situation. Oleander felt her stomach lurch as she looked at the display, which centered on their position and was slowly resolving other bodies in the system. The *Bright Crescent* was oriented inside the channel with the buoy to her stern.

She was the largest object identified on the display, embedded within a minefield.

"Is that movement out there, Chief?" Aquino asked.

Now they all saw it. Stavros changed the orientation of the display to show a two-dimensional slice that contained the buoy arrival channel. The mine coverage down the center of the arrival channel could still cause problems, if the *Bright Crescent* tried to move. Toward the edge of the minefield, an unseen semicircular shield appeared to be pushing mines, much like a waiter brushing crumbs from the tablecloth in a fancy restaurant.

Oleander watched Chief Serafin, who frowned and chewed her lip as she furiously tapped and examined diagrams. The chief wasn't one for making unjustified decisions.

"That's not a self-healing field, sir," Serafin said at last. "The individual mines aren't sophisticated enough, by my readings."

"And that movement?" Aquino asked.

"Independent of the field, sir. Whatever's doing that—"

"Whoa! Something happened out there. All my EM instruments were blinded." Muttering something about gain and saturation, Stavros adjusted her sensors. Heads lifted to watch the diagram, computationally constructed through multiple sensor inputs and readings. It warped, shuddered, and adjusted.

"Captain Stavros?" Lieutenant Colonel Aquino kept his attention on his navigation and sensors officer.

"Gotcha!" Stavros turned around to face the command chairs with a triumphant grin. "There *is* an artificial body out there."

"A ship?" Aquino asked.

"That's my guess, sir. It's actively shunting and redirecting EM radiation; that's *true* cloaking, if ever I saw it!" Stavros ran her words together in her excitement. "But there's something wrong with their profile. With that last surge, I managed to catch diffraction off hard corners—perhaps they've been damaged."

Aquino rotated to exchange a glance with Edones. Both commanders seemed thoughtful.

"It's a good bet that's *not* our isolationists, given the technology," Edones said.

Aquino nodded. "And more mines have to be cleared before the *Percival* drops in. They'd take damage from a detonation like the one we just handled."

There was a quiet pause. Nobody even fidgeted.

"Comm, prepare to send a tightbeam message to the position that Captain Stavros calculated." Edones's voice was so cool and conversational that his order didn't immediately register with Kozel.

With a start, the lieutenant acknowledged. "What channel, sir?"

"Use our standard emergency channel. Send in the clear and use low power, as if we were in local exchange range."

Lieutenant Kozel looked horrified. "Unsecured, sir? Even though tightbeam's directional—"

"Give me mike control, *Lieutenant*."

Oleander half expected icicles to grow on Lieutenant Kozel's nose, given Edones's tone. As it was, the young man's face did freeze. He gulped and set something on his console, presumably following orders.

"This is the *Bright Crescent*, registered with the Armed Forces of the Consortium, calling Knossos-ship. We request assistance, under the Phaistos Protocols." Edones repeated this twice, precisely enunciating each word.

What was a Knossos-ship? Why was he broadcasting in the clear? Oleander looked up to see the two noncoms on the control deck exchanging a tense glance.

"Acknowledged, Bright Crescent–ship. This is Knossos-ship, Warrior Commander speaking."

The response on the control deck was immediate and electrifying. Lieutenant Kozel jerked backward, and looked toward Aquino. The younger officers exchanged glances, eyes wide. Everyone recognized the voice as Minoan. Oleander turned to watch the commanders and saw a sight she'd never expected. Colonel Edones's face was pale and stark. Fear? Lieutenant Colonel Aquino didn't look any better.

Aquino whispered, "Holy Avatars of Gaia."

"They've mobilized a *Warrior*," Edones said quietly, a comment probably intended only for Aquino's ears.

CHAPTER 21

No better service can a son give his father than to sacrifice his life for the Cause, our Freedom from the interference of other cultures.

—*The Cause, Qesan Douchet*, est. 2073.011 UT, indexed
by *Heraclitus 24* under Conflict Imperative

Ariane didn't know how far off their stern the *Aether's Touch* rode. The small second-wave prospector ship didn't have weapons, unless one considered the rail guns. Every ship that traveled real-space sported at least one set of symmetrical, but independent, rail guns for clearing debris or for moving via momentum transfer. *Aether's Touch* had three pairs, of a caliber that she could barely accelerate by forty thousand meters per second squared, which might not get through the *Chasma's* active smart armor.

"It won't let me program a higher yield." Emery seemed fascinated with his weapon interface.

Tahir looked over his shoulder at the console. Ariane noticed that he still held his stunner; he hadn't relaxed, like Emery, and laid it down.

"That's because we're using test codes. Don't worry, we'll still destroy the buoy," Tahir said.

"And cause the sun to supernova," Ariane said. "That's what happens when a temporal-distortion wave flips out time dimensions at the quantum level."

Emery scowled and reached to caress his pistol. "Stay quiet, Major, or you'll be seeing your retribution early."

"Remember, completing her arc will also raise your kismet," Tahir said. "Don't listen to her. There won't be any nova."

Emery scowled at the mention of kismet, perhaps feeling he had no reason to fear justice from a higher power, or anyone else, for that matter. Ariane's opinion differed; she felt Colonel Dokos's tag against her rib whenever she pressed her elbow to her side. It fueled her anger, but she followed Tahir's lead and looked down to avoid antagonizing Emery.

She wondered why Tahir was lying. He acted as if he wanted to detonate this weapon, but she kept ready, watching. *What the hell is Tahir doing on this ship, and why did he drag me along?*

"I've lowered our deceleration. I'm shutting off the gravity generator. We'll be near arming position within the hour, so web in." Julian secured himself with his webbing.

She made motions to follow suit, awkwardly fiddling with tied hands so the quick-release tabs on her webbing were easily accessible. The isolationists had obviously disabled the safety protocols in the real-space piloting controls, but thank Gaia, Julian was competent enough to ensure they didn't end up as jelly on the bulkheads.

After that, everyone was quiet. Julian looked like he was still toughing out nausea. The other two men were probably contemplating their impending, glorious demise. She scowled. Cipher's attempt on her life had convinced her of one thing: She wasn't prepared to enter the afterlife. Not yet.

A call from Abram broke the reverie on the control deck. Since they had FTL comm, Emery answered from his console for a real-time conversation. Tahir floated to a position behind Emery's chair while Ariane pointedly showed no interest in the conversation.

"My team on the *Pilgrimage* reports an AFCAW cruiser has dropped into our minefield. Furthermore, some sort of standoff shield is moving mines." Abram's gravelly voice filled the deck and seemed flatter than she remembered. She saw all the men tense up.

"That's impossible. They don't have that kind of technology," Tahir said.

"They're Autonomist. You, *Major*. Do AFCAW ships have standoff debris shields?" Emery asked. Ariane turned to look at the business end of his flechette pistol.

"Maybe." She shrugged, but Emery wagged his pistol and gestured for more information. "If so, it's experimental."

Tahir's eyes narrowed as he watched her, but he made no comment as he turned back to face the cam-eye. He didn't believe her, but she realized he didn't care. *Why isn't he concerned about the AFCAW ship?*

Abram read off the identifier and Emery looked at her. "Are you familiar with that ship, *Major*?"

"No." She lied. There was plenty of information about the *Bright Crescent* in its public registry. Perhaps they'd take time to initiate a search in ComNet, since they had control of outbound comm.

"I want to know why they're capable of using a locked-down buoy." Abram's voice was colorless and, from the men's reaction, she got the feeling that Abram was enraged. Emery and Tahir both began babbling, each protecting his reputation at the detriment of the other.

"There're rumors of military override codes, but they won't be able to drop out," began Tahir.

"Tahir should have known this when he looked at the buoy's status," Emery said.

"We needed that controller, but Emery killed him."

"How do you know that I didn't stop him from opening the buoy?"

"Because you're so trigger-happy, we won't know anything now," Tahir snapped.

"Weren't your fancy mines supposed to take care of any incoming ships?"

"It doesn't matter." Abram's words doused the squabble as effectively as a foot grinding out a bug.

She watched them with her peripheral vision, amazed that Abram could engender so much fear in his son and nephew, even when he was a hundred million kilometers away.

"Your window for detonation has started," Abram said. "Your heroism will be remembered forever, your lives given for our freedom."

What a pompous ass! Glancing at the FTL swathe that Julian opened, Ariane first checked that *Aether's Touch* was off the display, then noticed the *Pilgrimage III* was *moving*. On the edge of the diagram, the ship was snuggling behind Sophia I so that it was entirely eclipsed, just as Laomedon currently eclipsed Priamos and Beta Priamos, just as Sophia II was eclipsing the remote science station—

Abram had planned for temporary protection of the system inhabitants. Sophia I and II, as well as Laomedon, had magnetospheres that could protect against intense solar radiation. Of course, this would work only if the sun didn't explode. It also meant these idiots were on a critical timetable.

"The detonation must occur within thirty minutes. I have to deal with a minor outbreak of vigilantism on Beta Priamos, so I'll be out of touch for a while. I pray for your success, my sons." Abram signed off after giving a cavalier salute.

She shut her eyes, outraged. Abram's unemotional selfishness was an insult to everyone who would die: the crews on any ships transitioning between real and N-space, the crew of the *Bright Crescent*, and yes, even these young men Abram tenderly called his sons. How many more would die as the coronal mass ejections and flares dragged on and the entire system had to fend for itself, unable to import food, drugs, or medical personnel and equipment? *That's only if we're lucky. If not, we all go out in a blazing nova.*

Even accounting for the time-saving efforts of the Minoans, it was tricky business clearing the channel before the *Percival* dropped. The rail guns on the *Bright Crescent* didn't have full coverage, so Oleander had Captain Janda rotate the ship within the tight confines of the safety route the Minoans had established.

Lieutenant Colonel Aquino authorized symmetrical rail firing, so Janda had an easier job keeping the ship in position. Momentum couldn't disappear and when a rail gun fired, the momentum from accelerating its ammunition transferred to the ship's structure. They tried to disperse the force about the structure through the programmable mounting shocks, but the momentum always affected ship position.

"Rotated off standard lateral axis by thirty degrees." Janda's voice came quietly, but clearly, from Oleander's ear bug.

"Firing rails one and four," Oleander said, using her implanted mike and the weapons channel so that she would be heard in the pilot and navigator ear bugs, as well as in the magazine-loading compartments.

Symmetrical firing of multiple rail guns brutally punished the ship's framework, but it saved them precious time. The isolationists had screwed up; somebody chose a neat mathematical dispersal of the mines, which allowed her to move mines with two slugs at once and drive them toward their brethren, causing fratricide. So far, their procedure was working, with only a few kilometers to go.

She tapped the fire command and felt the slight shudder. On the data diagram piped to her console, the targeted mines jerked into movement. Theoretically, the slug caliber they were using shouldn't trigger the mine proximity fuses, but again, that was *theoretical*. These were crude mines with old-fashioned chemical propellants. One began moving outward into the minefield, but the other exploded as the slug hit and caused several nearby mines to blow up simultaneously.

The alarm at the damage assessment console shrilled, making her wince. Albert turned it off almost immediately, calling out in a calm voice that briefly lost its drawl, "Smart armor reduced damage by sixty percent, but we've got buckling, possible decompression, at starboard dorsal section sigma."

That was the bulkhead of the troop compartment. Oleander paused and looked up at the status board.

"Decompression confirmed. Evacuation in progress. Damage assessment team arriving. We've got two casualties being transported to medical." The results of her shots, the shots intended to protect their ship, were coming out slowly in fragmented updates from multiple consoles.

"Lieutenant Oleander? We're in position for two more shots," Captain Janda's voice said quietly from her ear bug.

"Yes, sir." She looked forward to the pilot's seat, but Janda didn't turn around. The shaved skin on the back of his head was glistening and there were beads of sweat running down to the base of his neck. She was glad she wasn't the only one drenched in sweat. She adjusted the rail gun angles with trembling fingers.

"Firing rails two and five."

"Medical updated the personnel roster. We've got one commando fatality and one pulled off duty," Chief Serafin said crisply.

"We've moved out-channel another fifty meters, Lieutenant. Fire at will," Janda said.

"Firing rails one and four." She could no longer afford the time to check her results.

"The Minoans gave us data to fill in our holes. We can't find the *Pilgrimage Three* because it's nearly hidden by Sophia One. Here's our one-eighty of the solar system using light-speed data." Captain Stavros was briefing the command chairs. "The Minoans also recorded two ships—"

"Firing rails two and five."

"Far in-system by now. It looks like the *Candor Chasma*, that's the State Prince's retrofitted Gladiator, pursued or accompanied by a small prospecting ship registered as *Aether's Touch*. Their trajectory—" Stavros was rapid-firing her words.

"We're another fifty meters out-channel, Lieutenant, rotated positive thirty off lateral axis," Janda said.

"Firing rails one and four."

Another alarm shrilled, quickly silenced. She ground her teeth together and tried to concentrate on her next targets.

"Explosion near port ventral section lambda. Smart armor reports no structural damage," Albert said from damage assessment.

"Firing rails two and five." Even her fingertips were sweaty, sliding on the surface of the console.

"Can we catch them?" Aquino asked.

"At the speeds the Minoans projected, it'd take us almost five hours. If the *Percival* drops in on schedule, it could catch them in three," replied Serafin.

"Moved another fifty meters, Lieutenant," Janda said, tiny and clear, from her ear bug.

"Firing rails one and four."

"What about missiles?" Edones asked.

"That's a civilian ship," Aquino said.

"Firing rails two and five."

"Don't care. The *Candor Chasma* has to be taken out." Edones's tone was unyielding.

"*Percival*'s dropping into real-space, sir," Chief Serafin said.

"This is the last set, Lieutenant. I've got us lined up, so fire at will," Janda said.

"Firing rails one and four." Another fine adjustment to aim the slugs correctly; her fingers were still trembling. "Firing rails two and five."

"We're through. Good work, Oleander!" Stavros checked her light-speed data again. "Tell the *Percival* they've got a clear path. I see nothing their smart armor can't handle."

She leaned back in relief, although she couldn't stop thinking about the commando fatality. Perhaps she shouldn't have aimed at the center of mass of the mines, perhaps—

"Lieutenant Oleander, how many Assassinator missiles are we carrying?" Colonel Edones's voice broke through her thoughts.

"Sixteen, sir." She'd memorized the armament loads because the two crews had deliberated this to death. Edones and Hauser had approved the loads, although she didn't expect them to remember the details.

Lieutenant Colonel Aquino looked expectantly at Colonel Edones. An O-6, or full bird, had to approve the use of that expensive and controversial missile. On this ship, that meant the mission commander.

"Load all sixteen, Lieutenant, and program them for the *Candor Chasma*." Edones's voice was heavy and didn't have its customary crispness. "Captain Janda, take us a hundred kilometers off the arrival channel, any direction. Comm, relay to *Percival* that we'll be firing missiles as soon as we've plotted target positions. Stavros, get Tactical some starting trajectories."

The chorus of "Yes, sir" was subdued. Oleander relayed the order to the magazine crews, since the Assassinators weren't preloaded into missile tubes.

The Assassinator missile, by itself, got better net-think ratings than most pornographic v-plays. Half of net-think considered the Assassinator to be the surgically safest, albeit most expensive, weapon ever developed. It could withstand extreme gee and boost to point-nine light speed in minutes, not hours, before having to decelerate. The name resulted from missile programming: When an Assassinator decelerated to its final recon point, it would query for, search out, and destroy a specific preprogrammed ship profile. The ship had to be within ten thousand kilometers. The lauded safety of the missile involved a timer that couldn't go past five UT minutes. If the missile couldn't find the correct profile within that time, it defaulted to safe and disabled its warhead.

Detractors of the Assassinator, usually opponents of military spending and members of fiscally conservative political parties, complained that the missile was expensive and ineffective. Military ships had EM countermeasures and physical chaff for confusing and defeating missiles with active targeting or profile assessment.

Oleander sighed as she watched tube status, where the missiles showed themselves powering up and coming online. Firing an Assassinator at a civilian ship violated plenty of treaties and regulations. It could sink military careers, but in this case, it was Colonel Edones making the decision and she was only following orders.

The crew at Ura-Guinn only followed orders, and Terrans still call them war criminals. She watched sixteen missile status lights glow ready with a bright, happy green color. The *Candor Chasma* was a prior-military vessel and its profile was in the Assassinator database. It was the only ship in this system qualified to interface with the TD package and it was in position to trigger the design flaw that would arm the warhead. If the *Candor Chasma* carried the warhead, it could arm the warhead in less than twenty minutes and neither the *Bright Crescent* nor the *Percival* could prevent its detonation. Colonel Edones was taking the single practical action that might, just *might*, stop another Ura-Guinn from happening.

Sixteen green lights. Her mind cleared. "All missiles have accepted the profile and ID. They're ready for target positions," she said.

"Without FTL data, sir, we're guessing on their trajectory," Stavros said.

"Understood. Tactical?" Once Edones had approved the use of the Assassinator missiles, Aquino fully backed his decision. No one mentioned that if the ship's crew could track the incoming missiles on FTL and knew their limitations, they could maneuver out of range.

"I've got sixteen points plotted that provide coverage for where we think they're going." Serafin showed the circles, ten thousand kilometers in diameter. "They'd have to go wonky to avoid these missiles. Even so, they might get there too late."

No one questioned the chief's use of "wonky" as everyone looked at her plot, more concerned by the phrase "too late." There was silence as everyone digested the possibilities of surviving a TD wave.

"Weapons, download final recon points to the missiles and fire when ready. Comm, update the *Percival* with the targets—they should leave as soon as possible." Aquino broke up the moment of preoccupation.

"Downloading final recon coordinates," Oleander said. It took a moment for the missiles to update their targeting processors and she heard Lieutenant Kozel say that the *Percival* was away, but she concentrated on entering her authorization codes.

"Missiles away," she said.

The firing of the Assassinators was anticlimactic when compared to the rail guns. The missiles were smart delivery systems that were gently pushed out of their tubes. They used minimal crude chemical propellant to orient themselves before starting their boost engines.

Oleander looked up to watch, with the rest of the control deck, the plots of the missiles as they overtook and passed the TLS *Percival*. The missiles were death addressed to a specific type of ship and they paid no heed to the *Percival*.

This hadn't been the way they hoped things would play out, considering the *Percival* had more than twice as many rangers as the *Bright Crescent* had commandos. Those special forces would have been welcome in boarding and taking back the *Pilgrimage*, but somebody had to go after the *Candor Chasma*. State Prince Hauser was on the *Percival*, and he'd already stated that since a Terran weapon, a Terran design flaw, and Terran security procedures had precipitated this crisis, then it was only fair the *Percival* perform cleanup. Now the presence of the Minoans made "cleanup" an absolute necessity and had forced "plan B" into effect.

"Relay to the Warrior Commander that we'd like Knossos-ship to follow us to Sophia One and help with the *Pilgrimage Three*. We'll be sending boarding tactics for their review within the hour," Aquino said.

"What if they ask about the *Percival*?" Lieutenant Kozel looked terrified at the prospect of lying to a Minoan.

"Pass the comm to me if that happens," Edones said.

As Oleander watched the forward part of the missile traces, she wondered at the strange deficiency of curiosity in the Minoans. Luckily, the Knossos-ship didn't once question the use of the *Percival* for pursuing "criminals," as Edones had described the situation. The Minoans must have tracked the launch of the missiles, but still made no comment.

Both the Terrans and Autonomists preferred the Minoans never found out about the missing TD weapon, and this was higher priority than hiding it from the Pilgrimage ship line. Strictly speaking, this wasn't a treaty violation, but the Minoans might still invoke penalties.

As a result, the *Percival* was on a mission that bordered on dishonor. *If* they successfully stopped the *Candor Chasma*, their highest priority was to destroy all evidence that a TD weapon was involved. Rescuing any survivors was far down on their priority list, allowing for the possibility that there *were* survivors after the Assassinators were finished.

Tahir turned away from the display. The final approval that flashed in Abram's eyes made his heart beat faster. Then his rush of hope flattened when Abram also called Emery his son.

Didn't you say, Father, that everybody has a key? A weakness that can be exploited? Yours is that you fail to recognize

*your son has the same capacity for hate as you do—and you
fail to see my hatred is focused upon you.*

"Final boost for trajectory change," Julian said.

Emery was monitoring sensors and the weapon itself,
courtesy of the old control unit installed in this heap of
a ship. Tahir glanced at Major Kedros, who looked tense
and focused on Julian. He hadn't dared tell her what he
planned, but he had no doubt she'd cooperate when the
Great Bull–shit splattered, so to speak.

"We need more acceleration to fit the profile," Emery
said. "I'll display the specs on your console."

Julian slowly pushed up thrust from the boost engines,
and watched the diagram in front of him. The real-space piloting turned out to be tricky. They were dangerously close
to the sun and unable to bleed off excess gee that could
harm them.

"If your great leader had any respect for you, he'd have
had you do this around Laomedon," Major Kedros said in
a casual tone.

"Shut up," Julian returned automatically.

"I'm just saying that you could have lived through this,"
Kedros said.

Emery looked sideways at Tahir, who shook his head.
At this point, he couldn't afford to have Emery distrust the
flight profile.

Tahir was pleased that Kedros was distracting Julian.
He tried to catch her eye, hoping she'd understand his approval, but she was staring at Julian's profile.

"I think Laomedon would have worked," she said. "We
could have flown this profile around that gas giant, but
Abram didn't want the detonation to be anywhere near
him."

"Shut up. Besides, we're going up in a ball of fury once
the weapon goes off," Julian said, using a lofty tone.

Kedros laughed. It was so unexpected and lighthearted
that Tahir couldn't help grinning. Even Emery grunted out
a chuckle at Julian's expense.

"What?" Julian tried to spin his body around, forgetting that he was tied to a chair and they were now in free fall. Instead, his arm flailed. "What's so *fucking* funny?"

"Get back to the rest of the profile." Tahir grinned, but kept an eye on Emery's console, watching them fill the second half of the gee maneuver.

"Again, what's so funny?" Julian was back at the stick. Beside him, Kedros was leaning closer, smiling.

"Because you're going to die from *radiation*, flyboy. There's not going to be any *ball of fury*." Kedros's voice was smooth and spiteful.

Tahir wanted to see Julian's face, but time was getting short and he needed to watch Emery. Kedros found Julian's "key," exactly as Abram had. Julian had a death wish, what Abram called the blaze-of-glory syndrome that he'd looked for in the disaffected and the anarchist masses. These people wanted to die for a cause, any cause, as long as it invoked sincere feelings of justification and visions of grand immolation.

"Radiation *poisoning*?" From the sound of Julian's voice, he hadn't planned such an ignominious end.

"That's it, flyboy. You're going to be drilled so bad you'll be smoking." Kedros sounded happy.

"Shut up, bitch." Julian's return didn't sound so automatic this time. Besides, they were under high gee and he almost had to grunt to get out the plaintive words. "We have radiation shielding."

Ignoring Julian, Tahir watched Emery, who concentrated on his console. They were finishing their gee maneuver.

"Ease up, Julian," Emery said. "Slowly reverse thrust. Good. I'll load some vectors in for a flight plan."

They were now in free fall around a strong gravity well. They'd gone through their low to high gee conditions and were now floating. He heard Julian retch. Tahir felt fine, but the free fall finally affected Julian. He kept his hand on his loosened stunner as he hovered behind Emery. They both saw what they were waiting for; the controller displayed a flashing yellow signal that read ARMED.

"Why do you think everybody in this system is hiding behind planets with magnetospheres, Julian? This is just the start, flyboy." Kedros's voice whipped through the control deck like a lash. "This nausea is the beginning of the grand death your leader is expecting from you."

"Shut. Up. You. Bitch." Julian was struggling against the nausea and he hadn't used a bag. Instead, he tried to hold the liquid mess together in the folds of his elbow. The smell of vomit filled the control deck quickly.

"I've had it with the both of you." Emery released his webbing, pulled out his flechette pistol, and turned with a catlike grace, his free hand gripping the back of his seat.

From his position behind Emery, Tahir saw Kedros make her move. He brought his stunner up and pulled the trigger.

CHAPTER 22

I hate to see pilots approach N-space drops by numbly processing their checklists, not understanding the necessity of the buoy lock signal, or the creation of the Penrose Fold and Fold boundary.

—Rant: *Understanding Our Technology*, Lee Wan Padoulos, 2101.078.12.19 UT, indexed by *Democritus 20* under Metrics Imperative

As Ariane pushed toward Julian, she heard the sizzle-pop sound of a stunner. Her tied fists hit Julian square in the face and her knees grabbed the chair arm. Julian pushed back with one hand and the other arm drew back to hit her. They both had leverage.

Then came the slam of propellant from a flechette pistol and the whine of twisting bladed needles. Julian flinched and ducked his head, so she slammed him in the face again with her two-handed fist. There were free-floating needles everywhere. She closed her eyes and tried to keep her head down as she hit Julian again.

And again. Julian yelled incoherently. Needles were flying; she felt pricking pain in her left leg.

"Get off him, Major Kedros."

She looked up to see Tahir pointing a stunner at her. Most of the flechette ammo had buried itself in the soft displayable covering on the walls and Emery's console, but some needles still moved around in free fall. Floating about were drops of spit, blood, and vomit—she saw Emery lodged against the opposite wall, stunned. He must have pulled the trigger on his pistol as he went under.

"Yeth, ge'off, you bith," Julian mumbled.

She regretfully disengaged, floating backward toward her chair. Tahir stunned Julian and she raised her eyebrows.

"Sorry." Tahir grimaced and awkwardly motioned toward Emery. "He was aiming the pistol before I could stun him."

She pulled a few painful needles out of her thigh. As she looked up, she saw Tahir tap a command at the weapons console.

"What are you doing?"

"Releasing the weapon," he said.

"*What?* No!" She pushed toward him.

"Don't." He pointed the stunner in warning. "It's gone. It'll detonate in—"

"Seven minutes remaining," announced the *Candor Chasma*'s ship timer, which must have been set by Emery.

"That's enough time for you to get us out of this system."

With agony churning her stomach, she watched the display on the weapons console. *All this trouble and I still didn't stop it.* The weapon, released from its homemade clamps and holding its original velocity vector, was quickly diverging from the ship's path. The ship was now on a flight plan that Emery had loaded into the autopilot.

"We've got to catch it," she said.

"No, we're leaving. We're dropping to N-space before this thing blows. The civilized galaxy will finally be free of Abram."

"Not possible. The referential engine won't work without a license crystal, we've got no drugs, and we're—"

She was going to say they were too far from the buoy

to get a lock signal, but she stopped as he reached into his pocket and held up a license crystal.

"I've already loaded codes for the Pilgrimage buoy, and you've done this before, without drugs."

Her mind went into overdrive. There was time to catch up with the weapon, or there was time to get within lock-signal distance of the buoy, but *there wasn't time enough to do both before detonation*. They were still in free fall, floating between the weapons console and the pilot chair where Julian still sat.

Tahir nodded, taking her silence for cooperation. He holstered his stunner and turned toward the hatch, using his toes lightly against the deck. "I'll get this installed while you—"

Her zero-gee training kicked in as she turned and grabbed the back of Julian's chair. Using the chair as an anchoring pivot, she twisted and clipped Tahir in the back of the head with her boots. He grunted and flew forward into the hatch. She reached down and pulled Julian's stunner out as Tahir thrashed to turn around, using the hatch for leverage. She felt no guilt as she stunned him.

"Thanks." She grabbed the crystal as it careened past her face. "I'm going to need this."

                                        •

Joyce quickly reconsidered the wisdom of wreaking havoc on a station with only a stunner, particularly when he came up against projectile weapons. Not that getting hit with a stunner was any fun, but rubber riot-shot—*Where the hell did they get shotguns?*—was painfully debilitating and flechettes were deadly.

As flechettes flew upward past him, he knew he needed better weapons and a *plan*—that dirty four-letter word. It didn't have to be an elaborate one, because these guys were *stupid*. The proof was below him, as a crazy tried to shoot flechettes up the manual access tube, only to have them ricochet or fall back down.

"Hey!" The shooter retreated.

"Is he gone?" the second man asked anxiously. "He can get access to other corridors up there."

"Why don't *you* check?" snarled the first.

More discussion and bullying followed, all of which typified the split in the crazies. There were only two men below; he'd dropped the third with a stunner before climbing up the tube. The anxious one was in station maintenance overalls and, by his clothes and accent, the other appeared to be an outsider. Joyce considered the outsiders to be the true threat. They were the ones entrusted with dangerous weapons, while their converts from the station carried stunners. The outsiders were aggressive and often browbeat their converts.

"All right, I'll take a look," the second man said reluctantly.

There was a pause. Joyce pictured the maintenance worker peeking up, wondering what could be waiting above. He wasn't the man Joyce needed to take out.

"Go ahead. He's probably gone. I'll cover you." The crazy was obviously tense and holding his pistol ready.

Joyce set the ministunner to low power and zeroed the range. Without leaning over the tube, he set it against the anchor of the ladder in the tube and pulled the trigger. At that low setting and without the squirt of ions to carry the charge, the stunner made no sound. He was, however, using its charge.

"Ow! He's charged the ladder."

Joyce quickly changed stunner settings.

"What? You're an idiot—I don't feel anything."

Joyce leaned and fired down the shaft. It was difficult firing a stunner inside a metal tunnel, but he was three meters away and the access tube was wide. The crazy was exactly where he'd hoped; better yet, the man dropped his pistol as the charge hit him, so no ammo went flying. For good measure, Joyce hit him with a charge again, this time taking better aim. He smiled as he heard the running footsteps from the retreating maintenance worker. Now *that* wasn't a surprise.

Climbing down, he surveyed his sudden wealth. The deserter hadn't taken the weapons from his fallen comrades. Crumpled against the corridor wall and near the corner, the other maintenance worker lay next to his shotgun with rubber riot-shot. Joyce grimaced as he hefted the flechette pistol dropped by the crazy. Pulling the magazine out, he found it still had five rounds of compressed foil darts.

He snorted. He'd carry the shotgun as his primary weapon because he'd never liked flechette weapons. The only advantage of flechettes, here, was intimidating unprotected civilians or flouting the Phaistos Protocols, if one wanted to thumb their nose at the Minoans. He'd used flechette rifles during EVA and boarding assaults, but both his forces and the opposing Terrans had been equipped in full exoskeleton-supported armor and self-sealing suits. Flechettes and small-caliber slugs were the only effective ammunition under those circumstances. He blinked and shook his head to avoid seeing the scenes against his eyelids: comrades flailing and dying in space. Those memories were burned into his brain.

He double-checked the safety on the flechette pistol. *These should never be used against unarmored civvies.* He supposed that was why he was career-AFCAW, so Autonomist citizens could continue their naive lives in peace. He put the flechette pistol on his belt and the ministunner in his vest pocket.

"Fledgling to Mother Bird," he broadcasted, using the slate hooked to his coveralls. Even though the comm was encrypted, the crazies had the same Command Post equipment and could be roaming the channels. Having short and obscure conversations kept the crazies from triangulating his position or figuring out his intentions.

"Mother Bird here." Maria's voice was tiny, piped through his implanted ear bug for hands-free comm. He'd plugged the slate into the connector at the base of his neck.

"Two more down." He quick-tied his victims' hands behind their backs, courtesy of the pocket contents of one of the crazies.

"Found any doves yet?"

"No." He grunted as he shoved the unconscious bodies into the access tube. "Got an ETA on Vulture?"

"Approximately forty-five minutes."

He wanted to ask whether the *Golden Bull*'s crew had made it through the *Hesperus* and onto Beta Priamos, but they'd agreed that Maria would manage that operation. They uncoupled the two activities; there were no coordination points or dependencies. His mission lay in the opposite direction from the class B docks and was more important than freeing the *Golden Bull*'s crew. He quickly checked the time on the cuff of his coverall sleeve.

"Fledgling out."

"Mother Bird out."

Another agreed procedure was that he initiated all comm. The exception that Maria would send, if it happened, was the notification that she was overrun and losing control of CP.

He had three more locations to check in ring four. In unlocking a storage room, he found three women and two men, all original Beta Priamos maintenance. After explaining who he was and the situation as briefly as possible, he forestalled any more questions.

"I need weapons and I need people willing to wield them," he said. "I've got an elevator to ambush."

Missile with serial number 13628, from tube number sixteen, would be the first missile to reach its target recon point. It reversed its boost with force that would have jellied a biological organism and switched on its receiver, braking to its recon point in five seconds ... three seconds ... arrival recorded. It began its activity countdown and searched for a ship like the *Candor Chasma* within its area of responsibility.

*   *   *

"I just wish I knew the real story," Matt muttered.

His agony had started when the Minoans tracked the *Aether's Touch* tightly following the Terran ship *Candor Chasma* toward the inner system. Initially, he'd alternated between blaming Ari for endangering his ship and hoping that both would be safe. There wasn't anything he could do but pace, waiting for the Minoans to get free of the minefield and hoping he could convince them to follow the ships in-system. He tried to get Warrior Commander to issue a hail, but his request was flatly denied.

Matt looked at the three-dimensional tracking. He couldn't read the linear script the Minoans used as tags, but given the progress on the diagram, he guessed the ships were pushing the top-boost capability of *Aether's Touch*. They were taking an elliptical path that would bring them closer to the sun than advised by his ship's engineering specifications.

"What the hell is Ari doing?" he whispered to David Ray, pacing in front of the bench where the counselor sat.

David Ray shrugged and gave him a sympathetic grimace.

"Your ship appears to make mechanical course updates, as if performing on autopilot," Warrior Commander said.

Matt stopped in his tracks, struck dumb by a third possibility: Muse 3 might be *operating* his ship, because Ari wouldn't use autopilot in either close formation or pursuit. He exchanged a wide-eyed stare with David Ray, who imperceptibly shook his head. Understanding the don't-you-dare-tell-them-about-the-AI warning on David Ray's face, Matt tried not to groan in wild frustration.

The next complication occurred in the form of the *Bright Crescent*. Having once spent several frustrating days on that ship, he knew who commanded it. *Sleazy lying bastard—*

Colonel Edones's calm and cool voice was clear to all of them in the room, but Matt suspected the *Bright Crescent* could hear only Warrior Commander's voice. His fists tightened as Edones told the Minoans that the *Candor Chasma* carried criminals who had stolen military hardware. AF-CAW Intelligence didn't know the motives of the following ship; at this point, they gave equal weight to the possibility that the *Aether's Touch* was either pursuing or escorting the criminals.

Fuck you, Edones! Matt's blood pressure spiked as he immediately focused on Edones's insult to his ship. Then he took a deep breath and his logic slowly returned. The whole "criminal" story was a vat of shit dropped from the Great Bull himself; Edones was downplaying whatever was happening on those ships to ensure the Minoans would *not* pursue them.

Matt paced, his fists clenched, as Warrior Commander and Edones made plans. Another ship would be arriving, a Terran Space Force ship named the TLS *Percival*. Edones requested help clearing mines because the *Percival* had less armor and was more vulnerable. After the Minoans agreed, a younger voice replaced Edones's and began to coordinate the operation.

Matt sighed and wheeled about, almost bumping into the emissary Minoan. He started, jumping back to slide down the slimy wall and sit beside David Ray. Contractor Adviser had quietly moved behind him and now effectively blocked both of them.

"You appear agitated, Owner of Aether Exploration."

"I just wish I knew the real story," Matt muttered.

"Are you familiar with Colonel Commanding Bright Crescent–ship?"

"Yes. I know him." Matt didn't need David Ray's grip on his forearm to remind him to choose his words carefully. In retrospect, Matt could say that Edones never outright *lied* to him. Edones was more dangerous than that; he was a master of camouflage and *omitting* facts.

"Is Colonel Commanding Bright Crescent–ship trustworthy? You appear suspicious."

Damn, these emissary types were better at interpreting humans than he expected. He might spout off emotionally about Edones to friends and acquaintances, but he wasn't going to cast aspersions on the colonel to *aliens*. Besides, Edones worked for the Directorate of Intelligence. That made Edones, by definition, a professional liar, although he did it in the name of the Consortium.

"Colonel Commanding Bright Crescent–ship will perform his duty above all else, and that includes protecting Pax Minoica," Matt said.

That was the truth. It was also the source of Matt's difficulty with Edones: The colonel had been willing to even sacrifice Ari in the name of Pax Minoica. Matt's answer seemed to satisfy Contractor Adviser, who moved to stand near the spherical tracking display.

"Bright Crescent–ship has launched missiles," Warrior Commander said. "Percival-ship has dropped in safely and is pursuing Candor Chasma–ship."

"Missiles?" Matt hung his head and pushed his fists against his ears. This was a nightmare.

"The missiles are probably programmed for Candor Chasma–ship," Warrior Commander added.

"Yeah, but how accurate could they be?" Matt asked the floor. He didn't expect an answer, but he got one.

"The most recent tracking package used on the Consortium Assassinator Missile Two Alpha has a point-nine-eight-six-six probability of finding a programmed profile within the range of ten thousand kilometers, provided its sensors can work optimally." Warrior Commander was adjusting the tracking sphere zoom. "We are moving toward Pilgrimage-ship. A shuttle from Pilgrimage-ship appears to be dropping beacons along the orbital plane of Sophia One."

This interested David Ray and Matt, who rose and came closer. The Minoans stood on the other side of the three-dimensional spherical display. The light from the display glinted off their jewels and metalwork, making their robes look diaphanous but deepening the darkness about their faces. Warrior Commander twisted a jewel hanging from his torque and Sophia I loomed large inside the display.

"What are those beacons transmitting?" David Ray asked.

"Distress calls," Warrior Commander said. "My first analysis was incorrect. They're not beacons, they're—"

Four more Assassinator missiles arrived at their recon points and began searching for their targets. They operated at reduced efficacy due to the intense noise generated by the close G-type sun, which lessened their possibilities of detecting a ship meeting the preprogrammed profile.

The *Candor Chasma* had boosted into a different trajectory than initially plotted by Chief Serafin. Only two missiles of the original sixteen would come within ten thousand kilometers of the *Candor Chasma*. Those missiles would arrive at their target recon points within the next nine UT minutes.

"They're *people*!" cried Lieutenant Kozel. "They've shoved out people in suits, who are transmitting on the emergency channel."

Oleander heard Stavros swearing under her breath as she tried to get every bit of data out of the sensors. "They're all drifting on different vectors, sir. They've got no propulsion. So far there're five of them, strung about fifty kilometers apart."

"They've got to be civilians from the *Pilgrimage*," Lieutenant Colonel Aquino said.

"Delaying tactics. This explains why they aren't jamming us; they didn't want us to miss these victims." Edones's voice was cool and objective. "They're hoping the TD wave, or subsequent radiation bursts, will hit us before we can take cover."

"I've got voice transmission."

Lieutenant Kozel put the channel on speaker, so everyone on the control deck heard the transmission. The voice was adolescent, gasping, barely on the sane side of terror.

"Please, someone . . . don't come near us! They rigged us to explode!"

"Chief, you'd better take this call," Aquino said to Serafin, then rotated his chair to look at Sergeant Albert. "Start prepping a pinnace and assign a warrant officer to the helm. Find out how many explosive experts those commandos brought along."

"Yes, sir." Sergeant Albert looked doubtful.

Oleander kept an eye on her display while she listened to Serafin's side of the conversation with the terrified civilian. The chief was chatting quietly and normally with her implant mike, sounding as if she were preparing to bake cookies.

"What's your name, hon? Samuel . . . that's okay, it happens to all of us. Samuel, I need you to repeat what those bast—those men told you. . . . Well, a one-hundred-kilometer range is unlikely for a proximity fuse. Samuel? Don't panic. I need you to breathe slowly. That's good. Now I want you to describe what they hooked on your tanks. . . ."

"Sir, the Minoans say they can only offer limited assistance. They can't disarm the devices because they're *similar to the mines*," Lieutenant Kozel relayed.

"For once, their comments are helpful," Aquino said.

"Perhaps we should send Knossos-ship on to the *Pilgrimage*," Edones said.

"Let the Minoans board however they want? Exact their own punishment—let them decide who lives and who dies? We don't know what collateral damage might result." Lieutenant Colonel Aquino sounded appalled.

"It's not going to matter if the weapon detonates." Edones spoke calmly, but he made no move to call Knossos-ship.

If the weapon detonates . . . Oleander shivered.

"Sir, the *Rhapsody* is prepped. Master Sergeant Pike is

sending two explosive technicians, plus two 'fast learners,' as he called them. They can be ready and released in three minutes," Albert said.

"I can help."

At the sound of this voice, everyone looked over toward damage assessment. Major Phillips, their Terran Space Forces coordinator, was standing beside Senior Master Sergeant Albert.

"Uh, I don't think we can afford to lose our only Terran liaison officer. Right, Colonel Edones?" Albert had that familiar stricken look on his face that noncoms got when faced with a useless senior officer who intended to make a muddle of his operation.

Before Edones could answer, Phillips said, "There's nothing more to coordinate with the *Percival*. I've got medical training, which might be needed."

"Yes, but—"

"I was a Battlefield Medic and I'm *prior enlisted*." Phillips said the magic words.

"In that case, sir, how soon can you get to the *Rhapsody*?" Albert said, looking toward the mission commander's chair. Edones nodded curtly, and Phillips left for the pinnace deck.

"I think we're dealing with the same fuses we saw on the mines," Chief Serafin said. "I doubt they'd have anything better; this is their last gasp at holding us off."

"Give the *Rhapsody* all the information you've got, Chief," Aquino said.

"Hey, Oleander." Captain Janda had swiveled about to face her. His face was hollow and ghastly. Lucky for him, the second-shift pilot seat was relieving him soon. He rubbed his smooth head absently. "How's it going with the missiles?"

"The projections don't look good. By my calculations, six of these missiles arrived on target and had nothing to aim at. Most of the others will miss, except for two that might get a chance."

"They might change their vector. We could get lucky."

"I suppose so, sir." She continued to monitor her station.

"Sir, the Minoan ship relays that they're moving on to the *Pilgrimage*," Lieutenant Kozel said.

"Ask them to wait," Aquino said. "Sensors, can you track them?"

"Sir, I'm barely holding on to their one sharp edge as it is," Captain Stavros said. "They'll get to the *Pilgrimage* before us."

CHAPTER 23

The Terran Expansion League (TerraXL) and the Consortium of Autonomous Worlds (CAW), hereinafter referred to as the Parties, conscious that testing of temporal-distortion weapons degrades the fabric of the universe, have agreed upon the articles written in this Treaty. . . .

—Preamble to Temporal-Distortion (TD) Testing Treaty, First Treaty Signed under Pax Minoica, 2092.005.12.00 UT, indexed by Heraclitus 5 under Conflict Imperative

Ariane put the license crystal into her front pocket on her hip. With her hands still tied, she felt around Julian's vest for his knife.

She cut the quick-tie around her wrists, causing instant pain. Her fingertips felt numb as she entered and started a small boost to change their course and chase the weapon. That wasn't tough, since the package was inside a big aluminum can and was behaving like any other space junk jettisoned off a speeding ship near the sun. She couldn't grab it back; Tahir's primitive mounting system had blown its struts as part of the release procedure. If this ship was upgraded with external booms or manipulators, she didn't have time to find the interfaces.

"Six minutes, thirty seconds remaining," announced the *Candor Chasma*'s ship timer.

There was only one fast option: an N-space drop, made

without getting a buoy lock—meaning there'd be no coming back to real-space. She floated around Julian, avoiding globs of vomit, and started the initialization, knowing it would hold on "Install license crystal...."

She felt the forces change from the boost and she gripped the handhold tighter. The vomit and flechettes started drifting down to the floor. Emery and Tahir were sliding down the walls. Julian stayed, webbed into his chair.

Swinging through three handholds, she was out the main hatch. She dove forcibly down the vertical, catching herself at the bottom. The referential engine was always at the most forward part of the ship, usually under the control deck. She was familiar with the TM-8440 and found the license crystal slot quickly.

Back up to the control deck, she glanced at the three men. None were coming round. Good. She needed to concentrate. The initialization had finished and the engine was tuned well—not surprising, because the pilot had been running diagnostics two days ago.

"Five minutes remaining."

First, she calculated and programmed the drop time, ensuring it happened when the ship overtook the weapon. The time window was tight, barely covering the detonation point. She had to force the engine to accept the plan because they were too far from the buoy to get a lock. *We don't need a lock to drop out of real-space, only to get back* safely *from N-space*. Lucky for her, the isolationists had disabled the N-space safety protocols with the others they had to inhibit.

Second, she messed with the recently tuned engine, making it inefficient. This was a bit tricky and she thanked Gaia that she understood the physics behind referential engines, Penrose Folds, and Fold boundaries. If she managed to get off this ship in time and outside the Fold boundary, she could get extra push from the badly tuned engine and its waste of energy.

"Four minutes remaining."

Almost done. Before she turned away from the console, she brought up the full tactical display that Julian didn't want to bother watching. Everything within a half light-hour was displayed. There was *Aether's Touch*, fifty kilometers behind and slowly closing. She wished she could use comm to warn Joyce of her plan, but he wouldn't have Abram's authorized frequencies and she didn't have time to roam the comm spectrum. Besides, there would be severe interference this close to the sun. She could only hope that Joyce was paying attention.

"Three minutes, thirty seconds remaining."

She saw two blips streaking toward a point on the ship's trajectory, which didn't surprise her. She had expected Colonel Edones would authorize Assassinator missiles. *Good old Owen—at least he tried.* Unfortunately for her plan, if the *Candor Chasma* was damaged, the N-space drop might fail. One missile trace would intercept them, at the point when the ship caught up to the weapon, but before the Penrose Fold was established for the N-space drop. The missile would have to lock on to the *Candor Chasma* and it would suffer the same problem as the comm: the electromagnetic noise, this close to the sun.

"Three minutes remaining."

She pushed to the weapons console and frantically searched the different displays. She found the right display, with a command to release chaff. When she tapped it, the display responded as if there were a load of expanding foil specks and gas going out the tube. She could only pray that this, coupled with the interference from the sun, would confuse the missile.

"Two minutes, thirty seconds remaining."

Time to go. She looked at the three limp bodies, knowing she should try to save someone—and she didn't need Dokos's tag to remind her that it wouldn't be Emery. She'd serve out her own justice, at least this once. She cut webbing from the N-space seat.

With Tahir webbed to her back, she floated them both

through the corridor to the emergency evacuation modules. They were small, but some ships didn't have modules that separated. Finally, the oddities of the TM-8440 were working for her, rather than against her.

"One minute, thirty seconds remaining." How convenient. The ship's timer could announce inside the emergency evacuation module. She got both of them webbed in and hit the EJECT button. They pushed free with a strong boost.

"One minute remaining." The message had static, the EM noise affecting even close communications with the *Candor Chasma*.

"We're going to die here. We can't escape the effects of the quantum glitch on the sun's fusion." Tahir slurred his words. Julian's stunner must have been set on a light charge, if he was already waking.

She freed the stunner and kept it ready, but Tahir made no move other than to wiggle his fingers. "Emery and Julian?"

"They'll be waking up in N-space, if my drop goes correctly." She tapped the panel of their emergency capsule, trying to bring up a view of the outside.

"You're trying to dump the detonation to N-space." His eyes widened. "There'll be leakage. There was always leakage on the Terran tests. That means solar flares. G-145 will still suffer."

"I'm betting it'll be better than experiencing a full-fledged TD wave."

"Thirty seconds remaining."

He looked tired. "And we'll get sucked along with the ship and the weapon into N-space. My way, we would have lived—in real-space."

The *Candor Chasma* was still transmitting the countdown, which had gone below fifteen seconds. There was so much static that they couldn't understand the numbers, so she turned the volume down.

"Not if we're on, or outside, the Penrose Fold boundary.

And you'd better hope that Assassinator missile doesn't destroy the Penrose Fold before the ship drops. Wait for it. . . ." She paused, shoulders tensed.

He blanched, and sat quietly.

The last transmission—"zero point"—came at the same time as a gentle push on the capsule. They could hear something hitting the module. It was the chaff, and she smiled. The ship had pulled the TD weapon into N-space. She felt the tension rush out of her body.

"Ever wonder why some ships cause a brilliant burst of light in real-space when they drop out? Their engine is tuned badly."

"And you made use of excess boundary energy to push us away? Fine and good, you saved us, just to die from lack of air or worse, radiation."

"Don't worry. We'll be picked up and you'll face justice." At least, she *hoped* they'd be picked up. She hoped too that Owen hadn't also programmed a profile matching *Aether's Touch* into his Assassinators.

"Justice? That's the least of my worries," he said hoarsely. When she frowned, he added, "My father's still out there. If this mission doesn't kill us, then he'll make us wish it did."

An alarm over the hatch started beeping. It came from the radiation monitor.

Joyce told the civilians that Abram would use their friends and coworkers as shields. He also told them they had to kill, maim, or wound Abram's men, or everyone would suffer. Some of these civilians were going to be more reliable than others.

"Stunners are better than using *this*. I mean, it's positively medieval." Carly hefted the portable magnetic bolt grappler while looking up at Joyce through her lush eyelashes. Her fading and blotching green skindo only undermined her flirtations a little.

"Well . . ." Joyce carefully pushed the business end of

the grappler to the left so she no longer aimed it at his abdomen. "Those bolts can blow a hole in somebody's body."

He ignored her grimace and looked around at his ragtag team of armed—and he used that term loosely—volunteers. Being the smallest, Carly had the light, thirty-five-millimeter grappler with a muzzle energy of no more than one kilojoule, intended for personal EVA use. Melissa, who was significantly huskier than Carly, carried their other magnetic grappler. This grappler fired fifty-millimeter magnetic bolts with five kilojoules and was the civilian version of the SAL-50 that AFCAW issued to boarding teams. They'd emptied the monofilament canisters on both grapplers. Sophi, Paul, and Nikos carried the biggest plasma torches they had found, as they made their way toward the elevator. They also carried stunners.

"I still think I should have a stunner." Carly pouted. "This thing can only load four bolts at a time."

"Give it a rest, Carly. And stop batting your eyelashes at him." Sophi adjusted the torch tank coming over her left shoulder and checked the charge on the stunner she held in her right hand. "We've only got three stunners."

"If somebody's got a flechette weapon, you need to take them out with *lethal* force, before they've got their weapon pointed," Joyce said. "I don't care if it's one of your friends holding the weapon, because a stun doesn't stop somebody from firing."

The three carrying the stunners nodded. Sophi, Paul, and Nikos had prior military or civilian security experience. With their agreement, Joyce was satisfied that he'd distributed the weapons correctly. Stunners were trickier to use than the v-plays credited, and he didn't want his own people going down twitching due to excess or friendly current. He still carried the crazy's flechette pistol and the shotgun loaded with twelve cartridges of rubber-covered riot-shot. He double-checked the charge; he had plenty. Lack of ammo would be his problem.

The sound of the elevator's inner cargo hold sliding into its cradle stopped all further discussion.

"Take your positions, people," Joyce said.

Sophi and Nikos went to the maintenance bay on the left side of the elevator, while Paul and Melissa went to the bay on the right. The elevator airlock was wider than a standard-size airlock; double sets of doors equalized pressure between the elevator interior and the station. The elevator opened almost flush on the side of the corridor. Even though the bays could be used to ambush people coming out of the elevator, they could also turn into nice little shooting galleries, trapping their occupants.

That's why Joyce set himself up at the corner of an offset spoke hallway that met the perimeter corridor. He would try to draw the crazies out of the crate and toward the right. The converts, he predicted, would run, and he told his team to let them go.

Down the hallway behind him, Carly took cover in an open hatch. In theory, she was providing him backup, but she was there because he considered her the weakest link.

It went down pretty much as Joyce predicted.

Abram was prepared for problems on Beta Priamos, perhaps because of the fracas near the class B docks. Joyce drew back as he heard the doors open. A quick, one-eyed peek showed five converts forming the first rank. They hesitantly stepped out of the elevator, obviously knowing their purpose as a shield for the occupants behind them. Three carried stunners, all tensely pointed into the corridor.

He listened. He heard low mutters and a few shuffling steps. Luckily, these amateurs didn't understand the value of being silent and he waited until they were a meter or two out of the elevator and still unable to see into the maintenance bays on either side. Behind his corner, Joyce edged backward, breathed deeply, and took the shotgun off safety.

Quickly leaning out from cover, he fired three blasts with the shotgun, then pulled back. The advantage of not using a chemical propellant, such as gunpowder, was that the sound of the shotgun was hard to locate. The kick of the shotgun felt the same, and the riot-shot hurt badly, particularly within the fifteen-meter range. He heard shouts and yelps.

He leaned out again. Two of the men were down, writhing in pain. One was firing his stunner down the corridor in the opposite direction. He fired four more blasts, then leaned in. This time, two stunners fired back and hit short. They knew that hitting the wall would spread the charge along to the corner, even when covered with display material. *That* was why he wasn't snuggled up against the wall for cover, thank you very much.

The air crackled with ozone and various ionized particles, causing that specific odor from stunner fire that Joyce could never describe well. The mélange of stunner effluent, fried sweat and blood, and melted plastic from the display material on the deck and walls was overwhelming—then his nose shut down all input, in self-defense.

He'd hoped to make the converts run before this. He leaned out as he fired rapidly, and saw seven more men coming off the elevator. Their living shield was reduced to two men who were wavering; one had already run away and the two overwhelmed by the riot-shot were crawling away. His shotgun took down the final waverers.

The seven new targets carried flechette pistols. Joyce pulled back behind cover, dropped the spent shotgun, and pulled his own pistol. As expected, only Abram's men, the *real* crazies, had flechette weapons.

His team members in the maintenance bay, bless their civvy hearts, held their fire as he used his shotgun. As instructed, they waited until the crazies exited, then dropped two of them with stunners. Now, however, two men split off to close with the maintenance bays. There were screams on both sides as flechettes met bursts from plasma torches.

Three of the crazies were in emergency environmental suits, including the center one who turned toward Joyce. The suits gave partial protection against stunners, but only the faceplates would protect against flechettes. Joyce got a glimpse of wide, crazed-with-hate dark eyes before unloading a round of flechette ammo into the chest of the advancing suited man. As designed, the round expanded into twirling needles, hit the chest, and shredded the suit. The man's steps faltered from the impact, but he kept coming.

That bastard's got body armor, at least in the chest area. Joyce was sure he was Abram. So far, nobody had been equipped with armor, but this changed things and made Joyce's current tactics foolhardy.

Abram aimed his pistol. Joyce pulled back behind the corner quickly, but something slammed his shoulder. He heard a scream from Carly and, looking down, saw what was left of his right shoulder. *Now* the pain welled up and his sight blurred. As he backed away from the corner, he managed to get the flechette pistol into his left hand. He shouted, "Fall back," over his shoulder.

Abram came around the corner with the false confidence that armor gives nonprofessionals and Joyce fired his flechettes at Abram's lower arm and hand. Abram yelled and dropped his weapon.

"Fall back!" Still backing up, Joyce glanced over his shoulder and caught sight of Carly's backside. She was running in a full-fledged dangerous retreat. *You were supposed to fall back with your weapon pointed at the bad guys.* Simple enough instructions, he'd thought, but now he had no hope of getting cover fire from her.

Damn civvy. He was fucked. But he knew Carly might crumble, and that's why she wasn't in one of the maintenance bays. Turning back, he was astonished to see Abram already had the pistol off the floor and in his other hand. Abram shot before his pistol rose above knee level. The flechette round took out Joyce's right knee and left behind ground meat.

Please, Carly, turn around and shoot! As he fell, he brought up his left hand to fire the pistol, but that was also the arm and elbow he needed to cushion his fall. He pulled the trigger as he hit the floor and his shot went wide, up toward the ceiling where the flechette needles stuck in the display material.

Abram leapt forward and kicked the pistol out of his hand.

Carly, for the love of Gaia, shoot! He tried to grab Abram's leg but missed. Abram stomped, pinning his left hand and wrist. He felt a spike of pain as something broke. He looked up into Abram's faceplate and saw a rictus formed of hate and teeth.

Abram aimed his pistol at Joyce's unprotected neck, a killing shot. Abruptly, he staggered backward, a small magnetic bolt protruding from his chest. His other suited hand, the wounded one, flailed at it.

Good, Carly. You gotta hit him again. Abram was still standing, trying to get his shot off at Joyce. His armor had slowed the penetration of the small bolt.

Joyce's sight was fading as Abram's chest exploded above him. A shower of bloody viscera sprayed outward, bits landing on Joyce's face. The business end of a *big* magnetic bolt protruded and pushed Abram's rib cage outward. Abram's hand jerked, and the flechette round missed Joyce's neck and flayed the right edge of his chest.

Good civvies, good Melissa . . . He passed out as Abram sagged forward and fell on him.

The Minoan ship screamed and writhed in pain. Matt would have covered his ears, if he could have used his hands. As it was, his arms and legs pinwheeled about in an effort to protect his body. He wedged himself into a corner, with no time to consider that oddity in an originally oval room.

"Ooof!" David Ray suddenly pressed against his side.

"What the—"

The corner tightened and the ship held them, squeezing them into jelly—no, they were surrounded by jelly. Matt couldn't breathe.

*   *   *

"What's going on with the Minoan ship?" Aquino asked. "How come they're suddenly showing on our sensors?"

"Not sure, sir." Captain Stavros magnified the trace display, which showed the Minoan ship suddenly taking an erratic vector. This was the first time they could clearly detect the ship.

"Chief Warrant Officer Marinos on the *Rhapsody* reports one explosion has resulted in casualties—sending full report to Damage Assessment." Lieutenant Kozel turned to look at the trace of the Minoan ship. "Do you want me to query the Minoans regarding their course?"

"They made another course change," Stavros said. "Whoops—another one. Sir, they're going wonky, to quote the chief."

Oleander turned to watch Colonel Edones, who was frowning at the trace display.

Edones's cool blue glance moved to meet Oleander's. "Lieutenant, what's the status of our missiles? And what have we got on the light-speed data for the *Candor Chasma*, Captain Stavros?"

"Eleven of the missiles reported in, sir," Oleander said. "Eight of those suicided, with no target found. The others are in countdown, and I've lost comm with the twelfth."

"Sir, light-speed data indicates the *Candor Chasma* dropped to N-space. That report's delayed by—" An alarm on the sensor console distracted Stavros and she tapped acknowledgment, silencing it. "We're recording solar flares and rising radiation levels. Sorry, sir, I lost the Minoan ship. They apparently got their invisibility cloak back online."

"We'll assume they're back on course for boarding the *Pilgrimage*," Edones said smoothly and quickly. "Lieutenant Kozel, if we've still got comm with the *Rhapsody*, tell them to prepare for strong solar flare activity. Hope they can protect those poor sods in EVA suits and reduce their radiation doses, but make the point they're on their own. We're too far away to help."

"Pilot and navigator, fastest speed toward the *Pilgrim-*

age. Get us behind Sophia One and in the shelter of that magnetosphere." Aquino's commands were sharp. The *Bright Crescent* carried more effective shielding than a pinnace like the *Rhapsody*, but he apparently thought they'd be in danger also.

"Yes, sir." Captain Hoak now sat in the pilot seat, replacing the exhausted Captain Janda.

Oleander turned to see Aquino lean toward Edones. "What just happened?" Aquino asked in a low voice.

"I think someone tried to use N-space to swallow a TD explosion. Some of the TD wave will leak and cause problems for the sun, even if we can't detect it."

"Did the Minoans?" Aquino jerked his head toward the trace display.

"Perhaps." Edones looked thoughtful. "One practice they adamantly wanted stopped was the Terran 'secret' test procedure of shunting the TD wave into N-space. They were very insistent about enforcing the test treaty first."

"So we're safe now." Aquino's tone was half question, half statement. "There'll be no TD detonation."

"Well, we won't see a quantum glitch in the sun's fusion engine or any nova. However, we may still see strong coronal mass ejections."

Edones and Aquino lowered their voices and Oleander turned back to her console, but she could still hear scraps of their conversation. They discussed whether anything could be done to help those aboard the *Rhapsody* pinnace, the *Aether's Touch*, and the TLS *Percival*. All those occupants would experience a more severe dose of solar-generated radiation than the *Bright Crescent*.

"If they get a buoy lock, can they drop—"

"Not when the buoy's controlled by the isolationists. But perhaps—"

Oleander tried to ignore the quiet conversation behind her. She looked up at the trace diagram that Stavros displayed, which now included a snapshot of their half of the solar system out to Laomedon. The closest magnetosphere, for any of them, wrapped about and stretched behind Sophia I. However, the sensors and comm were degrading, due to interference from solar activity, and the ship traces were mostly intelligent guesswork. *Aether's Touch* and *Percival* were probably heading toward Sophia I with all the boost they had—*Percival* easily outrunning *Aether's Touch*, but not the EM radiation.

She finished her report on the release of the missiles, signing with her thumbprint. Without sensor support, her best guess was that only one of the missiles came close to the *Candor Chasma*. She figured the ship sucked it into N-space during the transition. It was gone; any vehicles that entered N-space and weren't attached to a buoy-locked referential engine, disappeared forever.

"Lieutenant Oleander, find your second-shift weapons officer and report to the boarding teams forming on deck three," Aquino said.

"Yes, sir." She stood up and stretched surreptitiously. This wasn't over, not by a long shot. She had to stop worrying about radiation exposure and move on to the business of taking back the *Pilgrimage III*.

CHAPTER 24

Ariane's jaw clenched at the scraping sounds; then she winced as she felt the module jerked about roughly by the manipulator booms.

"*Aether's Touch*," she said, in response to Tahir's questioning look.

Tahir looked shocked. Apparently, the idea of a ship following them never entered his head.

It took two minutes to get them into the large sample bay and secure their capsule. To her, it felt like hours and she cringed with every metallic screech, wondering if fragile joints on the manipulators were being damaged. At long last, the comm indicator lit.

"Whoever's at control better haul ass toward Sophia

One!" she said quickly. Since Matt would have brought them in without a scratch and was probably still on the *Pilgrimage*, she had to be talking to Joyce. She didn't think anybody else could have gotten past *Aether's Touch* security, bolstered by Muse 3.

"Ari, are you in need of medical care?"

She froze. The voice was Muse 3. While the AI could certainly run the autopiloting software, she didn't believe Beta Priamos would have released the ship under AI direction—unless it blew the ship away from the station, meaning there was damage. *We won't be able to dock until we fix the clamps*.

"No, Muse, we're not hurt. We have a—" She decided she better be specific. "We have a prisoner. And, ah, Muse? Is Joyce on the control deck?"

"No, Ari. The sample bay has been pressurized so you may leave the evacuation module."

This explained the clumsy use of the manipulator boom; Muse 3 was only able to use one manipulator to retrieve the module. The second manipulator was inside the forward sample bay and had to be operated by human hands.

"Open it." She gestured and pointed the stunner at Tahir, who moved to the hatch. While he opened the module, she ran through some instructions for Muse 3, realizing that the AI would be saving her a hefty and possibly debilitating radiation dose. "Muse, set the autopilot for maximum burn toward Sophia One, with final destination behind the planet. Have the autopilot plot a high-gee braking maneuver as close to the planet as possible. Don't set any economy parameters—we need to get into the protection of that magnetosphere as soon as possible."

"I understand, Ari."

She motioned, indicating Tahir should precede her through the small sample bay. She felt the ship begin its boost toward Sophia I, using the gravity generator to bleed off gee to N-space so they didn't get smeared across the bulkheads. What a miracle N-space was, that it could swallow TD waves and move gravitational force both ways. *Sort of like an interstellar energy dumping ground.*

"Where are we going? There's nowhere we'll be safe." Tahir protested as she pushed him up a level and along a corridor.

"We've got a protected data array compartment. This is a second-wave prospector and its most precious cargo is its data." She wasn't going to bother answering any more of his muttered questions. He was partially right; the *normal* layers of directional polymer, containing specially oriented superconducting strands combined with the *normal* layers of composite and aerogel, wouldn't protect against the bursts of radiation they'd receive from heavy coronal flaring.

She used her thumbprint to unlock the array compartment. Tahir stepped through the hatch and turned around in the small space, looking dismayed.

"This is going to be a tight space for three of us, isn't it?" he asked.

"Three? Oh—we'll fit okay. Muse will be down in a moment. He's small." She was tired and making mistakes. Tahir couldn't be witness to the illegal use of an AI.

She closed the hatch behind her and looked about. She hadn't been in this compartment since Athens Point. Matt had puttered about in here, but it was pristine as always. To her left, the console ran along the entire side of the compartment, which was barely two meters long. When inactive, the console was a bare counter with two undermounted stools and plenty of empty wall space—all covered with flexible displayable surface so that she or Matt could have hundreds of view ports open at one time.

"I don't think I've seen this much crystal before, other than in a tour of a vault." The right wall had distracted Tahir, where sapphire-shielded edges of the crystal arrays peeked out of their sockets and glowed in patterns.

"That's what *Aether's Touch* is. It can be fitted with

nearly half a vault of crystal." She glanced down as her fingers changed the setting on her stunner. "Think of this ship as one big spacefaring data array, operated by two humans and carrying around bunches of sensor equipment and bots to gather data."

"Are you going to cut power to these?" His face was turned away, so he didn't see her raise the stunner and press the trigger.

"Sorry," she said as he fell against the back wall and quivered down to slump on the floor. "You ask too many questions."

She regretted having to stun him, again, and at such a high setting, but she couldn't have him learning about Muse 3.

"Muse Three?" She told the AI which systems to shut down and which angle to orient the ship to have the most protection from solar radiation, using the Penrose Fold referential engine to their advantage. She had the AI echo its autopilot settings to the array room so she could double-check them; they were on the right course, using the ship's top boost that could bleed real-space gee to N-space through their gravity generator.

She also had to protect Muse 3. "Unload all the noncritical routines that you can from temporary memory."

"Yes, Ari."

She safed the stunner and strapped it to her leg, still easily accessible. Sitting with her back against the closed hatch, she relaxed.

"What the hell?" Matt gasped.

He was still gripped by the ship, but at least his face was uncovered. The room appeared empty and smaller than before. He moved his eyes back and forth, but his angle of view was too tight to see the whole room.

"Matt? You okay?" David Ray's voice came from his left. "I can't see anything. There's goo over my eyes."

"Yeah, I'm fine . . ." Matt's voice trailed off as he saw

Warrior Commander extrude from the wall across from him. The Minoan appeared more as a growth from the wall, than from within the wall. Its horns still caused the ceiling to pucker up to avoid it, but Matt thought Warrior Commander looked different. He couldn't identify the difference exactly; was it taller, was its torque different, or did the set of its shoulders look unusual?

Warrior Commander strode to the center of the room, still within Matt's view. The center platform suddenly rose from the floor; only then did Matt realize he'd missed its presence. While the body language of the Minoans, according to Terran *somaural* experts, wasn't open to interpretation, Matt thought the jerky, strong movements and the set of the shoulders indicated anger.

"Warrior Commander?" he ventured.

The tall dark figure wheeled around to look at him. Was it surprised? Why? Warrior Commander held a gloved hand out parallel to the floor, above the platform. A console rose and the Minoan's hand rested on it. After a moment, Warrior Commander nodded slowly.

"Can you release us?" Matt asked.

Warrior Commander turned back to the console, above which a three-dimensional hologram showed part of the *Pilgrimage* with the wartlike extension of the Minoan ship. They had apparently docked. The warrior reached to the beads dripping from its torque. With a quiet slurp, the walls released Matt by pushing him outward and into a standing position. The same happened to David Ray, to his left.

"What just happened, Warrior Commander?" David Ray asked. "Was Knossos-ship attacked?"

They waited for the answer while Warrior Commander appeared to evaluate what the console was displaying.

"Someone violated the 2092 Weapons Testing Treaties by sending a temporal-distortion wave into what you call nous-space. Do you know the violators?" Using a rougher voice than before, the tall Minoan took a long step toward them.

Matt's mouth opened in surprise. The warrior, big and

covered in flowing black, was *so* much taller when it came within arm's reach. Matt quickly stepped back. Temporal-distortion wave? Only TD weapons generated those and if someone had such a weapon here in G-145—*somebody's in trouble, by the looks of things*. He didn't want to think about what the Minoans might do about a treaty violation.

"We don't know anything about a TD wave. Do we still have the buoy?" David Ray was thinking faster than Matt.

Matt closed his mouth and berated himself silently. He hadn't realized they might be the next Ura-Guinn. TD weapons were the only way humankind could destroy a Minoan time buoy—not that any sane person would want to do that.

"The buoy cannot be assessed until we can run diagnostics. It may still be operational, because the violators pushed most of the temporal distortion into nous-space," Warrior Commander said, after a pause.

"Where's Contractor Adviser?" Matt asked.

"Contractor Adviser will not be activated until Pilgrimage-ship is secured." Warrior Commander reached into the wall and withdrew its baton.

Matt tried to remember where Warrior Commander's baton had been when all the weirdness started. He looked around, puzzled, as the Minoan stalked toward the wall, which sighed and opened.

"Wait! We have to go with you." David Ray's plea, plus scuttling close behind the Minoan and jumping into the opening, stopped Warrior Commander.

When Matt saw that the opening held and the wall didn't squeeze David Ray, he stepped forward to stand beside the counselor. Looking past Warrior Commander, he expected to see the hallway by which they'd first entered. Instead, they entered a semicircular room on the rounded side. It was large enough that the eight waiting guardians took up half the room's volume. He shook his head. He'd lived on habitats and ships all his life, but Knossos-ship confused him. It obviously had the capability to alter itself.

Warrior Commander looked down at David Ray. Matt thought the Minoan seemed a bit peeved by the delay. If so, there was nothing to lose by pushing for everything.

"We'll need weapons too." Matt pointed at the batons held by the guardians.

David Ray made a disapproving sound in his throat.

"Might as well ask." Matt shrugged. It couldn't hurt, could it? He squirmed as the silence grew, however, and when he looked up at Warrior Commander, he wished he hadn't been such a smart-ass. They waited.

"This will work temporarily, and only on Pilgrimage-ship. It will harm only evolved, multicellular organisms. If you wish, you may use it in hand-to-hand combat." Warrior Commander reached into the wall, withdrew a baton of the size used by the guardians, and handed it to Matt. "Knossos-ship will not be responsible for your safety, or the safety of the Pilgrimage-ship crew members."

"What about me?" David Ray raised his eyebrows.

"You are not qualified with projectile or stun weapons, and you have no hand-to-hand training. What can I provide you?"

"Then I'll stay with—er, Owner of Aether Exploration." David Ray looked at Matt, who shrugged again. He'd taken training classes, at Ari's recommendation, but he wasn't placing much hope on two-year-old instruction. He wondered how the Minoans knew about the training.

The warrior turned toward the guardians. Without any overt communication, the Minoans lined up and strode through an opening in the wall.

"That's not the same Warrior Commander. It even sounds different than the one we first met," Matt said softly.

"I noticed. I'm wondering if the first one got killed or destroyed—but right now, we'd better follow." David Ray ran for the same spot where the last guardian disappeared.

Matt winced, expecting David Ray to rebound off the wall. Instead, the counselor disappeared into something with the same consistency as the gelatinous goo they swam through to get into the ship. He sighed and followed.

"This sucks. As weapons officers, we should get the exciting jobs during boarding missions—but because this is a civilian habitat and we have all these commandos instead of our normal personnel, we have to sit around and do nothing." When Lieutenant Maurell sulked, his face looked disturbingly like Oleander's youngest brother, who was twelve.

"I'm kind of tired after doing *nothing*," Oleander said mildly. She queried her implant with her slate, noted the level of bright was falling in her bloodstream, and opted to take her next dose early.

"Oh. I meant that *I'm* doing nothing." He looked sideways at her. "Sorry, forgot you've already done a shift. But if we were boarding a military vessel, one of us would be on the bridge and the other would be leading—"

"Lieutenant Oleander?" boomed a fully armored commando who moved to stand at attention in front of her. She looked up at his faceplate, a good thirty centimeters above hers. His equipment, a self-sealing environmental suit with armor and exoskeleton, helped him tower over her. She and Maurell were equipped with standard AFCAW-issue suits, which were tougher than civilian, self-sealing environmental suits but had armor only in the torso area.

"Master Sergeant Pike?"

"Yes, ma'am." The commando pushed controls on his forearm and the faceplate swiveled back. His face was hard, with lines down the sides of his mouth. He had squint lines at the corner of his eyes that she thought could be laugh lines, under other circumstances. Right now, Sergeant Pike didn't look like he ever laughed and his expression discouraged even the suggestion of frivolity.

"We're ready to open the final doors, ma'am." He jerked his head toward the airlock, where two of his people worked to force the *Pilgrimage*'s external side open. As usual, the outer airlocks had no windows. "We have no idea what they've got on the other side."

"Where do you want us, Sergeant?"

Pike looked at her silently in a measuring manner, so she added, "Don't worry about asking us to stay out of your way."

One of his eyebrows rose and the corners of his eyes crinkled a little. "All right, Lieutenants—you can watch our backside. We need an alarm, ASAP, if we get flanked or cut off from the *Bright Crescent*."

Lieutenant Maurell blew his breath out audibly, sounding exasperated. When Oleander and Pike looked at him, he reddened and looked down at the deck. "Okay, okay. Just don't call me 'son,' and I can deal with this."

The crinkles deepened at the corners of Pike's eyes. "You've been issued combination combat rifles that do double duty as high-performance stunners, and yes, I checked your qualification records before approving the issue. I suggest you keep the weapons set to stunner. Orders of engagement say no firing at civilians unless necessary and *no* aggressive moves toward Minoans. We don't know if they think we're the good guys."

"Control deck is first priority?" Oleander asked.

"Yes, ma'am."

There were exclamations on the team channel and a woman's voice overrode them with, "Sergeant Pike, this is Greco. We've got smoke."

Pike turned toward the doors and pushed past commandos waiting on the shipside of the airlock. Most of them had been leaning against the bulkheads, bored, as their postures suggested. Everybody, Lieutenants Oleander and Maurell included, straightened and jostled to see into the airlock.

Pike's team had forced their way to the *Pilgrimage* side of the airlock. Through the interior windows was an obvious haze. If there was smoke, that meant fire, which space crews feared almost as much as vacuum.

* * *

Matt fell to his knees after pushing through the goo that the Minoans used to keep their ship sealed. The lingering stench made him retch. David Ray was standing, leaning over, and gagging, with his hands on his knees. Their noses had suddenly started working again.

Once they could move on, Matt noticed the Minoan ship had extended a fleshy tunnel into the *Pilgrimage*, forcing open all the airlocks. They walked out into the eerily empty docking ring. There was a light, smoky haze that might have made Matt panic and hit the fire alarms, but when he sniffed, he smelled nothing. If there was a sense crèche-get trusted implicitly, it was their sense of smell.

"Where'd the guardians go?" Matt whispered. "What's hanging in the air?"

"They went toward the control deck—fast." David Ray looked around. "Let's hope everybody's hunkered down in quarters or somewhere safe. I want to get to Lee's lab."

"Let me test this first." Matt frowned as he examined the baton closely. It was about as long as his arm and there were two studs about three-fourths of the way from one side. There were two little nibs on the other end, which he took to be sights.

"Be careful. You don't even know which end fires." David Ray looked impatiently around.

Making sure that neither end pointed toward an "evolved multicellular organism," Matt arranged the baton so the studs were closest to his hand and pressed the nearest stud. Smoke, or rather haze, gushed out the other end and expanded so fast that they couldn't see more than a meter down the hall. Strangely, they weren't coughing and they couldn't smell anything.

"Well, that explains things, doesn't it?"

"Come on, we've got to get to the labs."

"One minute." Carefully, Matt pressed the other stud and a thin yellow line of light came out the other end, quite visible in the haze. He released the stud quickly.

"Let's go—somebody's coming." David Ray pulled his arm and they went down an inward spoke hall. Matt heard the sound of boots, quite a few of them, moving at a jog in military precision.

The footsteps passed them by, continuing toward the control deck. Equipment squeaked and hissed in the hazy main corridor and Matt was happy to leave.

"I think the isolationists wanted something specific when they boarded *Pilgrimage*. Like our fertilization and genetic labs, our crèches." As he whispered, David Ray was moving quietly, pausing at corners.

The emptiness of the corridors was beginning to spook Matt. Where were the other seven hundred people on this ship? He scuttled behind David Ray, leaning around the older man with the baton ready. This reminded him too much of a v-play, such as *Temple of Terror*, where he felt the metal of the "weapon" from the v-play gloves, much like this baton felt.

"My guess is that Abram wants progeny—something the Minoans denied him." David Ray continued to mutter about what the isolationists had planned. Matt suspected that the counselor was worried, almost frantic, about Dr. Lee.

"So they show up with their own sperm, eggs, and TD weapon?" Matt asked. He didn't buy into David Ray's theories.

They'd reached the center corridors near the wheel and had seen no one. Matt started relaxing, perhaps too soon. He heard a boot scuff behind him. He whirled, but the short spoke corridor they'd detoured through was empty.

"I doubt they brought eggs—Qesan always diminished the female contribution. As for the weapon, we have to hope the buoy is still operational." David Ray shrugged.

Crèche-get were raised to be self-sufficient, but Matt wasn't as sanguine about the possibility of being cut off from the civilized worlds. He'd opted off before he was twenty, relatively, and his comfortable years on Athens

Point made him hope that Warrior Commander was correct and the buoy would be fine.

They stopped before turning onto the wheel's main
semicircular-shaped corridors. David Ray poked his head
out, and pulled it back to confer with Matt. Up to this point,
they'd been talking in low tones or whispers. David Ray
held his finger in front of his lips as a warning.

"We're going to have to run around this corridor, where
there'll be plenty of chances to be seen from connecting
spokes. No more talking. Move quickly and quietly." He
breathed his words softly.

David Ray looked around the corner again, and started
running. Matt followed behind, remembering Dr. Lee's
comment and again wondering how old the counselor was,
in absolute terms. David Ray was surprisingly spry.

They ran past several intersections. Turning, Matt saw
familiar corridors. *Going right back to where we started this
nightmare.* He adjusted his grip on the baton.

The birthing center doors were open, which was unusual. The first one they reached was to Birthing Center
Two, and David Ray stopped short, winded. Matt stepped
around him, holding the baton up, but didn't step into the
opening.

"Get out of the way!" shouted a rough male voice.

They heard the sound of equipment breaking.

"No! Don't hurt her—Allison!" This was Dr. Lee Pilgrimage's voice, shrill with anger. "Stop it. These embryos
were ordered by Abram."

"And his orders are clear. If we pull out or lose the system, we kill these things."

"These are children, not things," Lee said.

"My God, one of these is an abomination. Abram never
authorized *females*, not for first-born."

"Let me go!" Lee's voice sounded panicked.

Matt gripped the baton and readied himself. He leaned
into the opening to see a short, muscular man take Lee by
the shoulders, shake her, and throw her sideways against

the birth chamber wall. She collapsed like a rag doll, next to another crumpled body in a white lab coat. The man stepped back and, apparently intent upon destroying an occupied birth chamber, raised a weapon that looked like a slug pistol.

Matt steadied the baton over his other arm, lined up the small sights on the man's torso, and pressed the second stud. The man screamed. He turned toward Matt and started convulsing. Matt realized he was still pressing the stud and he released it. With no smoke or haze, he couldn't see the beam's path.

"Lee!" David Ray pushed past him.

Matt followed more slowly and looked numbly down at Lee's attacker, obviously in his death throes, the side and front of his chest looking like something had chewed its way out, rather than in. He felt like vomiting, but was distracted when David Ray tugged the leg of his coverall and pointed to the other technician.

This was obviously Allison, who must have hit her head going down. Her neck and back met in a strange angle, so Matt felt carefully for a pulse. He didn't feel anything. Beside him, David Ray cradled Lee in his lap while he muttered and prayed. Something about opting out, settling down together, just like he promised her, if only she was okay, please Gaia, let her be okay—

"Stand up, crèche-get."

Matt looked up to see another isolationist, with a squat, grav-hugger body, standing in the doorway and aiming a flechette pistol. His hand tightened on nothing; he'd set the Gaia-b'damned Minoan baton down somewhere. He started standing as the man was hit from behind with what sounded like a high-power stunner. The pistol flailed around before the man dropped, and Matt instinctively twisted and crouched down over David Ray and Lee. He yelped as he felt flechettes burn his right arm.

Quiet. He looked around to see two figures in environmental suits standing in the doorway over the body, holding

rearms that looked like rifles. The AFCAW crimson crest
f the Labrys Raptor on their shoulders stood out against
he white of their suits. He never thought he'd be so happy
o see that symbol.

The figure in front slung its rifle over its shoulder and
tepped forward. It pushed a button on its wrist. The reflec-
ve shield slid up, quickly followed by the regular shield, to
eveal Lieutenant Diana Oleander's green eyes and oval
ace.

Matt was bewildered. His right arm hurt and he wanted
o pull the needles out, but knew he shouldn't. His left hand
ept creeping toward his right arm.

"Matthew Journey, do you know me?" Her face looked
orried.

"Yes. Diana." Of course he knew her. She'd been nice
o him when Edones took him to Karthage on the *Bright
Crescent*. He felt dazed. She'd showed him around the ship.
Oh, she's wondering if I'm thinking straight. His right arm
nd hand were dripping blood.

"Matt, there's a problem."

Behind Lieutenant Oleander, the faceplate flipped up
n the second figure, exposing a young man. He started
alling in a medical emergency, four civilians wounded, two
ggressors down.

There's a problem? *No kidding. That's as obvious as the
Great Bull's balls.* Matt's vision blurred, and he tried to fo-
us on Diana's face.

"Matt, it's *Aether's Touch*. It's fried and coming in on
utopilot."

"Isrid? Answer me, please."

He opened his eyes to see Garnet's face above him, her
orehead lined with worry. "Chander?" he croaked, and her
ace smoothed into a smile.

"Sabina's with him. He's fine, physically, but they gave
im a sedative to calm him. He didn't get pumped full of
rugs." *Like you,* her eyes said. "When you're ready, you've

a lot to deal with—more than thirty contractors and civil-ians are dead. We've got fourteen prisoners."

He remembered. Abram. Major Kedros. *The stolen weapon.* He was lying on the smooth, cold floor. Garnet knelt beside him and a member of his security stood at the door, part of the security detail that he'd foolishly left on Beta Priamos.

"Kedros. My ship."

Garnet nodded. "They kidnapped Kedros, stole the *Candor Chasma*, and headed into a close orbit about the sun. Another ship followed, the *Aether's Touch*, but Mari doesn't know if it was stolen or not."

He managed to sit up, with Garnet's help. "They have one of our TD weapons. Do you know—"

"Maria monitored the FTL display. She says *Candor Chasma* dropped out of real-space. *Aether's Touch* turned about and headed toward Sophia One, before the interfer-ence blanked out our sensors. We're having bad solar flares so comm's out."

"She must have pushed the detonation into N-space."

"She?" Garnet was applying a cold pack to his face and it felt wonderful.

"Major Kedros. I'm betting that she saved us."

Garnet paused, her eyes turning cool. "The destroyer of Ura-Guinn just became a hero by saving G-145?"

"Maybe. But don't worry about thanking her, Garnet. I doubt she could have survived." He took a sip of water, feeling immensely better. "After all, I forgot to warn her of the solar side effects after she pushed the detonation into N-space."

CHAPTER 25

The Pilgrimage Criminal Justice System, as defined in *Pilgrimage Operating Manual*, Series 12, will apply to all civilian criminal offenses. AFCAW personnel will be adjudicated under the Consortium Uniform Code of Military Justice, unless . . .

—Status of Forces Agreement Between the Consortium of Autonomist Worlds and Pilgrimage Ship Line, 2085.210.12.00 US, indexed by Heraclitus 4 under Flux Imperative

The chaos had barely started. The Minoans had taken the control deck, because Warrior Commander's voice suddenly reverberated through the *Pilgrimage III*.

"To all isolationists. Please surrender to the nearest guardian." The Minoan voice was soulless and polite. After all, it said "please." There were no threats. There didn't have to be.

Abram's followers weren't tripping over themselves to turn themselves in; on the other hand, the guardians were tromping through every corridor on the *Pilgrimage*, searching. They opened hatches everywhere. Even where they shouldn't have access to search, they were. The isolationists couldn't find any safe haven.

Medics carefully lifted Dr. Lee to a stretcher and took her to the *Pilgrimage*'s medical center. She was alive, but unconscious, with internal bleeding and broken bones. Da-

vid Ray looked devastated, but Matt couldn't think of any
thing to say as the counselor trailed after the stretcher.

Matt tried to ignore the Minoans' repeated announce
ment and concentrate on Diana's words while an AFCAW
medic fixed his arm. According to her, *Aether's Touch* ha
been pursuing the Terran State Prince's ship, called *Cando
Chasma*, near the sun. The TLS *Percival* had been follow
ing them, but for some reason—here's where Diana wa
vague—*Candor Chasma* had dropped out of real-spac
and both *Aether's Touch* and *Percival* were heading back
under heavy radiation.

"Last I knew, Ari and Joyce were on Priamos. I'm nc
sure who's on *Aether's Touch*." Matt tried not to wince a
the medic pulled another flechette. Under anesthetic, it fe
strange, since the flechettes had tiny fins so they wouldn
come out of the flesh without a fight.

Diana's story matched what Matt already learned wit
the Minoans, with the exception of the *missiles* the *Brigh
Crescent* shot off. The first warrior commander called the
"Assassinators." When was she going to get to that part c
the story?

"Is the radiation due to the TD weapon?" He hoped t
jog more of the story free.

Diana's face took on the familiar, stubborn look tha
he'd seen before on Ari, Joyce, and Edones—the look tha
said he wasn't supposed to know certain things, that sai
she couldn't answer his questions.

"Look, Diana—the *Minoans* told us that a tempora
distortion wave was generated and pushed into N-spac
They *know*, and they seemed pretty pissed off by it." Ma
was irritated; this was exactly like talking to Ari, or eve
Edones.

Shock widened Diana's eyes. The medic working on hi
arm paused.

"Okay, don't tell me about the TD weapon. Where
Ari?" Matt closed his eyes.

"We think Major Kedros was on the *Candor Chasm*

with the isolationists, perhaps as hostage. When the *Candor Chasma* dropped out of real-space, they were too far away to get a lock on the buoy, even if they had authorized codes. *Percival* recorded an emergency pod ejected right before transition, and their last message said *Aether's Touch* took the time to pick up the pod. That was almost at the same point as the—the—I'm sorry, Matt, we don't know if Major Kedros made it off the *Candor Chasma*. The sun's going nuts and solar flares are playing havoc with comm. We can't talk to anyone, unless they're practically on our doorstep."

Ari might be lost in N-space, with the *Candor Chasma*. On the other hand, she might be on the *Aether's Touch*, fried by radiation, hurt, or perhaps just out of contact. Matt sighed heavily. *I'm going to be optimistic, until proven wrong.*

"The *Percival* is docking with radiation casualties." Diana grabbed Matt's attention. "The colonel wants you on the control deck, because we don't know if the *Aether's Touch* is coming in under control or not. You have remote command capability, right?"

Matt got to his feet, with the medic's help, and numbly followed Diana. She had said that *Aether's Touch* had taken the time to pick up the pod, meaning that the *Aether's Touch* had taken more radiation exposure. If the *Percival* had serious casualties, they would expect that Ari had suffered the same—but AFCAW personnel weren't familiar with the *Aether's Touch*.

When Matt got to the control deck, Edones turned toward him. The strain had taken its toll on the colonel. Edones's normally bland face was pale and lined with worry. He'd been looking at a casualty list displayed on the wall. At the top was the name "Alexander Joyce" and beside it was "Status: Critical" in red letters.

"What happened to Joyce?" he asked Diana.

"Abram took over Beta Priamos and Joyce took it back." Edones said before Diana had a chance to answer.

"By himself?" Matt was impressed.

"Almost. They don't expect him to make it, considering they can't get him here to the *Pilgrimage* because of the radiation. He needs organs grown and replaced, and only the *Pilgrimage* has the lab facilities for that, in this system."

Matt never thought he'd feel compassion for Edones, but he took pity, just this once.

"Remember, *Aether's Touch* has protected compartments with extra radiation shielding." Matt pointed to the name "Ariane Kedros" with "Status: Unknown" beside it. "If Ari's on *Aether's Touch*, she'll have gone to those compartments."

They waited. The chatter was cacophonous as controllers collected information from the recently docked *Percival* and *Rhapsody*. They were trying to piece together what was happening on the Priamos surface facilities, Beta Priamos Station, the mining station near Laomedon, the research platform orbiting Sophia II, and any other manned vehicle in the solar system. Communications throughout the system were down due to solar activity, so they gleaned what status they could from interviews and messages recorded prior to the TD wave.

A console displayed radiation readings and solar emission data, but everyone avoided reading it. Warrior Commander stood at an abandoned station to broadcast it periodical "surrender to the guardians" message. Commander Meredith walked about the consoles, checked on status, and tried to remind Warrior Commander about Pilgrimage sovereignty. All isolationists that the guardians arrested had to be confined on the *Pilgrimage III* for later arraignment—but no one knew if Warrior Commander was heeding Meredith's words.

Edones and Matt silently watched the casualty status list grow, with both civilian and military personnel. Matt watched as two Terran State Princes were added: SP Parmet had minor wounds but was stable; SP Hauser was listed as critical due to radiation exposure. The personnel on the *Percival* had prior prophylactic treatments, a well as military-grade shielding. Matt hoped the radiation shielding around *Aether's Touch* array compartment was as good as advertised.

The TLS *Percival* was faster than the *Aether's Touch*. Matt tensed his fists as his ship, *his own ship*, came around into the eclipsed area behind Sophia I, where the *Pilgrimage III* and its docked vessels clustered for protection. If Ari hadn't programmed the right parameters, if the ship wasn't braking with enough reverse thrust, then *Aether's Touch* might whip on by, given extra gravitational pull from Sophia I, and go into the inner solar system again. Worse, it could plow into the huge *Pilgrimage III*.

If the comm worked, Matt might be able to get control of the ship. He stood behind the controller at the comm station, tensely rising up and down on his toes. *Aether's Touch* didn't appear to be decelerating, from what they could determine with their sensors, hampered by noise from the irate sun. Matt took a deep breath. He might have to try remote braking from the *Pilgrimage*'s control deck.

"*Pilgrimage Three*, this is *Aether's Touch*. *Pilgrimage Three*, this is *Aether's Touch* on docking approach. Over."

Through the static, Matt recognized Ari's voice. He whooped in relief. She was alive, at least, and able to speak. The controller answered and asked for status and specifically, dosimeter readings. Her dose was still within a safe range, which caused cheers on deck.

"See, she stayed in the protected compartment," Matt said, turning to see Edones's face collapse with relief. The colonel probably hadn't intended a public display of—well, not affection, but concern, at least. Matt felt a hand on his shoulder, and turned toward Diana. He forgot she was standing at his side.

"I'm glad she's safe." Diana looked tired; there were shadows under her eyes.

Glancing about, Matt realized everyone looked haggard. He rubbed his chin, feeling several days' growth. *How much time has gone by since I thought life was normal and safe?* The problems he'd had when he first boarded the *Pilgrimage III* now seemed small.

Ari's voice came clearer now. "*Pilgrimage Three*, be advised I'm also carrying Tahir Dominique Rouxe, who is willing to turn himself in to Pilgrimage authorities. He requests asylum and protection from Abram Hadrian Rouxe. Over."

Matt felt both Colonel Edones and Diana stiffen. He realized that Warrior Commander had turned to pay close attention to Ari's message.

Ariane kept Tahir locked in the array compartment and spoke to him over internal comm. While she didn't know what had happened on Priamos, she *implied* that Abram's cause had failed.

"Is he alive?" He still sounded frightened of his father.

"I don't know. Comm with Priamos is impossible right now. You need to think about yourself, and pick your justice."

"What?"

"Everybody's going to want a piece of you, believe me. This system is currently under Pilgrimage sovereignty, but the Consortium, the League, and maybe even the Minoans might indict you and attempt extradition."

He was silent for a few moments, then said, "I don't think it matters, as long as I'm not confined with any of my people. After all, I'm the only one who failed to meet Qesan's directives."

She was tired and frustrated with his shortsightedness. Didn't he understand how much trouble he was in? She'd thrown the Minoan possibility out to scare him, but he continued to focus on Abram.

"Look, I recommend you turn yourself in *willingly* to Pilgrimage authorities and cooperate with them. It's the right thing to do, both morally and jurisdictionally, and when they learn more about Abram, they might be lenient."

"Certainly, Major. If you think it's best." His response was subdued.

She was on dock approach before she could make con-

tact with the *Pilgrimage*'s control deck. Luckily, the readings from her implant, as well as Tahir's, indicated they
wouldn't require medical treatement. She verified this by
passing their dosimeter readings to the *Pilgrimage*.

Before she released Tahir from the compartment, she
told him the third crew member, Muse, was resting. She also
warned him about the crowd waiting dockside. She'd seen
parts of the scene from the ship's cam-eye, but it wasn't until they were standing at the top of the ramp that they *both*
realized the extent of Tahir's difficulties.

Out of cam-eye range, to the right, stood a flotilla of
Minoans. She'd never seen so many guardians with both
an emissary and a *warrior*. She sharply drew her breath.
*I guess I wasn't bullshitting when I told Tahir the Minoans
would be interested.* Generational crew members clustered
in the center of the crowd surrounding the ramp and to the
left, she saw ranks of AFCAW and Terran Space Forces.
Three stun rifles were ready and aimed at Tahir.

The dock was strangely quiet. There was no motion, except for the Minoans' robes drifting about their bodies. She
saw Commander Meredith Pilgrimage, in uniform, standing at the bottom of the ramp. She prodded Tahir forward
and pointed to Meredith with her chin.

She walked behind him down the ramp, their boots
clunking dully. Tahir and Meredith spoke so quietly she
couldn't hear them, but she figured Tahir was asking to be
separated from all other isolationists. Meredith nodded
and gestured to the Minoans. To her surprise, two guardians moved forward to take Tahir away.

Suddenly, the quiet broke into ragged cheers. The crowd
surged toward her and the organized ranks dispersed. Matt
reached her first. He hugged her, nearly crushing the breath
out of her lungs.

"Are you all right?" he said in her ear.

"I'm great, and the ship is fine." She was breathless, perhaps because of the bear hug, perhaps because his arms
were still around her.

Matt glanced up the ramp. He squeezed her again, quickly, before running up the ramp to his first true love, probably going to the control deck to check on ship functions. She smiled; everything was getting back to normal.

There were others about her now, civilians and military, Autonomist and Terran, wishing her well, asking questions, slapping her on the back.

Owen stood in front of her. His colonel's black and blue uniform appeared pressed and clean, but he looked tired. When had he started to look so old? He was flanked by other AFCAW uniforms, perhaps, but she was getting tunnel vision. With shaking fingers, she reached into her jacket's inner pocket and handed him Dokos's name tag.

"She was executed. She died bravely." When Owen's warm hand closed over hers, she realized how cold her extremities were.

"Are you okay, Major?" Owen looked strange. He was still gripping her hand.

She was exhausted, running on adrenaline and nothing else. Out of the corner of her eye, she saw tall shadows and flinched. The Minoan emissary and warrior were focused intently upon her, and moving inexorably closer.

"You need food and rest," someone said in her ear. Owen? Her vision was going gray.

"Has Ariane woken yet?" David Ray asked.

"No. Colonel Edones said this is normal." Matt grimaced. He always felt a bad taste on his tongue whenever he mentioned Edones. "They pump nutrients into her and let her rest. Then she eventually wakes up—it has to do with her metabolism, supposedly."

David Ray nodded, but Dr. Lee Pilgrimage raised her eyebrows. Perhaps this vague description sounded as suspicious to her as it did to Matt. Holding firmly on to David Ray's hand, Lee was sitting in a slanted hospital bed. Broken bones were more serious for generational crew, particularly at her age, than for grav-huggers, and she was resting from the bone-stim. She'd fared better than Allison, her technician, who'd died instantly from a broken neck.

"I meet the strangest people hanging around outside Ari's room waiting for her to wake," Matt added. "In particular, *Warrior Commander*. "What's going on there, do you suppose?"

"I suspect the Minoans are less upset with the Terrans' losing a weapon than they are with Ariane sending the TD wave into N-space." David Ray clasped Lee's hand in both of his, looking down. "I'm thinking of taking a hiatus to study what the Minoans are doing here in G-145—they've been acting strangely ever since this system opened."

"A hiatus?" Lee looked startled. In shipspeak, that meant David Ray was taking a vacation from his duties on the *Pilgrimage*, perhaps preparing to opt off. "How are you going to get honest work in the meantime, David Ray?"

"He's going to be working for a small business," Matt said. "Namely, Aether Exploration."

"That's if I can handle the pay cut." David Ray winked. "Besides, I've heard a rumor the Minoans may attempt to use the Pilgrimage justice system to charge negligence, treaty violation, you name it. Even Terran State Princes want legal consultants, when facing Minoans."

David Ray and Lee stared at each other with we-have-to-talk looks. Lee's smile was brilliant. Matt looked away, a little envious, feeling like an interloper. He stood up.

"I've got to go. I offered to buy Diana Oleander a drink. Seems like the least I could do, considering she saved our lives."

"She's a bright young lady. With the advantage that she doesn't crew for you," David Ray added. Generational crews could be even pickier than the military about avoiding romance in the workplace, particularly because space was such a dangerous workplace.

"Beautiful too." Lee's eyes glinted wickedly as she watched Matt. "Lovely oval eyes and chestnut hair. With a complexion that makes us old ladies envious, don't you think?"

"Er—yes. S'pose so. Better get going." Matt retreated from the matchmaking environment as fast as he could.

When he was alone in the corridor, he ran his fingers through his short hair, remembering how Lieutenant Oleander had taken pity and befriended him. He'd been the only civilian on the *Bright Crescent*, unwelcome, and worried about Ari. Diana Oleander had made his tense sojourn pass more easily.

I must have crashed. Ariane woke up in a bed in the *Pilgrimage*'s clinic. To her right, she saw the shelter area, where they'd put bunks for the survivors who straggled in to get protection from the radiation. She closed her eyes.

"Major Kedros?"

She yawned and turned her head, running her fingers through her hair. A staff sergeant in green ops coveralls, with medical insignia, stood in the doorway.

"I'm not 'Major,' right now."

"Yes, you are." The sergeant smiled slightly and handed her a slate. "Colonel Edones put you on active-duty orders. I'll need your signature before I can release you from medical observation."

Ariane took the slate and looked at the effective datetime stamp. Was this to cover Edones's ass, or hers? Then she realized that AFCAW would have covered her medical bills, if she'd required more serious treatment. He was being more considerate than she gave him credit for—but it also meant that he had control over any sort of Intelligence data she might have gleaned in this period. So perhaps this action wasn't altruistic after all. It didn't matter; these emergency recall orders went into effect regardless of her opinion. She thumbed the slate and handed it back to the woman.

"You're free to go whenever you like, Major." She smiled and hesitated, drifting farther into the room. "By the way, as one of the three thousand survivors in this system—thank you. We all appreciate what you did."

"Oh. You're welcome." Ariane expected that Terra and CAW would have squelched all news of a "loose TD weapon"—but even the Directorate of Intelligence and yes, even Owen, were powerless in the face of rumor and gossip.

"And perhaps you should know," continued the sergeant, looking quickly out the door. "That creepy Minoan in black stops by three times a shift to see if you can be interviewed. You've got about an hour before it comes by again."

Ariane didn't have to be warned twice. There was one thing on her mind now, and she knew the *Pilgrimage III* well enough to find it. One deck up and she entered the crew lounge and bar. It was crowded, but with everybody hunkering behind anything with a magnetosphere right now, she wasn't surprised.

Two walls showed multiple feeds; a third wall had the bar. Across the lounge, Matt sat with the young woman lieutenant, whose name she couldn't remember, from the *Bright Crescent*. She took a step toward their table, but paused, feeling like she was intruding. Matt looked young and unscarred, making her feel bitter and scarred inside. He deserved someone more like himself: fundamentally happy, optimistic, and *with nothing to hide*. Ariane turned away from the couple.

"Ariane! Good to see you up and walking." Hal, the roadmaster she'd met on Beta Priamos Station, waved her over.

"Hal? What are you doing here?"

"We brought in your Sergeant Joyce. We loaded the *Golden Bull* with tons of extra shielding, making it the most expensive cargo run in my life. But we had to do it, to get him to medical support."

"Is he that bad?" Her spirits fell and her stomach felt hollow. "Maybe I should go see him."

"He can't have visitors. He's barely hanging on, but the

Pilgrimage has good facilities and they're hopeful he'll pull through, provided he can accept his own vat-grown organs."

"He can." Ariane didn't explain why she knew this. She glanced over her shoulder. Matt and his companion—name of Oleander, she remembered—were deep in conversation.

"So how 'bout a beer?" Hal asked, gesturing to the bar seat next to him. "I'll buy the first round."

Ariane watched Lieutenant Oleander lean forward and rest her hand on Matt's forearm. They were both laughing. She looked around the rest of the room. People were enjoying themselves, eating and drinking away the knowledge they'd come close to death. They'd felt the dank breath that usually chased them only in their dreams, and they wanted to forget it. Some knew just how close their sun had come to going nova, while others merely thought they'd escaped a madman's plan for an abysmal future. She cocked her head.

"What are you doing?" Hal's eyes narrowed.

"Listening."

"For what?"

She spent another moment absorbing the babble. If Major Tafani's voice was expressing disapproval inside her head she couldn't hear him. Likewise, no ghosts whispered.

"Nothing." She smiled, and reached for the beer that had appeared as if by magic in front of her. "Nothing at all."

TAYLOR ANDERSON

INTO THE STORM

Destroyermen, Book I

Pressed into service when World War II breaks out in the Pacific, the US *Walker*—a Great War-era destroyer—finds itself retreating from pursuing Japanese battleships. Its captain, Lieutenant Commander Matthew Patrick Reddy, desperately leads the *Walker* into a squall, hoping it will give them cover—only to emerge into an alternate world. A world where two species have evolved: the cat-like Lemurians and the reptilian Griks—and they are at war.

With its power and weaponry, the Walker's very existence could alter the balance of power. And for Reddy and his crew, who have the means to turn a primitive war into a genocidal Armageddon, one thing becomes clear. They must determine whose side they're on. Because whichever species they choose is the winner.

<u>Also Available</u>
Crusade
Maelstrom

Available wherever books are sold or at
penguin.com

S. M. STIRLING

From national bestselling author
S. M. Stirling comes gripping novels of
alternate history

Island in the Sea of Time

Against the Tide of Years

On the Oceans of Eternity

The Peshawar Lancers

Conquistador

Dies the Fire

The Protector's War

A Meeting at Corvallis

The Sunrise Lands

The Scourge of God

"First-rate adventure all the way."
—Harry Turtledove

Available wherever books are sold or at
penguin.com

THE ULTIMATE IN
SCIENCE FICTION AND FANTASY!

From magical tales of distant worlds to stories of technological advances beyond the grasp of man, Penguin has everything you need to stretch your imagination to its limits.

penguin.com

ACE
Get the latest information on favorites like
William Gibson, T.A. Barron, Brian Jacques,
Ursula K. Le Guin, Sharon Shinn, Charlaine Harris,
Patricia Briggs, and Marjorie M. Liu,
as well as updates on the best new authors.

ROC
Escape with Jim Butcher, Harry Turtledove, Anne Bishop,
S.M. Stirling, Simon R. Green, E.E. Knight, Kat Richardson,
Rachel Caine, and many others—plus news on the
latest and hottest in science fiction and fantasy.

DAW
Patrick Rothfuss, Mercedes Lackey, Kristen Britain,
Tanya Huff, Tad Williams, C.J. Cherryh, and many more—
DAW has something to satisfy the cravings of any
science fiction and fantasy lover.
Also visit dawbooks.com.

*Get the best of science fiction and fantasy
at your fingertips!*